LOYALTY IN DEATH

Also by Nora Roberts in Large Print:

Born in Shame
Captivated
Daring to Dream
From the Heart
Homeport
Inner Harbor
The Reef
River's End

Written as J. D. Robb:

Naked in Death

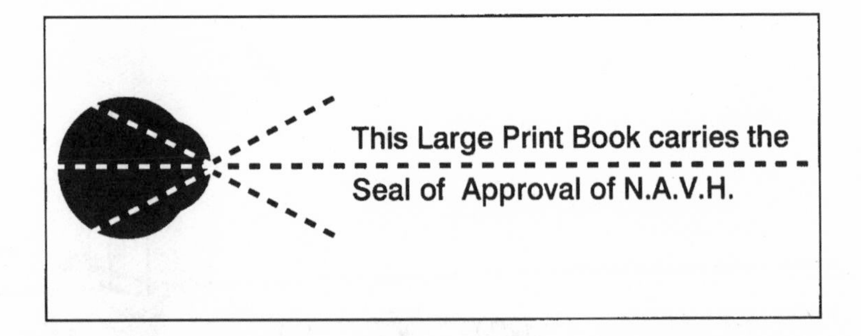

LOYALTY IN DEATH

J. D. Robb

Thorndike Press • Thorndike, Maine

This is a work of fiction. Names, characters, places and incidents are either the product of the author's imagination or are used fictitiously, and any resemblance to actual persons, living or dead, business establishments, events or locales is entirely coincidental.

Published in 2000 by arrangement with The Berkley Publishing Group, a member of Penguin Putnam, Inc.

Thorndike Press Large Print ® Americana Series.

The text of this Large Print edition is unabridged.
Other aspects of the book may vary from the original edition.

Set in 16 pt. Plantin by Minnie B. Raven.

Printed in the United States on permanent paper.

Library of Congress Cataloging-in-Publication Data

Robb, J. D., 1950–
Loyalty in death / J.D. Robb.
p. cm.
ISBN 0-7862-2443-6 (lg. print : hc : alk. paper)
ISBN 0-7862-2444-4 (lg. print : sc : alk. paper)
1. Dallas, Eve (Fictitious character) — Fiction.
2. Policewomen — New York (State) — New York — Fiction. 3. New York (N.Y.) — Fiction. 4. Large type books. I. Title.
PS3568.O243 L69 2000
813′.54—dc21 99-087731

For Vanessa Darby
because I really want to go to heaven

As flies to wanton boys,
are we to the gods;
They kill us for their sport.

— Shakespeare

Politics,
as the word is commonly understood,
are nothing but corruptions.

— Jonathan Swift

Prologue

Dear Comrade,

We are Cassandra.

It has begun.

All we have worked for, all we have trained for, all we have sacrificed for is in place. A dawn after so long a twilight. The goals set over thirty years ago will be achieved. The promises made will be kept. And the martyr's blood that was shed avenged at long last.

We know you are concerned. We know you are cautious. This is what makes you a wise general. Believe that we have taken your counsel and your warnings to heart. We do not break the moratorium on this righteous and bitter war with a battle we intend to lose. We are well-equipped, our cause well-financed, and all steps and options have been considered.

We send this transmission to you, dear friend and Comrade, as we joyfully prepare to continue our mission. Already, first blood has been spilled, and we rejoice. Circumstances have put an opponent in our path you would find worthy. We have attached to this transmission a dossier on Lieutenant Eve Dallas of the so-called New York City Police and Security Department so that you might familiarize yourself with this adversary.

Through the defeat of this enemy, our victory will be all the sweeter. She is, after all, another symbol of the corrupt and oppressive system we will destroy.

Your wise counsel directed us to this place. We have lived among these pitiful pawns of a weak-kneed society, wearing our smiling mask as we scorn their city and their system of repression and decay. We have to their blind eyes become one of them. No one questions us as we move about these immoral and filthy streets. We are invisible, a shadow among shadows as you, and the one we both loved, taught us the canniest soldier must be.

And when we have destroyed, one by one, the symbols of this overfed society, demonstrating our power and our clean-minded plan for the new realm, they will tremble. They will see us, and they will remember him. The first symbol of our glorious victory will be a monument to him. In his image.

We are loyal, and our memory is long.

You will hear the first rumble of battle to-morrow.

Speak of us to all the patriots, to all the loyal.

We are Cassandra.

Chapter One

On this particular night, a beggar died unnoticed under a bench in Greenpeace Park. A history professor fell bloodied, his throat slashed three feet from his front door for the twelve credits in his pocket. A woman choked out one last scream as she crumpled under her lover's pounding fists.

And not yet done, death circled its bony finger, then jabbed it gleefully between the eyes of one J. Clarence Branson, the fifty-year-old copresident of Branson Tools and Toys.

He'd been rich, single, and successful, a jolly man with reason to be as co-owner of a major interplanetary corporation. A second son and the third generation of Bransons to provide the world and its satellites with implements and amusements, he'd lived lavishly.

And had died the same way.

J. Clarence's heart had been skewered with one of his own multipower porta drills by his steely-eyed mistress, who'd bolted him to the wall with it, reported the incident to the police, then had calmly sat sipping claret until the first officers arrived on the scene.

She continued to sip her drink, settled cozily in a high-backed chair in front of a computer-generated fire while Lieutenant Eve Dallas examined the body.

"He's absolutely dead," she coolly informed Eve. Her name was Lisbeth Cooke, and she made her living as an advertising executive in her deceased lover's company. She was forty, sleekly attractive, and very good at her job. "The Branson 8000 is an excellent product — designed to satisfy both the professional and the hobbyist. It's very powerful and accurate."

"Uh-huh." Eve scanned the victim's face. Pampered and handsome, even though death had etched a look of stunned and sorrowful surprise on his face. Blood soaked through the breast of his blue velvet dressing gown and puddled glossily on the floor. "Sure did the job here. Read Ms. Cooke her rights, Peabody."

While her aide attended to the matter, Eve verified time and cause of death for the record. Even with the voluntary confession, the business of murder would follow routine. The weapon would be taken into evidence, the body transported and autopsied, the scene secured.

Gesturing to the crime scene team to take over, Eve crossed the royal red carpet, sat across from Lisbeth in front of the chirpy fire that blew out lush heat and light. She said nothing for a moment, waiting several beats to see what reaction she might get from the fashionable brunette with fresh blood splattered somehow gaily on her yellow silk jumpsuit.

She got nothing but a politely inquiring stare. "So . . . you want to tell me about it?"

"He was cheating on me," Lisbeth said flatly. "I killed him."

Eve studied the steady green eyes, saw anger but no shock or remorse. "Did you argue?"

"We had a few words." Lisbeth lifted her claret to full lips painted the same rich tone as the wine. "Most of them mine. J.C. was weak-minded." She shrugged her shoulders and silk rustled. "I accepted that, even found it endearing in many ways. But we had an arrangement. I gave him three years of my life."

Now she leaned forward, eyes snapping with the temper behind the chill. "Three years, during which time I could have pursued other interests, other arrangements, other relationships. But I was faithful. He was not."

She drew in a breath, leaned back again, very nearly smiled. "Now he's dead."

"Yeah, we got that part." Eve heard the ugly suck and scrape as the team struggled to remove the long steel spike from flesh and bone. "Did you bring the drill with you, Ms. Cooke, with the intention of using it as a weapon?"

"No, it's J.C.'s. He putters occasionally. He must have been puttering," she mused with a casual glance toward the body the crime scene team was now removing from the wall in a ghastly ballet of movements. "I saw it there, on the table, and thought, well, that's just perfect, isn't it? So I picked it up, flicked it on. And used it."

It didn't get much simpler, Eve mused, and rose. "Ms. Cooke, these officers will take you down to Cop Central. I'll have some more questions for you."

Obligingly, Lisbeth swallowed the last of the claret, then set the glass aside. "I'll just get my coat."

Peabody shook her head as Lisbeth tossed a full-length black mink over her bloody silks and swept out between two uniforms with all the panache of a woman heading out to the next heady social engagement.

"Man, it takes all kinds. She drills the guy, then hands us the case on a platter."

Eve shrugged into her leather jacket, picked up her field kit. Thoughtfully, she used solvent to clean the blood and Seal-It from her hands. The sweepers would finish up, then secure the scene. "We'll never get her on murder one. That's just what it was, but I'll lay odds it's pleaded down to manslaughter within forty-eight hours."

"Manslaughter?" Genuinely shocked, Peabody gaped at Eve as they stepped into the tiled elevator for the trip down to the lobby level. "Come on, Dallas. No way."

"Here's the way." Eve looked into Peabody's dark, earnest eyes, studied her square, no-nonsense face under its bowl-cut hair and police-issue hat. And was nearly sorry to cut into that unswerving belief in the system. "If the drill proves to be the victim's, she didn't bring a weapon with her. That cuts down on premeditation. Pride's got her now, and a good dose of mad, but after a few hours in a cell, if not before, survival instinct will kick in, and she'll lawyer up. She's smart, so she'll lawyer smart."

"Yeah, but we've got intent. We've got malice. She just made a statement for the record."

That was the book. As much as Eve believed in the book, she knew the pages often became blurred. “And she doesn’t have to renege on it, just embellish it. They argued. She was devastated, upset. Maybe he threatened her. In a moment of passion — or possibly fear — she grabbed the drill.”

Eve stepped off the elevator, crossed the wide lobby with its pink marble columns and glossy ornamental trees. “Temporary diminished capacity,” she continued. “Possibly an argument for self-defense, though it’s bullshit. But Branson was about six-two, two-twenty, and she’s five-four, maybe one-fifteen. They could make that work. Then, in shock, she contacts the police immediately. She doesn’t attempt to run or to deny what she did. She takes responsibility, which would earn points with a jury if it comes down to it. The PA knows that, so he’ll plead it down.”

“That really bites.”

“She’ll do time,” Eve said as they stepped outside into a cold as bitter as the scorned lover now in custody. “She’ll lose her job, spend a hefty chunk of credits on her lawyer. You take what you can get.”

Peabody glanced over at the morgue wagon. “This one should be so easy.”

“Lots of times the easy ones have the most angles.” Eve smiled a little as she opened the door of her vehicle. "Cheer up, Peabody. We'll close the case, and she won't walk. Sometimes that's as good as it gets."

"It wasn't like she loved him." At Eve's arched brow, Peabody shrugged. "You could tell. She was just pissed because he'd screwed around on her."

"Yeah, so she screwed him — literally. So remember, loyalty counts." The car 'link beeped just as she started the engine. "Dallas."

"Hey, Dallas, hey. It's Ratso."

Eve looked at the ferret face and beady blue eyes on-screen. "I'd never have guessed."

He gave the wheezy inhale that passed for a laugh. "Yeah, right. Yeah. So listen, Dallas, I got something for you. How 'bout you meet me and we'll deal. Okay? Right?"

"I'm heading into Central. I've got business. And my shift's over ten minutes ago, so —"

"I got something for you. Good data. Worth something."

"Yeah, that's what you always say. Don't waste my time, Ratso."

"It's good shit." The blue eyes skittered like marbles in his skinny face. "I can be at The Brew in ten."

"I'll give you five minutes, Ratso. Practice being coherent."

She broke the connection, swung away from the curb, and headed downtown.

"I remember him from your files," Peabody commented. "One of your weasels."

"Yeah, and he just did ninety days on a D and D. I got the indecent exposure tossed. Ratso likes to flaunt his personality when he's piss-faced. He's harmless," Eve added. "Mostly full of wind, but every now and again, he comes up with some solid data. The Brew's on the way, and Cooke can hold for a bit. Run the serial number on the murder weapon. Let's verify if it belonged to the victim. Then find the next of kin. I'll notify them once Cooke's booked."

The night was clear and cold with a stiff wind snapping down the urban canyons and chasing most of the foot traffic indoors. The glide-cart vendors held out, shivering in the steam and stink of grilling soy dogs, hoping for a few hungry souls hearty enough to brave February's teeth.

The winter of 2059 had been brutally cold, and profits were down.

They left the swank Upper East Side neighborhood with its clear, unbroken sidewalks and uniformed doormen and headed south and west where the streets went narrow and noisy and the natives moved fast, their eyes on the ground and their fists over their wallets.

Smashed against curbs, the remnants of the last snowfall was soot gray and ugly. Nasty patches of ice still slicked sidewalks and lay in wait for the unwary. Overhead, a billboard swam with a warm blue sea hemmed by sugar-white sand. The busty blonde frolicking in the waves wore little more than a tan and invited New York to come to the islands and play.

Eve entertained herself with thoughts of a couple of days in Roarke's island getaway. *Sun, sand, and sex,* she mused as she negotiated bad-tempered evening traffic. Her husband would be happy to provide all three, and she was nearly ready to suggest it. Another week or two maybe, she decided. After she cleared up some paperwork, finished some court appearances, tied a couple of dangling loose ends.

And, she admitted, felt a little more secure about being away from the job.

She'd lost her badge and had nearly lost her way too recently for the sting to have faded. Now that she had both back, she wasn't quite ready to set duty aside for a quick bout of indulgence.

By the time she found a parking space on the second-level street ramp near The Brew, Peabody had the requested data. "According to the serial numbers, the murder weapon belonged to the victim."

"Then we start off with murder in the second," Eve said as they trooped down to the street. "The PA won't waste time trying to prove premeditation."

"But you think she went there to kill him."

"Oh yeah." Eve crossed the sidewalk toward the murky lights of an animated beer mug with dingy foam sliding down the sides.

The Brew specialized in cheap drinks and stale beer nuts. Its clientele ran to grifters down on their luck, low-level office drones and the cut-rate licensed companions who hunted them, and a smatter of hustlers with nothing left to hustle.

The air was stale and overheated, conversation scattered and secret. Through the smeared light, several gazes slid to Eve, then quickly away.

Even without Peabody's uniform beside her, she whispered cop. They would have recognized it in the way she stood — the long, rangy body alert, the clear brown eyes steady, focused, and flat as they took in faces and details.

Only the uninitiated would have seen just a woman with short, somewhat choppily cut brown hair, a lean face with sharp angles and a shallow dent in the chin. Most who patronized The Brew had been around and could smell cop at a dead run in the opposite direction.

She spotted Ratso, his pointy rodent face nearly inside the mug as he sucked back beer. As she walked toward his table, she heard a few chairs scrape shyly away, saw more than one pair of shoulders hunch defensively.

Everyone's guilty of something, she thought, and sent Ratso a fierce, bare-toothed smile. "This joint doesn't change, Ratso, and neither do you."

He offered her his wheezy laugh, but his gaze had danced nervously over Peabody's spit-and-polish uniform. "You didn't hafta bring backup, Dallas. Jeez, Dallas, I thought we was pals."

"My pals bathe regularly." She jerked her head toward a chair for Peabody, then sat herself. "She's mine," Eve said simply.

"Yeah, I heard you got you a pup to train." He tried a smile, exposing his distaste for dental hygiene, but Peabody met it with a cool stare. "She's okay, yeah, she's okay since she's yours. I'm yours, too, right, Dallas? Right?"

"Aren't I the lucky one." When the waitress started over, Eve merely gave her a glance that had her changing directions and leaving them alone. "What have you got for me, Ratso?"

"I got good shit, and I can get more." His unfortunate face split into a grin Eve imagined he thought cagey. "If I had some working credit."

"I don't pay on account. On account of I might not see your ugly face for another six months."

He wheezed again, slurped up beer, and sent her a hopeful look out of his tiny, watery eyes. "I deal square with you, Dallas."

"So, start dealing."

"Okay, okay." He leaned forward, curving his skinny little body over what was left in his mug. Eve could see a perfect circle of scalp, naked as a baby's butt, at the crown of his head. It was almost endearing, and certainly more attractive than the greasy strings of paste-colored hair that hung from it. "You know The Fixer, right? Right?"

"Sure." She leaned back a little, not so much to relax but to escape the puffs of her weasel's very distasteful breath. "He still around? Christ, he must be a hundred and fifty."

"Nah, nah, wasn't that old. Ninety-couple maybe, and spry. You bet The Fixer was spry." Ratso nodded enthusiastically and sent those greasy strings bobbing. "Took care of himself. Ate healthy, got regular sex from one of the girls on Avenue B. Said sex kept the mind and body tuned up, you know."

"Tell me about it," Peabody muttered and earned a mild glare from Eve.

"You're giving me past tense here."

Ratso blinked at her. "Huh?"

"Did something happen to The Fixer?"

"Yeah, but wait. I'm getting ahead of things." He dug his skinny fingers into the shallow bowl of sad-looking nuts. Chomped on them with what was left of his teeth as he looked at the ceiling and pulled his easily scattered thoughts back into line. "About a month ago, I got some . . . I had me a view-screen unit, needed a little work."

Eve's eyebrows lifted under her fringe of bangs. "To cool it off," she said mildly.

He wheezed, slurped. "See, it got sorta dropped, and I took it in to Fixer so's he could diddle with it. I mean, the guy's a genius, right? Nothing he can't make work like brand-fucking-new."

"And it's so clever the way he can change serial numbers."

"Yeah, well." Ratso's smile was nearly sweet. "We got to talking, and The Fixer, he knows how I'm always looking for a little pickup work. He says how he's got this job going. Big one. Really flush. They got him building timers and remotes and little bugs and shit. Done up some boomers, too."

"He told you he was putting together explosives?"

"Well, we was sorta pals, so yeah, he was telling me. Said how they heard he used to do that kind of shit when he was in the army. And they was paying heavy credits."

"Who was paying?"

"I don't know. Don't think he did, either. Said how a couple guys would come to his place, give him a list of stuff and some credits. He'd build the shit, you know? Then he'd call this number they give him, leave a message. Just supposed to say like the products are ready, and the two guys would come back, pick the stuff up, and give him the rest of the money."

"What did he figure they wanted with the stuff?"

Ratso lifted his bony shoulders, then looked pitifully into his empty mug. Knowing the routine, Eve lifted a finger, turned it down toward Ratso's glass. He brightened immediately.

"Thanks, Dallas. Thanks. Get dry, you know? Get dry talking."

"Then get to the point, Ratso, while you

still have some spit in your mouth."

He beamed as the waitress came over to slop urine-colored liquid in his mug. "Okay, okay. So he says how he figures maybe these guys are looking to shake down a bank or jewelry store or something. He's working on some bypass unit for them, and he's clued in that the timers and remotes set off the boomers he's got going for them. Says maybe they'll want a little guy who knows his way under the street. He'll maybe put in a word for me."

"What are friends for?"

"Yeah, that's it. Then I get a call from him a couple weeks later. He's really wired up, you know? Tells me the deal isn't what he figured. That it's bad shit. Real bad shit. He ain't making any sense. Never heard old Fixer like that. He was real scared. Said something about being afraid of another Arlington, and how he needed to go under awhile. Could he flop with me until he figured out what to do next? So I said sure, hey sure, come on over. But he never did."

"Maybe he went under somewhere else?"

"Yeah, he went under. They fished him outta the river a couple days ago. Jersey side."

"I'm sorry to hear that."

"Yeah." Ratso brooded into his beer. "He

was okay, you know? Word I got is somebody cut his tongue right outta his head." He lifted his tiny eyes, fixed them mournfully on Eve. "What kinda person does that shit?"

"It's bad business, Ratso. Bad people. It's not my case," she added. "I can take a look at the file, but there's not a lot I can do."

"They offed him 'cause he figured out what they was gonna do, right? Right?"

"Yeah, I'd say that follows."

"So you gotta figure out what they're gonna do, right? You figure it out, Dallas, then you stop them and take them down for doing The Fixer like that. You're a murder cop, and they murdered him."

"It's not as simple as that. It's not my case," she said again. "If they fished him out in New Jersey, it's not even my damn city. The cops working it aren't likely to take kindly to me horning in on their investigation."

"How much you figure most cops gonna bother with somebody like Fixer?"

She nearly sighed. "There are plenty of cops who'll bother. Plenty who'll work their butt off trying to close the case, Ratso."

"You'll work harder." He said it simply, almost childlike faith in his eyes. And Eve felt her conscience stir restlessly. "And I can find out shit for you. If Fixer talked to me some, he coulda maybe talked to somebody else. He didn't scare easy, you know. He come through the Urban Wars. But he was plenty scared when he called me that night. They didn't do him that way 'cause they was gonna take out a bank."

"Maybe not." But she knew there were some who would gut a tourist for a wrist unit and a pair of airboots. "I'll look into it. I can't promise any more than that. You find out anything that adds to this, you get in touch."

"Yeah, okay. Right." He grinned at her. "You'll find out who did Fixer that way. The other cops, they didn't know about the shit he was into, right? Right? So that's good data I give you."

"Yeah, good enough, Ratso." She rose, dug credits out of her pocket, and laid them on the table.

"You want me to run down the file on this floater?" Peabody asked when they stepped back outside.

"Yeah. Tomorrow's soon enough." As they climbed back up to her vehicle, Eve dug her hands into her pockets. "Do a run on Arlington, too. See what buildings, streets, citizens, businesses, that kind of thing have that name. If we find anything, we can turn it over to the investigating officer."

"This Fixer, did he weasel for anybody?"

"No." Eve slid behind the wheel. "He hated cops." For a moment she frowned, drummed her fingers. "Ratso's got a brain the size of a soybean, but he's got Fixer down. He didn't scare easy, and he was greedy. Kept that shop of his open seven days a week, worked it solo. Rumor was he had his old army-issue blaster under the counter, and a hunting knife. Used to brag he could fillet a man as quick and easy as he could a trout."

"Sounds like a real fun guy."

"He was tough and sour and would sooner piss in a cop's eye than look at one. If he wanted out of this deal he was in, it had to be way over the top. Nothing much would've put this old man off."

"What's that I hear?" Cocking her head, Peabody cupped a hand at her ear. "Oh, that must be the sound of you getting sucked in."

Eve hit the street with a bit more bounce than necessary. "Shut up, Peabody."

She missed dinner, which was only mildly irritating. The fact that she'd been right about the PA and the plea bargain on Lisbeth Cooke was downright infuriating.

At least, Eve thought as she let herself into the house, *the twit could have stuck for murder two a little longer.*

Now, scant hours after Eve had arrested her in the wrongful death of one J. Clarence Branson, Lisbeth was out on bail and very likely sitting cozily in her own apartment with a glass of claret and a smug little smile on her face.

Summerset, Roarke's butler, slipped into the foyer to greet her with a baleful eye and a sniff of disapproval. "You are, once again, quite late."

"Yeah? And you are, once again, really ugly." She dropped her jacket over the newel post. "Difference is, tomorrow I might be on time."

He noted that she looked neither pale nor tired — two early signs of overwork. He would have suffered the torments of the damned before he would have admitted — even to himself — that the fact pleased him.

"Roarke," he said in frigid tones as she breezed by him and started up the steps, "is in the video room." Summerset's brow arched slightly. "Second level, fourth door on the right."

"I know where it is," she muttered, though it wasn't absolutely true. Still, she would have found it, even though the house was huge, a labyrinth of rooms and treasures and surprises.

The man didn't deny himself anything, she thought. Why should he? He'd been denied everything as a child, and he'd earned, one way or another, all the comforts he now commanded.

But even after a year, she wasn't really used to the house, the huge stone edifice with its juts and its towers and the lushly planted grounds. She wasn't used to the wealth, she supposed, and never would be. The kind of financial power that could command acres of polished wood, sparkling glass, art from other countries and centuries, along with the simple pleasures of soft fabrics, plush cushions.

The fact was, she'd married Roarke in spite of his money, in spite of how he'd earned a great portion of it. Fallen for him, she supposed, as much for his shadows as his lights.

She stepped into the room with its long, luxurious sofas, its enormous wall screens, and complex control center. There was a charmingly old-fashioned bar, gleaming cherry with stools of leather and brass. A carved cabinet with a rounded door she remembered vaguely held countless discs of the old videos her husband was so fond of.

The polished floor was layered with richly patterned rugs. A blazing fire — no computer-generated image for Roarke — filled the hearth of black marble and warmed the fat, sleeping cat curled in front of it. The scent of crackling wood merged with the spice of the fresh flowers spearing out of a copper urn nearly as tall as she and the fragrance of the candles glowing gold on the gleaming mantel.

On-screen, an elegant party was happening in black and white.

But it was the man, stretched out comfortably on the plush sofa, a glass of wine in his hand, who drew and commanded attention.

However romantic and sensual those old videos with their atmospheric shadows, their mysterious tones could be, the man who watched them was only more so. And he was in three glorious dimensions.

Indeed, he was dressed in black and white, the collar of his soft white shirt casually unbuttoned. At the end of long legs clad in dark trousers, his feet were bare. Why, she wondered, she should find that so ripely sexy, she couldn't say.

Still, it was his face that always drew her, that glorious face of an angel leaping into hell with the light of sin in his vivid blue eyes and a smile curving the poetic mouth. Sleek black hair framed it, falling nearly to his shoulders. A temptation for any woman's fingers and fists.

It hit her now, as it often did, that she'd started falling for him the moment she'd seen that face. On her computer screen in her office, during a murder investigation. When he'd been on her short list of suspects.

A year ago, she realized. Only a year ago, when their lives had collided. And irrevocably changed.

Now, though she'd made no sound, came no closer, he turned his head. His eyes met hers. And he smiled. Her heart did the long, slow roll in her chest that continued to baffle and embarrass her.

"Hello, Lieutenant." He held out a hand in welcome.

She crossed to him, let their fingers link. "Hi. What are you watching?"

"*Dark Victory*. Bette Davis. She goes blind and dies in the end."

"Well, that sucks."

"But she does it so courageously." He gave her hand a little tug and urged her down on the sofa with him.

When she stretched out, when her body curved easily, naturally against his, he smiled. It had taken a great deal of time and a great deal of trust between them to persuade her to relax this way. To accept him and what he needed to give her.

His cop, he thought as he toyed with her hair, with her dark corners and terrifying courage. His wife, with her nerves and her needs.

He shifted slightly, content when she settled her head on his shoulder.

Since she'd gone that far, Eve decided it would be a pretty good idea to pull off her boots and to take a sip from his glass of wine. "How come you're watching an old video like this if you already know how it ends?"

"It's the getting there that counts. Did you have dinner?"

She made a negative sound, passed him back his wine. "I'll get something in a bit. I got hung up on a case that came in right before end of shift. Woman screwed a guy to the wall with his own drill."

Roarke swallowed wine, hard. "Literally, or metaphorically?"

She chuckled a little, enjoying the wine as they passed the glass back and forth. "Literally. Branson 8000."

"Ouch."

"You betcha."

"How do you know it was a woman?"

"Because after she pinned him to the wall, she called it in, then waited for us. They were lovers, he was playing around, so she drilled a two-foot steel rod through his cheating heart."

"Well, that'll teach him." Ireland cruised through his voice like whiskey and had her tilting her head to look up at him.

"She went for the heart. Me, I'd've screwed it through his balls. More to the point, don't you think?"

"Darling Eve, you're a very direct woman." He lowered his head to touch his lips to hers — one brush, then two.

It was her mouth that heated, her hands that reached up to fist in his thick, black hair and drag him closer. Take him deeper. Before he could shift to set the wine aside, she flipped over, knocking the glass to the floor as she straddled him.

He lifted a brow, eyes glinting, as he used his nimble fingers to unbutton her shirt. "I'd say we know how this one ends, too."

"Yeah." Grinning, she bent down to bite his bottom lip. "Let's see how we get there this time."

Chapter Two

Eve scowled at her desk-link after she'd finished her conversation with the PA's office. They'd accepted a plea of man two on Lisbeth Cooke.

Second-degree manslaughter, she thought in disgust, for a woman who had coolheadedly, cold-bloodedly ended a life because a man couldn't control his dick.

She'd do a year at best in a minimum-security facility where she'd paint her nails and brush up on her fucking tennis serve. She'd very likely sign a disc and video deal on the story for a tidy sum, retire, and move to Martinique.

Eve knew she'd told Peabody to take what you could get, but even she hadn't expected it to be so little.

She damn well let the APA — and she'd told the spineless little prick in short, pithy terms — inform the next of kin why justice was too overworked to bother — why it had been in such a fucking hurry to deal it hadn't even waited to settle until she'd finished her report.

Setting her teeth, she rapped a fist against her computer in anticipation of its vagaries and called up the ME's report on Branson.

He'd been a healthy male of fifty-one, with no medical conditions. There were no marks or injuries to the body other than the nasty hole made by a whirling drill bit.

No drugs or alcohol in the system, she noted. No indication of recent sexual activity. Stomach contents indicated a simple last meal of carrot pasta and peas in a light cream sauce, cracked wheat bread, and herbal tea ingested less than an hour before time of death.

Pretty boring meal, she decided, for such a sneaky ladies' man.

And who, she asked herself, said he was a ladies' man but the women who'd killed him? In their damn rush to clear the dockets, they hadn't given her time to verify the motive for the pissy man two.

When it hit the media, and it would, she imagined a lot of dissatisfied sexual partners were going to be eyeing the tool closet.

Lover piss you off? she thought. *Well, see how he likes a taste of the Branson 8000 — the choice of professionals and serious hobbyists.* Oh yeah, she thought Lisbeth Cooke could work up a pretty jazzy ad campaign using that angle. Sales would shoot right up.

Relationships had to be society's most baffling and brutal form of entertainment. Most could make an arena ball playoff game look like a ballroom dance. Still, lonely souls continued to seek them out, cling to them, fret and fight over them, and mourn the loss of them.

No wonder the world was full of whacks.

The glint of her wedding ring caught her eye and made her wince. That was different, she assured herself. She hadn't sought anything out. It had found her, taken her down like a hard tackle to the back of the knees. And if Roarke ever decided he wanted out, she'd probably let him live.

In a permanent body cast.

Disgusted all around, she spun back to her machine and began to hammer out the investigative report the PA's office apparently didn't want to bother with.

She glanced up as E-Detective Ian McNab poked a head in her doorway. His long golden hair was braided today, and only one iridescent hoop graced his earlobe. Obviously to make up for the conservative touch, he wore a thick sweater in screaming greens and blues that hung to the hips of black pipe-stem trousers. Shiny blue boots completed the look.

He grinned at her, green eyes bold in a pretty face. "Hey, Dallas, I finished checking out your victim's 'links and personal memo book. The stuff from his office just came in, but I figured you'd want what I've got so far."

"Then why isn't your report on my desk unit?" she asked dryly.

"Just thought I'd bring it over personally." With a friendly smile, he dropped a disc on her desk, then plopped his butt on the corner.

"Peabody's running data for me, McNab."

"Yeah." He moved his shoulders. "So, she's in her cube?"

"She's not interested in you, pal. Get a clue here."

He turned his hand over, examined his nails critically. "Who says I'm interested in her? She still seeing Monroe, or what?"

"We don't talk about it."

His eyes met hers briefly, and they shared a moment of the vague disapproval neither of them liked to show for Peabody's continued involvement with a slick if appealing licensed companion. "Just curious, that's all."

"So ask her yourself." *And report back to me,* she added silently.

"I do." He grinned again. "Gives her a

chance to snarl at me. She's got great teeth."

He got up, paced around Eve's cramped box of an office. They both would have been surprised to realize their thoughts on relationships were, at that moment, running on parallel lines.

McNab's hot date with an off-planet flight consultant had cooled and soured the night before. She'd bored him, he thought now, which should have been impossible as she'd put her truly magnificent breasts on display in something sheer and silver.

He hadn't been able to work up any enthusiasm because his thoughts had continued to drift to the way a certain prickly cop looked in her starched uniform.

What the hell did she wear under that thing? he wondered now, as he had unfortunately wondered the night before. That speculation had caused him to end the evening early, annoying the flight consultant so that when he came to his senses — as he was sure he would — he'd never get another shot at those beautiful breasts.

He was, he decided, spending too many nights home alone, watching the screen.

Which reminded him.

"Hey, I caught Mavis's video on-screen last night. Frigid."

"Yeah, it's pretty great." Eve thought of her friend; even now on her first tour to promote her recording disc for Roarke's entertainment arm, singing her butt off in Atlanta. Mavis Freestone, Eve thought sentimentally, was a long way from shrieking her lungs out for the zoned and the glazed at dives like the Blue Squirrel.

"The disc is starting to take off. Roarke thinks it'll make the top twenty next week."

McNab jingled credit chips in his pocket. "And we knew her when, right?"

He was stalling, Eve thought, and she was letting him. "I think Roarke's planning a party or something once she gets back."

"Yeah? Great." Then he perked up at the unmistakable sound of police-issue shoes slapping worn linoleum. McNab had his hands in his pockets and a look of sheer disinterest on his face when Peabody came through the door.

"NJPSD came through with —" She broke off, scowled. "What do you want, McNab?"

"Multiple orgasms, but you guys copped that one out of the goodie bag."

A laugh tried to bubble into her throat, but Peabody controlled it. "The lieutenant doesn't have time for your pitiful jokes."

"Actually, the lieutenant kind of liked that

one," Eve said, then rolled her eyes when Peabody glared at her. "Take off, McNab, play period's over."

"Just thought you'd be interested," he continued, "that in running the 'links and memo books of the deceased, no calls, incoming and outgoing, were transmitted to a female other than his assailant or his office staff. No records of appointments appear in his log for *liaisons*," he said, rolling out the word with a smirk for Peabody, "other than those involving Lisbeth Cooke — who he often refers to as Lissy my love."

"No record of another woman?" Eve pursed her lips. "What about another guy?"

"Nope, no dates either way, and no indication of bisexuality."

"Interesting. Run the office logs, McNab. I wonder if Lissy my love was lying about her motive, and if so, why she killed him."

"I'm on it." As he strolled out, he paused just long enough to throw Peabody a loud, exaggerated kiss.

"He is such a complete asshole."

"Maybe he irritates you, Peabody —"

"There's no maybe involved."

"But he was smart enough to see that his report might change a few angles on this case."

The idea of McNab dipping his toe into

one of her cases, again, had Peabody bristling. "But the Cooke case is closed. The perpetrator confessed, has been charged, booked, and bonded."

"She got man two. If it wasn't a crime of passion, maybe we get more. It's worth finding out if Branson was bouncing on somebody on the side or if she made that up to cover another motive. We'll take a run over to his office later today, ask some questions. Meanwhile . . ." She wagged her curled fingers toward the disc Peabody still held.

"Detective Sally's primary," Peabody began as she handed Eve the disc. "He's got no problem cooperating. Basically because he's got nothing. The body'd been in the river at least thirty-six hours before discovery. He's got no witnesses. The victim wasn't carrying any cash or credits, but he did have ID and credit cards. He was wearing a wrist unit — Cartier knockoff but a good one — so Sally ruled out a standard mugging, especially when the autopsy didn't turn up a tongue."

"There's a clue," Eve muttered and slid the disc into a slot on her unit.

"ME's report indicates the tongue was severed with a serrated blade, premortem. However, lacerations and bruising at the back of the neck, and the lack of defensive indicate the victim was probably knocked unconscious before the impromptu surgery, then dumped in the river. They strapped his hands and feet before giving him the toss. Drowning's down as cause of death."

Eve tapped her fingers. "Any reason I should bother reading this report?" she asked and earned a grin.

"Detective Sally was talkative. I don't think he'd struggle if you wanted to take the case. He pointed out that since the victim lived in New York, it's a toss-up right now if he was killed here or on the other side of the river."

"I'm not taking the case, I'm just looking at it. You run Arlington?"

"Everything that popped is on side B of the disc."

"Fine. I'll skim through, then we'll head over to Branson's office."

Eve narrowed her eyes as a tall, gangly man in worn jeans and an ancient parka hesitated at her doorway. Early twenties, she judged, with a look of such open innocence in eyes of dreamy gray she could already hear the street thieves and hustlers lining up to pluck his pockets clean.

He had the thin, bony face she associated with martyrs or scholars, and brown hair worn in a smooth tail and liberally streaked from the sun.

His smile was slow and shy.

"Looking for someone?" Eve began. At the question, Peabody turned, gaped, then let out what could only be called a squeal.

"Hey, Dee." His voice creaked, as if he used it rarely.

"Zeke! Oh wow, *Zeke!*" She took one vaulting leap and jumped into long, welcoming arms.

The sight of Peabody in her ruthlessly pressed uniform with her regulation shoes dangling inches off the floor while she giggled — it was the only word to describe the sound — and pressed cheerful kisses onto the long face of the man who held her had Eve slowly rising to her feet.

"What are you doing here?" Peabody demanded. "When did you get here? Oh, it's so good to see you. How long can you stay?"

"Dee," was all he said, and hauled her up another inch to press his lips to her cheek.

"Excuse me." Well aware how quickly tongues could wag in the unit, Eve stepped forward. "Officer Peabody, I suggest you have this little reunion on your personal time."

"Oh, sorry. Put me down, Zeke." But she kept an arm wrapped possessively around him even when her feet hit the floor. "Lieutenant, this is Zeke."

"I got that far."

"My brother."

"Oh yeah?" Eve took another look, searching for family resemblance. There was none — not body type, not coloring, not in features. "Nice to meet you."

"Didn't mean to interrupt." Zeke flushed a little and held out a big hand. "Dee's had lots of good things to say about you, Lieutenant."

"Glad to hear it." Eve found her hand lost inside one the consistency of granite and as gentle as silk. "So which one are you?"

"Zeke's the baby," Peabody said with such adoration Eve had to grin.

"Some baby. What are you, about six-six?"

"And a quarter," he said with a shy smile.

"He takes after our father. They're both tall and skinny." Peabody gave her brother a fierce squeeze. "Zeke's a wood artist. He builds the most beautiful furniture and cabinets."

"Come on, Dee." The flush became a blush. "I'm just a carpenter. Handy with tools, that's all."

"There's a lot of that going around lately," Eve murmured.

"Why didn't you tell me you were coming to New York?" Peabody demanded.

"Wanted to surprise you. Didn't know for sure I'd come until a couple of days ago."

He stroked a hand over her hair in a way that made Eve think of relationships again. Some weren't about sex or power or control. Some were just about love.

"I got a commission to custom-build cabinets from these people who saw my work back in Arizona."

"That's great. How long will it take?"

"Don't know till they're done."

"Okay, well, you'll stay at my place. I'll get you the key and tell you how to get there. You'll take the subway." She gnawed her lip. "Don't go wandering around, Zeke. It's not like home. Are you carrying your money and ID in your back pocket, because —"

"Peabody." Eve held up a finger for attention. "Take the rest of the day on personal time, get your brother settled in."

"I don't want to be any trouble," Zeke began.

"You'll be more trouble if she's worried about you getting mugged six times before you get to her apartment." Eve added a smile to soften it, though she'd already decided the guy had M for *mark* all over his face. "Things are slow here, anyway."

"The Cooke case."

"I think I can handle it solo," Eve said mildly. "Anything pops, I'll tag you. Go show Zeke the wonders of New York."

"Thanks, Dallas." Peabody took her brother's hand, vowing that she'd make sure he didn't see the seamier side of those wonders.

"Nice to've met you, Lieutenant."

"You, too." She watched them go off, Zeke bending his body slightly toward Peabody as she bubbled with sisterly affection.

Families, Eve mused. They continued to baffle her. But it was nice to see that, occasionally, they worked.

"Everyone loved J.C." Chris Tipple, Branson's executive assistant, was a man of about thirty with hair approximately the same shade as the swollen red rims of his eyes. Even now he wept unashamedly, tears trickling down his chubby, pleasant face. "Everyone."

Which might have been the problem, Eve mused, and waited once again while Chris scrubbed his cheeks with his crumpled handkerchief. "I'm sorry for your loss."

"It's just impossible to believe he won't come through that door." His breath hitched as he stared at the closed door of the big, bright office suite. "Ever again. Everyone's in shock. When B.D. made the announcement this morning, no one could speak."

He pressed the handkerchief to his mouth as if his voice had failed him again.

B. Donald Branson, the victim's brother and partner, Eve knew, and waited for Chris to finish.

"You want some water, Chris? A soother?"

"I've taken a soother. It doesn't seem to help. We were very close." Mopping his streaming eyes, Chris didn't notice Eve's look of consideration.

"You had a personal relationship?"

"Oh yes. I'd been with J.C. for nearly eight years. He was much more than my employer. He was . . . he was like a father to me. Pardon me."

Obviously overcome, he buried his face in his hands. "I'm sorry. J.C. wouldn't want me to fall apart this way. It doesn't help. But I can't — I don't think any of us can take it in. We're closing down for a week. The whole operation. Offices, factories, everything. The memorial . . ." He trailed off, struggling. "The memorial service is scheduled for tomorrow."

"Quick."

"J.C. wouldn't have wanted it to be drawn out. How could she have done it?" He fisted the damp cloth in his hand, staring blindly at Eve. "How could she have done it, Lieutenant? J.C. adored her."

"You know Lisbeth Cooke?"

"Of course."

He rose to pace, and Eve could only be grateful. It was difficult to watch a grown man grieve while he was sitting in a chair shaped like a pink elephant. Then again, she was sitting in a purple kangaroo.

It was obvious, with one look at the late J. Clarence Branson's office, that he'd enjoyed indulging in his own toys. The shelves lining one wall were loaded with them, from the simple remote-control space station to the series of multitask minidroids.

Eve did her best not to look at their lifeless eyes and small-scale bodies. It was too easy to imagine them popping to life and . . . well, God knew what.

"Tell me about her, Chris."

"Lisbeth." He sighed heavily, then in an absent gesture adjusted the sunshade tint on the wide window behind the desk. "She's a beautiful woman. You'd have seen that for yourself. Smart, capable, ambitious. Demanding, but J.C. didn't mind that. He told me once if he didn't have a demanding woman, he'd end up puttering and playing his life away."

"They spent a lot of time together?"

"Two evenings a week, sometimes three. Wednesdays and Saturdays were standard — dinner with theater or a concert. Any social event that required his presence or hers, and Monday lunch — twelve-thirty to two. A three-week vacation every August wherever Lisbeth wanted to go, and five weekend getaways through the year."

"Sounds pretty regimented."

"Lisbeth insisted on that. She wanted conditions spelled out and obligations on both sides clear-cut and in order. I think she understood J.C's mind tended to wander, and she wanted his full attention when they were together."

"Any other part of him tend to wander?"

"Excuse me?"

"Was J.C. involved with anyone else?"

"Involved — romantically? Absolutely not."

"How about just sexually?"

Chris's round face stiffened, the puffy eyes went cool. "If you're insinuating that J. Clarence Branson was unfaithful to the woman he'd made a commitment to, nothing could be more false. He was devoted to her. And he was loyal."

"You can be sure of that? Without question?"

"I made all of his arrangements, all professional and personal appointments."

"Couldn't he have made some of his own, on the side?"

"It's insulting." Chris's voice rang out. "The man is dead, and you're sitting there accusing him of being a liar and a cheat."

"I'm not accusing him of anything," Eve corrected calmly. "I'm asking. It's my responsibility to ask, Chris. And to get him whatever justice I can."

"I don't like how you go about it." He turned away again. "J.C. was a good man, an honest man. I knew him, his habits, his moods. He wouldn't have entered into some illicit affair, and certainly couldn't have done so without my knowledge."

"Okay, so tell me about Lisbeth Cooke. What would she have to gain by killing him?"

"I don't know. He treated her like a princess, gave her everything she could possibly want. She killed the golden goose."

"The what?"

"Like in the story." He nearly smiled now. "The goose that laid the golden eggs. He was happy to give her whatever she wanted, and more. Now he's dead. No more golden eggs."

Unless, Eve thought as she left the office, she'd wanted all the eggs at one time.

She knew as she already consulted the animated map in the lobby that B. Donald Branson's office was at the opposite end of this level from his brother's. Hoping to find him in, she headed down. Many of the stations were unmanned, most of the glass doors locked with the offices behind them dark and empty.

The building itself seemed to be grieving.

At regular intervals, holograph screens were set up to show off Branson Tools and Toys' new or favored products. She stopped at one, watching with equal parts amusement and dismay as a uniformed beat cop action-droid returned a lost child to his tearfully grateful mother.

The cop faced the screen, its face sober and trustworthy, his uniform as severely pressed as Peabody's. "It's our job to serve and protect."

Then the image pulled back, spun slowly to give the viewer a three-sixty view of the product and accessories while the computer's voice stated product and pricing details. A street thief action-droid with air-skates was offered as a companion piece.

Shaking her head, Eve turned away. She wondered if the company produced LC droid figures, or illegals dealers. Maybe a couple of psychopaths just to keep the game interesting. Then, of course, you'd need victim-droids.

Jesus.

The clear glass doors opened as Eve approached. A pale and weary-eyed woman manned a sleek U-shaped console and fielded calls on a privacy headset.

"Thank you very much. Your call is being recorded and your condolences will be passed on to the family. Mr. Branson's memorial service is scheduled for tomorrow, at two o'clock at Quiet Passages, Central Park South. Yes, it's a great shock. A great loss. Thank you for calling."

She swiveled the mouthpiece aside and offered Eve a sober smile. "I'm sorry, Mr. Branson isn't available. These offices will be closed until Tuesday of next week."

Eve took out her badge. "I'm primary on his brother's homicide. Is he in?"

"Oh, Lieutenant." The woman touched her fingers briefly to her eyes, then rose. "One moment, please."

She slipped gracefully from behind the console, then after a quick knock on a tall white door, disappeared inside. Eve heard the soft beep of incoming calls from the multiline 'link, then the door opened again.

"Please come in, Lieutenant. Mr. Branson will see you. Is there anything I can get you?"

"No, I'm fine."

She entered the office. The first thing she noticed was that it was dramatically opposed to J.C.'s. This was cool colors, sleek lines, rich sophistication. No silly animal chairs or grinning droid dolls. Here the muted grays and blues were designed to soothe. And the wide surface of the desk, uncluttered with gadgets, clear for business.

B. Donald Branson stood behind that desk. He didn't have the bulk of his brother but was slim in a sleekly tailored suit. His hair was a dull gold, slicked back from a high forehead. Eyebrows, thick and peaked, were shades darker over tired eyes of pale green.

"Lieutenant Dallas, it's kind of you to come in person." His voice was as quiet and soothing as the room. "I meant to contact you, to thank you for your kindness when you called last night to inform me of my brother's death."

"I'm sorry to intrude at this time, Mr. Branson."

"No, please. Sit down. We're all trying to deal with it."

"I gather your brother was well liked."

"Loved," he corrected as they took their seats. "It was impossible not to love J.C. That's why it's so hard to imagine him gone, and in this way. Lisbeth, she was like part of the family. My God." He looked away for a moment, trying to compose himself.

"I'm sorry," he managed. "What can I do for you?"

"Mr. Branson, let me get this over with as quickly as I can. Ms. Cooke claims she discovered your brother was involved with another woman."

"What? That's absurd." Branson dismissed the idea with one angry wave of his hand. "J.C. was devoted to Lisbeth. He never looked at another woman."

"If that's true, why would she have killed him? Did they quarrel often, violently?"

"J.C. couldn't maintain an argument for five minutes," Branson said wearily. "It just wasn't in him. He had no violence, and he certainly was no womanizer."

"You don't believe he could have been interested in someone else?"

"If he was — which is difficult to believe — he would have told Lisbeth. He would have been honest with her and dissolved their relationship before starting another. J.C. had almost childishly honest standards."

"If I accept that, then I'm looking for motive. You and your bother were copresidents. Who inherits his share?"

"I do." He folded his hands on the desk. "Our grandfather founded this company. J.C. and I have been at the helm together over thirty years. In our business agreement it's stipulated that the survivor or the survivor's heirs inherit the partnership."

"Could he have designated any portion of it to Lisbeth Cooke?"

"Not of the company, no. We have a contract."

"Of his personal funds and holdings, then."

"Certainly, he'd be free to designate any or all of his personal estate to whomever he pleased."

"Would we be talking substantial?"

"Yes, I believe we would say substantial." Then he shook his head. "You think she killed him for money? I can't believe that. He was always very generous with her, and Lisbeth is — was — a well-paid member of this company. Money shouldn't have been an issue."

"It's an angle," was all Eve said. "I'd like the name of his lawyer, and I'd appreciate it if you'd clear it so I can have the terms of the will."

"Yes, of course." He tapped a finger on the top of his desk and the center drawer slid open. "I have one of Suzanna's business cards right here. I'll contact her right away," he added, rising as Eve did to hand her the card. "Tell her to give you whatever information you need."

"I appreciate your cooperation."

Eve checked her wrist unit as she left. She could probably hook up with the lawyer by midafternoon, she decided. And since she had some time, why not juggle in a trip to Fixer's shop?

Chapter Three

Peabody shifted two of the three bags of groceries and foodstuffs she'd stopped off for on the trip home and dug out her key. She'd loaded up on fresh fruits and vegetables, soy mix, tofu, dried beans, and the brown rice she'd disliked since childhood.

"Dee." Zeke set down the single duffel bag he'd packed for New York and added his sister's two sacks to the one he already carried. "You shouldn't have bought all this stuff."

"I remember how you eat." She grinned over her shoulder at him and didn't add that most of her larder consisted of things no respectable Free-Ager would consider consuming. Fat- and chemical-laden snacks, red meat substitutes, alcohol.

"It's robbery what they charge for fresh fruit here, and I don't think those apples you bought came off a tree in the last ten days." Plus he sincerely doubted they'd been organically grown.

"Well, we're kind of short on orchards in Manhattan."

"Still. You should've let me pay for it."

"This is my city, and you're the first of the family to visit me." She pushed open the door, turned to take the sacks.

"There's got to be some Free-Ager co-ops around."

"I don't really do any co-opping or bartering these days. Don't have the time. I pull in a decent salary, Zeke. Don't fuss. Anyway." She blew her hair out of her eyes. "Come on in. It's not much, but it's home now."

He stepped in behind her, scanned the living area with its sagging sofa, cluttered tables, bright poster prints. The windowshade was down, something she hurried over to remedy.

She didn't have much of a view, but she enjoyed the rush and rumble of the street below. When the light shot in, she noted that the apartment was every bit as untidy as the street below.

And remembered, abruptly, she'd left a disc text on the mind of the serial torture killer in her computer. She'd have to get it out and bury it somewhere.

"If I'd known you were coming, I'd've picked up a little."

"Why? You never picked up your room at home."

He grinned at her and headed to the tiny kitchen to set down the food sack. Actually, it relieved him to see her living space was so much like her. Steady, unpretentious, basic.

He noted a slow drip from the faucet, a blister burn in the countertop. He could fix those for her, he thought. Though it surprised him she hadn't done so herself.

"I'll do this." She stripped off her coat, her cap, and hurried in behind him. "Go put your things in the bedroom. I'll bunk on the couch while you're here."

"No, you won't." Already he was poking in cabinets to put things away. If he was shocked by the stock in her pantry, particularly the bright red and yellow bag of Tasty Tater Treats, he didn't mention it. "I'll take the sofa."

"It's a pull-out, and fairly roomy." And she thought she probably had clean sheets for it. "But it's lumpy."

"I can sleep anywhere."

"I know. I remember all those camping trips. Give Zeke a blanket and a rock, and he's down for the count." Laughing, she wrapped her arms around him, pressed her cheek to his back. "God, I missed you. I really missed you."

"We — Mom and Dad and the rest of us — hoped you'd make it home for Christmas."

"I couldn't." She stepped back as he turned. "Things got complicated." And she wouldn't speak of that, wouldn't tell him what had been happening, what had been done. "But I'll make time soon. I promise."

"You look different, Dee." He touched his big hand to her cheek. "Official. Settled in. Happy."

"I am happy. I love my work." She lifted her hand to his, pressed down on it. "I don't know how to explain it to you, to make you understand."

"You don't have to. I can see it." He pulled out a six-pack of juice tubes and opened the tiny friggie. Understanding wasn't always the answer. He knew that. Accepting was. "I feel bad about pulling you away from your job."

"Don't. I haven't had any personal time in . . ." She shook her head as she stuffed boxes and bags onto shelves. "Hell, who remembers? Dallas wouldn't have green-lighted it if we'd been jammed."

"I liked her. She's strong, with dark places. But she's not hard."

"You're right." Head angled, Peabody turned back to him. "And what did Mom tell you about peeking at auras without consent?"

He flushed a little, grinned around it.

"She's responsible for you. I didn't look that close, and I like to know who's looking out for my big sister."

"Your big sister's doing a pretty good job of looking out for herself. Why don't you unpack?"

"That'll take me about two minutes."

"Which is about twice the time it'll take me to give you the grand tour." She took his arm and led him across the living space into the bedroom.

"This is about it." A bed, a table, and lamp, a single window. The bed was made — that was habit and training. There was a book on the nightstand. She'd never understood why anyone could choose to curl up with a palm unit and disc. But the fact that it was a grisly murder mystery made her wince when Zeke flipped it over.

"Busman's holiday?"

"I guess."

"You always did like this kind of stuff." He set the book back down. It comes down to good and evil, doesn't it, Dee? And good's supposed to win when it's over."

"That's the way it works for me."

"Yeah, but what's evil there for in the first place?"

She might have sighed, thinking of all she'd seen, what she'd done, but she kept her gaze level on his. "Nobody's got the answer to that, but you've got to know it's there and deal with it. That's what I do, Zeke."

He nodded, studied her face. He knew it was different from the routine she'd had when she'd moved to New York and put on a uniform. Then it had been traffic incidents, squabbles to break up, and paperwork. Now she was attached to homicide. She dealt with death every day and rubbed shoulders with those who caused it.

Yes, she looked different, Zeke acknowledged. The things she'd seen and done and felt were there behind those dark, serious eyes.

"Are you good at it?"

"Pretty good." Now she smiled a little. "I'm going to be better."

"You're learning from her. From Dallas."

"Yeah." Peabody sat on the edge of the bed and looked up at him. "Before she took me on as her aide, I studied her. I read her files, I crammed on her technique. I never expected to be able to work with her. Maybe that was luck, maybe it was fate. We were taught to respect both."

"Yeah." He sat next to her.

"She's giving me a chance to find out what I can do. What I can be." Peabody drew in a long breath, let it out slowly. "Zeke, we were raised to take our own path, to pursue it, and to do the best we were capable of. That's what I'm doing."

"You think I don't approve, don't understand."

"I worry about it." She slid her hand down to the regulation stunner strapped to her belt. "About what you — especially you — feel."

"You shouldn't. I don't have to understand what you do to know it's what you need to do."

"You were always the easiest of us, Zeke."

"Nah." He bumped his shoulder against hers. "It's just when you're the last coming up, you get to watch how everyone else screws up. Okay if I take a shower?"

"Sure." She patted his hand and rose. "Water takes awhile to come up to temp."

"No hurry."

When he got his bag and took it into the bath, she pounced on the kitchen 'link, called Charles Monroe, and left a message on his service canceling their date that night.

However wise and broad-minded and adult he'd sounded, she didn't see her baby brother embracing her casual, and just lately spotty, relationship with a licensed companion.

* * *

She might have been surprised at just how much her little brother would understand. As he stood under the spray, let the hot water ease away the faint stiffness from travel, he was thinking of a relationship that wasn't — couldn't be — a relationship. He was thinking of a woman. And he told himself he had no right to think of her.

She was a married woman, and she was his employer.

He had no right to think of her as anything else, less to feel this shaky heat in his gut at the knowledge he would see her again very soon.

But he couldn't get her face out of his mind. The sheer beauty of it. The sad eyes, the soft voice, the quiet dignity. He told himself it was a foolish, even childish crush. Horribly inappropriate. But he had no choice but to admit here, in private, where honesty was most valued, that she was one of the primary reasons he'd taken the commission and made the trip east.

He wanted to see her again, no matter how that wanting shamed him.

Still, he wasn't a child who believed he could have whatever he needed.

It would be good for him to see her here, in her own home, with her husband. He liked to think it was the circumstances of how they'd met, of where they'd met, that had caused this infatuation. She'd been alone, so obviously lonely, and had looked so delicate, so cool and golden in the deep desert heat.

It would be different here because she would be different here. And so would he. He would do the job she had asked him to do and nothing more. He would spend time with the sister he had missed so deeply it sometimes made his heart ache. And he would see, at long last, the city and the work that had pulled her away from her family.

The city, he could already admit, fascinated him.

As he toweled off, he tried to see through the tiny, steam-misted window. Even that blurry, narrow view made his blood pump just a little faster.

There was so much of it, he thought now. Not the open vastness of desert and mountain and field he'd grown used to since his family had relocated in Arizona a few years before. But so much of everything rammed and jammed into one small space.

There was so much he wanted to see. So much he wanted to do. As he hitched on a fresh shirt and jeans, he began to speculate, to plot, and to plan. When he stepped back out into the living area, he was eager to begin.

He saw his sister busily tidying and grinned. "You make me feel like company."

"Well . . ." She'd tucked away every murder and mayhem disc and file she could find. It would have to do. She glanced over, blinked.

Wow, was all she could think. Why hadn't she noticed in her first rush of delight in seeing him? Her baby brother had grown up. And he was a genuine eye treat. "You look good — sort of filled out and everything."

"It's just a clean shirt."

"Right. Do you want some juice, some tea?"

"Ah . . . I really want to go out. I've got this whole guidebook thing. I studied it on the way east. You know how many museums there are in Manhattan alone?"

"No, but I bet you do." Inside her regulation shoes, Peabody's toes curled and flexed. Her feet, she decided, were about to get a workout. "Let me change, and we'll check them out."

An hour later, she was almost tearfully grateful for the airsoles, for the thick soft wool of her slacks, and the lining of her winter coat. It wasn't just museums Zeke was after. It was everything.

He took videos with the palm unit he told her he'd splurged on for the trip. It would have been ripped off a dozen times if she hadn't kept her eyes peeled for street thieves. No matter how often she lectured him to watch himself, to recognize the signs and the moves, he just smiled and nodded.

They rode to the top of the Empire State Building, stood in the freezing, bitter wind until the tips of her ears went numb. And his pale gray eyes glowed with the wonder of it. They toured the Met, gawked at the storefronts along Fifth, stared up at the tourist blimps, bumped along the sky glides, and gnawed on stale pretzels he'd insisted on buying from a glide-cart.

Only deep and abiding love could have convinced her to agree to skidding over the ice rink at Rockefeller Center when her calf muscles were already weeping from three hours of urban hiking.

But he made her remember what it was to be stunned by the city, to see all it had to offer. She realized, watching him be awed, time after time, that she'd forgotten to look.

And if she had to flash the badge she'd tucked in her coat pocket at a gimlet-eyed grifter looking to score the tourist, it didn't spoil the day.

Still, by the time she finally talked him into stopping for a hot drink and a bite to eat, she'd decided it was imperative she outline some very specific do's and don'ts. He was going to be on his own a great deal when he wasn't working, she thought. He might have been twenty-three, but he had all the naive trust in his fellow man of a sheltered five-year-old.

"Zeke." She warmed her hands on a bowl of lentil soup and tried not to think about the soy-beef burger she'd spied on the menu. "We should talk about what you're going to do while I'm working."

"I'll be building cabinets."

"Yeah, but my hours are . . ." She gestured vaguely. "You never know. You'll be spending a lot of time on your own, so —"

"You don't have to worry about me." He grinned at her, spooned up his own soup. "I've been off the farm before."

"You've never been here before."

He sat back, shot her the exasperated look brothers reserve for nagging sisters. "I carry my money in my front pocket. I don't talk to the people who cart around those cases full of wrist units and PPCs, and I don't move in to play that card game like the one they had going on Fifth Avenue, even though it looks like fun."

"It's a con. You can't win."

"Still looked like fun." But he wouldn't brood on it, not when she had that line dug between her eyebrows. "I don't strike up conversations on the subway."

"Not with a chemi-head looking to score." She rolled her eyes. "Jesus, Zeke, the guy was practically foaming at the mouth. Anyhow." She waved that away. "I don't expect you to lock yourself into the apartment on your free time. I just want you to be careful. It's a great city, but it eats people every day. I don't want one of them to be you."

"I'll be careful."

"And you'll stick to the major tourist areas, carry your palm-link?"

"Yes, Mom." He grinned at her again, and looked so young Peabody's heart stuttered. "So, you up for the Fly Over Manhattan tour?"

"Sure." She managed to smile instead of wince. "You bet. Soon as we're done here." She took her time with the soup. "When are you supposed to get started on this job?"

"Tomorrow. We set it all up before I left. They approved the plans, the estimates. They paid for my transpo and expenses."

"You said they saw your work when they were out in Arizona on vacation?"

"She did." And just thinking of it had his pulse running a little faster. "She bought one of the carvings I'd done for Camelback Cooperative Artworks. Then she and Silvie — I don't think you ever met Silvie, she's a glass artist. She was running the co-op that day and she mentioned how I'd designed and built the cabinets and counters and the displays. And then Mrs. Branson mentioned how she and her husband were looking for a carpenter, and —"

"What?" Peabody's head snapped up.

"They were looking for a carpenter, and —"

"No, what was that name?" She grabbed his hand, clamped down. "Did you say Branson?"

"That's right. The Bransons hired me. Mr. and Mrs. B. Donald Branson. He owns Branson T and T. Good tools."

"Oh." Peabody set down her spoon. "Oh, shit, Zeke."

Fixer's was a grungy smear in an area not known for its tidiness. Just off Ninth, a bare block from the entrance to the tunnel, Fixer's was a dilapidated storefront mined with security bars, patched with intercoms and peek lenses, and as welcoming as a cockroach.

The one-way windows offered the passerby a dingy field of black. The door was reinforced steel, studded with a complicated series of locks that made the police seal look like a joke.

People who loitered in the area knew how to mind their own business — which was usually second-story work. One glance at Eve had most of them finding something else to do and somewhere else to do it.

Eve used her master on the police seal, relieved that the sweeper team hadn't engaged Fixer's locks. At least she wouldn't have to spend time decoding them. It made her think of Roarke and wonder how long it would have taken him to slide right through them.

Since a part of her would have enjoyed watching him do just that, she scowled as she stepped inside and shut the door behind her.

It smelled — not quite foul but close, she decided. Sweat, grease, bad coffee, old piss. "Lights, full," she ordered, then narrowed her eyes at the sudden brightness.

The interior of the shop was no more cheerful than the exterior. Not a single chair invited a customer to sit and relax. The floor, the sickly green of baby vomit, carried the grime and scars of decades of wear. The way her boots stuck and made sucking noises as she walked told her that mopping up hadn't been a major occupation of the deceased.

Gray metal shelves rose up one wall and were jammed full in a system that defied all logic.

Miniscreens, security cams, porta-links, desk logs, communication and entertainment systems crowded together in varying stages of repair or harvesting.

Jumbled on the other side of the room were more units she took to be complete as the hand-lettered sign above warned that pickup must be made within thirty days or the customer defaulted the merchandise.

She counted five No Credit Given postings in a room no larger than fifteen feet wide.

Fixer's sense of humor — for lack of a better term — was evidenced by the dangling human skull over the cashier's counter. The sign under the sagging jaw read The Last Shoplifter.

"Yeah, that's a laugh riot," Eve murmured and huffed out a breath.

Damn if the place didn't give her the creeps, she realized. The only window was behind her and barred. The only outside door mired with locks. She glanced up, studied the security monitor. It had been left running and gave her a full view of the street. On another, securing the interior, she could study herself on the crystal-clear screen.

Nobody got in, she decided, unless Fixer wanted them in.

She made a note to ask Sally at NJPSD for copies of the security discs, exterior and interior.

She crossed to the counter, noted that the computer stationed there was an ugly hybrid of scavenged parts. And in all probability, she mused, ran with more speed, efficiency, and reliability than the one in her office at Cop Central.

"Engage, computer."

When nothing happened, she frowned and attempted to boot it manually. The screen shimmered.

Warning: This unit protected by fail safe. Code proper password or voice print within thirty seconds of this message or disengage.

Eve disengaged. She'd see if Feeney, top dog in the Electronic Detective Division, had the time and inclination to play with it.

There was nothing else on the counter but some greasy fingerprints, the dull sheen left by the sweepers, and a scatter of parts she couldn't identify.

She uncoded the door leading to the back area and stepped into Fixer's workshop.

The guy could've used a few elves, she thought. The place was an unholy mess with the bones and sinews of dozens of electronic devices scattered around. Tools were hung on pegs or tossed wherever they landed. Minilasers, delicate tweezers, and screwdrivers with bits hardly wider than a single hair.

If he'd been attacked here, how the hell would you tell? she wondered, nudging the shell of a monitor with her boot. But she didn't think he had been. She'd only dealt with Fixer a handful of times and hadn't seen him in a couple of years, but she remembered he kept his place and his person in constant disarray.

"And they wouldn't have gotten into this dungeon unless he'd wanted them to," she murmured. The man had been seriously paranoid, she mused, checking out yet more monitors overhead. Every inch of his space and several feet outside the shop were all under surveillance twenty-four/seven.

No, they didn't take him from inside, she decided. If he was panicked, as Ratso had said, he'd have been all the more careful. Still, he hadn't felt safe enough to simply barricade himself inside and wait it out. So he'd called a friend.

She moved into the tiny room beyond, scanned the mess of Fixer's living space. A cot with yellowed sheets, a table with a jury-rigged communications center, a pile of unwashed clothes, and a narrow bathroom with hardly enough room for the skinny shower stall and toilet.

The kitchenette was a turnaround space packed with a fully loaded AutoChef and a minifridge stocked to bursting. Canned and dry goods were stacked in a wall as high as her waist.

"Jesus, he could have waited out an alien attack in here. Why go out to go under?"

Shaking her head, she tucked her thumbs in her pockets and turned a slow circle.

No windows, no outside doors, she noted. He'd lived in a fucking box. She studied the monitor across from the bed, watched the traffic move along Ninth. No, she corrected. Those were his windows.

She closed her eyes and tried to picture him there, using the image of him she remembered. Skinny, grizzled, old. Mean.

He's scared, so he moves fast, she thought. *Takes only what he needs. He's former military. He knows how to decamp fast. Some clothes, some money. Not enough money on him for a man going under,* she realized. *Not nearly.*

Greed, she thought. That was another facet of the man. He'd been greedy, hoarding his money, overcharging his clients who paid because of his magic hands.

He'd have taken cash, credits, bank and brokerage passkeys.

And where was his bag? He'd have packed a bag. Could be in the river, too, she decided, hooking her thumbs in her front pockets. Or whoever killed him took it.

"He'd've had money," she thought aloud. "He sure as hell wasn't spending it on home decorating or personal hygiene and enhancements."

She'd check into his finances.

He packs a bag. Going under, she thought again. *What does he put into it?*

He'd have taken a palm-link, a PPC. He'd have wanted his logs, his connections. And weapons.

She moved back out, poked under the counter. She found an empty rack with a quick-release bar. Hunkering down, she narrowed her eyes as she studied it. Had the old bastard really had an illegal blaster? Was this some kind of weapon holder? She'd check the sweepers' report, see if they'd confiscated a weapon.

She hissed out a breath, picked up the rack to examine it. She didn't have a clue what an army-issue blaster circa the Urban Wars looked like.

Then she sighed, pushed the rack into her evidence bag. She knew where to find one.

Chapter Four

Because she wanted to speak to Feeney in person, Eve swung back to Cop Central. She took the glide up to EDD, hopping off long enough to hit up a vending machine for a nutra-bar.

The Electronic Detective Division was a hive of activity. Cops were working on computers, tearing them apart, rebuilding them. Others sat in privacy booths playing and copying discs from confiscated 'links and logs. Nevertheless, the beeps and buzzes and whines of electronics crowded the air and made her wonder how anyone could manage to squeeze in a stray thought.

Despite the noise level, the door of Captain Ryan Feeney's office was open. He sat at his desk, his shirtsleeves rolled up to the elbows, his wiry, rust-colored hair standing up on end, his droopy eyes enormous behind the lenses of microgoggles. While Eve watched from the doorway, he plucked a tiny translucent chip from the guts of the computer upended on his desk.

"Gotcha, you little bastard." And with the

delicacy of a surgeon, he slid the chip into an evidence bag.

"What is it?"

"Hah?" Behind the goggles, his hound dog eyes blinked, then he shoved the goggles up to his forehead and focused on her. "Hey, Dallas. This little darling? It's basically a counter." He tapped the bag and smiled a little. "Bank teller with a talent for e-work installed it in her unit at work. Every twenty transfers, a deposit got zipped into an account she'd set up for herself in Stockholm. Pretty slick."

"You're slicker."

"Damn right. What are you doing over here?" He continued to work as he spoke, methodically tagging evidence. "Want to hang out with real cops?"

"Maybe I missed your pretty face." She eased a hip onto the corner of his desk, grinning when he snorted. "Or maybe I wondered if you had any spare time."

"For what?"

"You remember The Fixer?"

"Sure. Bad attitude, magic hands. The son of a bitch's nearly as good as I am. He can take a unit like this XK-6000 here, strip her down, harvest her, and spread her into six other units before she cools down. He's goddamn good."

"Now he's goddamn dead."

"Fixer?" Genuine regret showed in his eyes. "What happened?"

"He took a last swim." She filled him in quickly, moving from her meeting with Ratso through her quick tour of the shop.

"Had to be something big and something bad to scare an old warhorse like Fixer," Feeney mused. "You say they didn't take him from inside?"

"I'd say that would've been next to impossible. He had full security scan. Interior and exterior. A hive of locks. One exit — reinforced — and one window, one-way luminex, barred. Oh, and I checked his supplies. He had enough unperishables and bottled water to last a man used to rations a good month."

"Sounds like he could've held off an invasion."

"Yeah. So why run?"

"Got me. The Jersey primary cleared you to look into it from this end?"

"Well, he's got nothing. I haven't got much more," she admitted. "The story's from my weasel, and he tends to spook easy. But Fixer was into something, and they took him out. They didn't get into his place, so they didn't get to his equipment. He's got a fail-safe on his shop unit. I thought you could play with it, see if you can get past it."

Feeney scratched his ear, reached absently for a handful of the sugared nuts in a bowl on his desk. "Yeah, I can do that. Gotta figure he'd've taken his logs with him if he was going under. But he was smart. Might've left a copy behind. So I'll look."

"Appreciate it." She straightened. "I'm just juggling this in for now. I haven't run it by the commander."

"Let's see what I find; then we'll take it to him."

"Good." She snatched some of the nuts before she headed for the door. "So how much did she get? The bank teller?"

Feeney glanced down at the microtimer. "Three million and change. If she'd settled for the three and skipped, she might've gotten away with it."

"They always want more," Eve said.

She munched on nuts as she headed to her own office. The detective's bullpen clattered with voices, curses, and whines from suspects, from victims giving statements, the incessant trill of 'links, and the quick screams and scratches as two women went at each other with teeth and nails over a dead man they both claimed to love.

Eve found the atmosphere oddly soothing after her trip to EDD.

As a professional courtesy, she stepped in and hauled one of the shrieking women up in a headlock while the detective in charge struggled with the other.

"Thanks, Dallas." Baxter grinned at her.

She only sneered. "You were enjoying that, weren't you?"

"Hey, nothing like a catfight." He cuffed his charge to a chair before she could slice at him. "If you'd have waited another minute, clothes might've gotten ripped off."

"You're so sick, Baxter." Eve bent close to the woman's ear. "You hear that?" she murmured, tightening her grip just a little as the woman continued to squirm like a fish. "You go after her again, the guys in the squad are going to get off on it. Is that what you want?"

"No." She bit the word off, then sniffled. "I just want my Barry back!" she wailed.

The sentiment set the other woman off, so that the room was filled with the wild sobbing of women. Seeing Baxter wince, Eve smiled thinly and pushed the woman to him. "There you go, pal."

"Thanks a lot, Dallas."

Satisfied with her part in the little drama, Eve went into her office, shut the door. In the relative peace, she sat down and contacted Suzanna Day, the late J. Clarence

Branson's attorney.

After being passed from reception to assistant, Eve watched Suzanna's face swim on-screen. She was a sharp-looking woman of perhaps forty. Black hair was cut short and sleek around an attractive face. Her complexion was dark and deep as onyx, her eyes like jet. Her unsmiling mouth was painted a rich crimson that matched the tiny bead pierced through the trailing tip of her left eyebrow.

"Lieutenant Dallas. B.D. told me you'd be in touch."

"I appreciate you taking the time to speak to me, Ms. Day. You're aware I'm primary in the matter of J. Clarence Branson's death?"

"Yes." Her mouth thinned. "I'm also aware, through a contact at the PA's office, that Lisbeth Cooke is being charged with man two."

"You're not happy with that decision."

"J.C. was a friend, a good one. No, I'm not happy that the woman who killed him will do hardly more than turnaround time in a high-class cage."

PAs make the deals, Eve thought sourly. Cops take the heat. "It's not my job to make that determination, but it is to gather all possible evidence. Mr. Branson's will could shed a different light on matters."

"The will is to be read tonight, in the home of B. Donald Branson."

"You already have the information as to the beneficiaries."

"I do." Suzanna paused, seemed to struggle with herself. "And I can't reveal any of the terms before the official reading, as per my client's instructions when the document was drawn up. My hands are tied here, Lieutenant."

"Your client didn't expect to be murdered."

"Regardless. Believe me, Lieutenant, I'm already skimming corners by insisting the reading be held tonight."

Eve considered a moment. "What time tonight?"

"Eight o'clock."

"Any legal reason why I can't be there?"

Suzanna lifted her ornamented eyebrow. "No, not if Mr. and Mrs. Branson clear it. I'll speak to them about it, get back to you."

"Good. I'm going out in the field, but I'll get the message. Just one more thing. Did you know Lisbeth Cooke?"

"Very well. I often socialized with her and J.C."

"Opinion?"

"She's ambitious, determined, possessive. And hot-tempered."

Eve nodded. "You didn't like her."

"On the contrary, I liked her very much. I admire a woman who knows what she wants, gets it, and hangs on to it. She made him happy," she added and pressed her lips together as tears swam into her eyes. "I'll get back to you," she said and broke transmission.

"Everybody loved J.C.," Eve murmured, then, shaking her head, began to gather her things. Her communicator beeped before she got to the door. She tugged it out. "Dallas."

"Lieutenant."

"Peabody. I figured you'd have your brother out on the town."

"Try vice versa." On-screen, Peabody rolled her eyes. "I've already been to the top of the Empire State Building, taken the glide around the Silver Palace twice, gawked at skaters in Rockefeller Center —" Not under the tortures of hell would she admit she'd strapped on skates herself. "And I walked my feet off in two museums. He's dying to do the Fly Over Manhattan tour. It leaves in fifteen."

"Tons of fun," Eve commented as she made her way to the elevator that would take her down to her car.

"Zeke's never been to the city before. I've

had to stop him from talking to every LC and beggar on the street. Jesus, Dallas, he wanted to play three-card monte."

Eve grinned. "Good thing his sister's a cop."

"You're telling me." Then she sighed. "Look, this probably doesn't mean anything, but it's weird, and I thought I should let you know."

Eve stepped out of the elevator into the garage. "What?"

"You know how Zeke said he came out because he had a commission? Building custom cabinets and stuff? Well, it turns out his commission is from B. Donald Branson."

"Branson?" Eve pulled up short. "Branson hired your brother?"

"Yeah." Peabody studied Eve out of unhappy eyes. "What are the odds?"

"Low," Eve murmured. "Pretty low. How'd Branson hear about Zeke?"

"Mrs. Branson, actually. She was out in Arizona at some spa and was shopping, saw his work in one of the artists' co-ops. Zeke does a lot of custom work, built-ins, furniture. He's really good. She asked about the craftsman, and they put her in touch with Zeke. One thing led to another, and here he is."

"It sounds normal, logical." She slipped into her car. "Has he been in touch with them since he got in?"

"He's calling now. Their name just came up, and I told him. He thought he should call Mrs. Branson and see if she wanted to put off the work."

"Okay. Don't worry about it, Peabody. But let me know how they handle it. And if he hasn't already spilled it about having a cop for a sister, tell him to keep that little bit of data to himself."

"Sure. But it's not like the Bransons are suspects. We've got the killer."

"Right. Let's just be cautious. Go play tour guide. I'll see you tomorrow."

Coincidence, Eve mused as she drove out of the garage. She really hated coincidence. But no matter how she played the information through her mind, she couldn't come up with anything off about the family of her murder victim hiring Peabody's brother to do carpentry work.

J. Clarence had been alive when Zeke had been hired. Neither of the Bransons were involved in his death. There was no way to stretch it into anything shaky.

Sometimes coincidence was just coincidence. But she pushed the information into a corner of her mind and let it stew there.

* * *

There was music playing softly when Eve walked in the house. Summerset entertaining himself, she decided as she stripped off her jacket, while he went about doing whatever the hell it was he did all day.

She tossed the jacket over the newel post as she started upstairs. He would know she was home, she thought. The man knew every damn thing. He also hated to have his routine, whatever it was, disturbed. It was unlikely he would bother her.

She turned, walked down the corridor to the tall double doors of Roarke's weapon room. Frowning a little, she hitched her bag on her shoulder more securely. She was aware that only Roarke, Summerset, and she could gain access to this room.

Roarke's collection was legal — at least it was legal now. She had no idea if every piece had been obtained by legal means. She doubted that sincerely.

Eve laid her hand flat on the palm plate, waited while the cool green light shimmered on to take her print, then stated her name, and finally used the key code.

The security computer verified her identification, and the locks snicked open.

She stepped inside, closed the door behind her, and let out a long breath.

Weapons of violence through the ages were displayed, somehow elegantly, in the great room. Encased in glass, showcased in beautiful cabinets, gleaming on the walls were guns, knives, lasers, swords, pikes, maces. All testaments, she thought, to man's continued ambition to destroy man.

And yet, she knew the weapon strapped to her side was as much a part of her as her arm.

She remembered the first time Roarke had showed her this room, when her instinct and her intellect had been waging a battle. One telling her he could be the killer she sought, the other insisting it wasn't possible.

The first time he'd kissed her had been here, in this private museum of war. And another element had been added to her personal battle: her emotions. She'd never quite gotten her emotions back on track when it came to Roarke.

Her gaze skimmed over a case of handguns, all illegal but for collections like this since the Gun Ban implemented decades before. Clumsy, she thought, with their bulk and their weight. Lethal with their propulsion of hot steel into flesh.

Taking such impulsive killing devices off the street saved lives, she was sure. But as Lisbeth Cook had proved, there were always new ways to kill. The human mind never tired of dreaming them up.

She took the rack out of her bag, then studied her choices to find one that would fit.

She'd narrowed it down to three side arm types when the door behind her opened. She turned, intending to scald Summerset for interrupting, and Roarke strolled in.

"I didn't know you were here."

"I'm working at home today," he told her and lifted a brow. She looked a little frazzled, he noted, a bit distracted. And alluring.

"Do I assume the same for you, or are you just playing with guns?"

"I've got a case, sort of." She set the rack down, gestured to it. "Since you're here, you'd be better at this. I need an army-issue blaster, Urban War style, that would fit into this rack."

"U.S. Army?"

"Yeah."

"European style's a bit different," he commented as he walked to a display cabinet. "The U.S. had two hand blasters during that period, the second — toward the end of the war — was lighter, more accurate."

He chose a piece with a long double over-and-under barrel and molded grip in a dull gray. "Infrared sight, heat-seeking directional. The blast can be toned down to stun — which would drop a two-hundred-pound man to his knees and have him drooling for twenty minutes — or tuned up to shoot a fist-sized hole in a charging rhino. It can be pinpointed or scattered to wide range."

He turned the weapon over, showing Eve the controls on either side. She held out her hand, testing the weight when Roarke passed the weapon to her.

"Can't weigh more than five pounds. How does it charge?"

"Battery card in the butt. Same principle as a clip on an old-fashioned automatic."

"Hmm." She turned and tried it in the rack. It slid in, settled snug, like a foot in a comfortable shoe. "Looks like a winner. Are there many of these around?"

"That depends on if you choose to believe the U.S. government, which claims that the vast majority were confiscated from its troops and destroyed. But if you believed that, you wouldn't be the cynic I know and love."

She grunted. "I want to test this out. You've got a battery card, right?"

"Of course." He picked up the gun and rack himself, walked to the wall, and opened the panel. Frowning a little, Eve got on the elevator with him.

"Don't you have to go back to work?"

"That's the beauty of being the boss." He smiled as she hooked her thumbs in her pockets. "What's this about?"

"I'm not sure. Probably a waste of time."

"We don't get to waste nearly enough time together."

The doors opened to the lower-level target range with its high ceilings and sand-colored walls. He hadn't indulged his appreciation for comfort here. This room was spartan and efficient.

Roarke ordered the lights, set the rack on a counter area on the long glossy black console. He took a slim battery card from a drawer. He slid it into a slot on the butt of the weapon, gave it a quick shove with the heel of his hand.

"Fully charged," he told her. "You've only to activate. A thumb flick on the side here," he showed her. "Set your preferences and let it rip."

She tried it out, nodded. "It's fast, efficient. If you were worried about an attack, you'd have it on, already set." Experimentally, she laid it against her own weapon harness. "With decent reflexes, you could have it out, aimed, and fired in seconds. I want to discharge it a couple of times."

He opened another drawer, took out earplugs and safety goggles. "Hologram or still target?" Roarke asked as she put them on, then laid his palm on the identiscreen so that console lights glowed on.

"Hologram. Give me a couple of guys, night scene."

Obligingly, Roarke programmed the target range, then settled back to enjoy the show.

He'd given her two bulky men who were nonetheless fast on their feet. Their images came at her from both sides. With a quick pivot, she blasted them both.

"Too easy," she complained. "You'd have to be a one-armed moron with a vision impairment to miss with this thing."

"Try it again." He reprogrammed while she balanced on the balls of her feet and tried to imagine herself a scared old man getting ready to run.

The first one came at her fast, out of the shadows, and head-on. She shifted, firing in a crouch, then swiveling around in anticipation. It was closer this time. The second man had a steel bat lifted, had started into his swing. She rolled clear, fired up, and took his face off.

"Christ, I love to watch you work," Roarke murmured.

"Maybe he wasn't as fast," she considered

as she rose. "Maybe they knew about the blaster. But it would've given him the edge. And I had it on pinpoint. If he'd put it on wide range, he'd have taken out half the block in one swing."

To demonstrate, she switched it herself, then using a two-handed grip sprayed the street scene. The vehicle parked on the opposite curb went up in flames, window glass shattered, alarms screamed.

"See?"

"As I said." He stepped forward to take the weapon from her. Her hair was a tousled mess, and in the hard light every shade upon shade, every tone upon tone in the mix of brown showed. "I do love watching you work."

"They didn't just step up and knock him cold when he had one of those," she insisted. "They had to distract him, send in a decoy or someone he trusted. They needed enough time to blindside him and not get blown to hell while they were at it. He didn't have a vehicle, and he didn't call for transport. I checked. So he'd've been on foot. Armed, ready, street savvy. But they took him out as quick and easy as plucking a Nebraskan tourist's pocket in Times Square."

"You're sure it was quick and easy?"

"He had a blow to the head, no defensive

wounds. If he'd fired that thing and the blast didn't go into someone, there'd be a sign of the discharge. It isn't neat."

She blew her hair out of her eyes, shrugged. "Maybe he was just old and slow after all."

"Not everyone reacts to fear clearheadedly, Lieutenant."

"No, but I'd have bet the bank he would." She moved her shoulders again. "I say they were armed. One of them drew his attention." She began to set a new program herself as she thought it through. To put herself more into the scene she was devising, she removed her safety gear. "When he's focused on that target . . ."

She took the weapon back from Roarke, engaged the program, slid herself into it. One man slipping out of the shadows, swing toward him, reach for your weapon. Even as she flicked it on, pivoted, she felt the slight shock of a computer hit on her upper shoulder.

She'd gotten off a shot, that was true, she mused as she absently rubbed her shoulder. But she was young and fit, and her mind was cool.

"He was old and scared, but he figured himself tough, too smart for them. But they flanked him, somewhere between his door and the subway stop. He goes for one, and the other stuns him. A stun's not going to show up on autopsy unless it was a severe shock to the nervous system. They don't need that. They just need to jolt him, then they can knock him out and haul him off."

She laid the weapon down. "Anyway, I've got some answers. I just have to figure out where they fit."

"Then I take it this little demonstration is concluded."

"Yeah. I'm just going to — Hey," she protested when he reached out and yanked her against him.

"I'm remembering the first time with you." He expected her to resist a little, at first. It would only make her surrender sweeter. "It started right here." He lowered his mouth to graze her cheek, sampling the taste he intended to devour. "Nearly a year ago. Even then, you were everything I wanted."

"You just wanted sex." Even as she twisted, she angled her head so that his clever mouth could skim down her throat. Under her skin dozens of pulse points awakened.

"I did." He chuckled as his hands roamed down to mold and squeeze. "I still do. Always with you, darling Eve."

"You're not going to seduce me in the middle of a workday." But he was circling her toward the elevator, and she wasn't putting up much of a fight.

"Did you take a lunch break?"

"No."

He leaned back long enough to grin. "Neither did I." Then his mouth was hot and demanding on hers, taking her in quick, greedy gulps that had her nerve ends going from alert to sizzle.

"Oh hell," she muttered and groped clumsily for her communicator with one hand while she hung onto him with the other. "Wait, stop. Hold it a minute. Block video." She let out a breath. God, the man could do the most amazing things with his tongue. "Dispatch, Dallas, Lieutenant Eve."

He dragged her into the elevator, pressed her against the wall, and savaged her neck.

Dispatch, acknowledged.

"I'm taking an hour personal time." She bit back a moan when his hand closed roughly over her breast. And his other hand slipped between her legs, the heel pressed firmly against her where the heat built fever bright.

The first helpless orgasm had her fighting a scream.

Dallas, Lieutenant Eve, on personal time. Affirmative. Dispatch out.

She barely managed to end transmission before he was tugging her shirt open. She fumbled for the release on her weapon harness, then grabbed a handful of his hair. "This is crazy," she panted. "Why do we always want to do this?"

"I don't know." He swung her out of the elevator, then into his arms for the quick trip across the room to the big bed. "I just thank God for it."

"Put your hands on me. I want your hands on me." And they were, even as she fell beneath him onto the bed.

"A year ago." His lips traced over her face, along her jaw. "I didn't know your body, your moods, your needs. Now I do. It only makes me want you more."

It was insane, she thought dimly, as she met his mouth with the same urgent hunger that touching him, tasting him, always caused this deep ache to grind inside her.

Whether they loved fast and furious such as now, or with sweeping tenderness, that ache, that want never seemed to lessen.

He was right. He knew her body now, as she knew his. She knew where to touch to make his muscles tense, where to stroke to make them quiver. And that knowledge, that familiarity was unbearably seductive.

She knew what he would bring her, this time, every time, whether it was a slow, burning build or one breathless burst: pleasure, deep and dazzling, with the excitement that shimmered around it.

He found her breast, giving himself the thrill of taking her into his mouth. Soft, firm, his. Her back bowed, her breath caught, and beneath his busy tongue, her heart hammered.

His hand closed around the teardrop diamond she wore — a symbol that she had learned to take what he so needed to give her.

Then they rolled, tugging at clothes so flesh could slide and stroke torturously against flesh.

Her breathing quickened, firing his blood. She who was strong and steady could be made to tremble under him. He could feel her body straining toward release, see in her face those flickers of shock and delight as it built.

As he took her over, he closed his mouth over hers and swallowed her long, shuddering moan.

It wouldn't be enough. Even as her system started that lovely glide toward contentment, she knew he would drive her back up again. Drive her to where every pulse in her body pounded, every nerve sparked.

Braced and ready, she reached for him, struggling to give back even as her mind shattered and emptied, her system careened helplessly back into the heat.

She said his name, only his name, and arched up to take him inside her. The joining was smooth, and it was hot. Agile, eager, she pistoned her hips to meet each thrust. She could drive him as well as be driven. His fingers clamped down on hers, locked tight. Another layer of intimacy.

She could see in his eyes, so wildly blue, that he was as lost as she in this moment, this magic.

Only you. She knew he thought it, even as she did. Then those glorious eyes went opaque. With one breathless cry, she clung to his hands and threw herself over with him.

He lowered himself, sighing as he stretched out to rest his head between her breasts. Beneath him her body had gone lax as water. He knew she'd spring up soon enough, throw on her clothes, and go back to the work that consumed her.

But for now, for just a few moments more, she was content to drift.

"You should come home for lunch more

often," he murmured.

She laughed.

"Fun time's over. I've got to get back."

"Mm-hmm." But neither of them made a move to rise. "We have dinner at eight at The Palace with some top-level staff and their spouses from one of my transportation arms."

She frowned a little. "Did I know that?"

"Yes."

"Oh. I've got this thing at seven."

"What thing?"

"Will reading. At B. D. Branson's."

"Ah. No problem, I'll shift dinner to eight-thirty and we'll go by Branson's first."

"There's no *we* here."

He lifted his head from her breast, smiled. "I think I just proved you wrong."

"It's a case, not sex."

"All right, I won't have sex with you at Branson's, but it might have been interesting."

"Look, Roarke —"

"It simply makes sense, logistically." He gave her cheek a pat and rolled aside. "We'll go from Branson's to the hotel where dinner is set."

"You can't just sit in on a will reading. It's not a public event."

"I'm sure B.D. has some comfortable

place where I can wait for my wife without intruding, if that's necessary. As I recall, he has a very spacious home."

She didn't bother to grumble. "I guess you know him."

"Of course. We're competitors — not unfriendly ones."

She blew out a breath as she sat up and eyed him. "I'll see if the lawyer approves it, so pending that, fine. And maybe later, you'll give me your opinion of the Branson brothers."

"Darling, I'm always delighted to help."

"Yeah." This time she did grumble. "That's what worries me."

Chapter Five

Eve fidgeted in the back of the limo. It wasn't the mode of transport she'd have chosen when she considered herself on duty. The fact was, she preferred being at the wheel when she was on the clock. There was something just plain decadent about streaming along in a mile-long limo under any circumstances, but in the middle of an investigation, it was, well, embarrassing.

Not that she would use the words *decadent* or *embarrassing* to Roarke. He'd enjoy her dilemma entirely too much.

At least the long, somewhat severe black dress she wore was suitable enough for both a will reading and a business dinner. It was straight and simple, covering her from neck to ankle. She considered it practical, if foolishly expensive.

But there was no place to strap on her weapon without looking ridiculous, no place for her badge but the silly little evening purse.

When she squirmed again, Roarke draped an arm over the backseat and smiled at her. "Problem?"

"Cops don't wear virgin wool and ride in limos."

"Cops who are married to me do." He skimmed a finger over the cuff beneath the sleeve of her coat. He enjoyed the way the dress looked on her — long, straight, unadorned so that the body under it was quietly showcased. "How do you suppose they know the sheep are virgins?"

"Ha ha. We could have taken my ride."

"Though your current vehicle is a vast improvement over your last, it hardly provides this kind of comfort. And we wouldn't have been able to fully enjoy the wines that will be served with dinner. Most importantly . . ." He lifted her hand, nipped at her knuckles. "I wouldn't be able to nibble on you along the way."

"I'm on duty here."

"No, you're not. Your shift ended an hour ago."

She smirked at him. "I took an hour's personal time, didn't I?"

"So you did." He shifted closer, and his hand slid up her thigh. "You can go back on the clock when we get there, but for now . . ."

She narrowed her eyes as the car swung to the curb. "I haven't gone off the clock, ace. Move your hand, or I'll have to arrest you for assaulting an officer."

"When we get home, will you read me my rights and interrogate me?"

She snorted out a laugh. "Pervert," she muttered and climbed out of the car.

"You smell better than a cop's supposed to." He sniffed at her as they walked toward the dignified entrance of the brownstone.

"You squirted that stuff on me before I could dodge." He tickled her neck, made her jerk back. "You're awfully playful tonight, Roarke."

"I had a very satisfying lunch," he said soberly. "Put me in a cheerful mood."

She had to grin, then cleared her throat. "Well, shake it off, this isn't exactly a festive occasion."

"No, it's not." He stroked an absent hand down her hair before ringing the bell. "I'm sorry about J.C."

"You knew him, too."

"Well enough to like him. He was an affable sort of man."

"So everyone says. Affable enough to cheat on his lover?"

"I couldn't say. Sex causes the best of us to make mistakes."

"Really?" She arched her brows. "Well, if you ever feel like making a mistake in that area, remember what an annoyed woman can do with a Branson power drill."

"Darling." He gave the back of her neck a quick squeeze. "I feel so loved."

A solemn-eyed maid opened the door, her slick, black jumpsuit conservatively cut, her voice smooth and faintly British. "Good evening," she began with the faintest of nods. "I'm sorry, the Bransons aren't accepting visitors at the moment. There's been a death in the family."

"Lieutenant Dallas." Eve took out her badge. "We're expected."

The maid studied the badge for a moment, then nodded. It wasn't until Eve saw the quick jitter in the eyes that indicated a security probe that she tagged the maid as a droid.

"Yes, Lieutenant. Please come in. May I take your coats?"

"Sure." Eve shrugged out of hers, then waited until the maid neatly laid it and Roarke's over her arm.

"If you would follow me. The family is in the main parlor."

Eve glanced around the foyer with its atrium ceiling and graceful curve of stairs. Urban landscapes done in spare pen and ink adorned the pearl gray walls. The heels of her dress boots clicked on tiles of the same hue. It gave the entranceway and wide hall a misty, sophisticated ambiance. Light slanted down from the ceiling like moonbeams through fog. The staircase, a pure white sweep, seemed to be floating unsupported.

Two tall doors slid silently into the wall at their approach. The maid paused respectfully at the entrance. "Lieutenant Dallas and Roarke," she announced, then stepped back.

"How come we don't have her instead of Summerset?"

Eve's muttered question earned her another light neck squeeze from her husband as they walked into the room.

It was high-ceilinged, spacious, the lighting muted. The monochromatic theme carried through here, this time in layers of blue from the delicate pastels of fan-shaped conversation pits to the cobalt tiles of the fireplace where flames flickered.

Silver vases of varying sizes and shapes were arranged on the mantel. Each held white lilies. The air was ripely funereal with their scent.

A woman rose from the near curve of the seating area and crossed the sea of carpet toward them. Her skin was white as the lilies against her black suit. She wore her wheat-colored hair pulled severely back, knotted at the nape in smooth, snaking twists, in a way only the most confident and beautiful of women would dare. Unframed, her face was stunning, a perfect creation of planed cheekbones, slim, straight nose, smooth brow, shapely, unpainted lips all set off with large, lushly lashed eyes of dark violet.

The eyes grieved.

"Lieutenant Dallas." She held out a hand. Her voice reminded Eve of her skin — pale and smooth and flawless. "Thank you for coming. I'm Clarissa Branson. Roarke." In a gesture that was both warm and fragile, she offered him her free hand so that, for a moment, the three of them stood joined.

"I'm very sorry about J.C., Clarissa."

"We're all a little numb. I saw him just this weekend. We had . . . we all had brunch on Sunday. I don't — I still don't —"

As she began to falter, B. D. Branson stepped up, slid an arm around her waist. Eve watched her stiffen slightly, saw the gorgeous eyes lower.

"Why don't you get our guests a drink, darling."

"Oh yes, of course." She released Eve's hand to touch her fingers to her temple. "Would you like some wine?"

"No, thanks. Coffee, if you have it."

"I'll arrange for some to be brought in. Excuse me."

"Clarissa's taking this very hard," Branson said quietly, and his gaze never left his wife.

"She and your brother were close?" Eve asked.

"Yes. She has no family, and J.C. was as much a brother to her as he was to me. Now we only have each other." He continued to stare at his wife, then seemed to pull back into himself. "I didn't make the connection until you'd left my office today, Lieutenant. Your connection to Roarke."

"Is that a problem?"

"Not at all." He managed a small smile for Roarke. "We're competitors, but I wouldn't say we're adversaries."

"I enjoyed J.C.," Roarke said briefly. "He'll be missed."

"Yes, he will. You should meet the lawyers, so we can get on with this." A bit grim around the mouth now, he turned. "You've spoken with Suzanna Day."

Catching Branson's eye, Suzanna came over. Handshakes were brisk and impersonal before Suzanna ranged herself beside Branson. The final person in the room rose.

Eve had already recognized him. Lucas Mantz was one of the top and priciest criminal defense attorneys in the city. He was trim, slickly attractive, with waving hair of streaked white on black. His smile was cool and polite, his smoky eyes sharp and alert.

"Lieutenant. Roarke." He nodded to both of them, then took another sip from the straw-colored wine he carried. "I'm representing Ms. Cooke's interests."

"She didn't spare any expense," Eve said dryly. "Your client figuring on coming into some money, Mantz?"

His eyebrows lifted in an expression of amused irony. "If my client's finances are in question, Lieutenant, we'll be happy to provide you with records. Once you provide a warrant. The charges against Ms. Cooke have been filed and accepted."

"For now," Eve told him.

"Why don't we get on with the business at hand." Branson once more looked toward his wife who was directing the maid to position the coffee cart. "Please, let's sit down." He gestured toward the seating area.

Once they took their places and coffee was served, Clarissa sat beside her husband, her hand clinging to his. Lucas Mantz shot Eve one more cool smile, then settled on the far end. Suzanna sat in a facing chair.

"The deceased left personal bereavement discs to his brother and sister-in-law, to Ms. Lisbeth Cooke, and to his assistant, Chris Tipple. Those discs will be hand delivered to the appropriate parties within twenty-four hours of the reading of his will. Mr. Tipple was advised of tonight's reading but has declined to attend. He is . . . unwell."

She took a document out of her briefcase and began.

The opening was technical and flowery. Eve doubted the language for such things had changed in two centuries. The formal acknowledgment of one's own death had a long tradition, after all.

Humans, she thought, had a tendency to start planning for their end well in advance. And to be pretty specific about it. There was the betting pool with life insurance. *I bet so much a month that I'll live till I die,* she mused.

Then there were cemetery plots or cremation urns, depending on your preferences and income. Most people bought them in advance or gave them as gifts, picking out a sunny spot in the country or a snazzy box for the den.

Buy now, die later.

Those little details changed with the fashions and societal sensibilities. But one constant in the business end of life to death appeared to be the last will and testament. Who got what and when and how they got all the goodies the dead had managed to accumulate through the time fate offered.

A matter of control, she'd always thought. The nature of the beast demanded control be maintained even after death. The last grip on the controls, the last button pushed. For some, she imagined, it was the ultimate insult to those who had the nerve to survive. To others, a last gift to those loved and cherished during life.

Either way, a lawyer read the words of the dead. And life went on.

And she who dealt with death on a daily basis, who studied it, waded through it, often dreamed of it, found the whole business slightly offensive.

The minor bequests went on for some time, giving Eve a picture of the man who'd enjoyed foolish chairs and purple dressing gowns and carrot pasta with peas and cream sauce.

He'd remembered the people who'd had a part in his routine, from his doorman to the 'link operator at his office. He left his attorney, Suzanna Day, a Revisionist sculpture she had admired.

Her voice hitched over that, then Suzanna cleared her throat and continued.

"To my assistant, Chris Tipple, who has been both my right and left arms, and often most of my brain as well, I leave my gold wrist unit and the sum of one million dollars, knowing he will treasure the former and make good use of the latter.

"To my beautiful and beloved sister-in-law, Clarissa Stanley Branson, I leave the pearl necklace my mother left to me, the diamond heart brooch that was my grandmother's, and my love."

Clarissa began to weep silently into her hands, her slender shoulders shaking even when her husband draped his arm around them.

"Hush, Clarissa," Branson murmured in her ear, barely loud enough for Eve to hear. "Control yourself."

"I'm sorry." She kept her head lowered. "I'm sorry."

"B.D." Suzanna paused, casting Clarissa a glance of quiet sympathy. "Would you like me to stop for a few moments?"

"No." Jaw set, mouth grim, he kept his arm firmly around his wife and stared straight ahead. "Please, let's finish."

"All right. To my brother and partner, B. Donald Branson." Suzanna took a breath. "The disposition of my share of the business we ran together is set down in a separate document. I acknowledge here that all my interest in Branson Toys and Tools is to be transferred into his name upon my death should he survive me. If he should predecease me, that interest is to be transferred to his spouse or any children of that union. In addition, I hereby bequeath to my brother the emerald ring and diamond cufflinks that were our father's, my disc library including but not exclusive to all family images, my boat the *T and T*, and my air cycle in the hopes he'll finally try it out. Unless, of course, he was right, and my crashing it is the reason this will is being read."

Branson made a sound, something that might have been a short, strained laugh, then closed his eyes.

"To Lisbeth Cooke." Suzanna's voice chilled several degrees as she spared Mantz one glimmering stare of dislike. "I leave all the rest of my personal possessions, including all cash, bank and credit accounts, real estate, financial holdings, furnishings, art, and personal property. Lissy my love," Suzanne continued, biting off the words, "don't grieve too long."

"Millions." Branson got slowly to his feet. His face was deathly pale, his eyes brilliant. "She murders him and stands to gain millions. I'll fight this." Hands clenched, he turned on Mantz. "I'll fight this with everything I have."

"I understand your distress." Mantz rose

as well. “However, your brother’s wishes were clearly and legally outlined. Ms. Cooke has not been charged with murder but with second-degree manslaughter. There are legal precedents that protect her inheritance.”

Branson bared his teeth. Even as he lunged, Eve sprang up to block him. Before she could, Roarke was doing so.

“B.D.” Roarke spoke calmly, but he had Branson’s arms pinned firmly to his sides. “This won’t help you. Let your lawyer handle it. Your wife’s very distraught,” he continued as Clarissa curled into a ball and wept wildly. “She should lie down. Why don’t you take her upstairs, give her a soother.”

The bones in Branson’s face stood out in sharp relief, so keen it seemed they might cut right through the flesh. “Get out of my house,” he ordered Mantz. “Get the hell out of my house.”

“I’ll see him out,” Roarke said. “Take care of your wife.”

For one long moment, Branson strained against Roarke’s hold; then he nodded, turned. He gathered his wife up, cradling her as he would a child, and carried her from the room.

“You’re done here, Mantz.” Eve faced

him. "Unless you want to see if the Bransons have a dog you could kick."

He acknowledged this, picked up his own briefcase. "We all do our jobs, Lieutenant."

"Right, and yours is to run to a murderer and tell her she just got rich."

His eyes never wavered. "Life is very rarely black and white." He nodded to Suzanna. "Good evening, Counselor," he murmured and left.

"He's right." Suzanna sighed and sat again. "He's only doing his job."

"Will she inherit?" Eve demanded.

Suzanna pinched the bridge of her nose. "As things stand, yes. With charges of second-degree manslaughter, it can be argued she killed J.C. in a moment of jealous passion. His will was a sealed document. We can't prove she had prior knowledge of its contents or that those contents in any way influenced her. Under current law, she can gain by his death."

"If the charges are bumped up?"

Suzanna dropped her hand into her lap, regarding Eve thoughtfully. "Then things change. Is there a chance of that? I was under the impression the case was closed."

"Closed doesn't mean locked."

"I hope you'll keep me updated," Suzanna said as she rose and walked out with them to where the maid waited with their coats.

"I'll let you know what I can when I can." When they stepped outside, Eve slid her hands into her pockets. The limo was waiting. She struggled not to be embarrassed by it.

"Can we give you a lift home, Ms. Day?" Roarke asked.

"No, thanks. I could use a walk." She paused a moment and her sigh puffed out a thin stream of white. "As an estate lawyer, I deal with this sort of thing all the time. Grief and greed. But it's rare it hits this close to home. I really liked J.C. Some people you think will live forever." Shaking her head, she walked away.

"Well, that was fun." Eve started toward the car. "Wonder if Lissy my love will shed half as many tears over this guy as Clarissa. You know her very well?"

"Hmm, no." Roarke slid into the car beside her. "In that false intimacy of social acquaintances, I run into the Branson brothers at events occasionally. Clarissa and Lisbeth were usually with them."

"I'd've reversed it."

Roarke sat back, lighted a cigarette. "Meaning?"

"I'd put Clarissa with J.C. Just going by

what I've learned about him, he was lighter, less driven, more emotional than his brother. Clarissa comes off fragile, nearly tender — seems a little . . . intimidated by Branson. She doesn't seem like your slick corporate wife. The man's running a big, international company. Why doesn't he have a slick corporate wife?" Even as she posed the question, Roarke was grinning, making her narrow her eyes. "What?"

"I was going to say that he might have fallen for a different type. It happens, even to the heads of big, international companies."

Now her narrowed eyes glinted. "Are you saying I'm not a slick, corporate wife?"

He drew contemplatively on his cigarette. "If I said you were, you'd try to hurt me, then we'd end up wrestling back here. One thing would lead to another and we'd be very late for a business dinner."

"I'd be real sorry about that," she muttered. "You're not exactly the typical cop's spouse either, pal."

"If you said I was, we'd end up wrestling back here, and so on." He stubbed out his cigarette, then trailed a fingertip down the center of her body from throat to waist. "Wanna?"

"I didn't get all polished up so you could

leave fingerprints all over me."

He smiled and cupped her breast. "Darling, I never leave prints."

During the evening of dinner and conversation, Eve managed to slip away long enough to request a warrant to access data on Lisbeth Cooke's finances. She cited the sizable inheritance as cause and got lucky with a judge who either agreed with her or was too tired to argue the point.

As a result, she was alert and edgy when they arrived home.

"I've got some stuff I want to check out," she told Roarke when they walked into the bedroom. "I'm going to change and work in my office awhile."

"On . . . ?"

"I asked for a warrant to access Cooke's financial data." She wiggled out of the dress, tossed it aside, then stood there, much to her husband's interest, in two tiny scraps of black and high leather boots. "It came through during the dessert course."

"I must have a whip around here," he murmured.

"A what?"

Grinning, he started toward her, amused when her eyes narrowed threateningly. "Keep your distance, ace. I said I have work."

"I can access that information in half the time you can. I'll help you out."

"I didn't ask for help."

"No. But we both know I can do it faster and interpret it without getting a tension headache. And all I want in return is one little thing."

"What little thing?"

"That when we're finished you're still wearing this very interesting getup."

"Getup?" She glanced over, caught a glimpse of herself in the mirror, and blinked in shock. "Jesus, I look like —"

"Oh yes," Roarke agreed. "Yes, you do."

She looked back at him, struggled to ignore the slick ball of lust the gleam in his eyes caused. "Men are so weird."

"Then have pity on us."

"I'm not parading around in my underwear so you can cook up some sordid little fantasy."

"That's all right," he said as she snatched up a robe and bundled into it. "It's already cooked. We can do this faster in my office."

As she belted the robe, she eyed him suspiciously. "Do what faster?"

"Why, access the data, Lieutenant. What else?"

She refused to acknowledge the little tug of disappointment. "This is official business. I want the search initialized from my machine."

"You're the boss." He took her hand to lead her out.

"Just remember that."

"Darling, with what you're wearing under that robe forever imprinted on my memory, how could I forget?"

"All roads," she said dryly, "don't lead back to sex."

"The best ones do." He gave her butt a friendly pat as she preceded him into her office.

Galahad was curled up in her sleep chair. The cat raised his head in obvious annoyance at the disturbance. Since neither of them headed for the kitchen, he closed his eyes again and ignored them.

She slid the warrant into a slot on her computer, engaged it. "I know how to do a financial search. You're just here to interpret and tell me if you think she's got anything buried under layers."

"I'm here to serve."

"Cut that out." She dropped into the chair at her desk and called up Lisbeth Cooke's case file. "Hold current data," she ordered, "and initiate search of financial records on subject's name and identification number. All accounts, cash, credit, and debit. Start with one-year period back from this date."

Working. . . .

"Personal property?" Roarke asked.

"I'll get to it. We'll do the bucks first."

Data complete. Cooke, Lisbeth has four cash/credit accounts active.

"Scroll data on-screen."

Acknowledged. . . .

Eve made a low sound as the data popped. "Over two million in New York Security, another one and a half in New World Bank, just under a mil in American Trust, and a quarter million in Credit Managers."

"The last would be for living expenses," Roarke told her. "The other three are security and brokerage type accounts. Primarily long-term investments, managed by financial teams endorsed by those particular institutions. It's smart business. She's mixing high risk, big gain, with conservative interest income."

"How can you tell that from the names of the banks and the amounts in them?"

"It's my business to know the nature of banks. If you break this down to the next level, you'll see she likely has a balanced mix of stocks, bonds, mutuals, and fluid cash to float into new investments as the market fluctuates."

He ordered the breakdown himself and tapped a finger on the screen. "There, you see she believes in her own company. There's a healthy chunk of stocks in Branson T and T, but she hedges her bets. She also has stocks in several other companies, including a number of mine. And including three that are in direct competition with Branson. She doesn't invest her money emotionally."

"She's calculating."

"When it comes to her finances, she's smart and she's realistic."

"And she's got over four million to play with. Seems like a lot for an ad exec. Computer, detail on-screen deposits and e-transfers during the one-year period."

Working. . . .

When the data appeared, Eve lifted her eyebrows. "Look at that. An e-transfer from J. Clarence Branson's account to her living expense account. A quarter million every three months. A fucking million a year. Computer, list all transfers from subject Branson's account into the name of Lisbeth Cooke."

Working. . . . Data complete. Initial transfer of one hundred and fifty thousand dollars made July second, 2055. Transfers every quarter in that amount for period of one year. Transfers increased to two hundred thousand on July second, 2056, continuing at six-month increments until July second 2057, when transfers were increased to two hundred and fifty thousand.

"Nice work if you can get it," Eve muttered.

"He provided her with a steady and generous income." From behind her chair, Roarke rubbed absently at the tension in Eve's shoulders. "Why kill him?"

"A million a year?" She glanced back at him. "That would be nothing to you."

"Darling, it's all something."

"You probably blow that on shoes."

Chuckling, he pressed a kiss to the top of her head. "If your feet aren't happy, you aren't happy."

She grunted, tapped her fingers on the desk. "So what if she got greedy, got tired of hanging out for a million a year? Kill him, and do it right, and she gets it all and gets it now."

"It's a big risk. It goes wrong, she's charged with murder and gets nothing but a cage for her trouble."

"She's calculating. She'd figure the odds. Computer, what is the value of J. Clarence Branson's personal estate, not including any holdings in Branson Toys and Tools."

Working. . . .

Roarke moved away to pour himself a brandy. He knew Eve would drink nothing — save coffee — while she worked like this. And since he wanted her to sleep, he bypassed the AutoChef.

She was up and pacing when he turned back. The belt of her robe had loosened, reminding him he had plans for her before sleep. Very specific, interesting plans.

Data complete. Estimated value, including appraisals of real estate, transportation vehicles, art, and jewelry is two hundred and sixty-eight million dollars.

"That's a hell of an increase in salary." Eve scooped her hair back with her hand. "You deduct the minor bequests, the death taxes, and he'd have finagled some there to cut them back, and she stands to get about two hundred million."

"Mantz will argue she didn't know about the inheritance."

"She knew. They'd been together over three years. Damn straight she knew."

"How much am I worth, Eve, and how are the bequests in my will distributed?"

She glanced up briefly, irritation in her eyes. "How the hell would I know?" When he smiled at her, she blew out a breath. "That's different. We didn't make a business arrangement."

"True enough. But Mantz will still argue it."

"He can argue until his tongue falls out. She knew. I'm going to talk to her again, hit her tomorrow. Her story about the other woman and her insane fit of jealousy just isn't holding up for me."

She swung back behind the desk and called up the debit data. Dissatisfied, she studied it, sliding her hands into her pockets. "Expensive taste, but nothing out of line with her income. She bought a lot of men's jewelry, clothing. Maybe she had a guy on the side. That's an angle worth looking into."

"Hmm." Her robe was open now, revealing a delightful strip of flesh, black silk, and leather. "I suppose all of that has to wait until tomorrow."

"Not much more I can do here tonight," she agreed.

"On the contrary." He moved quickly, tugging the robe off, then running his hands over her. "I can think of a great deal more."

"Oh yeah?" Her blood was already on boil. The man had the most creative hands. "Such as?"

"Why don't I make a few suggestions." With his lips curving against hers, he backed her up against the wall. The first one murmured against her ear made her eyes cross.

"Wow. That's a good one. I'm just not sure it's physically possible."

"Never know until you try," Roarke said, and began to demonstrate.

Chapter Six

Peabody was already waiting when Eve arrived in her office in the morning. "Thanks for the time off, Dallas."

Eve eyed the slim vase of red, hothouse roses on her desk. "You bought me flowers?"

"Zeke did." The smile Peabody offered managed to be both whimsical and wry. "He does stuff like that all the time. He wanted to thank you for yesterday. I told him you weren't the type for flowers, but he thinks everyone is."

"I like flowers." Feeling slightly defensive about Peabody's take on her, Eve deliberately bent down and sniffed them. Twice. "What's not to like? So what's baby brother up to today?"

"He's got a list of museums and galleries. A long list," Peabody added. "Then he's going to go down and stand in line for discount theater tickets for tonight. He doesn't care what show, as long as he gets to see something on Broadway."

Eve studied Peabody's face, the concerned eyes, the teeth McNab had admired busily gnawing her bottom lip. "Peabody, people manage to do all the things he's planning and survive New York every day."

"Yeah, I know. And we went over all the warnings. Six or seven times," she added with a wry smile. "But he's just so . . . Zeke. Anyway, first he's going to contact the Bransons, again, see what they want him to do. He couldn't reach them yesterday."

"Hmm." Eve sat and began to poke through the interoffice and outside mail Peabody had already brought in and stacked. "Roarke and I sat in on the will reading last night. Cooke terminates her lover and inherits millions." Eve shook her head. "We're going to drop by her place this morning, have a little chat about that. Who the hell is Cassandra?"

"Who?"

"That's what I said." Frowning, Eve turned over the disc pouch. "Outside package — return address in the Lower East Side. I don't like packages from people I don't know."

"All outside deliveries are scanned for explosives, poisons, and hazardous materials."

"Yeah, yeah." But instinct had her reaching in a drawer for a can of Seal-It and coating her fingers before she opened the pouch and took out the disc. "The virus killer on this thing in working order?"

Peabody looked sadly at Eve's computer. "Your guess is as good as mine."

"Fucking piece of junk," Eve muttered and slipped the disc into a slot. "Computer, engage and run disc."

There was a low buzzing, like a distant swarm of angry bees on the rise. Her screen blinked on, off, then with a whine came on again.

"First chance I get," Eve vowed, "I'm paying a personal visit to those clowns in maintenance."

Disc in text only. Message as follows. . . .

Lieutenant Eve Dallas, New York Police and Security, Cop Central, Homicide Division.

We are Cassandra. We are the gods of justice. We are loyal.

The present corrupt government with its self-serving and weak-stomached leaders must and will be destroyed. We will dismantle, we will remove, we will annihilate as it becomes necessary to make way for the republic. No longer will the masses tolerate the abuse, the suppression of ideas and voices, the neglect of the pitiful few who cling to power.

Under our rule, all will live free.

We admire your skills. We admire your loyalty in the matter of Howard Bassi, known as The

Fixer. He was useful to us and terminated only because he proved defective.

Eve slammed another disc into a slot. "Computer, copy disc currently running."

We are Cassandra. Our memory is long. We are prepared. We will make our needs and demands known to you, in time. At nine-fifteen this morning, we will provide a small demonstration of our scope. You will believe. Then you will listen.

"A demonstration," Eve said when the message ended. With a quick check of her wrist unit, she grabbed both discs, sealed the original. "We've got less than ten minutes."

"To do what?"

"They gave us an address." She tapped a finger on the pouch, scooped up her jacket. "Let's check it out."

"If these are the people who took out Fixer," Peabody began as they strode to the elevator, "they already know you're looking into it."

"Not that hard to know. I've been in contact with New Jersey, I went to his shop yesterday. Run the address, Peabody, see what it is. Apartment, private home, business."

"Yes, sir."

They climbed into the car. Eve reversed, spun into a neat one-eighty, and shot out of the garage. "Display map," she ordered, heading south. "Lower East Side, sector six." When the street grid of the proper area shimmered onto her view screen, she nodded. "That's what I thought. It's a warehouse district."

"The building in question is an old glass factory slated for rehab. It's listed as unoccupied."

"Maybe the address is bogus, but they expect us to check it out. We won't disappoint them. Time?"

"Six minutes."

"Okay. We're going up." Eve punched the warning siren, hit vertical lift, and shot over the roofs of southbound traffic.

She swung east, passed reconditioned lofts where young professionals liked to live and shop and eat in overpriced cafés with bad lighting and good wine.

Barely a block over, the ambiance changed to disuse, disrepair, and despair. Misery walked the streets below in the guise of the unemployed and the unwashed, the failed and the desperate.

South of there, the old factories and warehouses loomed, nearly every one abandoned. Bricks were soot gray from smoke, smog, time. Window glass was in shards and sparkling on ground littered with garbage and straggling with weeds that struggled out of broken concrete.

Eve set the car down, briefly studied the square six-story building of brick closed in behind a security fence. The gate was equipped with a card lock but was wide open.

"I'd say we're expected." She drove through, scanning the building for any sign of life. Then, frowning, she stopped the car, climbed out. "Time?"

"About a minute," Peabody told her as she got out the opposite door. "Are we going in?"

"Not quite yet." She thought of Fixer and his nasty little shop. "Call for backup. Let Dispatch know where we are. I don't like the feel of this."

It was as far as she got. There was a rumble, and the ground shook under her feet. A series of flashes bloomed in the broken windows of the building and had her swearing.

"Take cover!" Even as she started to dive behind the car, the air exploded and gave her a hot little slap that had her skidding on her knees. The noise was huge, slamming against her eardrums, shooting a high-pitched wine through the center of her skull.

Bricks rained. A smoldering chunk

smashed into the ground inches from her face as she rolled under the car. Her body bumped solidly into Peabody's.

"You hurt?"

"No. Jesus, Dallas."

A wave of heat swarmed over them, brutally intense. The air was screaming. Debris flew overhead, battering the car like hot, furious fists. This is what the end of the world would feel like, Eve thought as she fought to catch her breath. Hot and filthy and full of noise.

Above them, the car rocked, bucked, shuddered. Then there was no sound but the ringing in her ears and Peabody's ragged pants. No movement but the wild hammering of her own heart.

She lay there another moment, assuring herself she was still alive, that all her parts were intact. There was a burning sensation where she'd met the concrete. Her fingers came away wet with blood as she probed the area. That disgusted her enough to have her bellying out from under the car.

"Goddamn it, goddamn it! Just look at my ride."

The car was dents and scorch marks, the windshield a fancy web of cracks. The roof carried a fist-sized hole.

Peabody crawled to her feet, coughed at

the smoke that was stinking the air. "You don't look so good yourself, sir."

"It's just a scratch," Eve muttered and wiped her bloody fingers on her ruined trousers.

"No, I meant as a whole."

Scowling, Eve glanced over, then narrowed her eyes. Peabody's face was smeared with black, making the whites of her eyes stand out like moons. She'd lost her uniform cap and her hair was standing wildly on end.

Eve rubbed her fingers over her own face, studied the now blackened tips, and swore. "Shit. That caps it. Call this in. Get some units out here for crowd control. We're going to have a hell of a crowd once people in this area crawl out from under their beds. And get —"

At the sound of a car, she whirled, one hand on the butt of her weapon. She wasn't sure if she was relieved or annoyed when she recognized the vehicle that pulled in behind hers.

"What the hell are you doing here?" she demanded when Roarke got out of the car.

"I could ask the same. Your leg's bleeding, Lieutenant."

"Not much." She rubbed a hand under her nose. "I've got myself a crime scene here, Roarke, and a hazardous area. Go away."

He took a handkerchief out of his pocket and, crouching down, examined the cut before tying the cloth over the wound. "You'll need that tended. It's full of grit." Rising, he stroked a hand over her hair. "Interesting do, and somehow you."

She caught Peabody's smirk out of the corner of her eye but decided to let it pass. "I don't have time for you, Roarke. I'm working."

"Yes, I can see that. But I think you'll want to make time." His eyes were cold and flat as he scanned the smoldering rubble. "This used to be my building."

"Oh hell." Eve shoved her hands into her pockets, paced away, back, away again. "Hell," she repeated and glared at him.

"I knew you'd be delighted." He took a disc pouch out of his pocket, offered it to her. He'd already copied the disc and secured it. "I received that this morning. It's a text message from a group calling themselves Cassandra. Basically, it calls me a capitalist opportunist — which of course is absolutely true — and states that I've been chosen in their first demonstration. There's some tired and tedious political jargon thrown in. The redistribution of wealth, the exploitation of the poor by the rich. Nothing terribly original."

His words might have been casual, but the tone was much too controlled. And she knew him. Beneath those cool eyes, violence was bubbling.

She handled it the only way she knew how, with professional dispatch. "I'm going to need you to come in so I can take a detailed statement. I'll have to take this as evidence."

She broke off as the violence in his eyes swam to the surface. No one, she thought fleetingly, no one could look more dangerous than Roarke in an icy temper.

Abruptly, he swung away from her to stride through the smoking bricks.

"Damn it." Impatient, she scooped a hand through her disordered hair and tossed a glance at Peabody.

"Units are on the way, Dallas."

"Stand at the gate," Eve ordered. "Secure it if necessary."

"Yes, sir." With some sympathy, Peabody watched as Eve walked over to deal with her husband.

"Look, Roarke, I know you're pissed off. I don't blame you. Somebody blows up one of your buildings, you've got a right to be pissed."

"Damn right I do." He spun back to her, fury ripe in his eyes. The fact that she'd nearly backed up a step in the face of it both mortified and infuriated her. She compensated by leaning forward until her boots bumped his shoes.

"This is a goddamn crime scene, and I don't have the time or inclination to stand around and pat you on the head because one of your six million buildings got blown to hell. Now, I'm sorry about it, and I understand you feel ticked off and violated, but don't take it out on me."

He gripped her arms and hauled her up to her toes in a move guaranteed to make her snarl and spit. If his property hadn't been heaved out in a half-block pile of stinking ruin, she might have decked him.

"Do you think that's the problem?" he demanded. "Do you think the fucking warehouse is the problem?"

She struggled to think through her own temper. "Yes."

He hauled her up another inch. "You're an idiot."

"I'm an idiot? *I'm* an idiot? You're a moron if you think I'm going to stand here making clucky noises to your ego while I've got somebody blowing up buildings on my watch. Now, get your hands off before I take you down."

"How close were you to going in?"

"That's not —" She broke off, deflating as it hit her. It wasn't the building that put that wicked light in his eyes. It was her. "Not that close." She said it quietly as she unclenched her fists. "Not that close, Roarke. I didn't like the setup. I'd just ordered Peabody to call it in, send for a couple of backup units. I know how to handle myself."

"Yeah." He took a hand off her arm to brush his fingertips over her filthy cheek. "It shows." Then he released her completely, stepped back. "Have that leg tended to. I'll meet you at your office."

When he started to walk away, she jammed her hands in her pockets, pulled them out. Rolled her eyes. Damn it, she did know how to handle herself. She just didn't always know how to handle him. "Roarke."

He stopped, glanced back. And nearly smiled when he watched the obvious struggle between duty and heart on her face. Looking over to make certain Peabody had her back discreetly turned, she crossed to him, lifted a hand to his cheek.

"Sorry. I was a little pissed off, myself. Having a building blow up in my face does that to me." When she heard the approaching sirens, she dropped her hands, frowned. "No kissing in front of the uniforms."

Now he did smile. "Darling, no kissing until you wash your face. I'll meet you at your office," he repeated and walked away.

"Give it a couple of hours," she called out. "I'll be tied up here at least that long."

"Fine." He stopped by her car, angling his head as he studied it. "Actually, this suits you better now."

"Bite me," she said with a laugh, then put on her official face for the bomb squad.

When she returned to Cop Central, Eve hit the showers and washed off the stink and soot. She remembered the gash in her leg when the hot water stung. Setting her teeth, she cleaned the wound herself, dug out a first-aid kit, and went to work on it. She figured she'd watched the med-techs poke around her body often enough to handle a few cuts.

Satisfied, she rooted through her locks for her spare set of clothes and made herself a memo to bring more in. Those she'd been wearing went straight into the recycler as a dead loss.

She found Roarke in her office, having a cozy chat with Nadine Furst from Channel 75.

"Scram, Nadine."

"Come on, Dallas, a cop nearly gets

blown up when her husband's building is destroyed by person or persons unknown, it's news." She offered Eve one of her pretty cat smiles, but there was concern in her eyes. "You okay?"

"I'm fine, and I wasn't nearly blown up. I was yards away from the building at the time of the explosion. I've got nothing official to give you at this time."

Nadine merely recrossed her legs. "What were you doing at the building?"

"Maybe I was scoping out my husband's property."

Nadine snorted and managed to make the sound ladylike. "Yeah, and maybe you've decided to retire and raise puppies. Give a little, Dallas."

"The building was abandoned. I'm homicide. There was no homicide. I suggest you stroll on up to Explosives and Bombs."

Nadine's eyes slitted. "It's not your case?"

"Why would it be? Nobody died. But if you don't get out of my chair, somebody might."

"All right, all right." With a shrug, Nadine rose. "I'll go charm the boys in E and B. Hey, I caught Mavis's video yesterday. She looked fantastic. When's she due back?"

"Next week."

"We'll have a welcome home party for

her," Roarke put in. "I'll let you know the details."

"Thanks. You're so much nicer than Dallas." With a cocky grin, Nadine strolled out.

"I'm going to remember that crack the next time she wants a one-on-one," Eve muttered and closed her door.

"What didn't you tell her?" Roarke asked.

Eve dropped into her chair. "It's going to take time for E and B to scan and sweep the site. At this point, they have some pieces and suspect there were at least six explosive devices, likely on timers. It'll be a couple of days before I have a cohesive report."

"But it's your case."

"At this point, it appears the explosion is linked to a homicide I'm investigating." Fixer was hers now. She'd arranged it. "The people responsible for both contacted me. I have a meeting with Whitney shortly, but yeah, until he says differently, it's mine. Did you ever have any dealings with Fixer?"

Roarke stretched out his legs. "Is that an official question?"

"Shit." She closed her eyes. "That means you did."

"He had magic hands," Roarke said, examining his own.

"I'm getting really tired of hearing that

from people who should know better. Give."

"Five, maybe six years ago. He worked on a little device for me. Security probe, a very cleverly designed code breaker."

"Which I suppose you designed."

"For the most part, though Fixer had some interesting input. He was brilliant with electronics, but not completely trustworthy." Roarke plucked a stray speck of lint from his smoke gray slacks. "I decided it was unwise to use his services again."

"So nothing recent."

"No, nothing, and we parted ways amicably enough. I've no links to him, Eve, that should worry you or would complicate your investigation."

"What about this warehouse? How long have you owned it?"

"About three months. I'll get you the exact date of purchase and the details. It was intended for renovation. As the permits just came through, work was to begin next week."

"Renovating it into what?"

"Housing units. I also own the buildings on either side, and I have a bid on another in the area. They're to be rehabbed as well. Markets, shops, cafés. Some offices."

"Will that sector support that kind of thing?"

"I believe it will."

She shook her head, thinking of the income level and street crime. "You'd know more about that sort of thing, I guess. The building was insured."

"Yes, for little more than the purchase price at this point. The project's worth a great deal more to me." Taking the neglected, the disdained and giving it value meant a very great deal to him. "The building was old, but it was sound. The problem with progress is that it often sweeps aside, destroying rather than respecting what others have built before us."

She knew of his affection for old things but wasn't sure there was a point here. She'd seen little more than a pile of bricks, and that was before it had been blown up.

His money, she thought with a shrug. His time.

"Do you know anyone name Cassandra?"

Now he smiled. "I'm sure I do. But I sincerely doubt this is a former lover's jealous snit."

"They had to get the name from somewhere."

He moved his shoulders. "Maybe from the Greeks."

"Greek Town isn't anywhere near that sector."

For a moment he just stared at her; then he laughed. "The ancient Greeks, Lieutenant. In mythology, Cassandra could foretell the future, but no one believed her. She warned of death and destruction and was dismissed. Her predictions always came true."

"How do you know all this shit?" She waved the question away before he could answer. "So what's this Cassandra predicting?"

"According to my disc, the uprising of the masses, the toppling of corrupt governments — which is one of those annoying redundancies — and the overthrow of the greedy upper class. Of which I am a proud member."

"Revolution? Killing an old man and blowing up an empty warehouse is a pretty petty way to revolt." But she wouldn't dismiss the possibility of political terrorists. "Feeney's working on Fixer's office unit. It had a fail-safe feature, but he'll get by it."

"Why didn't they?"

"If they'd had anyone good enough to break into that fortress of his, they wouldn't have needed him in the first place."

Roarke considered, nodded. "Good point. Do you need me for anything else?"

"Not now. I'll keep you updated on the investigation. If you do a press release, keep it minimal."

"All right. Did you have your leg looked at?"

"I took care of it."

He raised his brow. "Let me see."

Instinctively, she tucked her legs under the desk. "No."

He only rose and stepped over to bend down and tug her leg up. At her sputtering protest, he tightened his grip and rolled up her trousers.

"Are you crazy? Stop that." Mortified, she reached out to slam the door shut. "Somebody could come in."

"Then stop squirming," he suggested, and gently peeled back the bandage. He nodded in approval. "You did a decent job." Even as she hissed at him, he lowered his head and touched his lips to the cut. "All better," he said with a grin just as the door opened.

Peabody gaped, flushed, then stammered out, "Excuse me."

"Just leaving," Roarke said, patting the bandage back in place while Eve ground her teeth. "How did you come through this morning's excitement, Peabody?"

"Okay, it was . . . well, actually." She cleared her throat and shot him a hopeful glance. "I got this little nick right here." She rubbed her finger at her jawline, heart fluttering pleasantly when he smiled at her.

"So you do." He stepped to her, angled his head, and touched his lips to the tiny cut. "Take care of yourself."

"Man, man, oh man," was the best she could manage when he'd left. "He's got such a great mouth. How do you stop yourself from just biting it?"

"Wipe the drool off your chin, for Christ's sake. And sit down. We've got a report to write for the commander."

"I almost got blown up and got kissed by Roarke all in the same morning. I'm writing it on my calendar."

"Settle down."

"Yes, sir." She took out her log and got to work. But with a smile on her face.

Commander Whitney was an imposing figure behind his desk. He was a big man with beefy shoulders and a wide face. There were lines scored in his forehead his wife fussed at him to have smoothed away. But he knew that when furrowed, that brow symbolized authority and power to his officers. He'd sacrifice vanity for results every time.

He'd called in the top people in the required units. Lieutenant Anne Malloy from E and B, Feeney from EDD, and Eve. He listened to the reports, dissected, calculated.

"Even using three shifts," Anne continued, "I'm projecting at least thirty-six hours before we've swept the site. The fragments coming in indicate multiple devices, using plaston explosives and intricate timers. This tells me the work was both expensive and sophisticated. We're not dealing with vandals or a scatter group. More likely we have an organized, well-funded operation."

"And the likelihood you'll be able to trace any of the fragments?"

She hesitated. Anne Malloy was a small woman with a pretty, caramel-colored face and wide eyes of quiet green. She wore her blond hair in a bouncy ponytail and had a reputation for being both cheerful and fearless.

"I don't want to make promises I can't keep, Commander. But if there's anything to trace, we'll trace it. First we've got to put the pieces together."

"Captain?" Whitney shifted his attention to Feeney.

"I'm down to the last couple of layers in Fixer's unit. I should have it bypassed by the end of the day. He put in a maze, but we're working through it, and we'll have whatever data there is. I've got some of my best going through his equipment at his shop now. If, as we believe, he was connected with this morning's explosion, we'll find the link."

"Lieutenant Dallas, according to your report, the subject was never connected with any political group or involved in any terrorist activity."

"No, sir. He was a loner. Most of his suspected criminal activity was in the area of robbery, security bypass, small explosives used in those fields. After the Urban Wars, he retired from the army. He was reputed to have become disenchanted with the military, the government, and people in general. He established himself as a freelance electronics artist, with his repair shop as a front. In my opinion, it was for those very reasons that once he discovered he hadn't been hired to take out a bank but to be a part in something much larger, he panicked, attempted to go under, and was killed."

"That leaves us with a dead electronics man who may or may not have recorded data on his activities, a previously unknown group with as yet undetermined purposes, and a privately owned building that's been destroyed with enough overkill to spew debris over a two-block area."

He leaned back, folded his hands. "Each of you will work on your particular angle, but I want all efforts coordinated. Data is to be shared. We were told this morning was a demonstration. They may not choose an uninhabited building in a scantily populated area the next time. I want this shut down before we're picking fragments of civilians as well as explosives out of the rubble. I want progress reports by end of shift."

"Sir." Eve stepped forward. "I'd like to take copies of both discs and each report to Dr. Mira for analysis. We could use a more detailed profile on the kind of people we're dealing with."

"Granted. The media will be given only the information that this explosion was a deliberate act and is under investigation. I want no leaks regarding the discs or the possible connection to a homicide. Work fast," he ordered and dismissed them.

"Normally," Anne said when the three of them moved down the corridor together, "I'd arm wrestle you for primary on this little project, Dallas."

Eve slid her eyes over, sized up Anne's tiny frame, and snorted. "I'd hurt you, Malloy."

"Hey, I'm little, but I'm tough." She bent

her arm, flexing her biceps. "In this case, however, the ball bounced to you first, and these jerks contacted you personally. I'll give way here." As if to symbolize it, she gestured Eve onto the glide ahead of her, then winked at Feeney and hopped on.

"I've got some of my top people on site," she continued. "I juggled the budget to work them round the clock, but it won't shake loose for that kind of OT in the lab. IDing and tracing these parts and pieces after a major explosion takes time. It takes manpower. It takes some hot fucking luck."

"We coordinate what you find with what my team comes up with at Fixer's, we might find some of that luck," Feeney said. "We could get even luckier, and I'll find names, dates, and addresses on his hard drive."

"I'll take luck, but I'm not going to count on it." Eve tucked her hands in her pockets. "If this is a well-funded, organized group, Fixer wouldn't have joined, but he wouldn't have run, either. Not as long as they were paying. He ran because he was scared. I'm going to tag Ratso again, see if he left anything out. What does Arlington mean to you, Feeney?"

He started to shrug, but Anne shot her hand between them, grabbed Eve's arm. "Arlington? Where does that play?"

"Fixer told my weasel he was afraid of another Arlington." She stared into Anne's troubled eyes. "Mean something to you?"

"Yeah, Christ, yeah. And to any E and B man. September 25, 2023. The Urban Wars were basically over. There was a radical group, terrorists — assassinations, sabotage, explosives. They'd kill anyone for a price and justified it as revolution. They called themselves Apollo."

"Oh shit," Feeney breathed when the name hit home. "Holy Mother of God."

"What?" Frustrated, Eve gave Anne a quick shake. "History's not my strong suit. Give me a lesson here."

"They're the ones who took responsibility for blowing up the Pentagon. Arlington, Virginia. They used what was then a new material known as plaston. They used it in such amounts and in such areas that the building was essentially vaporized.

"Eight thousand people, military and civilian personnel, including children in the care center. There were no survivors."

Chapter Seven

In Peabody's apartment, Zeke cleaned and repaired the recycler and replayed the 'link conversation with Clarissa Branson on the kitchen unit.

The first time he played it back, he told himself he was just making sure of the details, of what time he was to report to work, the address.

The second time he played it, he convinced himself he'd missed something vital in the instructions.

By the third time, the parts of the recycler lay neglected while he stared at the screen and let her soft voice wash over him.

I'm sure we have everything you need in the way of tools. She smiled a little as she spoke and made his heart beat just a little faster. *But you've only to ask if there's anything else you want.*

It shamed him that what he wanted was her.

Before he could give in and replay the transmission one more time, he ordered the 'link off. Color rose into his cheeks as he thought of his own foolishness, his own dishonor in coveting another man's wife.

She'd hired him to do a job, he reminded himself. That was all there was between them. All there ever could be. She was a married woman, as removed from him as the moon, and had never done anything to encourage these yearnings in him.

But as he rebuilt the recycler with the energy of the guilty, he thought of her.

"How much more can you tell me?" Eve asked.

Rather than squeeze into her office, she'd set them up in a conference room. Already, she had Peabody setting up crime scene photos and available data on a board. Right now, the board was very thin.

"Arlington's something anyone who wants into E and B studies." Anne sipped the stale black coffee the room's AutoChef offered. "The group had to have recruited inside people, probably both military and civilian. An instillation like the Pentagon just isn't easily infiltrated, and during that period, security was very tight. The operation was very slick," she continued. "The investigation indicated that a trio of explosive devices loaded with plaston were placed in all five sides, more in the underground facilities."

Restless, she rose, glancing at the board as she paced. "At least one of the terrorists must have had high clearance in order to set the bombs underground. There was no warning, no contact demanding terms. The entire facility went up at eleven hundred hours, detonated by timers. Thousands of people were lost. It wasn't possible to identify all the victims. There wasn't enough left of them."

"What do we know about Apollo?" Eve asked her.

"They took credit for the bombing. Boasted that they could do the same again, anywhere, at any time. And would unless the president resigned and their chosen representative was established as leader of what they called their new order."

"James Rowan," Feeney put in. "There's a dossier on him, but I don't think there's much data. Paramilitary type, right, Malloy? Former CIA operative with ambitions toward politics and lots of bucks. They figured him for the head guy, and likely the inside man at the Pentagon. But somebody took him out before it was verified."

"That's right. It's assumed he was head of the group; that he was pushing the buttons. After Arlington, he went public with video transmissions and on-air speeches. He was charismatic, as a lot of fanatics are. There was a lot of panic, pressure on the administration to cave rather than to risk another slaughter. Instead, they put a price on his head. Five million, dead or alive. No questions asked."

"Who did him?"

Anne looked back at Eve. "Those files are sealed. That was part of the package. His headquarters — a house outside of Boston — was blown up with him in it. His body was ID'd, and the group scattered, fell apart. Splinter groups formed, managed to do some damage here and there. But the tide of the Wars had turned — at least here in the States. By the late twenties, the core of the original group was either dead or in cages. Over the next decade, others were tracked down and dealt with."

"And how many slipped through?" Eve wondered.

"They never found his right hand. Guy named William Henson. He'd been Rowan's campaign manager during his political runs." Anne rubbed a hand over her slightly queasy stomach and set her coffee aside. "It was believed he was top level in Apollo. It was never proven, and he disappeared the same day Rowan went up. Some speculate he was inside when the bomb went, but that could be wishful thinking."

"What about their holes, headquarters, arsenals?"

"Found, destroyed, confiscated. It's assumed everything was found, but if you ask me, that's a big assumption. A lot of the data's sealed tight. Rumor is that a lot of the people taken in were killed without trial, tortured. Family members unlawfully imprisoned or executed." Anne sat again. "It might be true. It couldn't have been pretty, and there's no way it was by the book."

Eve rose, studied the photos on the board. "In your opinion, this deal is linked with what happened in Arlington?"

"I want to study the evidence more closely, pull the available data on Arlington, but it follows." She hissed out a breath. "The names — both mythical types — the political crap, the material used for explosives. Still, there are variations. It wasn't a military target, there was a warning, no lives were taken."

"Yet," Eve murmured. "Shoot me whatever data you spring on this, will you? Peabody, Fixer was army during the Urban Wars, let's take a closer look at his service record. Feeney, we need everything he put on that office unit."

"I'm on it." He rose. "Let me put McNab

on that service record. He'll be able to melt through any seals quicker."

Peabody opened her mouth, then shut it again in a thin line at one warning look from Eve.

"Tell him to send data to me as he gets it. Let's ride, Peabody. I want to find Ratso."

"I can access military data," Peabody complained as they headed down to the garage. "It's just a matter of going through channels."

"McNab can swim the channels faster."

"He's a show-off," she muttered and made Eve roll her eyes.

"I'll take a show-off as long as he gets the job done fast. You don't have to like everyone you work with, Peabody."

"Good thing."

"Shit, would you look at this?" Eve stopped to study her battered and abused car. Some joker had put a hand-lettered sign on the cracked rear window that read: Show mercy. Terminate me now.

"That's Baxter's warped sense of humor." Eve ripped the sign away. "If I turn this sucker in to maintenance, they'll just screw it up." She got behind the wheel. "And they'll take a month to do it. I'll never get it back the way it was."

"You're going to have to have the windows replaced at least," Peabody pointed out and tried to squint through the starburst of cracks on her side.

"Yeah." She pulled out, wincing when the car shuddered. Glancing up, she saw the sky through the hole in the roof. "Let's hope the temp controls still work."

"I can put in a request for a replacement."

"This *is* a replacement, remember?" Sulking, Eve headed south. "I'm going to take grief for this."

"I can ask Zeke to take a look at it."

"I thought he was a carpenter."

"He's good at everything. He can tinker with the innards, then you just get the glass replaced, the roof patched. It won't be pretty, but you won't have to turn the whole deal over to maintenance or enter the black hole of requisitions."

Something inside the dash controls began to rattle ominously. "When could he do it?"

"Soon as you want." She slid Eve a sidelong glance. "He'd really like to see your house. I told him about it, how you've got that mag old wood and furniture and stuff."

Eve shifted in her seat. "I thought you were going to a play or something tonight."

"I'll tag him, tell him not to get the tickets."

"I don't know if Roarke has plans."

"I'll check with Summerset."

"Shit. All right, okay."

"That's so gracious of you, sir." Happily, Peabody took out her palm 'link to call her brother.

They found Ratso at The Brew, contemplating a plate of what looked like undercooked brains. He blinked up as Eve slid into the booth across from him.

"These are supposed to be eggs. How come they ain't yellow?"

"Must be from gray chickens."

"Oh." Apparently satisfied with that, he dug in. "So what's up, Dallas? You got the guys who done Fixer?"

"I've got some lines to tug. What have you got?"

"Word is nobody sees Fixer that night. Don't expect to, 'cause he don't come out at night usual. But Pokey — you know Pokey, Dallas, he deals some Zoner if he scores enough, and does some street work as an LC."

"I don't believe Pokey and I are acquainted."

"Pokey's all right. Mostly he minds his own, you know? He says how he was doing street work that night. Not much business 'cause it's too fucking cold to fuck, you know? But he was tapped out, so he's out on the stroll, and he sees a van down from The Fixer's place. Nice new one. Figures how somebody's come around looking for some action, but there ain't nobody in it he can see. Said he scoped it out awhile in case somebody comes back and wants a quick poke. That's why they call him Pokey, he gives a real quick poke."

"I'll keep that in mind. What kind of van was it?"

Ratso toyed with his eggs and tried to look sly. "Well, see, I told Pokey you'd want to know stuff, and if it was solid data, you'd pay."

"I don't pay until I get the data. Did you tell him that?"

Ratso sighed. "Yeah, guess I did. Okay, okay, he says it was one of them fancy Airstreams, looked spanking, was black. Had zap security." Ratso smiled a little. "He knows 'cause he tried to get in and got the zap. So he's dancing and blowing on his hand and he hears a kinda commotion down the street."

"What kind of commotion?"

"I dunno. Like noise and maybe somebody yelling, and people coming. So he ducks around the corner in case who owns the van maybe saw him trying to break in. What he sees is two guys and one of 'em's carrying this big bag over his shoulder. The other — get this — is holding what Pokey says looks like a gun — like he's seen on-screen and on discs and shit. So they toss this bag in the back, and it makes a thump when it hits. Then they get in the front and drive away."

He scooped up more eggs, washed them down with the pissy-looking liquid in his glass. "I'm just sitting here thinking on it and wondering if I should tag you and fill you in, then here you are." He grinned at her. "Maybe it was Fixer in that bag. Maybe they took him off in it, and did him and tossed him in the river. Maybe."

"Pokey get the vehicle ID?"

"Nah. Pokey, he's not too smart, you know. And he said his hand was on fire and he didn't think nothing of it until I come around asking about Fixer."

"Black Airstream van?"

"Yeah, with the zapper. And oh yeah, he says how it had the full blast entertainment center in the dash. That's how come he thought maybe to get in. Pokey, he sometimes trades off electronics."

"Sounds like a real solid citizen."

"Yeah, he votes and everything. So how about it, Dallas, that's good data, right?"

She took out twenty. "If it leads anywhere,

there's twenty more. Now, how much do you know about Fixer's military history?"

The twenty vanished inside one of the pockets in Ratso's dirty coat. "History?"

"What he did in the army? He ever talk to you about it?"

"Not much. Couple times when we was drinking and he sucked down too many. He said he took out plenty of targets during the Wars. Said how the army called 'em targets 'cause they didn't have the balls to call them people. He had a real hard-on for the army. Said how he gave them every fucking thing he had, and they took everything. Um, how they thought they could throw money at him to make it right. He took their money and screw 'em. Screw the cops, too, and the CIA and the goddamn president of the U.S. of A., too. But that was only when he was sloppy. Otherwise, he never said nothing."

"Have you ever heard anything about Apollo or Cassandra?"

Ratso swiped a hand under his nose. "Table dancer over at the Peek-A-Boo goes by Cassandra. She got tits like watermelons."

Eve shook her head. "No, this is something else. You ask around, Ratso, but ask around real careful. And if you hear anything, don't wonder if you should tag me. Just do it."

"Okay, but I'm kinda low on operating expenses."

She rose, then tossed another twenty on the table. "Don't waste my money," she warned. "Peabody."

"I'll start the run on Airstream vans," Peabody said, "New York and New Jersey registrations."

"Goddamn it!" Eve dashed toward her vehicle. "Look at this shit, would you?" she demanded, jerking a thumb toward the bright red frowny face someone had painted on her dented hood. "No respect. No respect whatsoever for city property."

Peabody coughed, forced her face into stern, disapproving lines. "It's a disgrace, sir. Absolutely."

"Was that a smirk, Officer?"

"No sir, it certainly was not a smirk. It was a scowl. A righteous scowl. Should I canvas the area for spray cans, Lieutenant?"

"Kiss my ass." Eve slammed into the car, giving Peabody just enough time to snort out the laugh that had been burning in her chest.

"I do," she murmured. "Constantly." She let out a long breath, shook off the grin, and climbed in the passenger seat.

"We'll finish out the shift at my home office. I'll be damned if I'm going to park this thing in the garage and have the precinct snickering."

"That works for me. You've got better food." And there'd be no chance of McNab swinging through to do one of his tap dances.

"Have you got Lisbeth Cooke's address? We can swing by and see if we can catch her before we take the rest of this home."

"Yes, sir, I believe it's on the way." Peabody called it up. "That's just off Madison at Eighty-third. Should I call and set up an interview?"

"No, let's surprise her."

It was obvious they did, and that Lisbeth didn't care for surprises. "I don't have to speak to you," she said when she opened the door. "Not without my attorney present."

"Call him," Eve suggested. "Since you've got something to hide."

"I've got nothing to hide. I've given you my statement, I've interviewed with the prosecuting attorney's office. I've taken the plea, and that's it."

"Since it's all neat and tidy, it shouldn't bother you to talk to me. Unless everything you stated was a lie."

Lisbeth's eyes flashed. Her chin jutted. Pride, Eve saw, had been the right target.

"I don't lie. I insist on honesty, for myself

and the people I'm involved with. Honesty, loyalty, and respect."

"Otherwise, you kill them. We've established that."

Something flickered in Lisbeth's eyes, then her mouth thinned and they were cool and hard again. "What do you want?"

"Just a few questions to tidy up my case file." Eve angled her head. "Don't you include neatness in your list of required virtues?"

Lisbeth stepped back. "I warn you, the minute I feel you're out of line, I'm calling my representative. I can file harassment charges."

"Note that down, Peabody. No harassing Ms. Cooke."

"So noted, Lieutenant."

"I don't like you."

"Aw well, now you've hurt my feelings."

Eve studied the living area, the absolute order, the flawless taste. Style, she mused, she had to admit the woman had style. She could even admire it, in the twin streamlined sofas in deep green and blue stripes that looked as comfortable as they did attractive. In the trim, smoked glass tables and the vivid paintings of seascapes.

There was a case filled with books with faded leather bindings she knew Roarke would approve of, and a view of the city neatly framed with swept-back curtains.

"Nice place." Eve turned to study the perfectly groomed woman in casual at-home wear of buff-colored slacks and tunic.

"I don't believe you're here to discuss my decorating skills."

"J. Clarence help you pick out your knickknacks?"

"No. J.C.'s taste ran the gamut from the absurd to the tacky."

Rather than wait for an invitation, Eve sat on the sofa, stretched out her legs. "You didn't seem to have much in common."

"On the contrary, we enjoyed a great many of the same things. And I believed he had a warm, generous, and honest heart. I was wrong."

"A couple hundred million seems pretty damn generous to me."

Lisbeth merely turned away, took a bottle of water from a built-in minifridge. "I wasn't speaking of money," she said, and poured the water into a heavy, faceted glass. "But of spirit. However, yes, J.C. was very generous with money."

"He paid you to sleep with him."

Glass snapped against glass as Lisbeth slammed down her water. "He certainly did not. The financial arrangement was a separate matter, a personal one mutually agreed to. It kept us both comfortable."

"Lisbeth, you were taking the guy for a million a year."

"I was not *taking* him for anything. We had an agreement, and part of that agreement included monetary payments. Such arrangements are often made in relationships when one party has considerable financial advantage over the other."

"You have considerable financial advantage now that he's dead."

"So I'm told." She picked up her glass again, watched Eve over the rim. "I was unaware of the terms of his will."

"That's hard to believe. You had an intimate relationship, a long-term and intimate relationship that included, at your own admission, regular monetary payments. And you never discussed, never questioned what would happen in the event of his death."

"He was a robust, healthy man." She tried for a smooth shrug, but it came off in a jerk. "His death wasn't something we focused on. He did tell me I'd be taken care of. I believed him."

She lowered her glass and passion leapt into her eyes. "I believed him. I believed *in* him. And he betrayed me in the most insulting, the most intolerable of ways. Had he come to me and told me he wanted to end our arrangement, I would have been unhappy. I would have been angry, but I would have accepted it."

"Just like that?" Eve lifted her eyebrows. "No more payments, no more fancy trips and expensive gifts, no more boinking the boss?"

"How dare you! How dare you lower what we had to such crude terms. You know nothing, *nothing* about what was between J.C. and me." Her breath began to heave, her hands to clench. "All you see is the surface because you don't have the capability to see beneath it. And you, you're *boinking* Roarke; you wangled marriage out of him. How many fancy trips and expensive gifts are you raking in, Lieutenant? How many million a year goes in your pockets?"

With an effort, Eve kept her seat. Temper had washed ugly color into Lisbeth's face, turned her eyes into hot green glass. For the first time she looked fully capable of punching a drill through a man's heart.

"I haven't killed him," Eve said coolly. "And now that you mention it, Lisbeth, why didn't you wangle marriage out of J.C.?"

"I didn't want it," she snapped. "I don't believe in marriage. It was something we disagreed on, but he respected my feelings. I will have respect!" She'd taken three long strides toward Eve, fists clenched, when a movement from Peabody stopped her.

She seemed to tremble, and her knuckles went white with strain. The lips she'd peeled back in a snarl relaxed slowly and the wild color began to fade from her cheeks.

"That's some trigger you've got there, Lisbeth," Eve said mildly.

"Yes. Part of my plea bargain is to enter anger control therapy. I begin sessions next week."

"Sometimes it's not better late than never. You claim you went off when you learned J.C. was cheating on you. Yet no one knows of another woman in his life. His personal assistant swears there was no one but you."

"He's mistaken. J.C. deceived him even as he deceived me. Or he's lying," she said with a shrug. "Chris would have cut off his hand for J.C., so lying would be nothing."

"Why lie? Why cheat if, as you just told me, all he had to do was come to you and end the arrangement?"

"I don't know." She pushed an agitated hand through her hair, disturbing its perfect order. "I don't know," she repeated. "Perhaps he was like other men after all and found it more exciting to cheat."

"Don't like men much, do you?"

"As a whole, no."

"So, how'd you find out about this other woman? Who is she? Where is she? How is it no one else knows about it?"

"Someone does," Lisbeth said evenly. "Someone sent me photos of them together, discs of conversations. Conversations where they talked about me. Laughed at me. God, I could kill him all over again."

She whirled around, yanked open a cabinet, and pulled out a large pouch. "Here. These are copies. We gave the PA the originals. Look at him, with his hands all over her."

Eve tapped out the contents, frowned. They were decent shots. The man was very clearly J. Clarence Branson. In one, he sat on what looked like a park bench with a young blonde in a short skirt. His hand was resting high on her thigh. In the next, they were kissing with apparent passion, and the hand was under her skirt.

The others looked to be taken in a privacy room at a club. They were grainy, which fit if they'd been duped from disc. A club could lose its sex license if the management was caught running video of privacy rooms.

But grainy or not, they clearly showed J.C. and the blonde in various and energetic sexual acts.

"When did you receive these?"

"I've given all that information to the PA's office."

"Give it to me," Eve said shortly. And she was damn well going to find out why the PA hadn't bothered to pass these tidbits on to the primary investigator.

"They were in my mail slot when I got home from work. I opened them, I looked at them. I went directly to J.C. to confront him. He denied it. He actually stood there and denied it, told me he didn't know what I was talking about. It was infuriating, insulting. I lost my temper. I was blind with rage. I grabbed the drill and . . ."

She trailed off, remembering herself and her lawyer's instructions. "I must have lost my mind, I can't remember what I was thinking, what I was doing. Then I called the police."

"Do you know this woman?"

"I've never seen her before. Young, isn't she?" Lisbeth's lips trembled before she firmed them. "Very young and very . . . agile."

Eve slid the photos and discs back in the pouch. "Why are you keeping these?"

"To remind me that everything we had together was a lie." Lisbeth took the bag back, placed it in the cabinet again. "And to remind me to enjoy every cent of the money he left me."

She picked up her water glass again, lifted it as if in a toast. "Every goddamn cent."

Eve got back in her car, slammed the door. And brooded. "It might have happened just the way she said. Hell." She rapped a fist on the wheel. "I hate that."

"We can run the photo of the woman, try to get an ID. Something may pop."

"Yeah, shuffle it in when you have time. And when we have the goddamn photos." Disgusted, Eve pulled away from the curb. "No way to prove she knew about the will or that was her motive. And damn it, after seeing her in action up there, I tend to believe her story."

"I thought she was going to try to rip your face off."

"She wanted to." Then Eve sighed. "Anger control therapy," she muttered. "What next?"

Chapter Eight

"Snag on system," Eve muttered as she pushed away from her desk-link. "The PA's office said we didn't get the photos and discs on the Branson case because there was an SOS. My ass." She rose to pace. "SOS also stands for sack of shit."

She heard the snicker, turned to glare at Peabody. "What are you grinning at?"

"It's your way with words, sir. I do so admire your way with words."

Eve dropped into her chair again, leaned back. "Peabody, we've been working together long enough for me to know when you're gassing me."

"Oh. Is that also long enough for you to appreciate our personal rapport?"

"No."

To help put the Branson matter out of her mind for the moment, Eve squeezed the heels of her hands on either side of her head. "Okay, back to priorities. Run the vans while I see how much McNab's shaken loose on Fixer's military record. And why don't I have any coffee?"

"I was just wondering the same thing." To avoid another snarl, Peabody hurried into the kitchen.

"McNab," Eve said the minute she had him on-screen. "Gimme."

"Just got the basic front stuff for now. I'm weaving through." He recognized the view out the window behind her and pouted. "Hey, you working at home today? How come I'm not there, too?"

"Because, thank God, you don't live here. Now, let's have it."

"I'll shoot it to your home unit, but the quick rundown is as follows. Bassi, Colonel Howard. Retired. Enlisted in 1997, enrolled officer's training. Top scores. As a first lieutenant, he worked with STF — Special Training Forces. Elite, real hush-hush stuff. I'm working on that, but at this point, I'm just getting commendations — he had a hat full — and remarks about his expertise with electronics and explosives. He made captain in 2006, then worked his way right up the ranks until he was given a field promotion to full colonel during the Urban Wars."

"Where was he stationed? New York?"

"Yeah, then he was transferred to East Washington in . . . wait, I've got it. 2021. Had to put in for a special family transfer package because most military weren't allowed to take their families along during that period."

"Family?" She held up a hand. "What family?"

"Ah . . . military records have him down for a wife Nancy, civilian, and two kids, one of each. He got the transfer because his spouse was a civilian liaison between army and media. Like, you know, public relations."

"Hell." Eve rubbed her eyes. "Run the wife and kids, McNab."

"Sure, they're on the list to do."

"No, now. You've got the ID numbers there." She glanced over as Peabody brought in coffee. "Do a quick run on date of death."

"Shit, they're not old," McNab muttered, but he turned away to check the records. "Man, Dallas, they all bought it. Same DOD."

"September 25, 2023, Arlington County, Virginia."

"Yeah." He let out a sigh. "They must have been taken out with the Pentagon. Christ, Dallas, the kids were only six and eight. That bites."

"Yeah, I'm sure Fixer agreed with you. Now we know why he turned."

And, she thought, why he ran. How could

he expect to be safe, even in his dirty little fortress, if he was up against the kind of people who could wipe out the most secure military establishment in the country?

"Keep up the search," she ordered. "See if you can find anybody he worked with who's still around and no longer military. Somebody who got transferred with him, in his same unit. If he was STF, he probably had some part in dealing with Apollo."

"I'm on it. Hey, Peabody." He wiggled his brows when she came into view, and sliding his hand under his bright pink shirt mimed a thumping heart.

"Asshole," she muttered and stepped aside.

Scowling, Eve cut him off. "Roarke thinks he's got a thing for you."

"He's got a thing for breasts," Peabody corrected. "I happen to have a pair. I caught him eyeballing Sheila's from Records, and hers aren't as good as mine."

Thoughtfully, Eve glanced down at her own. "He doesn't look at my tits."

"Yes, he does, but he's careful because he fears you nearly as much as he fears Roarke."

"Only nearly? I'm disappointed. Where's my data on the vans?"

"Here." With a smug smile, Peabody

tapped a disc into the desk unit. "I used the one in the kitchen to run it. We've got fifty-eight hits, but that's with factory-installed zappers. If we consider that they were installed privately, we more than triple that number."

"We'll start with the big number, check and see if anyone reported their vehicle stolen during the forty-eight hours around the murder. If we don't hit there, eliminate families. I can't see a professional mother running the kids to arena ball practice in the afternoon, then Daddy transporting corpses in it at night. Look for registration to companies and males. We'll run females if we crap out on those.

"Use this unit," Eve told her and rose. "I can make calls on the one in the other room."

She contacted Mira and set up a meeting for the following day. The closest she could get to Feeney was his e-mail announcement that he was on a priority and could only take emergency transmissions.

Deciding to leave him to what he did best, she tagged Anne Malloy in the field.

"Hey, Dallas, your sexy husband just left."

"Oh yeah." Eve could see the rubble and the E and B teams sifting through it.

"He wanted to see what we had going here, which isn't any more than you already know, at this point. We've transported fragments to the lab. We're finding more. Your man took a look at a piece of one of the devices and said it was a chunk of high-impact politex, like they use in space construction. Probably from a remote. He could be right."

He would be right, Eve thought. *He was rarely otherwise.*

"What does that tell you?"

"A couple of things," Anne said. "One, at least some of the devices were made from space salvage or parts manufactured for that use. And two, your man's got a sharp eye."

"Okay." She scooped a hand through her hair. "If he's right, can you trace it?"

"It narrows the field. I'll be in touch."

Eve sat back, then out of curiosity looked up politex and its manufacturers.

It didn't surprise her to see Roarke Industries as one of the four interplanetary companies that made the product. But it did have her rolling her eyes. She noted Branson Toys and Tools also manufactured it. Smaller scale, she noted. On planet only.

She decided to save time and simply ask Roarke for a rundown on the other two companies, then spent the next hour backtracking, picking through old data, weeding through the fresh data McNab transmitted. She was about to go in and harass Peabody for results on the vehicle search when her 'link beeped.

"Dallas."

"Hey, Dallas!" Mavis Freestone's delighted smile filled the screen. "Catch this."

Beside the table, a column of air shimmered, then, in a blink, the hologram image of Mavis standing in the kitchen on skinny ruby heels with bright pink feathers drifting over her toes. She wore a short robe in eye-watering swirls of the same two tones that drooped off one shoulder to display a tattoo of a silver angel playing a gilt harp.

Her hair tumbled in spiraling curls as fat as soy sausages in a mix of gold and silver and glinted with a metallic sheen.

"Mag, huh?" She laughed and did a little bump and grind dance around the kitchen. "My room's got this way fine holo feature on the 'link. How do I look?"

"Colorful. Nice tattoo."

"That's nothing, get this." Mavis tugged the robe down her other shoulder to reveal a second angel with a little whip tail who carried a pitchfork and wore a maniacal grin. "Good angel, bad angel. Get it?"

"No." But Eve grinned. "How's the tour going?"

"Dallas, it is like wow! We're going just everywhere and the crowds are panic city when I perform. And Roarke's got us the most amazing transpo and all the hotels are absolutely the ult."

"Ult?"

"Ultimate. Today, I've got this appearance at a music center to sign discs and a bunch of interviews with media, then a gig at the Dominant here in Houston. It's like packed. I hardly have time to do hair."

Eve skimmed her gaze off the shiny curls. "But you manage."

"Yeah, I'd never get it all done if Leonardo hadn't come with me. Hey, Leonardo, I've got Dallas here. Come say hi." Mavis laughed and bounced on her heels. "She doesn't care if you're naked."

"Yes, she does," Eve corrected. "You look happy, Mavis."

"Beyond. Dallas, I'm totally D and D."

"Drunk and disorderly."

"No." Mavis giggled again and turned circles. "Dazed and delirious. It's everything I always wanted and didn't know. When I come back, I'm going to kiss Roarke all over his face."

"I'm sure he'll enjoy that."

"I know I will." This time Mavis cackled. "Leonardo says he's not jealous, and maybe he'll kiss Roarke, too. Anyway, how are things on the home front?" Before Eve could answer, Mavis tilted her head, then sighed. "You haven't seen Trina."

Eve paled a little, squirmed in her chair. "Trina? Trina who?"

"Come on, Dallas, you said you were going to get her to come by and do your hair and stuff while I was gone. You haven't had a salon date in weeks."

"Maybe I forgot."

"Maybe you thought I wouldn't notice. But that's okay, we'll have her give us both the works when I get back."

"Don't threaten me, pal."

"You'll cave." Mavis twirled a silver curl around her finger, then grinned. "Hey, Peabody!"

"Hi, Mavis." Peabody stepped closer. "Great hologram."

"Roarke has the best toys. Whoops, gotta go. Leonardo says it's time to get ready. Watch this." She twirled, blowing kisses, then winked away.

"How does she move like that on those heels?" Peabody wondered.

"Just one of the many Mavis mysteries. What have you got on the van?"

"Pretty sure I tagged it. Black Airstream, 2058 model, loaded." She offered Eve a hard copy data printout. "Registered to Cassandra Unlimited."

"Bull's-eye."

"But I checked the address. It's bogus."

"Regardless, it ties Fixer in and gives us a target. Did you do a search on Cassandra Unlimited?"

"Not yet. I wanted to give you this first."

"All right. Let's just see." Eve swiveled back. "Computer, search and report all data on Cassandra Unlimited."

Working. . . . No data in banks on Cassandra Unlimited.

"Yeah," Eve murmured. "That would've been too easy." She sat back a moment, closing her eyes as she considered. "Okay, try this, search and list all companies and businesses with Cassandra in the title. Keep it to New York and New Jersey."

Working. . . .

"You think they'd use the name?" Peabody asked her.

"I think they're smart, but they're cocky. There's a way to run it down. There's always a way."

Data complete. List as follows. . . . Cassandra's House of Beauty, Brooklyn, New York. Cassandra's Chocolate Delights, Trenton, New Jersey. Cassandra Electronics, New York, New York.

"Stop. All data on Cassandra Electronics."

Working. . . . Cassandra Electronics, 10092 Houston, established 2049, no financial or employee data in banks. A branch of Mount Olympus Enterprises. No available data. Encoded block illegal under federal law and will be reported automatically to CompuGuard.

"Yeah, you do that. The data's there. It'll be there somewhere. Verify address on Houston."

Working. . . . Address is invalid. No such address exists.

Eve rose, circled the room. "But they put it in. Why bother to register the companies, risk an automatic search by CompuGuard, an IRS probe?"

Peabody took the opportunity to program more coffee. "Because they're cocky?"

"That's just exactly right. They don't know the van was spotted and tagged, but they had to know I'd do a run on the name Cassandra and click into it."

She took the coffee Peabody offered absently. "They want me to waste my time on it. If they can get an illegal into the data system, they've got funds and superior equipment. They aren't worried about CompuGuard."

"Everybody's worried about Compu-

Guard," Peabody disagreed. "You can't get by them."

Eve sipped her coffee and thought of Roarke's private room, his unregistered equipment, and his talent for skimming smoothly by CompuGuard's all-seeing eye. "They did," was all she said. "We'll dump this on EDD." Officially, Eve thought. Unofficially, she would ask her clever husband what he could do. "For now we'll just wait."

She turned back to the machine, called up the four companies that manufactured politex. Roarke Industries, she noted, Branson Toys and Tools, Eurotell Corporation, and Aries Manufacturing.

"Peabody, any of these named for those god people?"

"God people? Oh, I get it. Aries. I think he's a god of something or other, and I know he's a sign of the Zodiac."

"Greek?"

"Yeah."

"Let's see if they follow pattern." She ordered the data search and found Aries listed at an invalid address and attached to Mount Olympus.

"They're certainly tidy." Eve stepped back, leaned against the counter. "If they have a pattern, we can start predicting. Like

Cassandra," she said with a cool smile.

She sent Peabody off to transfer the data and start an updated report. Then, switching to privacy mode, she called Roarke's office.

"I need to speak with him," she told Roarke's terrifyingly efficient assistant. "If he's available."

"Just one moment, Lieutenant. I'll pass you through."

One hand to her headphones, Eve moved quietly to the doorway, saw Peabody hard at work at the desk. With only a slight tug of guilt, she slipped back out of sight. She wasn't deceiving her aide, she told herself. She was preventing Peabody from stepping into the shadowy area between the law and justice.

"Lieutenant? What can I do for you?"

Eve blew out a breath and stepped into those shadows. "I need a consult."

"Oh? Of what sort?"

"Of the unofficial sort."

A glimmer of a smile worked around his mouth. "Ah."

"I hate when you say 'ah' that way."

"I know."

"Look, I'm not in a position to explain right now, but if you don't have anything on for tonight —"

"But I do. We do," he reminded her. "You invited guests."

"I invited?" She went totally blank. "I never invite anybody. You're the one."

"Not this time. Peabody and her young brother? Ring a bell?"

"Oh hell." Dragging a hand through her hair, Eve paced in a circle. "I can't get out of that. I can't tell her the truth, and if I make some lame excuse, she'll pout. You can't work with her when she pouts."

She picked up her coffee, drank with a scowl on her face. "Are we like feeding them and everything?"

He laughed, adoring her. "Eve, you are the most gracious of hosts. Personally, I'm looking forward to meeting Peabody's brother. Free-Agers are so soothing."

"I'm not much in the mood for soothing." But she shrugged. "Well, they have to go home sometime."

"They certainly do. I'll be home in a couple of hours. That should give you time to fill me in."

"Okay, we'll play it that way. You ever hear of Aries Manufacturing?"

"No."

"Mount Olympus Enterprises?"

She had his interest now. "No. But Cassandra slides right in, doesn't she?"

"Looks that way. I'll be home when you get here," she told him and signed off.

She solved the first problem by sending Peabody back to Cop Central with the updated report and instructions to pass what they had on to Feeney and McNab.

With the idea of clearing her head before she worked on the rest of the problem, she headed downstairs. A quick workout, she decided, might jar something loose in her brain.

Summerset stood at the base of the stairs. He studied her baggy sweater and ancient trousers with a cool and derisive eye. "I trust you intend to change into something more appropriate before dinner this evening."

"I trust you'll continue to be an asshole for the rest of your life."

He drew air sharply through his nose, and because he knew she despised it, took her arm before she could swing by him. She bared her teeth. He smiled. "There is a messenger coming to the door with a package for you."

"A messenger." Though she yanked her arm free as a matter of principle, she shifted to stand between Summerset and the door. Her hand moved automatically to rest on her weapon. "Did you scan?"

"Naturally." Puzzled, he lifted a brow. "It's a registered delivery service. The driver is a young female. The scan showed no weapons."

"Call the delivery service and verify," she ordered. "I'll take care of the door." She started forward, tossed a glance over her shoulder. "You scanned for explosives?"

He paled a little but nodded. "Of course. Gate security is very thorough. Roarke designed it himself."

"Call and verify," she repeated. "Do it from the back of the house."

Eyes grim, Summerset drew out his palm 'link but moved no farther than the parlor doorway. He'd be damned if he'd allow Eve to shield him as she'd done once before.

Eve watched the miniscooter approach on the security monitor. The logo for Zippy Service was clearly printed on the fuel tank. The driver wore the standard bright red uniform, goggles, and cap. She flipped them up as she stopped the scooter, then stood gaping at the house.

She was young, Eve noted, her cheeks still pudgy with baby fat. Her eyes were wide and dazzled as she craned her head back to try to see the top of the house as she moved forward.

She tripped on the steps, then blushed as

she looked around to see if anyone noticed. In one hand she carried a disc pouch. She used the other to hitch down her jacket, then ring the bell.

"The delivery is verified," Summerset said from behind Eve and nearly made her jolt.

"I told you to call from the back of the house."

"I don't take orders from you." He reached for the door, blocking her, then yelped in absolute shock when Eve stomped hard on his instep.

"Get back," she snapped. "Stupid son of a bitch." She muttered it as she yanked the door open. Before the delivery girl could give her standard greeting, Eve had dragged her inside, shoved her face first against the wall, and secured her hands behind her back.

"You got a name?"

"Yes, yes, ma'am. Sherry Combs. I'm Sherry Combs." She had her eyes squeezed shut. "I'm with Zippy. I have a delivery. Please, lady, I don't carry any money."

"Is that the right name, Summerset?"

"Yes. She's just a child, Lieutenant, and you've frightened her."

"She'll live through it. How'd you get the delivery, Sherry?"

"I—I—I . . ." She gulped audibly, kept her eyes shut. "I'm on rotation."

"No, how did the package come in?"

"Oh, oh, oh, drop box. I think. I'm pretty sure. Golly, I don't know. My supervisor just told me to bring it here. It's my job."

"Okay." Eve eased back, patted Sherry's shoulder. "We've been getting a lot of solicitations," she said with a smile. "We really hate that here." She pulled out a fifty-credit chip and pressed it into the girl's sweaty palm. "You drive careful."

"Okay, right, thanks, gosh." She started for the door, then turned back, almost tearfully. "Man, gee lady, you're supposed to sign for it, but you don't have to if you don't want to."

Eve simply jerked her head toward Summerset, then started upstairs with the pouch. She heard him murmur to the girl. "I'm terribly sorry. She hasn't had her medication today."

Despite the fact that she'd seen the return address on the pouch, Eve had to grin. But the humor didn't last long. Her eyes were cool when she walked back into her office. She sealed her hands, opened the pouch, then slipped the disc it held into her machine.

We are Cassandra.

We are the gods of justice.

We are loyal.

Lieutenant Dallas, we hope our demonstration of this morning was enough to convince you of our capabilities and the seriousness of our intent. We are Cassandra, and we predict that you will show your respect to us by arranging for the release of the following political heros now wrongly imprisoned in the gestapo facilities of Kent Prison in New York: Carl Minnu, Milicent Jung, Peter Johnson, and Susan B. Stoops.

If these patriots of freedom are not released by noon tomorrow, we will be forced to sacrifice a New York landmark. A symbol of excess and foolishness where mortals gawk at mortals. You will be contacted at noon for verification. If our demands are not met, all lives lost will be on your head.

We are Cassandra.

Susan B. Stoops, Eve thought. Susie B, former nurse, who had poisoned fifteen elderly patients at the rehab facility where she'd worked. Claiming they had all been war criminals.

Eve had been primary, had taken her in, and knew Nurse Susie B was doing five terms of life in the mentally defective ward at Kent Prison.

She had a feeling the other "political heros" would have similar histories.

She copied the disc and called Whitney.

"It's out of my hands, at least for now," Eve told Roarke as she paced the main parlor. "The political heads are doing their circle and spin. I wait for orders. I wait for contact."

"They won't agree to terms."

"No. You add up the body count the four names they want are responsible for, you come up with over a hundred. Jung blew up a church claiming all religious symbols were tools of the hypocritical right. A kids' choir was rehearsing inside. Minnu burnt down a café in SoHo, trapping over fifty people inside. He claimed it was a front for the fascist left, and Johnson was a hired assassin who killed anyone for the right price. What the hell's the connection?"

"Maybe there isn't one. It may just be a test. Will the governor acquiesce, or will he refuse?"

"They have to know he'll refuse. They've left us no way to negotiate."

"So you wait."

"Yeah. What place in New York symbolizes excess and foolishness?"

"What place doesn't?"

"Right." She frowned, paced. "I did a run on that Cassandra — the Greek one. It said how she was given her gift of prophecy by Apollo."

"I'd say this group enjoys symbolism." He glanced toward the doorway when he heard voices. "That'll be Peabody. Put it out of your mind for a couple of hours, Eve. It might help."

Roarke walked over to greet Peabody, to tell her she looked lovely, to shake hands with Zeke. He was so damn smooth, Eve thought. It never failed to fascinate her how he could shift from mode to mode without a single visible hitch.

Beside Zeke — gangling, his smile awkward as he struggled very obviously not to gawk — the contrast was only more marked.

"Give her the thing, Zeke," Peabody demanded and added a quick, sisterly jab in the ribs.

"Oh yeah. It's not much of anything." He offered that shy smile to Eve, then took a small wood carving out of his pocket. "Dee said you had a cat."

"Well, one lets us live here." Eve found herself grinning down at a thumb-sized carving of a sleeping cat. It was rough and simple and cleverly done. "And this, next to eating, is what he does best. Thanks, it's great."

"Zeke makes them."

"Just for fun," he added. "I saw your vehicle outside. It looks a little rough."

"It sounds rougher."

"I can take a look at it, tinker around."

"I'd appreciate it." She started to suggest he do just that, now, when she caught Roarke's warning look and bit the words back. "Ah, let me get you a drink first."

Damn party manners, she thought.

"Just some water, or juice maybe. Thanks. There's beautiful work in this house," he said to Roarke.

"Yes, there is. We'll show you through after dinner." He ignored Eve's grimace and smiled. "Most of the wood is original. I appreciate craftsmen who build to last."

"I didn't realize so much of the nineteenth- and twentieth-century interior work was left in an urban area like this. When I saw the Branson home today, I was just staggered. But this —"

"You were at the Bransons'?" Eve had finished scratching her head over the choices of juice Summerset had arranged. She poured something rose-colored into a glass.

"I called this morning to express my condolences and to ask if they'd prefer to postpone the work they'd contracted for." He took the glass she offered with a smile of thanks. "But Mrs. Branson said they'd appreciate it if I'd come by and look things over today. This afternoon, after the memorial service. She said the project might help take their minds off things."

"Zeke says they have a fully equipped workshop on the lower level." Peabody wiggled her eyebrows at Eve. "Apparently B. Donald likes to putter."

"Runs in the family."

"I still haven't met him," Zeke put in. "Mrs. Branson showed me around." He'd spent time with her, just a little time. And his system was still revving on it. "I'll get started tomorrow, work right there in the house."

"And get roped into doing odd jobs," Peabody said.

"I don't mind. Maybe I should go take a look at the car, see what I can do." He looked at Roarke. "Do you have any tools I could borrow?"

"I think I have what you need. They're not Branson, I'm afraid. I use Steelbend."

"Branson's good," Zeke said soberly. "Steelbend's better."

Sending his wife a blinding smile, Roarke laid a hand on Zeke's shoulder. "Let's go see what we've got."

"Isn't he great?" Peabody sent a look of

affection after her brother. "Twenty minutes at the Bransons' and he was repairing some plumbing blip. There's nothing Zeke can't fix."

"If he can keep that car out of the hands of the monkeys in maintenance, I'll owe him for life."

"He'll do it."

She started to bring up her newest worry. Something in Zeke's eyes, in his voice, when he spoke of Clarissa Branson. Just a crush, Peabody assured herself. The woman was married, years older than Zeke. Just a little crush, she told herself again, and decided her lieutenant was hardly the person to share foolish sisterly concerns with. Certainly not in the middle of a difficult investigation.

Peabody blew out a breath. "I know this isn't a great time for socializing. As soon as Zeke's done, we'll take off."

"We'll feed you. Look, there's this stuff all ready." Eve gestured absently to a tray of beautifully arranged canapés. "You might as well eat them."

"Well, since you insist." Peabody plucked one up. "No word from the commander?"

"Nothing yet. I don't expect to hear anything before morning. Which reminds me, I'll need you to report to Central at oh-six-hundred."

Peabody swallowed the canapé before she choked. "Six. Great." She blew out a breath and snagged another canapé. "Looks like it's going to be a very early evening."

Chapter Nine

Dear Comrade,

We are Cassandra.

We are loyal.

It has begun. The preliminary stages of the revolution have proceeded precisely as outlined. Our symbolic destruction of the property of the capitalist Roarke was pitifully simple. The slow-witted police are investigating. The first messages of our mission have been transmitted.

They will not understand. They will not comprehend the magnitude of our power and our plans. Now, they scramble like mice, chasing down the crumbs we've left for them.

Our chosen adversary studies the deaths of two pawns, and sees nothing. Today, unless we were mistaken in her, she will go where we have led her. And be blinded to the true path.

He would be proud of what we accomplish here.

After this bloody battle is won, we will take his place. Those who have stood for us, for him, will join us. Comrade, we look forward to the day we raise our flag over the new capital of the new order. When all those responsible for the death of the martyr die in pain and terror.

They will pay, in fear, in money, in blood, as one by one and city by city, we who are Cassandra destroy what they worship.

Gather the faithful today, Comrade. Watch the screen. I will hear your shouts of triumph across the miles that separate us.

We are Cassandra.

Zeke Peabody was a conscientious man. He believed in doing a job well, in giving it all his time, his attention, and his skill. He'd learned carpentry from his father, and both father and son had been proud when the boy had outdistanced the man.

He'd been raised a Free-Ager, and the tenets of his faith suited Zeke like his skin. He was tolerant of others; part of his beliefs included the simple knowledge that the human race was made up of diverse individuals who had the right to go their own way.

His own sister had gone hers, choosing to become a cop. No true Free-Ager would ever carry a weapon, much less use one against another living thing. But her family was proud of her for following her own path.

That, after all, was the foundation of Free-Agism.

One of the sweetest benefits of the job he'd taken here was the chance it gave him to spend time with his sister. It gave him a great deal of pleasure to see her in what had become her milieu, to explore the city she'd made her home. And he knew he amused her by dragging her around to every clichéd tourist attraction he could find on his guide disc.

He was very pleased with her superior. Dee had called and written home countless details about Eve Dallas that Zeke had arranged into a very complex and fascinating woman. But seeing her for himself was better. She had a strong aura. The dark shimmer of violence might have troubled him a bit, but the heart of it had been bright with compassion and loyalty.

He'd wanted to suggest that she try meditation to dull that shimmer, but he'd been afraid she'd take offense. Some people did. He'd also thought, perhaps, that nimbus of darkness might be necessary for her line of work.

He could accept such things, even if he never fully understood them.

In any case, he was satisfied that when the job was finished, he could return home content that his sister had found her place and was with the people she needed in her life.

As instructed, he went to the service entrance of the Branson brownstone. The servant who admitted him was a tall male with cool eyes and a formal manner. Mrs. Branson — she'd told him to call her Clarissa — had told him that all staff members were droids. Her husband considered them less intrusive and more efficient than their human counterparts.

He was shown to the lower-level workshop, asked if he required anything, then left alone.

And alone, he grinned like a boy.

The shop was nearly as well-equipped and organized as his own back home. Here, though he had no intention of using them, were the additions of a computer and telelink system, a wall screen, VR unit and mood tube, and a droid assistant that was currently disengaged.

He ran his hands over the oak he knew would be a joy to work with, then took out his plans. They were on paper rather than disc. He preferred to create his drawings with a pencil as his father had, and his grandfather before him.

It was more personal, Zeke thought, more a part of himself. He spread the diagrams out neatly on the workbench, took his bottle of water from his sack, and sipped contemplatively while he visualized the project, stage by stage.

He offered the work up to the power that had given him the knowledge and skill to build, then took his first measurements.

When he heard Clarissa's voice, his pencil faltered. The flush was already working up his neck as he turned. The fact that there was no one there only made the blush deepen. He'd been thinking too much about her, he told himself. And had no right to think about another man's wife. No matter how lovely she was, no matter if something in her big, troubled eyes called to him.

Especially because of that.

Because he was flustered, it took him a moment to realize the murmur of sound he heard was coming through the old vents. They should be sealed, he mused. He would ask her if she wanted him to take care of that while he was here.

He couldn't quite make out the words — not that he would have tried, he assured himself. Not that he would ever, ever, intrude on another's privacy. But he recognized her tone — the smooth flow of it, and his blood moved a little faster.

He laughed at himself, went back to his

measuring with the assurance that it was all right to admire a woman because of her beauty and gentle manner. When he heard a voice join hers, he nodded. Her husband. It was good to remember she had a husband.

And a lifestyle, he added, lifting a board with a casual strength his gangly body disguised. A lifestyle that was far removed from his own.

Even as he carried the board to the braces for his first cuts, he heard the tones change. Voices raised in anger now, loud and clear enough for him to catch a few words.

"Stupid bitch. Get the hell out of my way."

"B.D., please. Just listen."

"To what? More whining? You make me sick."

"I only want to —"

There was a thump, a crash that made Zeke wince, and the sound of Clarissa's voice, begging now: "Don't, don't, don't."

"Just remember, you pathetic cunt, who's in charge."

Another bullet of sound, a door slamming. Then a woman's wild and miserable weeping.

He'd had no right, Zeke told himself, no right to listen to the intimacies of a marriage. No right to want to go upstairs and comfort her.

But, my God, how could anyone treat their life partner so callously, so cruelly? She should be cherished.

Despising himself for imagining doing just that, of going upstairs, gathering Clarissa against him, Zeke slipped on his ear protectors and gave her the privacy that was her right.

"I appreciate you changing your schedule and coming here." Eve scooped her jacket off her ratty chair and tried not to obsess that her tiny, cluttered office was a far cry from the elegant Dr. Mira's work space.

"I know you're working against the clock on this one." Mira glanced around. Odd, she thought, she'd never been in Eve's office before. She doubted Eve realized just how completely the cramped little room suited her. No fuss, no frills, and very little comfort.

She took the chair Eve offered, crossed her smooth legs, lifted a brow when Eve remained standing.

"I should have come to you. I don't even have any of that tea you drink in here."

Mira merely smiled. "Coffee would be fine."

"That I've got." She turned to the AutoChef, which did little more than spit at her. Eve rammed it with the heel of her hand. "Goddamn budget cuts. One of these days I'm taking every lousy piece of equipment in this room and chucking it out the window. And I hope to God every piss-head in maintenance is down below when I do."

Mira laughed and glanced at the narrow slit of grimy glass. "You'd have a hard time fitting anything through that window."

"Yeah, well, I'd manage. It's coming up," she said as the AutoChef gave a coughing hum. "The rest of the team is working in their areas. We're meeting in an hour. I want to be able to take them something."

"I wish I had more to give you." Mira sat back, accepting the mug of coffee Eve offered. It was barely seven A.M., yet Mira looked as elegant and polished as fine glass. Her sable-toned hair waved gently back from her serene face. She wore one of her trim suits, this one in a quiet sage green she'd accented with a single strand of pearls.

In her tired jeans and bulky sweater, Eve felt scruffy, gritty-eyed, and unkempt.

She sat, thinking Roarke had said basically the same thing to her in the early hours of the morning. He'd continued to search, but he was up against equipment and minds as clever and complex as his own. It could be hours, he'd explained, or days before he broke through the tangled blocks and reached the core of Cassandra.

"Give me what you've got," Eve said shortly to Mira. "And it'll be more than I have now."

"This organization is exactly that," Mira began. "Organized. It would be my supposition that whatever they intend to do has been planned out meticulously. They wanted your attention, and they have it. They wanted the attention of the powers of the city, and have that as well. Their politics, however, elude me. The four people they're demanding be released are from variable points on the political compass. Therefore, this is a test. Will their demands be met? I don't believe they think they will."

"But they've given us no mechanism to negotiate."

"Negotiation isn't their goal. Capitulation is. The destruction of the building yesterday was merely a show. No one was hurt, they can say. We're giving you a chance to keep it that way. Then, they ask for the impossible."

"I can't link any of the four on the list together." Eve rested a booted ankle on her knee when she sat. She'd spent hours the night before trying to find the connection while Roarke had worked on Cassandra. "No political tenet, as you said. No associations, no memberships. Ages, personal and criminal histories. Nothing connects them. I say they picked those four names out of a hat, for the hell of it. They couldn't care less if those people are back on the street or not. It's smoke."

"I agree. Knowing that, however, doesn't ease the threat of what they'll do next. This group calls itself Cassandra, links itself to Mount Olympus, so the symbolism is clear. Power and prophecy, of course, but more a distance between them and mere mortals. A belief, an arrogance, that they, or whoever heads them, has the superior knowledge and ability to direct us. Perhaps even to care for us in the ruthlessly cold directives of gods. They'll use us — as they did Howard Bassi — when we have the potential to be useful. And when they are done, we are rewarded or punished as they see fit."

"This new republic, new realm?"

"Theirs, of course." Mira sampled the coffee, delighted to discover it was Roarke's marvelous blend. "With their tenets, their rules, their people. It's the tone that troubles me more than the content, Eve. Underlying what is said is a glee in saying it. 'We are Cassandra,' " she added. "Is that the group, or one person who believes himself to be many? If the latter is partially true, you're dealing with a clever and damaged mind.

'We are loyal.' Loyal, we can assume, to the organization, the mission. And to the terrorist group Apollo from which Cassandra was given its prophetic powers."

" 'Our memory is long,' " Eve murmured. "It would have to be. Apollo was broken more than thirty years ago."

"You'll note the constant use of the plural pronoun, the short declarative sentences followed by political jargon, propaganda, accusations. There's nothing new in that part of it, nothing original. It's recycled, and a great deal older than three decades. But don't take this to mean they're not advanced in the ways and means in which they operate. Their foundation may be tired and trite, but I believe their intentions and capabilities are vital.

"They came to you," she continued, "because they respect you. Possibly admire you — soldier to soldier. Because when they win, as they believe they will, victory will have a more satisfying taste if their opponent was worthy."

"I need their target."

"Yes, I know you do." Mira closed her eyes a moment. "A symbol. Again, it would be something worthy. A place of excess, they said, and foolishness. Where mortals gawk at mortals. Perhaps a theater."

"Or a club, an arena. It could be anything from Madison Square to a sex joint on Avenue C."

"More likely the first than the second." Mira set her coffee aside. "A symbol, Eve, a landmark. Something that would have impact."

"The first hit was an empty warehouse. Not much impact."

"It was Roarke's," Mira pointed out and watched Eve's eyes flicker. "It got your attention. They mean to keep your attention."

"You think they'll target one of his properties again." Eve pushed to her feet. "Well, that narrows it down. The man owns most of the damn city."

"Does that bother you?" Mira began, then caught herself and nearly chuckled. "Sorry, knee-jerk psychologist's question. I think it's a good possibility since they've targeted you that they may focus on Roarke's properties. It's certainly not conclusive, no more, really, than what you'd term a hunch. But you have to look somewhere."

"All right, I'll contact him."

"Concentrate on important buildings, something with tradition."

"Okay, I'll get started."

Mira got to her feet. "I haven't given you much help."

"I didn't give you much to work with." Then Eve jammed her hands in her pockets. "I'm not really in my area here. I'm used to dealing with straight murder, not the threat of wholesale annihilation."

"Are the steps that different?"

"I don't know. I'm still feeling my way around. And while I am, somebody's got their finger on the button."

She tried Roarke in his home office first, and got lucky. "Do me a favor," she said immediately. "Work at home today."

"For any particular reason?"

Who was to say, she thought, that the sumptuous lobby, the theaters and lounges in his midtown office building didn't make it the target?

And, if she told him that, he'd be down there in a heartbeat, doing a search and scan personally. She wouldn't risk it.

"I don't like asking, but if you could keep on that project we were dealing with last night, it would help a lot."

He studied her face. "All right. I can shift some things around. I've got an auto-search going in any case."

"Yeah, but you get things done faster when you're working them yourself."

He lifted a brow. "I believe that was very

nearly a compliment."

"Don't get puffed up about it." She leaned back, tried to look casual. "Look, I'm kind of pressed right now, but can you shoot me some data here?"

"Of what kind?"

"Your properties in New York?"

Now both eyebrows winged up. "All?"

"I said I was pressed for time," she said dryly. "I don't have a decade or so to deal with this. Just the really jazzy ones. Jazzy old stuff."

"Why?"

Why? Shit. "I'm just doing a cross-check. Loose ends. Routine."

"Darling Eve." He didn't smile when he said it, and she began to drum her fingers on the desk.

"What?"

"You're lying to me."

"I am not. Jesus, ask a guy for some basic data, data which as his wife I'm entitled to, and he calls you a liar."

"Now I know you're lying. You don't give two damns about my properties, and you hate when I call you my wife."

"No, I don't. It's this certain tone you use that I object to. Forget it," she said with a shrug. "It's not important anyway."

"Which one of my properties do you

believe is the target?"

She hissed out a breath. "If I knew, don't you think I'd tell you? Just send me the goddamn data, will you, and let me do my job."

"You'll have it." His eyes were as cool as his voice now. "And if you find the target, let me know. You can reach me at my midtown office."

"Roarke, damn it —"

"Do your job, Lieutenant, and I'll do mine."

Before she could swear at him again, he'd cut her off. She kicked the desk. "Stubborn, tight-assed son of a bitch." Without hesitation, she tossed procedure out the window and called Anne Malloy.

"I need an E and B team at a midtown address. Full search and scan."

"You located the target?"

"No." She said that much between her teeth, then forced her jaw to relax. "It's a personal favor, Anne, I'm sorry to ask. Mira believes one of Roarke's properties will likely be today's target. He's going into his office, and I —"

"Give me the address," Anne said briskly, "and it's done."

Eve closed her eyes, breathed out slowly. "Thanks. I owe you."

"No, you don't. I've got a man of my own.

I'd do the same thing."

"I owe you anyway. I've got data coming in," she added when her machine beeped. "It's a place to start. I'll be sifting through it, hopefully have it narrowed down by our meeting."

"Fingers crossed, Dallas," Anne said and signed off.

"Peabody." Eve signaled her aide. "My office."

She sat, tunneled her fingers through her hair, then called up the data Roarke had sent her.

"Sir." Peabody stepped into the room. "I got the reports back on the Cassandra discs. Analysis doesn't show anything. Standard units, no initializations or prints. No way to trace."

"Pull up a chair," Eve ordered. "I've got a list here of potential targets. We'll run a probability scan, try to slim it down."

"How did you generate the list?"

"Mira's take is that we're likely looking for a club or theater. I agree with that. She thinks it's a pretty good bet they'll go for one of Roarke's again."

"Follows," Peabody said after a moment, then sat down next to Eve. And gaped at the list scrolling on-screen. "Man, those are his? He *owns* all that?"

"Don't get me started," Eve muttered. "Computer, analysis current data, select properties considered landmarks or traditional symbols of New York, and list. Ah, add buildings constructed on historic sites."

Working. . . .

"That's a good call," Peabody said. "You know, I was in a lot of these places with Zeke. We'd have been even more impressed if we'd known you owned them."

"Roarke owns them."

Task complete, the computer announced with such efficiency Eve eyed it suspiciously.

"Why do you think this thing's working so well today, Peabody?"

"I'd knock wood when I make statements like that, Lieutenant." Peabody's brows drew together as she studied the new list. "That didn't whittle it down by a whole lot."

"That's what he gets for liking old things. The guy has a real obsession for old shit." She let out a breath. "Okay, we're thinking club or theater. Mortals gawking at mortals. Computer, which of this list runs matinees today?"

Working. . . .

"They want people inside," Eve murmured as the computer burped rudely. "Lives lost. Not just a couple of tour groups, not just employees. Why not go for a full house. Impact."

"If you're right, we could still have time enough to stop it."

"Or we could be peeking in the wrong window and some bar downtown blows up. Okay, okay." Eve nodded when the new data emerged. "That's better, that's workable. Computer, copy current list to disk, print hard copy."

Eve checked the time, rose. "Let's get this in to the conference room." She snatched up the hard copy, stared at it. "What the hell is this?"

Peabody looked over her shoulder. "I think it's Japanese. I told you to knock on wood, Dallas."

"Get the damn disc. If it's in Japanese, Feeney can run it through a translator. Out the fucking window," she muttered as she strode from the room. "One of these days, out the fucking window."

The disc proved to be in Mandarin Chinese, but Feeney dealt with it and put it on the wall screen.

"Mira's preliminary profile," Eve began, "and the computer analysis of data and supposition indicates these are the most likely targets. All are entertainment complexes, either landmarks or constructed on the site of destroyed landmarks. All have performances scheduled this afternoon."

"That's a good angle." Anne tucked her hands in her back pockets as she read the screen. "I'll send out teams for a search and scan."

"How much time will you need?" Eve asked her.

"Every damn bit of it." She whipped out her communicator.

"No uniforms and unmarked vehicles," Eve said quickly. "They may have the buildings under surveillance. Let's not tip them off."

With a nod, Anne began to bark orders into her communicator.

"We got through the fail-safe." Feeney picked up with EDD's progress. "The old bastard coded his data. I'm running a code breaker, but he used a good one. It's going to take more time."

"Let's hope it's something worth looking at."

"McNab tracked down a couple of names from Fixer's old unit. Men still in the area. I've got interviews set up for noon today."

"Good."

"Teams are moving." Anne tucked her communicator away. "I'll be in the field. You'll know when I know. Oh, Dallas," she added as she headed for the door. "That address we discussed earlier? It's clean."

"Thanks."

Anne sent her a grin. "Any time."

"I'll be on the code until we have something to move on." Feeney rattled his bag of candied nuts. "This kind of shit went on all the damn time during the Urban Wars. Mostly we suppressed and subdued, but there's bigger and better shit out there now."

"Yeah, but we're bigger and better, too."

It made him smile a little. "Goddamn right."

Eve rubbed her eyes when she was alone with Peabody. The scant three hours' sleep she'd managed was threatening to fog her brain. "Man the computer in here. As Malloy's teams report in, adjust the list. I'll report in to Whitney, then I'll be in the field. Keep me updated."

"You could use me in the field, Dallas."

Eve thought of how close she'd come to getting her aide blown to pieces once already and shook her head. "I need you here," was all she said, and headed out.

An hour later, Peabody swung between being miserably bored and outrageously edgy. Four buildings had been tagged clean, but there were another dozen to go with just under two hours until noon.

She wandered the room, drank too much coffee. She tried to think like a political terrorist. Eve could do that, she knew. Her lieutenant could slide into the mind of a criminal, walk around in it, visualize a scene from the eyes of a killer.

Peabody envied that skill, though it had occurred to her more than once it couldn't be a comfortable one.

"If I were a political terrorist, what building in New York would I want to take out to make a statement?"

Tourist traps and lures, she thought. The problem was she'd always avoided that kind of thing. She'd come to New York to be a cop and had deliberately — as a matter of pride, she supposed — avoided all the usual tourist havens.

The fact was, she'd never been inside the Empire State or the Met until Zeke . . .

Her head came up, her eyes brightened. She'd call Zeke. She knew he'd studied his guide disc front and back and sideways. So where would he, as an eager tourist from Arizona, most like to attend a weekday matinee?

She turned from the window to start toward the 'link, then scowled when McNab strolled in.

"Hey, She-Body, they dump you on desk duty, too?"

"I'm busy, McNab."

"Yeah, I can see that." He wandered to the AutoChef, poked. "This thing's out of coffee."

"Then go drink somewhere else. This isn't a damn café." She wanted him out and gone on general principles, and because she didn't want him smirking when she called her little brother.

"I like it here." Partially because he wanted to know, and partially to annoy her, he leaned over her monitor. "How many have been eliminated?"

"Get away from there. I'm manning this unit. I'm working here, McNab."

"What are you so touchy about? You and Charlie have a spat?"

"My personal life is none of your business." She tried for dignity, but something about him always put her back up. She marched over, elbowed him aside. "Why don't you go play with your motherboard?"

"I happen to be part of this team." To irritate her, he plopped his butt on the table. "And I outrank you, sweetheart."

"Only through some obvious glitch in the system." She jabbed her finger in his chest. "And don't call me sweetheart. The name is

Peabody, Officer Peabody, and I don't need some half-wit, skinny-assed e-man breathing down my neck when I'm on assignment."

He glanced down at the finger that had jabbed twice more into his chest. When he lifted his gaze, she was mildly surprised to see his usually cheerful green eyes had gone to pricks of ice. "You want to be careful."

The chilly steel of his voice surprised her, too, but she was too far in to back off. "About what?" she said and gleefully jabbed him again.

"About physically assaulting a superior officer. I'll only tolerate so much of your abuse before I start dishing it back out."

"*My* abuse. You come sniffing around every time I blink with your lame comments and innuendos. You try to horn in on my cases —"

"*Your* cases. Now she's got delusions of grandeur."

"Dallas's cases are my cases. And we don't need you poking into them. We don't need you strolling in for comic relief with your stupid jokes. And *I* don't need you asking questions about my relationship with Charles, which is completely private and none of your damn business."

"You know what you do need, Peabody?"

Since she'd raised her voice to a shout, he did the same. And he was up, toe to toe, nearly nose to nose.

"No, McNab, just what do you think I need?"

He hadn't intended to do it. He didn't think. Well, maybe he had. Either way, it was done. He'd grabbed her arms, he'd yanked her hard, and his mouth was currently doing a damn fine job of devouring hers.

She made a sound, something that was reminiscent of a swimmer inhaling water by mistake. Somewhere under his bubbling temper was the knowledge that she was likely to kick his ass the minute she recovered from the shock. So, what the hell, he gave the moment all he had.

He trapped her between the table and his body, and took as much of her in as a man could in one, long, greedy gulp.

She was paralyzed. It was the only rational explanation as to why the man still had his mouth on her instead of lying broken and bleeding on the floor.

She'd had some sort of a stroke or . . . Oh my God, who'd known an annoying little twit could kiss like this?

The blood simply drained out of her head and left it buzzing. And she discovered she wasn't paralyzed after all, when her arms locked around him, and her mouth began to meet his assault with one of her own.

They grappled, groping and biting. Somebody moaned. Somebody swore. Then they were staring at each other, panting.

"What the — what the hell was that?" Her voice came out in a squeak.

"I don't know." He managed to suck in air, release it. "But let's do it again."

"Jesus Christ, McNab!" Feeney exploded from the doorway and watched the pair of them jump apart like rabbits. "What the sweet hell are you doing?"

"Nothing. Nothing." He wheezed, coughed, tried to blink his vision clear. "Nothing," he said for a third time. "At all. Captain."

"Holy Mary McGuire." Feeney rubbed his hands over his face, kept them there. "We'll all just pretend I didn't see that. I didn't see a goddamn thing. I've just now this second walked into this room. Is that understood?"

"Sir," Peabody said snappily, and prayed the blush she could feel burning her face would fade sometime before the end of the decade.

"Yes, sir." McNab took a long sideways step away from Peabody.

Feeney lowered his hands, studied the two

of them. He'd locked less guilty-looking pairs in cages, he thought with an inner sigh. "Target's been located. It's Radio City."

Chapter Ten

They had time. They still had time, was all Eve allowed herself to think. She wore riot gear: the full antiflak jacket, the assault helmet, and face visor. All of which, she knew, would prove as useless as fresh, pink skin if they didn't have time.

So they did. That was the only choice for her, for the E and B team, and for the civilians they were working feverishly to evacuate.

The Great Stage at Radio City had pulled in a full house: tourists, locals, preschoolers with parents or caretakers, classroom groups with teachers and chaperons. The noise level was huge, and the natives weren't just restless, they were pissed.

"Seats run between one hundred and two hundred and fifty." The six-foot blonde, who'd identified herself as the theater manager, galloped beside Eve like a Viking warhorse. Outrage and distress had gone to battle in her voice. "Do you have any idea how complicated it's going to be to arrange alternate dates or refunds? We're sold out through the run of the show."

"Look, sister, you'll be holding your run of the show in pieces blown over to Hoboken if you don't let us do our job." She elbowed the woman aside and pulled out her communicator. "Malloy? Status."

"Multiple devices detected. We've located and neutralized two. Scan indicates six more. Teams already deployed. The stage has four elevators, every one of them can go down twenty-seven feet into the basement of this place. We got hot ones in all of them. Working as fast as we can here."

"Work faster," Eve suggested. She jammed the communicator back in her pocket and turned to the woman beside her. "Get out."

"I certainly will not. I'm the manager."

"That doesn't make you captain of this sinking ship." Because the woman outweighed her by a good fifty pounds and looked frazzled enough to put up a good, entertaining fight, Eve was tempted to haul her along personally. It was too bad she couldn't spare the time. Instead, she signaled to a couple of beefy uniforms, indicated the woman with a jerk of her thumb.

"Move this," was all she said and pushed her way through the noisy, complaining crowd of evacuees.

She could see the impressive block-long expanse of stage. A full dozen cops in riot gear were posted on it to keep any ticket holders from scrambling in that direction. The heavy red curtain was raised, the stage lights brilliant. No one, she thought dryly, would mistake the helmeted figures onstage for The Rockettes.

Babies wailed, the elderly griped, and a half dozen schoolgirls clutching their souvenir Rockette dolls wept silently.

The cover story of a water main leak had staved off panic, but it didn't make for cheerful cooperation from the civilians.

The evacuation teams were making progress, but it was no easy task to move several thousand annoyed ticket holders out of a warm theater and into the cold. The main lobby area was jammed shoulder to shoulder.

And there were countless other rooms, lounges, lobbies. Beyond the public areas there were dressing rooms, control centers, offices. Each one had to be searched, emptied, secured.

Add panic to annoyance, Eve mused, and you'd have several hundred casualties before they hit the doors. She slapped on her headset and climbed onto a wide Art Deco table to look down on the grumbling horde being pushed along through the grandiose lobby with its stylized glass and chrome.

She switched on her mike. "This is the NYPSD," she announced over the echoing din. "Your cooperation is appreciated. Please don't block the exits. Continue to move outside." She ignored the shouts and questions thrown at her and repeated her statement twice more.

A woman in her matinee pearls curled a hand around Eve's booted ankle. "I know the mayor. He's going to hear about this."

Eve nodded pleasantly. "Give him my best. Please proceed in an orderly fashion. We apologize for any inconvenience."

The word *inconvenience* pushed the bitch button. The shouts increased even as uniforms firmly led people through the doors. Eve had just swiveled her mouthpiece aside, pulled out her communicator for another status check when she saw someone come in instead of out.

Her blood went instantly on boil as Roarke slid gracefully through the crowd toward her.

Her teeth were grinding as she stared down at him. "What the hell do you think you're doing?"

"Insuring that my property — and my wife," he added just deliberately enough to make her snarl, "remain in one piece."

He hopped agilely beside her. "May I?" he began and snatched her headset.

"That's police property, ace."

"Which means it's an inferior product, but it should do the job."

Then, looking cool and sleek, he addressed the disorderly crowd. "Ladies and gentlemen, the staff and performers of Radio City apologize for this difficulty. All tickets and transportation costs incurred will be fully refunded. An alternate date will be set for today's matinee at no charge to any ticket holders who wish to attend. We appreciate your understanding."

The noise level didn't abate, but the tone of it altered dramatically. Roarke could have told Eve that money, unfailingly, talks.

"Pretty slick, aren't you?" she muttered and swung down behind the table.

"You need them out," he said simply. "What's your status?"

She waited until he stood down with her, then contacted Anne. "We're about fifty percent evacuated. It's moving, but slow. Where are you?"

"About the same. We've got half. Cooled one in the organ console. Working on one in the orchestra pit now. This one's almost a lock, but they're scattered all over hell and back. I've only got so many men."

Out of the corner of her eye, she saw Roarke checking a handheld scanner. It sank sickness into her gut. "Keep me posted. You," she said as she turned to him. "Get out."

"No." He didn't bother to look up but did lay a hand on her shoulder to prevent her from moving in on him. "There's one up on the catwalk. I'll take that one."

"You're taking nothing but a hike, and now."

"Eve, we both know there's no time to argue. If these people have the building under surveillance, they know you've tagged them. They could decide to detonate any time now."

"Which is why all civilians —" She broke off rather than talk to his back. He'd already turned away and was slipping quickly through the oncoming crowd. "Goddamn it, goddamn it, goddamn it." Fighting off panic, she muscled her way through after him.

She caught up just as he was unlocking a side door and managed to push her way in behind him.

It slammed, locked, and they eyed each other narrowly. "I don't need you here," they said together. Roarke very nearly chuckled.

"Never mind. Just don't crowd me." He moved fast up narrow metal steps, moved quickly along twisting corridors.

Eve saved her breath. They were in it now, win or lose.

She could hear the echoes of voices from below, just a hum as the walls were thick. Here the theater was plain and functional, like an actor without costume or makeup.

Roarke took another set of steps, more narrow than the last, and came out on what looked to Eve like the deck of a ship.

It swung out over the plush seats, gave a full view of the stage far below. As heights weren't on her list of favorite things, she turned away and studied the massive and complicated control panels, puzzled over the thick hanging hanks of rope.

"Where . . ." she began, then lost all power of speech as he stepped through an opening and out into space.

"I won't be long."

"Jesus, Roarke. Jesus!" She scrambled over, saw he was not actually walking on air. But from her perspective, he might as well have been. The platform was no more than two feet wide, a kind of bridge that spanned above the theater, slicing through huge hanging lights, more ropes and pulleys, metal beams.

Even as she stepped onto it after him, her ears began to buzz. She'd have sworn she could feel her brain start to swim in her skull.

"Go back, Eve. Don't be so stubborn."

"Shut up, just shut up. Where is the fucker?"

"Here." For both their sakes, he put her fear of heights out of his mind. And hoped she could do the same. Nimbly, he pivoted, knelt, then leaned over in a way that made Eve's stomach flip in one long, slow rotation. "Under this catwalk."

He ran the scanner as Eve gratefully lowered to her hands and knees. She kept her teeth gritted and told herself to watch him. Don't look down. Don't look down.

Of course, she looked down.

The crowd was thin now, just a few dozen stragglers being hurried along by uniforms. The trio of E and B men in the orchestra pit looked like toys, but she heard their shout of triumph through the ocean roar of blood in her ears.

"They took out another one."

"Mmm," was Roarke's only comment.

With sweaty fingers, she took out her communicator and answered Anne's beep. "Dallas."

"We've got two more down. Closing in.

I'm sending a team to the catwalk and another —"

"I'm on the catwalk. We're working on this one."

"We?"

"Just do the rest." She blinked her vision clear and saw Anne stride out onstage, look up. "We're under control here."

"I hope to Christ you are. Malloy out."

"Are we under control here, Roarke?"

"Hmm. It's a clever little bastard. Your terrorists have deep pockets. I could use Feeney," he said absently, then held out a minilight. "Hold this."

"Where?"

"Just here." He indicated, then glanced at her, noted she was dead pale and clammy. "On your belly, darling. Breathe slow."

"I know how to breathe." She snapped it out, then bellied down. Her stomach might have been doing a mad jig, but her hand was rock steady.

"Good, that's good." He stretched out across from her so they were nearly nose to nose and went to work with a delicate tool that glinted silver in the lights. "They want you to snip these wires here. If you do, you'll be blown into several unattractive pieces. They're a front," he went on conversationally while he carefully removed a cover. "A lure. They've made it to appear to be a second-rate boomer when in reality . . . Ah, there's that little beauty. When in reality, it's top of the line, plaston-driven, with compu-remote trigger."

"That's fascinating." Her breath wanted to come in pants. "Kill the bastard."

"Normally, I admire your kick-in-the-face style, Lieutenant. But try that with this, and the two of us will be making love in heaven tonight."

"Heaven wouldn't have either of us."

He smiled. "Wherever, then. It's this chip I need. Turn the light a bit. Aye, that's the way. I'll need both hands here, Eve, so I'll need one of yours as well."

"For what?"

"To catch this when it pops out. If they're as clever as I think, they'd have used an impact chip. Which means if this little darling falls, hits below, it'll take out a good dozen rows and put a very nasty crater in my floor. Very possibly shaking us off our perch here with the backwash. Ready?"

"Oh sure. Absolutely." She rubbed her sweaty hand on her butt, then held it out. "So you figure we can still have sex, wherever?"

He glanced up long enough to grin at her. "Oh sure. Absolutely." He took her hand, squeezed it once, then lowered it. You're going to need to lean out a bit. Keep your eye on what I'm doing. Watch the chip."

She emptied her mind, shifted so that her head and shoulders were unsupported. She stared at the little black box, the colorful wires, the dull green of the miniboard.

"This one." He touched the point of his tool to a gray chip no bigger than the first knuckle on a baby's pinkie.

"I've got it. Finish the job."

"Don't squeeze it. Be gentle. On three then. One, two." He slid the tip around the edge of the chip, pried it gently. "Three." And it snapped out with a quiet click that sounded like a bomb blast to Eve's ears.

It hit her cupped palm, bounced. She rolled her fingers into a loose fist. "Got it."

"Don't move."

"I'm not going anywhere."

Roarke pushed up to his knees, took out a handkerchief. Taking Eve's hand, he uncurled her fingers and placed the chip in the center of the silk, folded it, folded again. "Not much padding, but better than nothing. He slipped it into his back pocket. "As long as I don't sit on it, we'll be fine."

"Be careful. I like your ass too much to see it blown off. Now, how the hell do we get off of here?"

"We could go back the way we came." But there was a glint in his eye as he stood. "Or we can have some fun with it."

"I don't want any fun."

"I do." He took her hand to help her to her feet, then reached out to grip a rope and pulley. "Do you know what today's matinee was?"

"No."

"A revival of that longtime children's favorite, *Peter Pan*. Hold tight, darling."

"Don't." But he'd already pulled her close and in automatic defense, her arms locked around him. "I'll kill you for this."

"The pirates look great swinging to stage on these. Inhale," he suggested, then with a laugh swung free.

She felt a rush of wind that took her stomach and flung it behind her. Before her glazed eyes, she watched color and shape fly. The only thing that stopped her from screaming was pride, and even that was nearly used up as they flew over the orchestra pit.

Then the crazy man she was somehow married to closed his mouth silkily over hers. A hot little ball of pure lust burned along with terror, and both managed to jelly her knees so they buckled clumsily when her boots hit the stage.

"You're dead. You're meat."

He kissed her again and chuckled against her mouth. "It was worth it."

"Nice entrance." Feeney, his face rumpled and weary, walked toward them. "Now, if you kids have finished playing, we've got two more of these bastards still armed."

Eve elbowed Roarke aside and managed to stand on her own. "Civilians out?"

"Yeah, we're clear there. If they stick to deadline, we should make it. Cutting it damn close, but —"

He broke off as the rumble sounded below and the stage shook beneath their feet. Above, lights and cables swung wildly.

"Oh hell, oh shit." Eve slapped her communicator into her hand. "Malloy? Anne? Report. Give me a report. Anne? Do you copy?"

The answering buzz had her gripping Feeney's shoulder, then there was a crackle. "Malloy here. We had it contained. No injuries, no casualties. The timer went and we had to contain and detonate. Repeat, no injuries. But this understage area is one holy mess."

"Okay. All right." Eve rubbed a hand over her face. "Status?"

"We got them all, Dallas. This building's clean."

"Report to the conference room at Central when you're secured here. Good work." She broke transmission, spared Roarke a quick glance. "You're with me, pal." She offered Feeney a brief nod before striding off. "We'll need all security data on this building, a complete list of personnel — techs, performers, maintenance, managerial. Everyone."

"I ordered that for you when I learned the target. It should be waiting for you at Central."

"Fine. Then you can go back to buying the planet and stay out of my hair. Give me the chip."

He lifted a brow. "What chip?"

"Don't be cute. Let me have the impact chip or whatever it's called."

"Oh, that chip." With the appearance of cooperation, he took out his handkerchief, unfolded it. And revealed nothing. "I seem to have lost it somewhere."

"Like hell. Give me the goddamn chip. Roarke. It's evidence."

Smiling blandly, he shook the handkerchief, shrugged.

She moved in until her toes bumped his. "Give me the damn thing, Roarke." She hissed it out. "Before I order you strip-searched."

"You can't do that without a warrant. Unless, of course, you'd like to do it yourself, in which case I'd be more than delighted to waive a few of my civil rights."

"This is an official investigation."

"It was my property, twice. My woman, twice." His eyes had gone very cool. "You know where to find me if you need me, Lieutenant."

She grabbed his arm. "If 'my woman' is your new way of saying 'my wife,' I don't like it any better."

"I didn't think you would." He gave her a friendly kiss on the brow. "See you at home."

She didn't bother to snarl. Instead, she contacted Peabody to let the rest of the team know they were heading in.

Clarissa raced into the workroom where Zeke was quietly fashioning the grooves for the tongue-and-groove joints on his cabinet. He glanced up in surprise, noted that her eyes were huge, her face flushed.

"Did you hear?" she demanded. "Someone tried to set off a bomb in Radio City."

"In the theater?" His brow furrowed as he set down his tools. "Why?"

"I don't know. Money or something, I suppose." She brushed a hand over her hair.

"Oh, you're not using the entertainment center. I thought you would have heard. They aren't giving out any real details, just that the building's been secured and there's no danger."

She fluttered her hands as if she didn't know what to do with them now. "I didn't mean to interrupt your work."

"It's all right. That's such a beautiful old place. Why would anyone want to destroy it?"

"People are so cruel." She ran a fingertip along one of the smoothly sanded boards he had stacked on a worktable. "Sometimes there's no reason for it at all. It just is. I used to go to the Christmas show there every year. My parents would take me." She smiled a little. "Good memories. I suppose that's why I got so upset when I heard the news. Well, I should let you get back to work."

"I was about to take a break." She was lonely — and more. He was sure of it. Out of politeness, he avoided looking beyond, scanning her aura. He could see enough in her face. She'd used enhancers carefully, but the faint bruise on her cheek showed, as did the results of weeping.

He opened his lunch sack, took out his bottle of juice. "Would you like a drink?"

"No. Yes. Yes, I suppose I would. You

don't have to bring your lunch Zeke. The AutoChef is fully stocked."

"I'm sort of used to my own." Because he sensed she needed it, he smiled. "Got any glasses?"

"Oh, of course." She walked to a doorway, disappeared through it.

He tried not to pay close attention. Really, he did. But it was such a pleasure to watch her move. All that nervous energy just under the seamless grace. She was so tiny, so beautiful.

So sad.

Everything inside him wanted to comfort her.

She came back with two tall, clear glasses, then set them down so she could study his work. "You've already done so much. I've never seen the stages of something being built by hand, but I thought it would take much more time."

"It's just a matter of sticking with it."

"You love what you do." She looked back at him, her eyes just a little too bright, her smile just a little too wide. "It shows. I fell in love with your work the first time I saw it. With the heart of it."

She stopped, laughed at herself. "That sounds ridiculous. I'm always saying something ridiculous."

"No, it's not. It's what matters to me, anyway." He picked up a glass he'd filled, offered it. He didn't feel tongue-tied and miserably shy around her as he often did with women. She needed a friend, and that made all the difference. "My father taught me that whatever you put of yourself in your work, you get back twice over."

"That's nice." Her smile softened. "It's so important to have family. I miss mine. I lost my parents a dozen years ago and still miss them."

"I'm sorry."

"So am I." She sipped the juice, stopped, sipped again. "Why, this is wonderful. What is it?"

"It's just one of my mother's recipes. Mixed fruit, heavy on the mango."

"Well, it's marvelous. I drink entirely too much coffee. I'd be better off with this."

"I'll bring you a jug if you like."

"That's kind of you, Zeke. You're a kind man." She laid a hand over his. As their eyes met, he felt his heart stumble in his chest, fall flat. Then she slid her hand, and her gaze, aside. "It, ah, smells wonderful in here. The wood."

All he could smell was her perfume, as soft and delicate as her skin. The back of his hand throbbed where her fingers had skimmed it. "You've hurt yourself, Mrs. Branson."

She swung around quickly. "What?"

"There's a bruise on your cheek."

"Oh." Panic shadowed her eyes as she lifted her hand to the mark. "Oh, it's nothing. I . . . tripped earlier. I tend to move too fast and not watch where I'm going." She set her glass down, lifted it again. "I thought you were going to call me Clarissa. Mrs. Branson makes me feel so distant."

"I can make you a salve for the bruise. Clarissa."

Her eyes filled, threatened to overflow. "It's nothing. But thank you. It's nothing at all. I should go, let you get back to work. B.D. hates it when I interrupt his projects."

"I like the company." He stepped forward. He could imagine himself reaching out, taking her into his arms. Just holding her there. Nothing more than that. But even that, he understood, was too much. "Would you like to stay?"

"I . . ." A single tear spilled over, slipped beautifully down her cheek. "I'm sorry. I'm so sorry. I'm not myself today. My brother-in-law — I suppose, the shock. Everything. I haven't been able to . . . B.D. hates public displays."

"You're not in public now."

And he was reaching out, taking her into his arms where she fit as if she'd been designed for him. He held her there, nothing more than that. And it wasn't too much at all.

She wept quietly, almost silently, her face buried against his chest, her fists clenched against his back. He was tall, strong, innately gentle. She'd known he would be.

When the tears began to slow, she sighed once, twice. "You are kind," she murmured. "And patient, letting a woman you barely know cry on your shoulder. I really am sorry. I suppose I didn't realize I had all that pent up."

She eased back, offered him a watery smile. Her eyes glimmered with tears as she lifted to her toes to press a light kiss to his cheek. "Thank you." She kissed his cheek again, just as lightly, but her eyes had darkened, and her heart tripped against his chest.

The hands balled against his back opened, spread, stroked, her breath trembled out through lips just parted.

Then somehow, without thought or reason, his met them. Naturally as breathing, soft as a whispered promise. He drew her in, she drew him down into a kiss that spun delicately out until there was no time, no place for him but here and now.

She seemed to melt against him, muscle by muscle and bone by bone as if to prove she was as lost in that moment as he. Then she trembled, then shuddered until her body quaked almost violently against his.

She yanked back, her color high, her eyes huge and shocked. "That was — that was entirely my fault. I'm sorry. I wasn't thinking. I'm sorry."

"It was my doing." He was as pale as she was flushed, and every bit as shaken. "I beg your pardon."

"You were just being kind." She pressed a hand against her heart as if to stop it from bounding out of her chest. "I'd forgotten how that is. Please, Zeke, let's forget it."

He kept his eyes locked on hers, nodded slowly while his pulse beat like a thousand drums. "If that's what you want."

"It's what has to be. I stopped having choices a long time ago. I have to go. I wish —" She bit back whatever she'd intended to say, shook her head fiercely. "I have to go," she said again and dashed from the room.

Alone, Zeke laid his hands against the workbench, leaned in, and closed his eyes. What in God's name was he doing? What in God's name had he done?

He'd fallen flat-faced in love with a married woman.

Chapter Eleven

"Sir." The minute Eve walked into the conference room, Peabody was on her feet. Strain showed in the tightness around her mouth. "You received another communication."

Eve pulled off her jacket. "Cassandra?"

"I didn't open the pouch, but I had it scanned. It's clean."

With a nod, Eve took the pouch, turned it over in her hand. It was identical to the first. "The rest of the team's on the way in. Where's McNab?"

"How would I know?" It came out in something close to a squeak that had Eve glancing over to watch Peabody stuff her hands in her pockets, take them out, fold her arms over her chest. "I don't keep tabs on him. I don't care where he is."

"Tag him, Peabody," Eve said with what she considered admirable patience. "Bring him in."

"Ah, the superior officer should send for him."

"*Your* superior officer is telling you to get

his skinny butt in here. Now." Annoyed, Eve dropped into a chair and ripped open the pouch. She examined the disc briefly, then plugged it into the computer.

"Run disc."

Running. . . . contents are text only as follows. . . .

We are Cassandra.

We are the gods of justice.

We are loyal.

Lieutenant Dallas, we enjoyed today's events. We are in no way disappointed in our choice of you as adversary. In less than our projected time allotted, you located the described target. We are pleased with your skills.

Perhaps you believe you won this battle. Though we congratulate you on your quick and decisive work, we feel, in fairness, we should inform you today's work was only a test. A preliminary round.

The first wave of police experts entered the target building at eleven hundred hours and sixteen minutes. Evacuation proceedings began within eight minutes. You arrived at target twelve minutes after evacuation had begun.

At any time during this process, the target could have been destroyed. We preferred observing.

We found it interesting that Roarke became personally involved. His arrival was an unexpected bonus and allowed us to study you working together. The cop and the capitalist.

Forgive us for being amused by your fear of heights. We were impressed that despite it, you performed your duties as the tool of the fascist state. We had expected no less from you.

In triggering the last device, we allowed time for containment. Lieutenant Malloy will confirm that without this time, without this containment, several lives and a great deal of property would have been lost.

We will not be as accommodating with the next target.

Our demands must be met within forty-eight hours. To those initial demands, we now demand a payment of sixty million dollars in bearer bonds in increments of fifty thousand dollars. The capitalistic figureheads that line their pockets and break the back of the masses must be made to pay in coin they worship.

Once confirmation of the liberation of our compatriots is assured, instructions on delivery of the monetary penalty will be issued.

To prove our commitment to the cause, a small demonstration of our power will be

made at precisely fourteen hundred hours.
We are Cassandra.

"A demonstration?" Eve glanced at her wrist unit. "In ten minutes." She pulled out her communicator. "Malloy, are you still in the target?"

"Just securing."

"Get everybody out, keep out for another fifteen minutes. Run another scan."

"This place is clean, Dallas."

"Run it anyway. After the fifteen, have Feeney send a unit of exterminators in. The building's full of bugs. They were watching every move. We'll need the bugs brought in for analysis, but get out and stay out of the building until after fourteen hundred."

Anne opened her mouth, obviously decided to save her questions, then nodded. "Affirmative. ETA to Central thirty minutes."

"Do you think they got a bomb past the scan?" Peabody asked when Eve broke transmission.

"No, but I'm not taking the chance. We can't track every damn building in the city. They want to show us how big and bad they are. So they're going to take something out." She pushed away from the desk, walked to the window. "There's not a fucking thing I can do to stop them."

She scanned her view of New York, the old brick, the new steel, the crowds of people jammed onto glides or sidewalks, the nervous, edgy traffic in the streets, the rumble of it in the air.

Serve and protect, she thought. That was her job. That was her promise. And now all she could do was watch and wait.

McNab came in, looked anywhere but at Peabody. He preferred to pretend she wasn't in the room. "You sent for me, Lieutenant?"

"See what you can do with the disc I just ran. Make copies for my files and for the commander. And what is the status on Fixer's code?"

McNab allowed himself a small, smug smile and a sly sidelong glance at Peabody. "I just cracked it." He held up his own disc and struggled not to scowl as Peabody turned her head away and studiously examined her nails.

"Why the hell didn't you say so?" Eve strode over to snatch it out of his hand.

Insulted, McNab opened his mouth, then shut it tight when he caught Peabody's smirk out of the corner of his eye. "I'd just run the backups when you sent for me," he said stiffly. "I didn't take the time to read the contents comprehensively," he continued as Eve jammed the disc home. "But a quick skim indicates he lists all materials used, all devices made, and there are enough of them to wipe out a Third World country."

He paused, deliberately moving to the other side of Eve as Peabody shifted closer to see the screen. "Or a major city."

"Ten pounds of plaston," Eve read.

"An ounce would take out half this level of Cop Central," he told her. When Eve shifted to the wall screen, he moved another lateral foot away from Peabody, and she from him.

"Timers, remotes, impacts, sound and motion activated." Eve felt the ice crawl into her stomach. "They didn't miss a trick. Plenty of security, sensors, surveillance toys, too. He put together a goddamn warehouse for them."

"They paid him plenty," Peabody murmured. "He's got his costs, his fees, his profits all listed nice and tidy beside each unit."

"Hell of a businessman. Guns." Eve's eyes narrowed. "He got hold of banned weapons for them. Those are Urban War era."

"Is that what they are?" Interested, McNab leaned closer. "I didn't know what the hell he was talking about there, but didn't take time to run a check. Fifty ARK-95s?"

"Riot dispersers, military. A troop could take down a city block of looters — stunned or terminated — with a couple of passes."

Roarke had one in his collection. She'd tested it herself and had been stunned by the hot ripple of power up her arms at discharge.

"Why would they need guns?" Peabody wondered.

"When you start a war, you arm the troops. It's not a damn political statement." She shoved back. "That's smoke. They want the city, and they don't much care if it's in rubble." She blew out a breath. "But what the hell do they want to do with it?"

She shifted to continue the run. Without thinking, both Peabody and McNab moved in. Their shoulders bumped. Eve glanced back with a baffled scowl when they leaped widely apart.

"What the hell are you doing?"

"Nothing. Sir." Peabody snapped to attention even as color washed into her cheeks.

"Well, stop dancing around and contact the commander. Request he join us for debriefing and update as soon as possible. Inform him of the new deadline."

"Deadline?" McNab asked.

"New communication. A promised demonstration at fourteen hundred." Eve looked at her wrist unit. "Less than two minutes from now." Nothing to be done, she thought, but deal with the after. She turned back to the screen.

"We've got what he made them and how many. We don't know, however, if he was their only source. From his list here, we can calculate that he was paid more than two million, cash, over a period of three months. I suspect they put that money back into their pie when they took him out."

"He knew they meant to." McNab glanced over. "Scan down to page seventeen. He adds a sort of journal there."

Eve did as he suggested, then slid her hands into her pockets and read.

It's my own fault, my own fucking fault. You keep looking at the money, you get blinded. So the assholes sucked me in, and sucked me deep. This ain't no bank job. They could take out the National fucking Mint with what I've put together for them. Maybe it's money, maybe it's not. I don't give a rat's ass.

Guess I thought I didn't give that rat's ass about nothing. Until I started thinking. I started remembering. It's smarter not to re-

member. You got a wife and kids once, they get blown to pieces, no point in thinking about it the rest of your life.

But I'm thinking about it now. I'm thinking what's in the works here is another Arlington.

These two jokers I've been dealing with figure I'm old and greedy and stupid. But they're off. I got enough brain cells left to know they aren't running this song and dance. Fucking-A. Mechanical muscle's all they are. Muscle with dead eyes. When I started to tip to how things were, I added a little bonus to one of the transmitters. Then all I had to do was sit and wait and listen.

Now I know who they are and what they want. Bastards.

They're going to have to take me out. It's the only way they can cover their asses. One day soon, one of them's walking in here and slicing my throat.

I've got to go under. I've built and handed over to them enough to blow me out of here as soon as they're done with me. I've got to take what I can and go under deep. They won't get inside my place, not for a while, and they don't have the brain power to get to the data on here. This is my backup. The proof, the money, they're going with me.

Jesus, Jesus, I'm scared.

I gave them everything they need to blow this city to hell. And they'll use it. Soon.

For money. For power. For revenge. And God help us all, for the fun.

It's a game, that's all. A game played in the name of the dead.

I have to go under. I have to get out. Need time to think, to figure things out. Christ, I might have to go to the cops with this. The fucking bastard cops.

But first I'm getting out. If they come after me, I'm taking the two drones down with me.

"That's it." Eve curled her hands into fists. "That's all. He had names, he had data. Why didn't the stubborn old fuck put the info on his machine?" She whirled away to pace. "Instead, he takes it with him, whatever he had on them, he takes with him. And when they off him, they have it all."

She stalked to the window. Her view of New York hadn't changed. It was five after two. "Peabody, I need everything you can get on the Apollo group. Every name, every incident they took responsibility for."

"Yes, sir."

"McNab." She turned, stopping when Feeney stepped into the doorway. His face was drawn, his eyes too dark. "Oh hell.

What did they hit?"

"Plaza Hotel. The tea room." He walked slowly to the AutoChef, jabbed his finger into the controls for coffee. "They took it out, and the lobby shops, most of the goddamn lobby, too. Malloy's headed to the scene. We don't have a body count yet."

He took out the coffee, drank it down like medicine. "They'll need us."

She'd never lived through war. Not the kind that killed in indiscriminate masses. Her dealings with death had always been more personal, more individual. Somehow intimate. The body, the blood, the motive, the humanity.

What she saw now had no intimacy. Wholesale destruction accomplished from a distance erased even that nasty bond between killer and victim.

There was chaos, the screams of sirens, the wails of the injured, the shouts of onlookers who stood nearby, both shocked and fascinated.

Smoke continued to stream out of the once-elegant Fifth Avenue entrance of the revered hotel to sting the air and the eyes. Hunks of brick and concrete, jagged spears of metal and wood, glittering remnants of marble and stone lay heaped with grim pieces of flesh and gore scattered over them.

She saw tattered rags of colorful cloth, severed limbs, hills of ash. And a single shoe — black with a silver buckle. A child's shoe, she thought, unable to stop herself from crouching down to study it. It would have been shiny, a little girl's dress-up-for-tea shoe. Now it was dull and splattered with blood.

She straightened, ordered her heart to chill and her mind to clear, then began to make her way over, around the rubble and waste.

"Dallas!"

Eve turned, saw Nadine picking her way through the filth in lady heels and thin hose. "Get back behind the press line, Nadine."

"No one's put up a line." Nadine lifted a hand to push at her hair while the wind blew it back in her face. "Dallas. Sweet God. I was finishing up a luncheon speech deal over at the Waldorf when this came through."

"Busy day," Eve muttered.

"Yeah. All around. I had to pass on the Radio City story because I was committed to the lunch. But the station kept me updated. What the hell's going on? Word was you evacuated over there."

She paused, scanned over the destruction.

"It wasn't any water main problem. And neither was this."

"I don't have time for you now."

"Dallas." Nadine caught at her sleeve, held firm. Her eyes, when they met Eve's, were ripe with horror. "People have got to know." She said it quietly. "They have a right to."

Eve jerked her arm free. She'd seen the camera behind Nadine and the remote mike pinned to her lapel. Everyone had their jobs. She knew it, understood it.

"I don't have anything to add to what you see here, Nadine. This isn't the time or the place for statements." She looked down again at the small shoe, the silver buckle. "The dead make their own."

Nadine held up a hand to signal her camera operator back. Lifting a hand, she closed it over her mike and spoke softly. "You're right, and so am I. And just now, it doesn't matter a damn. If there's anything I can do — any sources I can tap for you, just let me know. This time, it's for free."

Nodding, Eve turned away. She saw the MTs scurrying, a team of them working frantically on the bloody mess that must have been one of the doormen. Most of him had been blown clear, a good fifteen feet from the entrance.

She wondered if they'd ever find his arm.

She stepped away and through the blackened hole into what was left of the lobby.

The fire sprinklers had gone off so that streams and puddles of wet ran through the waste. Her feet squelched as she pushed through. The stench was bad, very bad. Blood and smoke and ripe gore. She forced herself not to think about what littered the floor, ordered herself to ignore the two emergency workers who were weeping silently as they marked the dead, and looked for Anne.

"We'll need extra shifts at the morgue and the labs, to deal with IDs." Her voice was rusty, so she cleared it. "Can you clear that with Central, Feeney?"

"Yeah, goddamn it. I brought my daughter here on her sixteenth birthday. Fucking pigs." He yanked out his communicator and turned away.

Eve kept going. The closer she came to point of impact, the worse it got. She'd been there once before, with Roarke. She remembered the opulence, the elegance. Cool colors, beautiful people, wide-eyed tourists, excited young girls, groups of shoppers crowding at tables to experience the old tradition of tea at The Plaza.

She fought her way through rubble then

stared, cold-eyed, at the blackened crater.

"They never had a chance." Anne stepped up beside her. Her eyes were wet and hot. "Not a fucking chance, Dallas. An hour ago there were people in here, sitting at pretty tables, listening to a violinist, drinking tea or wine and eating frosted cakes."

"Do you know what they used?"

"There were children." Anne's voice rose, broke. "Babies in strollers. It just didn't mean a damn. Not one damn to them."

Eve could see it, and much too well. She already knew it would come back to her in dreams. But she turned, faced Anne. "We can't help them. We can't go back and stop it. It's done. All we can do is move forward and try to stop the next. I need your report."

"You want business as usual?" In a move Eve didn't bother to block, Anne snagged her by the shirt front. "You can stand here and look at this and want business as fucking usual?"

"They do," Eve said quietly. "That's all this is to them. If we're going to stop them, we have to do the same."

"You want a goddamn droid. You can go to hell."

"Lieutenant Malloy." Peabody stepped forward, laid a hand on her arm.

Eve had forgotten Peabody was there, and

now shook her head. "Stand back, Officer. I'll settle for a droid if you can't give me your report, Lieutenant Malloy."

"You'll get a report when I've got something to give you," Anne snapped. "And right now I don't need you in my face." She shoved Eve aside and pushed her way through the ruins.

"She was off, Dallas, way off."

"Doesn't matter." But it stung, Eve realized, more than a little. "She'll pull herself back together. I want you to edit that from the record. It isn't pertinent. We'll need masks and goggles from the field kit. We won't be able to work in here otherwise."

"What are we going to do in here?"

"The only thing we can at this point." Eve rubbed her stinging eyes. "Help the emergency team collect the dead."

It was miserable and gruesome work — the kind that would live inside you always unless you turned off everything you were.

It wasn't people she was dealing with, she told herself, but pieces, evidence. Whenever her shield began to slip, whenever the horror of it crept through, she yanked it up again, blanked her mind, and went on with the job.

It was dark when she stepped outside with Peabody. "You all right?" Eve asked.

"I'll get there. Jesus, Dallas, sweet Jesus."

"Go home, take a soother, get drunk, call Charles and have sex. Use whatever works, but blank it out."

"Maybe I'll go for all three." She tried for a half-hearted smile, then spotted McNab coming their way and stiffened like a flagpole.

"I need a drink." He looked directly, deliberately at Eve. "I need a whole bunch of drinks. Do you want us back at Central?"

"No. We've had enough for one day. Report at eight hundred hours."

"You got it." Then, following the lecture he'd given himself off and on throughout the day, he made himself look at Peabody. "You want a lift home?"

"I — well . . ." Flustered, she shifted from foot to foot. "No, um. No."

"Take the lift, Peabody. You're a mess. No point in fighting public transpo at this hour."

"I don't want . . ." Before Eve's baffled eyes she blushed like a schoolgirl. "I think it would be better . . ." She coughed, cleared her throat. "I appreciate the offer, McNab, but I'm fine."

"You look tired, that's all." And Eve watched in amazement as his color rose as well. "It was rough in there."

"I'm okay." She lowered her head, stared at her shoes. "I'm fine."

"If you're sure. Well, ah, eight hundred hours. Later."

With his hands in his pockets and his shoulders hunched, he headed off.

"What's the deal here, Peabody?"

"Nothing. No deal." Her head came up sharply, and despising herself, she watched McNab walk away. "Not a deal. Not a thing. Nothing going on."

Stop it, she ordered herself as babbling continued to stream out of her mouth. "Zip. Zero happening here. Oh look." With outrageous relief for the distraction, she saw Roarke step out of a limo. "Looks like you've got a lift. A class one."

Eve looked across the avenue, studied Roarke in the blinking red and blue emergency lights. "Take my vehicle and go home, Peabody. I'll get transpo to Central in the morning."

"Yes, sir," she said, but Eve was already crossing the street.

"You've had a lousy day, Lieutenant." He lifted a hand, started to stroke her cheek, but she stepped back.

"No, don't touch me. I'm filthy." She saw the look in his eyes, knew he'd ignore her, and yanked the door open herself. "Not yet.

Okay? God, not yet."

She climbed in, waited for him to settle beside her, order the driver to take them home, then lift the privacy screen.

"Now?" he said quietly.

Saying nothing, she turned to him, turned into him. And wept.

It helped, the tears and the man who understood her enough to offer nothing more until they were shed. When they were home, she took a hot shower, and the wine he poured her and was grateful he said nothing.

They ate in the bedroom. She'd been certain she wouldn't be able to swallow. But the first spoonful of hot soup hit her raw stomach like a blessing.

"Thanks." She sighed a little, leaned her head back against the cushions in the seating area. "For giving me an hour. I needed it."

She needed more than an hour, Roarke thought, studying the pale face, the bruised eyes. But they'd take it a step at a time. "I was there earlier." He waited while her eyes opened. "I would have done what I could to help you, but civilians weren't permitted."

"No." She closed her eyes again. "They're not."

But he had seen, briefly at least, he had seen the carnage, the horrors, and her. He had seen her deal with it, her hands steady, her eyes dark with the pity she thought she hid from everyone.

"I don't envy you your job, Lieutenant."

She nearly smiled at that. "You can't prove that to me when you're always popping up into it." With her eyes still closed, she reached out for his hand. "The hotel was one of yours, wasn't it? I didn't have time to check."

"Yes, it was one of mine. And so are the people who died in it."

"No." Her eyes flashed open. "They're not."

"Only yours, Eve? Are the dead your exclusive property?" He rose, restless, poured a brandy he didn't want. "Not this time. The doorman who lost his arm, who may yet lose his life, is a friend of mine. I've known him a decade, brought him over from London because he had a yen to live in New York."

"I'm sorry."

"The wait staff, the musicians, the desk and bell staff, every one of them died working for me." He turned back, and a fierce and cold fury rode in his eyes. "Every guest, every tourist who wandered through, every single person was under my roof. By Christ, that makes them mine."

"You can't take it personally. No, you can't," she repeated when his eyes flashed. She got up, gripped his arm. "Roarke, it's not you or yours they're interested in. It's their point, it's the power."

"Why should it matter to me what they're interested in beyond using that to find them?"

"It's my job to find them. And I will."

He set his brandy down, caught her chin in his hand. "Do you think you'll close me out?"

She wanted to be furious, and part of her was, if for nothing more than the proprietary way he held her face. But there was too much at stake, too much to lose. And he was much too valuable a source. "No."

His grip gentled, his thumb skimmed over the shallow dent in her chin. "Progress," he murmured.

"Let's understand each other," she began.

"Oh, by all means."

Now she did suck in a breath. "Don't start that with me. By all means, my butt. Makes you sound like some sort of snotty blue blood, and we both know you grew up scrambling for marks in Dublin alleys."

Now he grinned. "See, we already understand each other. You don't mind if I get comfortable before the lecture, do you?" He sat again, took out a cigarette, lighted it, then picked up his brandy while she smoldered.

"Are you trying to irritate me?"

"Not very hard, but it rarely takes true effort." He drew in smoke, blew out a fragrant stream. "I don't really need the lecture, you know. I'm sure I have the salient points memorized. Such as this is your job, I'm not to interfere. I'm not to explore any angles on my own, and so on."

"If you know the points, why the hell don't you follow them?"

"Because I don't want to — and if I did, you wouldn't have Fixer's data decoded." He grinned again when she gaped at him. "I had it late this morning and slipped the code into McNab's unit. He was close, but I was faster. No need to mention that," Roarke added. "I'd hate to dent his ego."

She frowned at him. "Now I suppose you think I should thank you."

"Actually, I was hoping you would." He crushed out his cigarette, set aside his barely touched brandy. But when he reached for her hand, she folded her arms over her chest.

"Forget it, pal. I've got work."

"And you'll reluctantly ask me to assist you with it." He hooked his fingers in her waistband and tugged until she tumbled on top of him. "But first . . ." He rubbed his mouth persuasively against hers. "I need you."

Her protest would have been lukewarm in any case. But those words melted it away. She skimmed her fingers through his hair. "I guess I can spare a couple of minutes."

He laughed, and tucking her close, reversed position. "In a hurry, are you? Well then."

Now his mouth crushed down on hers, hot, greedy, and with enough bite to shoot her pulse from steady to screaming. She hadn't expected it, but then she never quite did expect what he could do to her with a touch, with a taste, with as little as a look.

All the horror, the pain, the misery she'd waded through that day fell away in the sheer drive to mate.

"I am. In a big hurry." She tugged at the hook of his trousers. "Roarke. Inside me. Come inside me."

He yanked down the soft slacks she'd slipped into after her shower. Mouth still devouring mouth, he lifted her hips. And he plunged into her.

Into the heat and the welcome and the

wet. His body shuddered once as he swallowed her groan. Then she was moving under him, driving him, setting a frantic pace that ripped her to peak and over before he could catch his breath.

She closed around him, vise tight, erupted around him, nearly dragged him off that fine edge with her. Gasping for air, he lifted his head, watched her face. God, how he loved to watch her face when she lost herself. Those dark blind eyes against flushed skin, that mouth full and soft and parted. Her head tipped back, and there was that long smooth throat, its pulse wildly beating.

He tasted her there. Flesh. Soap. Eve.

And felt her building again, fast and sure, her hips pistoning as she climbed, her breath ragged as the wave swept in.

And this time, when it crested, he buried himself deep and let it swamp them both.

He collapsed on her, let out a long, contented sigh as his system shimmered. "Let's get to work."

Chapter Twelve

"We're not doing this in here because I want to get around CompuGuard." Eve took her stand in the center of Roarke's private office while he settled down at the control console of his unregistered — and illegal — equipment.

"Mmmm," was his response.

She narrowed her eyes to slits. "It's not the issue here."

"That's your story, and I'll stick with it."

She gave him a scalpel-thin smile. "Stick your smart-ass comments, pal. The reason I'm going this route is because I've got good reason to believe Cassandra's got just as many illegal toys as you do, and likely just as much disregard for privacy. It's possible they can slide into my equipment here or at Central. I don't want to chance them getting a line on any part of the investigation."

Roarke leaned back, nodded soberly. "And it's a very good story, too, well told. Now, if you've finished soothing your admirable conscience, why don't you get us some coffee?"

"I really hate when you snicker at me."

"Even when I have cause?"

"Especially." She strode to the AutoChef. "What I'm dealing with here is a group that has no kind of conscience, that has what appears to be heavy financial resources, expert technical skills, and a knack for getting by tight security."

She brought both mugs to the console, smiled again. "Reminds me of someone."

"Does it really?" He said it mildly as he took the coffee she offered.

"Which is why I'm willing to use everything you've got on this one. Money, resources, skills, and that criminal brain of yours."

"Darling, they are now and always at your service. And following that line, I've made some progress on Mount Olympus and its subsidiaries."

"You got something?" She went on full alert. "Why the hell didn't you tell me?"

"There were other matters. You needed an hour," he reminded her. "I needed you."

"This is priority," she began, then stopped herself with a shake of her head. Complaining was a waste of time. "What have you got?"

"You could say, nothing."

"But you just told me you'd found them."

"No, I said I'd made progress, and that progress is nothing. They're nothing. They don't exist."

"Of course they exist." Frustration shimmered around her. She hated riddles. "They appeared all over the computer — electronics companies, storage companies, office complexes, manufacturers."

"They exist only on the computer records," he told her. "You might call Mount Olympus a virtual company. But IRL — in real life — it's nothing. There are no buildings, no complexes, no employees, no clients. It's a front, Eve."

"A virtual front? What the hell is the point of that?" Then she knew, and swore. "A distraction, a time waster. Energy defuser, whatever. They knew I'd do a search and scan on Cassandra, that it would lead me to this Mount Olympus, and then to the other fake companies. So I waste time chasing down what was never there in the first place."

"Not very much time," he pointed out. "And whoever set up the maze — and a very complex and well-executed maze it was — doesn't know you've gotten from one end to the other."

"They think I'm still looking." She nodded slowly. "So I continue to search through

EDD, tell Feeney to take it slow so Cassandra thinks we're still running into walls."

"Building their confidence while you concentrate in other areas."

She grunted and, sipping her coffee, paced. "Okay, I'll handle that. Now, I need to know all I can about the Apollo group. I gave Peabody the assignment, but she'll have to go through channels and won't find enough data, not fast, anyway. I don't just want their party line," she added, turning back to him. "I want what's under it. I've got to get a handle on them and hope that gives me one on Cassandra."

"Then that's where we'll start."

"I need names, Roarke, of known members, living or dead. I need to know where they are, what happened to them. Then I need names and locations of family members, lovers, spouses, siblings, children, grandchildren."

She paused, her eyes going cop flat. "In Fixer's little journal, he mentioned revenge. I want survivors and loved ones. And I want those closest to James Rowan."

"The FBI will have files, sealed, but they'll have them." He lifted a brow, amused by the obvious struggle on her face. "It'll take some time."

"We're a little pressed in that area. Can

you zing whatever you pull up into one of the auxiliary units? I can start a comparison run on ID, see if I can tag anyone connected who worked or works in the three target buildings."

He nodded toward a machine on the left of his console. "Help yourself. I'd focus on lower-level positions," he suggested. "Security checks are likely to be spottier there."

She settled down, spending the next twenty minutes reviewing everything she could find on the Pentagon bombing. At the control center, Roarke went coolly about the business of bypassing FBI security and delving into sealed files.

He knew the route — had taken it before — and slid through the locked levels like a shadow through the dark. Occasionally, for his own amusement, he checked in to see just what the Bureau had in their file marked Roarke.

It was surprisingly lean for data on a man who had been and done and acquired all he had been and done and acquired. Then again, he'd erased and destroyed a great deal of that data, or at least altered it, when he'd still been a teenager. Files at the FBI, Interpol, IRCCA, and Scotland Yard contained nothing he didn't care for them to contain.

It was, he liked to think, a matter of privacy.

He regretted only mildly the fact that since he'd met Eve, none of those agencies had cause to add any interesting facts about his activities.

Love had him walking the straight and narrow, with only the occasional step into the dark.

"Incoming," he murmured, and had Eve's head coming up.

"Already?"

"It's only the FBI," he pointed out, and tipping back in his chair, ordered data onto the wall screen. "There's your head man. James Thomas Rowan, born in Boston, June 10, 1988."

"They so rarely look like madmen," Eve murmured, studying the image. A handsome face with sharp bones, easily smiling mouth, clear blue eyes. His dark hair was shot with distinguished gray, lending him the look of a successful executive or politician.

"Jamie, as he was called by friends, came from good, solid, New England stock." Roarke angled his head as he read data. "And healthy Yankee money. Prep schools, Harvard. Poli-sci major. Likely being groomed for politics. Did his military stint

— angled into Special Forces. He did some work for the CIA. Parents deceased, one sibling. Sister. Julia Rowan Peterman."

"Professional mother, retired," Eve read. "She lives in Tampa. We'll check her out."

She rose as much to stretch her legs as to get a closer look at the screen. "Married Monica Stone, 2015. Two children: Charlotte, DOB September 14, 2016, and James Junior, DOB February 8, 2019. Where's Monica?"

"Display current data on Monica Stone Rowan," Roarke ordered. "Split screen."

Going by the age of the subject, Eve decided the picture was fairly recent. So the Bureau was keeping tabs. She'd probably been an attractive woman once. The bones were still good, but lines had dug deep around her mouth, her eyes, and both the mouth and eyes carried bitterness. Her hair had gone gray and was carelessly cut.

"She lives in Maine." Eve pursed her lips. "Alone and unemployed. Pulls in a retired professional mother's pension. I bet it's stinking cold in Maine this time of year."

"You'll have to wear your long johns, Lieutenant."

"Yeah. It'll be worth a little chill to talk to Monica. Where are the kids?"

Roarke called the data up and had Eve

raising her brow. "Believed dead. Both of them? Same date? Get me more here, Roarke."

"One minute. You'll note," he added as he bent to the task, the dates of death coincide with the date James Rowan was killed."

"February 8, 2024. I saw that."

"Explosion. The feds blew up his house, though the public stand is he did the job himself." He glanced up again, face blank and set. "But that's confirmed in this file — time, unit, authorization to terminate. It appears he had his children in the house with him."

"You're telling me the FBI bombed his house to take him out, and took two kids along for the ride?"

"Rowan, his children, the woman he'd taken as his lover. One of his top lieutenants and three other members of Apollo." Roarke rose, moved to get more coffee. "Read the file, Eve. They'd tagged him. They'd been hunting him since his group had claimed responsibility for the Pentagon bombing. The government wanted payment, and they were pissed."

He brought fresh coffee to Eve. "He'd gone under, moved from location to location. Using new names, new faces when necessary." Roarke settled behind her as they read the data. "He still managed to make his videos and get them on air. But he stayed a step or two ahead of the hounds for several months."

"With his kids," she murmured.

"According to these files, he kept them close. Then the FBI ran him to ground, surrounded his house, moved in, and did the job. They wanted to take him out and break the back of the group. That's what they did."

"It didn't have to be done that way."

"No." He met her eyes. "It's rare in war for either side to consider the innocent."

Why hadn't they been with their mother? It was her first thought, one that came unwillingly to mind. What did she know of mothers? she reminded herself. Her own had left her in the hands of the man who'd beaten and raped her throughout her childhood.

And would the woman who had given birth to her have carried the same bitter look in her eyes as the woman now onscreen? Would she have had that same tight-lipped scowl?

What did it matter?

She shoved the thought aside, sipped her coffee again. For once, Roarke's superior blend left a bitter taste in her mouth.

"Revenge," she said. "If Fixer was right and that's part of the motive, this could be the root of it. 'We are loyal,'" she murmured. "Every message they send has that phrase in it. Loyal to Rowan? To his memory?"

"A logical step."

"Henson. Feeney said a man named William Henson was one of Rowan's top men. Do we have a dead list on here?"

Roarke brought it up to the wall screen. "Christ Jesus," he said quietly. "There are hundreds."

"From what I was told, the government hunted them down for years." Quickly, Eve scanned the names. "And they weren't too particular about it. Henson's not on here."

"No. I'll run a check on him for you."

"Thanks. Shoot this much through to my machine here, and keep digging."

He stopped her by brushing a hand over her hair. "It hurts you. The children."

"It reminds me," she corrected, "of what it's like to have no choice, and to have your life in the hands of someone who thinks of you as a thing to be used or discarded as the mood strikes."

"Some love, Eve, and fiercely." He pressed his lips to her forehead. "And some don't."

"Yeah, well, let's see what Rowan and his group loved, and fiercely."

She turned away to man her computer.

The answer, she thought, was in the series of statements on file that Apollo had issued during its three-year run.

We are the gods of war.

Each statement began with that single line. Arrogance, violence, and power, she thought.

We have determined the government is corrupt, a useless vehicle for those inside it, used for exploitation of the masses, for suppression of ideas, for the perpetuation of futility. The system is flawed and must be eradicated. Out of its smoke and ashes, a new regime will rise. Stand with us, you who believe in justice, in honor, in the future of our children who cry for food and comfort while the soldiers of this doomed government destroy our cities.

We who are Apollo will use their own weapons against them. And we will triumph. Citizens of the world, break the chains binding you by the establishment with their fat bellies and bloated minds. We promise you freedom.

Attack the system, she decided, cry out for the common man, for the intellect. Justify the mass murder of innocents, and promise a new way.

We are the gods of war.

Today at noon, our wrath struck down the military establishment known as the Pentagon. This symbol and structure of this faltering government's military strength has been destroyed. All within were guilty. All within are dead.

Once again, we call for the unconditional surrender of the government, a statement by the so-called Commander-in-Chief resigning all power. We demand that all military personnel, all members of the police forces lay down their weapons.

We who are Apollo promise clemency for those who do so within seventy-two hours. And annihilation for those who continue to oppose us.

It was Apollo's most sweeping statement, Eve noted. Broadcast less than six months before Rowan's house had been destroyed, with all its occupants.

What had he wanted, she wondered, this self-proclaimed god? What all gods wanted. Adulation, fear, power, and glory.

"Would you want to rule the world?" she asked Roarke. "Or even the country?"

"Good God, no. Too much work for too little remuneration, and very little time left over to enjoy your kingdom." He glanced over. "I much prefer owning as much of the world as humanly possible. But running it? No thanks."

She laughed a little, then propped her elbows on the counter. "He wanted to. When you take out all the dreck, he just wanted to be president or king or despot. Whatever the term would be. It wasn't money," she added. "I can't find a single demand for money. No ransoms, no terms. Just surrender, you fascist pig cops, or resign and tremble, you big fat politicians."

"He came from money," Roarke pointed out. "Often those who do fail to appreciate its charms."

"Maybe." She skimmed back to Rowan's personal file. "He ran for mayor of Boston twice. Lost twice. Then he ran for governor and didn't pull it off, either. You ask me, he was just pissed. Pissed and crazy. The combo's lethal more often than not."

"Is his motive important at this point?"

"You can't get a full picture without it. Whoever's pushing the buttons in Cassandra's linked to him. But I don't think they're pissed."

"Just crazy then?"

"No, not just. I haven't figured out what else yet."

She shifted, rolled her shoulders, then set up to run comparisons on the names Roarke had fed into her machine.

It was a slow process, and a tedious one that depended more on the computer than its operator. Her mind began to drift as she watched names, faces, data, skim over the screen.

She didn't realize she'd fallen asleep. Didn't know she was dreaming when she found herself wading through a river of blood.

Children were crying. Bodies littered the ground, and the ones that still had faces begged for help. Smoke stung her eyes, her throat, as she stumbled over the wounded. Too many, she thought frantically. Too many to save.

Hands snatched at her ankles, some no more than bones. They tripped her up until she was falling, falling into a deep, black crater piled with still more bodies. Stacked like cordwood, ripped and torn like broken dolls. Something was pulling her in, pulling her down until she was drowning in that sea of dead.

Gasping, whimpering, she clawed her way back, crawled frantically up the slippery side of the pit until her fingers were raw and bloody.

She was back in the smoke, crawling still, fighting to breathe, to clear her mind of panic so that she could do something. Do what needed to be done.

Someone was crying. Softly, secretly. Eve stumbled forward through the stinking, blinding mist. She saw the child, the little girl huddled on the ground, balled up, rocking herself for comfort as she wept.

"It's all right." She coughed her throat clear, knelt down, and pulled the girl into her arms. "We'll get out."

"There's no place to go." The little girl whispered in her ear. "We're already there."

"We're getting out." They had to get out, was all Eve could think. Terror was crawling over her skin like ants, crab claws of ice were scraping the inside of her belly. She dragged the child up and began to carry her through the smoke.

Their hearts thudded against each other's, hard and in unison. And the girl's fingers gripped like thin wires when voices slithered through the mist.

"I need a goddamn fix. Why the hell isn't there money for a goddamn fix?"

"Shut the fuck up."

Eve stopped cold. She hadn't recognized

the woman's voice, but the man's, the one who'd answered with that sharp, sneering snap. It was one that lived in her dreams. In her terrors.

Her father's voice.

"You shut the fuck up, you bastard. If you hadn't got me knocked up in the first place, I wouldn't be stuck in this hole with you and that whiny little brat."

Breath shallow, the child like a stone doll in her arms, Eve crept forward. She saw figures, male, female, hardly more than smudges on the smoke. But she recognized him. The build, the set of his shoulders, the tilt of his head.

I killed you, was all she could think. *I killed you, you son of a bitch. Why won't you stay dead?*

"They're monsters," the child whispered to Eve. "Monsters never die."

But they did, Eve thought. If you stood up long enough, they did.

"Should've gotten rid of it while you had the chance," the man who had been Eve's father said with a careless shrug. "Too late now, sweetie-pie."

"I wish to Christ I had. I never wanted the little bitch in the first place. Now you owe me, Rick. Give me the price of a corner fix, or —"

"You don't want to threaten me."

"Goddamn you, I've been in this hole all day with that sniveling kid. You fucking *owe* me."

"Here's what I owe you." Eve cowered back at the sound of a fist smashing into bone. The sharp cry that followed.

"Here's what I fucking owe both of you."

She stood paralyzed as he beat the woman, as he raped her. And realizing the child she held tight in her arms was herself, she began to scream.

"Eve, stop. Come on now, wake up." Roarke had bolted out of his chair at the first scream, had her up and into his arms by the second. And still she thrashed.

"It's me." She shoved at him, kicked. "It's me, and I can't get out."

"Yes, you can. You're out now. You're with me now." Shifting her, he pressed the mechanism on the wall and brought out the bed. "Come on, all the way back. You're with me. Understand?"

"I'm all right. Let go. I'm okay."

"Not a chance." She was shaking even as he sat on the edge of the bed and cradled her in his lap. "Just relax. Just hold onto me and relax."

"I fell asleep, that's all. I nodded off for a minute." He eased her back to study her face. It was the understanding in his eyes, those fabulous eyes, the patience there and the love that did her in. "Oh God." Surrendering, she pressed her face to his shoulder. "Oh God, oh God. Just give me a minute."

"All you need."

"I guess I hadn't let go of today. Everything. All those people — what was left of them. You can't let it get in the way of the job, or you can't do the job."

"So it slices you up when you shut down."

"Maybe. Sometimes."

"Darling Eve." He brushed his lips over her hair. "You suffer for all of them. And always have."

"If they're not people to me, what's the point?"

"None. Not for you. I love who you are." He drew back again to stroke her cheek. "And still, it worries me. How much can you give and still stand up to it?"

"As much as it takes. It wasn't only that." She drew a breath, then another, steadying herself. "I don't know if it was a dream or a memory. I just don't know."

"Tell me."

She did, because with him she could. She told him of finding the child, of the vague figures in the smoke. Of what she'd heard, and what she'd seen.

"You think it was your mother."

"I don't know. I have to get up. I have to move." She rubbed her hands over her arms when he released her. "Maybe I was — what do they call it? Projecting or transposing. What the hell. I'd been thinking of Monica Rowan, what kind of woman would have turned her kids over to a man like James Rowan. Like I said before, it reminded me."

"We don't know that she did."

"Well, he had them, anyway, just like my father had me. It's probably all it was. I've never had any memory of her. I've got nothing of her."

"You've remembered other things," he pointed out, and rose to warm her arms himself. "This could be one of them. Eve, talk to Mira."

"I'm not ready for that." She pulled back immediately. "I'm not ready. I'll know when I am. If I am."

"It eats at you." And at him, when he saw her suffering like this.

"No, it doesn't drive my life. It just gets in the way of it sometimes. Remembering her, if there's anything to remember, isn't going to bring me any peace, Roarke. To me, she's as dead as he is."

And that, Roarke thought as he watched Eve turn back to her machine, wasn't nearly dead enough.

"You need some sleep."

"Not yet. I can do another hour."

"Fine." He walked to her and had her up and over his shoulder before she could blink.

"Hey!"

"An hour should be just about right," he decided. "You rushed me earlier."

"We're not having sex."

"Okay, I'll have sex. You can just lie there." He rolled onto the bed with her.

There was something miraculous about the way his body fit to hers. But she wasn't going to pay any attention to that little miracle. "What part of no didn't you get?"

"You didn't say no." He lowered his head to nuzzle her cheek. "You said you weren't having sex, which is entirely different. If you'd said no . . ." His fingers busily unbuttoned her shirt. "I would, of course, respect that."

"Okay, listen up."

Before she could speak, his mouth was on hers, soft, seductive. And wonderfully sly. His hands were already sliding, slipping, searching over her. She didn't quite choke back the moan.

"Fine." She gave up and sighed when his lips laid a hot trail down her throat. "Be an animal."

"Thank you, darling. I'd love to."

He took every bit of the hour, while the machines hummed away. He pleased her, and himself, knowing when her body went lax with release under his, she would tumble mindlessly into sleep.

And for a night, at least, there would be no more dreams.

It was dark in the room when she awoke, with just the lights from the console and screens flickering. Blinking, her brain still musty, she sat up and saw Roarke at the controls.

"What time is it?" She didn't remember she was naked until she swung her legs from the bed.

"Just six. You have some matches here, Lieutenant. They're on disc and hard copy."

"Did you sleep?" She started to search for her pants, and saw the robe neatly laid across the foot of the bed. The man never missed a damn step.

"Yes. I haven't been up long. I assume you're going straight in today?"

"Yeah. Team briefing at eight hundred."

"The report on Henson — what there is of it — is printed out."

"Thanks."

"I have a number of things to see to today, but you can reach me if you need to." He rose, looking dark and dangerous in the half light, the night's growth of beard shadowing his face, the black robe carelessly belted. "There are a couple of names on the match list I recognize."

She took the hard copy he offered. "I guess it was too much to expect otherwise."

"Paul Lamont rings the clearest bell. His father fought in the French Wars before the family immigrated here. Paul's father was very skilled and passed considerable knowledge on to his son. Paul is a member of the security team for one of my businesses here in New York. Autotron. We make droids and various small electronics."

"You pals?"

"He works for me — and we . . . developed a project or two several years ago."

"And it's not the kind of project a good cop needs to know about."

"Exactly. He's been with Autotron for more than six years now. We haven't had contact beyond that relationship for nearly that amount of time."

"Uh-huh. And what are these skills his dear old dad passed along to him?"

"Paul's father was a saboteur. He specialized in explosives."

Chapter Thirteen

Peabody hadn't slept well. She dragged into work heavy-eyed and vaguely achy, as if she were coming down with some nasty little bug. She hadn't eaten, either. Though her appetite was dependable — sometimes too dependable — she expected few could eat hearty after spending several hours tagging body parts.

That she could have lived with. That was the job, and she had learned how to channel all thoughts and energies into the job during the months she'd worked under Eve.

What she couldn't live with, and what spread a thin layer of cranky over fatigue, was the fact that a great deal of her thoughts — and not pure ones — and entirely too much of her energies had been centered on McNab during the long night.

She hadn't been able to talk to Zeke. Not about this sudden weird compulsion for McNab. McNab, for Christ's sake. And she hadn't wanted to talk about the bombing at The Plaza.

He'd seemed distracted himself, she

thought now, and they'd circled each other the night before and again that morning.

She'd make it up to him, Peabody promised herself. She'd carve out a couple of hours that night and take him to some funky little club for a meal and music. Zeke loved music. It would do them both good, she decided as she stepped off the guide and tried to rub the stiffness out of the back of her neck.

She turned toward the conference room and rammed straight into McNab. He sprang back, collided with a pair of uniforms who toppled into a clerk from Anticrime.

Nobody took his apology very well, and he was red-faced and sweaty by the time he managed to look Peabody in the eye again. "You, ah, heading into the meeting."

"Yeah." She tugged at her uniform coat. "Just now."

"Me, too." They stared at each other a moment while people shoved by them.

"You shake anything loose on Apollo?"

"Not much." She cleared her throat, tugged her coat again, and finally managed to start moving. "The lieutenant's probably waiting."

"Yeah, right." He fell into step beside her. "You get any sleep?"

She thought of warm slick bodies . . . and stared straight ahead. "Some."

"Me, either." His jaw ached from gritting his teeth, but it had to be said. "Look, about yesterday."

"Forget it." She snapped it out.

"I already have. But if you're going to walk around all tight-assed about it —"

"I'll walk any way I want, and you just keep your hands off me, you moron, or I'll rip your lungs out and use them for bagpipes."

"Same goes, sweetheart. I'd rather kiss the back end of an alley cat."

Her breath was coming quick now. Outrage. "I bet that's just your style."

"Better that than a stiff-necked uniform with an attitude."

"Asshole."

"Twit."

They turned together into an empty office, slammed the door. And leapt at each other.

She bit his lip. He nipped her tongue. She body pressed him against the wall. He managed to get his hands under her thick coat to squeeze her ass. The moans that ripped from their throats came out as one single, tortured sound.

Then her back was against the wall and he

filled his hands with her breasts.

"Oh God, you're built. You are so built."

He was kissing her as if he could swallow her whole. As if the universe centered on that one taste. Her head was spinning too fast for her to catch her own thoughts. And somehow the bright buttons of her uniform were open and his fingers were on her flesh.

Who'd have thought the man had such fabulous fingers?

"We can't do this." Even as she said it she was scraping her teeth along his throat.

"I know. We'll stop. In a minute." The scent of her — all starch and soap — was driving him crazy. He was fighting with her bra when the 'link behind them beeped and had them both muffling a scream.

Panting like dogs, clothes twisted, eyes glazed, they stared at each other with a kind of horror. "Holy God," he managed.

"Step back, step back." She shoved him hard enough to knock him back on his heels and began to fumble with her buttons. "It's the pressure. It's the stress. It's something, because this is *not* happening."

"Right, absolutely. If I don't have sex with you, I think I'm going to die."

"If you'd die, I wouldn't have this problem." She did her buttons up wrong, swore, and fumbled them open again.

Watching her, he felt his tongue go thick. "Having sex would be the mother of all mistakes."

"Agreed." She buttoned her uniform again, then met his eyes dead-on. "Where?"

"Your place?"

"Can't. My brother's staying with me."

"Mine then. After shift. We'll just do it, and it's done and we'll, you know. Get it out of the way and be back to normal."

"Deal." With a brisk nod, she bent and picked up her cap. "Tuck in your shirt, McNab."

"I don't think that's a good idea quite yet." He grinned at her. "Dallas might wonder why I've got a hard-on the size of Utah."

Peabody snorted, straightened her cap. "Your ego, maybe."

"Baby, we'll see what you say about that after shift."

She felt a little tingling between her thighs, but sniffed. "Don't call me baby," she told him and yanked open the door.

She kept her head up and her eyes straight ahead as she walked the rest of the way to the conference room.

Eve was already there, which gave Peabody a quick twinge of guilt. Three boards were set up, and her lieutenant was busy covering the last of them with hard copy data.

"Glad you could make it." Eve said it dryly without turning around.

"I ran into . . . traffic. Do you want me to finish that for you, sir?"

"I've got it. Get me coffee, and program the screen for hard copy. We won't be using discs on this."

"I'll get the screen," McNab volunteered. "And I could use some coffee, too. No discs, Lieutenant?"

"No, I'll update when the full team's here."

They went to work quietly, so quietly that Eve got an itch between her shoulder blades. The two of them should've been sniping at each other by now, she thought, and glanced over her shoulder.

Peabody had given McNab his coffee, which was weird enough. But while she printed out hard copy of her own discs, she smiled at him. Well, not really a smile, Eve mused, but close.

"You two take happy pills this morning?" she asked, then frowned when they both blushed. "What's the deal?" she began, then shook her head when Anne Malloy and Feeney came in. "Never mind."

"Dallas." Anne stayed in the doorway.

"Can I talk to you a minute?"

"Sure."

"Make it quick," Feeney suggested. "Whitney and the chief are heading in."

"I'll keep it short." Anne drew a breath when Eve joined her at the door. "I want to apologize for yesterday. I had no call coming down on you that way."

"It was a tough scene."

"Yeah. I've done tough scenes before." She glanced into the room, lowered her voice another notch. "I didn't handle it well, and that won't happen again."

"Don't beat yourself up over it, Anne. It wasn't a big deal."

"Big enough. You're heading this investigation, and you have to count on all of us. I blew it yesterday, and you need to know why. I'm pregnant again."

"Oh." Eve blinked, shifted her feet. "Is that good?"

"It is for me." With a little laugh, Anne laid a hand on her belly. "Nearly four months into it now, and I'll tell my shift commander in a couple weeks. I've done it twice before and it hasn't interfered with my job. It did yesterday. It was the kids that got me, Dallas, but I've got a handle on it now."

"Fine. You're not feeling . . . weird or anything?"

"No, I'm good. I just want to keep it quiet for a few more weeks. Once everybody finds out, they start the betting pool and the jokes." She lifted her shoulders. "I'd like to close this case before all that gets going. So, are we square here?"

"Sure. Here come the brass," she murmured. "Give Peabody your report and evidence discs. We'll be using hard copy."

Eve remained in the doorway, at attention. "Commander. Chief Tibble."

"Lieutenant." Tibble, a tall, nearly massive man with sharp eyes, nodded as he walked by her into the room. He glanced at the boards, then as was his habit, linked his hands behind his back. "If everyone would please be seated. Commander Whitney, would you close the door?"

Tibble waited. He was a patient man and a thorough one, with a mind like a street cop and a talent for administration. He scanned the faces of the team Whitney had put together. Neither approval nor disapproval showed on his face.

"Before you begin your reports, I've come to tell you that both the mayor and the governor have requested a federal antiterrorist team to assist in this investigation."

He watched Eve's eyes flash and narrow and silently approved her control. "This is not a reflection on the work being done here. Rather it's a statement as to the scope of the problem itself. I have a meeting this morning to discuss the progress of the investigation and to make the final decision as to whether a federal team should indeed be called in."

"Sir." Eve kept her voice level and her hands on her knees. "If they're called in, which team heads the investigation?"

His brows lifted. "If the feds come in, the case would be theirs. You would assist. I don't imagine that sits well with you, Lieutenant, or any of your team."

"No, sir, it doesn't."

"Well then." He moved to a chair, sat. "Convince me that the investigation should remain in your hands. We've had three bombings in this city in two days. What have you got, and where are you going with it?"

She rose, moved to the first board. "The Apollo group," she began and went step by step through all the gathered data.

"Henson, William Jenkins." She paused there as the square-jawed, tough-eyed face flashed on-screen. She hadn't had time to closely review the data Roarke had accessed for her, so she went slowly here. "He served as Rowan's campaign manager, and according to sources, a great deal more. It's believed he acted as a kind of general in Rowan's revolution. Assisting and often devising the military strategies, selecting targets, training and disciplining the troops. Like Rowan, he had a background in the military and in covert work. Initially, it was believed he was killed in the explosion that destroyed Rowan's Boston headquarters, but several subsequent sightings of the subject negated that belief. He's never been located."

"You believe he's part of this current group, Cassandra." Whitney studied the face on-screen, then looked at Eve.

"There's a connection, and it's my belief he's one of the links. The FBI files on Henson remain open." She shifted gears and relayed the information on the maze of false companies inputted into the data banks.

"Apollo," she continued. "Cassandra, Mount Olympus, Aries, Aphrodite, and so on. It all connects. Their expert manipulation of data banks, the high quality of the materials used in their explosives, the employment of a disenfranchised former soldier to manufacture their equipment, the tone and content of their transmissions all connect and echo back to the original group."

Because it seemed so foolish, she let out a little breath before she spoke again. "In

Greek mythology, Apollo gave Cassandra the power of prophecy. Eventually, they had a disagreement, and that's when he fixed it so she could predict, but nobody would believe her. But I think the hook is she got her power from him. This Cassandra doesn't really care if we believe her or not. She's not trying to save, but to destroy."

"That's an interesting theory, Lieutenant. And logical enough." Tibble sat back, listened, watched the facts and images flash on-screen. "You've made the connections, have at least partial motives. It's good work." Then he glanced back at her. "The FBI antiterrorist team would be very interested in how you came by a great deal of this information, Lieutenant."

She didn't so much as blink. "I used what sources were available to me, sir."

"I'm sure you did." He folded his hands. "As I said, good work."

"Thank you." She moved past the second board to the third. "The current line of investigation corroborates our conclusions that there's a connection between the old Apollo group and Cassandra. Fixer believed there was, and though any evidence he may have gathered in that area is likely destroyed, the connection continues to hold through this second line. The tactics used by both groups are similar. In Dr. Mira's report, she terms Cassandra's political creed as a recycling of Apollo's. Following this angle, I believe that the people who formed Cassandra have connections to or were once a part of Apollo."

Tibble held up a hand. "Isn't it possible these people studied Apollo — just as you are — and chose to mirror that group as closely as possible?"

"It's not impossible, sir."

"If it's a copycat," Feeney put in, "it's going to be tougher."

"Even a copycat has to have a connection," Eve insisted. "The Apollo group was essentially disbanded when Rowan and some of his top people were killed. That was over thirty years ago, and the public was never privy to any but the sketchiest of details about him and his organization. Without a connection, who cares? It was over years ago, a lifetime ago. Rowan's not even a smudge in the history books because it was never proven — in reports to media — that he was the head of Apollo. Files verifying this are sealed. Apollo claimed responsibility for some bombings and for Arlington, then essentially vanished.

"There's a connection," she finished. "I don't believe it's a mirror, sir, but a personal stake. The people who head Cassandra killed hundreds yesterday. And they did it to prove they could. The bombs at Radio City were a tease, a test. The Plaza was always the target. And this echoes the theme used by Apollo."

She nodded toward the screen again, shifted to new copy. "The first building Apollo claims to have destroyed was an empty storehouse outside of what was then the District of Columbia. The local police were alerted, and there were no injuries. Following that, the locals were tipped that there were explosives in the Kennedy Center. All but one bomb was defused, the building was successfully evacuated, and the single explosive discharged caused only minor damage and injury. But this was immediately followed up by a bombing in the lobby of the Mayflower Hotel. There was no warning given. Casualties were steep. Apollo took responsibility for all three incidents, but only the last was reported in the media."

Whitney leaned forward, studying the screen. "What was next?"

"The newly refurbished U-Line Arena during a basketball game. Fourteen thousand people were killed or injured. If Cassandra runs true to form, I'm looking at

Madison Square or the Pleasure Dome. By keeping all data out of the mainframe and within this room, there's no way for Cassandra to know our current avenue of investigation. We should be a step ahead of them."

"Thank you, Lieutenant Dallas. Lieutenant Malloy, your report on the explosives?"

Anne rose, moved to the middle board. The next thirty minutes were technical: electronics, triggers, timers, remotes, materials. Rate of detonation, scope of impact.

"Pieces of the devices are still being gathered on-scene and are under lab analysis," she concluded. "At this time we know we're working with intricate, handmade units. Plaston appears to be the material of favor. Analysis is incomplete as to the capabilities of distance on the remotes, but it appears to be extreme long range. These aren't toys, no homemade boomers, but high-level military-style explosives. I concur with Lieutenant Dallas's opinion on Radio City. If this group had wanted it blown, it'd be dust."

She sat, giving way to Feeney. "This is one of the surveillance cameras my team swept out of Radio City." He held up a small round unit hardly bigger than the circle made by his thumb and forefinger. "It's damn well made. We tagged twenty-five of them from scene. They watched every step we took and could have blown us to hell in a heartbeat."

He slipped the bug back into its seal. "EDD is working with Malloy and her people to develop a longer-range, more sensitive bomb scanner. Meanwhile, I'm not saying the feds don't have good people, but so do we. And it's our damn city. Added to that, this group contacted Dallas. They targeted her. You pull her back now, and us with her, you're going to change the balance. Once it tips, we could lose it all."

"So noted. Dallas?" Tibble lifted a finger. "An opinion on why this group contacted you?"

"Only conjecture, sir. Roarke owns or has interests in the targets thus far. I'm connected to Roarke. It amuses them. Fixer referred to it as a game. I think they're enjoying it. He also spoke of revenge."

She rose again, shifted the image of Monica Rowan on-screen. "She'd have the most cause to enjoy some revenge, and as Rowan's widow, would be the most likely person to have personal and inside knowledge of his group."

"You and your aide are cleared for immediate travel to Maine," Tibble told her. "Commander? Comments?"

"This team has put together an impressive amount of evidence and probability in a short amount of time." Whitney rose. "It's my opinion that a federal team would be superfluous."

"I believe the lieutenant and her team have given me enough balls to juggle for the politicians." Tibble got to his feet as well. "Dallas, you remain in charge until further notice. I expect updates on every step. It's our city, Captain Feeney," he added as he turned to the door. "Let's keep it intact."

"Whew." McNab let out a huge sigh when the door closed again. "Dodged that beam."

"And if we want to keep this case where it belongs, we're going to work our butts off." Eve smiled at him thinly. "Your social life just went down the sewer, pal. We need that long-range scanner. And I want every arena and sports complex in every borough scanned. New Jersey as well."

"Christ, Dallas, with our equipment and manpower, that'll take a week."

"You've got a day," she told him. "Get in touch with Roarke." She jammed her hands in her pockets. "Odds are, he's got some toy that fits what you're looking for."

"Hot damn." McNab rubbed his hands

together and grinned at Anne. "Wait till you see what this guy's got."

"Feeney, is there any way you can block the unit in here? Jam it? Or better yet, come up with a new, unregistered unit with a shield."

His hangdog face brightened as he smiled at Eve. "Guess I could jury-rig something. Not that we ever fiddle with unregistereds over at EDD."

"Of course not. Peabody, you're with me."

"Hey, when are you getting back?" McNab called out.

Eve turned, stared at him, while Peabody wished herself invisible. "When we're finished, Detective. I think you have enough to keep you busy in the meantime."

"Oh sure, I just wondered. Just wondered." He grinned foolishly. "Have a nice trip."

"We're not going for lobster," Eve muttered and, shaking her head, walked out.

"We'll be back before end of shift, don't you think? Sir?"

Eve shrugged into her jacket as she strode to the elevator. "Look, if you've got a hot date, you'll just have to cool your glands."

"No, I didn't mean . . . Ah, I just want to let Zeke know if I'm going to be on OT, that's all." And it shamed her that she hadn't given her brother a thought.

"It takes as long as it takes. We've got a stop to make before we snag transpo north."

"I don't suppose we'll be taking one of Roarke's private jets?" When Eve merely eyed her balefully, Peabody hunched her shoulders. "Nope, guess not. It's just that they're so much faster than public shuttles."

"And you're just interested in speed, right, Peabody?" Eve stepped onto the elevator, pushed for garage. "It has nothing to do with plush, roomy seats, the fully stocked galley, or the screen selection."

"A comfortable body produces a sharp mind."

"That's lame. You're usually better than that when you try to hose me. You're off today, Peabody."

She thought of that wild interlude with McNab in an empty office. "You're telling me."

Zeke worked steadily, precisely, doing his best to focus his mind on the wood and his pleasure in it.

He'd known his sister hadn't slept well the night before. He'd heard her stirring and pacing while he'd laid awake on the living room pull-out. He'd wanted to go to her, offer to meditate with her, or to make her one of his organic soothers, but he hadn't been able to face her.

His mind was full of Clarissa, of the way she'd felt snuggled into his arms, of how sweet her lips had tasted. It shamed him. He believed strongly in the sanctity of marriage. One of the reasons he'd never pursued a serious relationship was that he'd promised himself when he took those vows to another, he would keep them throughout his life.

There had been no one he'd loved enough to make promises to.

Until now.

And she belonged to someone else.

Someone who didn't appreciate her, he thought now as he had during the night. Someone who mistreated her, made her unhappy. Vows were meant to be broken when they caused pain.

No, he couldn't talk to Dee when thoughts like that were skimming through his head. When he couldn't get Clarissa out of his mind and offer his own sister comfort.

He'd seen the reports of the bombing on the news the evening before. It had horrified him. He understood that not everyone embraced the cause-no-harm tenets that formed the foundation of the Free-Agers. He knew that even some Free-Agers modified that foundation to suit their lifestyles, and after all, the religion was designed to be fluid.

He knew cruelty existed. That murder was done every day. But he had never seen the kind of terrible disregard for life as he had on the viewing screen at his sister's apartment the evening before.

Those who were capable of it had to be less than human. No one with heart and soul and guts could destroy lives in that way. He believed that, clung to the hope that such a thing was an aberration, a mutation. And that the world had evolved beyond acceptance of wholesale death.

It had been a shock when he'd seen Eve moving through the carnage. Her face had been blank, he remembered, her clothes splattered with blood. He'd thought she'd looked exhausted, and hollow, and somehow courageous. Then it had struck him that his sister must have been there as well, somewhere in the horror of all that.

Eve had only spoken to one reporter, a pretty, foxy-faced woman whose green eyes had mirrored her grief.

"I don't have anything to add to what you see here, Nadine," she'd said. "This isn't the time or place for statements. The dead make their own."

And when his sister had come home, with that same exhausted look on her face, he'd left her alone.

He hoped now that he'd done so for her sake and not his own. He hadn't wanted to talk about what she'd seen and done. Hadn't wanted to think about it. Or about Clarissa. And while he'd been able to control his mind enough to blank out those images of death, he hadn't had the power to do so with the woman.

She would stay away from him now, he thought. They would stay away from each other, and that was best. He would finish the job he'd promised to do, then he would go back to Arizona. He'd fast and he'd meditate and he'd purge his system of her.

Maybe he'd camp in the desert for a few days, until his mind and heart were in balance again.

Then the sounds came through the vent. The angry laugh of the man, the soft pleas of the woman.

"I said I want to fuck. It's all you're good for, anyway."

"Please, B.D., I'm not feeling well this morning."

"I don't give a damn how you feel. It's your job to spread your legs when I tell you to."

There was a thud, then a cry sharply cut off. The crash of glass.

"On your knees. On your knees, you bitch."

"You're hurting me. Please —"

"Use that mouth of yours for something besides whining. Yeah, yeah. Put some effort into it, for Christ's sake. It's a miracle I can get it up with you in the first place. Harder, you whore. You know where I had my cock last night? You know where I had what you've got in your whiny mouth? In that new 'link operator I hired. I got my money's worth there."

He was panting now, grunting like an animal, and Zeke squeezed his eyes shut and prayed for it to stop.

But it didn't, it only changed, with the sounds of Clarissa weeping, then pleading. He was raping her now, there was no way to mistake those sounds.

Zeke caught himself at the foot of the steps, shocked to find his hand curled around the haft of a hammer. The blood was roaring violently in his ears.

My God, dear God, what was he doing?

Even as he set the hammer aside with a shaky hand, the sounds quieted. There was only weeping now. Slowly, Zeke climbed the steps.

It had to stop. Someone had to stop it. But he would face Branson empty-handed, and as a man.

He walked through the kitchen. Neither of the two remote domestics who worked there paid any attention to him. He moved into the wide hallway beyond, past the beautiful rooms and toward the sweep of floating stairs.

Perhaps he had no right to intrude, he thought, but no one, no one had a right to treat another human being as Clarissa was being treated.

He moved down the hallway to the right, judging which room would be directly over the workshop. The door was ajar; he could hear her crying inside. Placing his fingertips against the polished wood, he eased it open. And saw her curled on the bed, her naked body already blooming with bruises.

"Clarissa?"

Her head came up, eyes wide, and her swollen lips trembled. "Oh God. No, no, I don't want you to see me like this. Go away."

"Where is he?"

"I don't know. Gone. Oh please, please." She pressed her face to the tangled sheets.

"He can't be. I just came up the front stairs."

"The side entrance. He uses the side. He's

gone, already gone. Thank God. If he'd seen you come up . . ."

"This has to stop." He came to the bed, gently untangled a sheet, and draped it over her. "You can't let him hurt you this way."

"He doesn't mean — He's my husband." She let out a sigh that ripped at Zeke's heart. It was so hopeless. "I have no place to go. No one to go to. He wouldn't have to hurt me if I wasn't so slow and stupid. If I'd just do what he says. If I —"

"Stop that." It came out sharper than he'd intended, and when he laid a hand on her shoulder, she flinched. "What happened here wasn't your fault, it was his."

She needed counseling, he thought. She needed cleansing. A safe place to stay. Both her body and her self-esteem had been battered, and such things harmed the soul. "I want to help you. I can take you away from here. You can stay at my sister's until you decide what to do. There are programs, people you can talk to. The police," he added. "You need to file charges."

"No. No police!" She gathered the sheet close and struggled up. Her dark violet eyes were brilliant with fear. "He'd kill me if I did. And he knows people on the force. High-up people. I can never call the police."

She'd begun to tremble, so he soothed.

"That's not important now. Let me help you get dressed. Let me take you to a healer — the doctor," he corrected, remembering where he was. "Then we'll talk about what's next."

"Oh, Zeke." Her breath shuddered out as she lay her head on his shoulder. "There is no next. Don't you see this is it for me? He'll never let me go. He's told me. He's told me what he'd do to me if I try to leave. I'm just not strong enough to fight him."

He slipped his arms around her, rocked her. "I am."

"You're so young." She shook her head. "I'm not."

"That's not true. You feel helpless because you've been alone. You're not alone now. I'll help you. My family will."

He brushed at her loose and tangled hair, cloud soft under his hand. At home, my home," he said, keeping his voice a reassuring murmur. "It's peaceful. Remember how big and open and quiet the desert is? You can heal there."

"I was almost happy for those few days. All that space. The stars. You. If I believed there was a chance —"

"Give me the chance." Gently, he tipped her face back. The bruises on her face nearly broke his heart. "I love you."

Tears swam into her eyes. "You can't. You don't know what I've done."

"Nothing he's made you do counts. And it doesn't matter what I feel, but what you need. You can't stay with him."

"I can't drag you into this, Zeke. It's wrong."

"I won't leave you." He pressed his mouth to her hair. "When you're safe, if you want me to go, I will. But not until you're safe."

"Safe." She barely breathed the word. "I stopped believing I could be safe. If there's a chance . . ." She drew back, looked into his eyes. "I need time to think."

"Clarissa —"

"I have to be sure I can go through with it. I have to have time. Please, try to understand. Give me today." She closed a hand over his. "He can't hurt me any more than he already has. Give me today to look inside myself and see if there's anything there worth offering you. Or anyone else."

"I'm not asking for anything."

"But I am." Her lips trembled into a smile. "Finally, I am. Will you give me a number where I can reach you? I want you to go home now. B.D. won't be back until tomorrow afternoon, and I need this time alone."

"All right. If you promise that whatever

you decide, you'll call."

"I will." She picked up a memo from the bedside table and offered it. "I'll call you by tonight. I promise." When he'd entered the number, she took it from him, slipped it into the drawer. "Please, go now. I need to see how many pieces I can pick up on my own."

"I won't be far away," he told her.

She waited until he reached the door. "Zeke? When I met you in Arizona — when I saw you, looked at you . . . something inside me I'd thought had died seemed to stir again. I don't know if it's love. I don't know if I have love anymore. But if I do, it's for you."

"I'll take care of you, Clarissa. He'll never hurt you again."

Opening the door and leaving her was the hardest thing he'd ever done.

Chapter Fourteen

Eve gave her battered vehicle one long scowl as she strode across the garage. It wasn't that appearance mattered much. Since Zeke and Roarke had played with it, the heap was back in top running condition. But it was, by God, a heap.

"It's goddamn pitiful when a homicide lieutenant has to drive around in a wreck like this while those bozos in Illegals get zoomers." She gave the shiny, streamlined all-terrain two spaces down from hers an avaricious glare.

"Just needs some body work, some paint, a little new shielding." Peabody opened her door.

"It's the principle. Murder cops always get the shaft." Eve slammed in her side, a mistake, as the door popped right back open. "Oh fine, great."

"I noticed that little hitch yesterday when I took it home. What you have to do is lift up some, kind of jiggle it and slide it home. Zeke'll fix it for you first chance he gets. I forgot to mention it to him last night."

Eve held up her hands, took several slow, deep breaths. "Okay, no point in bitching about it."

"But you have such a smooth bitching style, sir."

Eve slanted Peabody a look as she went to work on the door. "That's better. You were starting to worry me. I've hardly heard a single smart-ass remark out of you for two days."

"I'm off my rhythm," Peabody muttered, and pressed her lips together. She could still taste McNab.

Eve secured the door. "Problem?"

"I —" She wanted to tell someone, but it was just too humiliating. "No, no problem. Where's the first stop?"

Eve lifted her brows. It was rare for Peabody not to walk through a door she'd opened. Reminding herself that personal lives were personal lives for a reason, Eve backed out of her slot. "Autotron. Get the address."

"I know it. It's a few blocks west of my place, on Ninth. Ninth and Twelfth. What's there?"

"A guy who likes bombs."

She filled Peabody in on the way.

When she pulled into the garage at Autotron, gate security took one look at her car and strode over snappily to glance at the badge she held up for view.

"You've already been cleared, Lieutenant. Your space is reserved. Slot thirty-six, level A. It's just up on your left."

"Who cleared me?" Though she wondered why she bothered to ask.

"Roarke. Take the first bank of elevators to the eighth floor. You'll be met."

Her eyes flashed once, then she drove in. "He just doesn't know when to step out."

"Well, it speeds things up. Saves time."

She wanted to say she wasn't in any hurry, but it was such a ridiculous lie Eve clamped her mouth shut. And smoldered. "If he's already questioned Lamont, I'm tying his tongue into a knot."

"Can I watch?" Peabody grinned as Eve braked hard in her parking slot. "I'm getting my rhythm back."

"Lose it." Irritated, she slammed the door before she remembered, then cursed roundly when the leading edge of it bounced on the concrete floor. "Son of a bitch." She kicked it, only because it seemed called for, then muscled it back into the frame. "Say nothing," she warned Peabody, then stalked to the elevator.

Peabody stepped into the elevator, folded her hands, and studiously studied the ascending numbers over the door.

The eighth floor was a wide, airy office and reception area filled with clerks and drones and snazzily suited execs. It was done in navys and grays with the startling slap and dash of wild red flowers streaming along under the windows and around a central console.

She thought that Roarke had a thing about flowers in the businessplace — anyplace, really. His main headquarters in midtown was alive with them.

She'd barely stepped out, had yet to reach for her badge, when a tall man in a severely cut black suit came toward her with a polished smile.

"Lieutenant Dallas. Roarke's expecting you. If you and your aide would follow me?"

A nasty part of her wanted to tell him to inform his boss to keep his pretty nose out of her business, but she sucked it in. She needed to talk to Lamont, and if Roarke had decided to be the line to him, it would take more time and energy than she had to waste to go around him.

She followed him through the cubicles, past snazzier offices, more flowers, and through open double doors to a spacious conference room.

The center table was a thick, clear slab,

lined with matching chairs with deep blue cushions, seat and back. A quick glance showed it held all the comforts and over-the-top technology she expected from anything Roarke had his hand in or his name on.

There was a maxi AutoChef and cold box, a fully equipped communications center, a rather jazzy entertainment console, and a wide window with full security and sun shade.

On the enormous wall screen an animated schematic twirled and spun. The man at the head of the table turned his attention from it, lifted a cocky brow, and gave his wife a charming smile.

"Lieutenant, Peabody. Thank you, Gates." He waited until the doors were closed, then gestured. "Have a seat. Would you like some coffee?"

"I don't want a seat or any damn coffee," Eve began.

"I'd like some coffee." Peabody winced under Eve's withering stare. "On the other hand . . ."

"Sit," Eve ordered. "Quiet."

"Sir." She sat, she was quiet, but sent Roarke a sympathetic glance before she did her best to become blind, deaf, and invisible.

"Did I ask you to have me cleared?" Eve began. "Did I ask you to be here when I came in to interview Lamont? I'm in the middle of an extremely sensitive investigation, one the feds would like to snatch out from under me. I don't want your name in my reports any more often than absolutely necessary. You got that?"

She'd marched to him as she spoke and ended by jabbing a finger at his shoulder.

"God, I love it when you scold me." He only smiled when she hissed breath between her teeth. "Don't stop."

"This isn't a joke. Don't you have worlds to conquer, small industrial nations to buy, businesses to run?"

"Yes." The humor cleared out of his eyes, leaving them dark and intense. "And this is one of them. Just as the hotel where people died yesterday is one of them. If someone in my employ turns out to be connected in any way, it's my business as much as yours, Lieutenant. I thought that was understood."

"You can't blame yourself for yesterday."

"If I say the same to you, will you listen?"

She stared at him a moment, wishing she didn't see his side so clearly. "Did you question Lamont?"

"I know better than that. I rescheduled my morning, arranged for your clearance, and made sure that Lamont was in the lab. I haven't sent for him yet. I assumed you'd want to rail at me a bit first."

If she was that predictable, Eve decided it was time for some realigning. "I'll take that coffee before you send for Lamont."

He skimmed his fingers along the tips of her hair before turning to deal with it. Eve dropped down in a chair, scowled at Peabody. "What are you staring at?"

"Nothing. Sir." Deliberately, Peabody looked away. It was so fascinating to watch them together, she mused. An education in the tug-of-war of relationships. And the way they looked at each other when their minds came together. You could actually see it.

She couldn't imagine what it was like to be that connected. So meshed that the brush of fingertips over your hair was a simple and absolute declaration of love.

She must have sighed. Roarke angled his head as he set her coffee in front of her. "Tired?" he murmured, and laid a hand on her shoulder.

Peabody felt she was entitled to the lovely flush of heat and mild lust she experienced nearly every time she looked at that spectacular face of his. But she didn't think Eve would appreciate it if she sighed again. "Rough night," she said and dipping her head, concentrated on her coffee.

He gave her shoulder a quick squeeze that sent her heart on a gallop, then turned back to Eve. "Lamont will be right up. I'd like to stay while you interview him. And," he continued holding up a hand, "before you tell me why I can't be here during an official interview, I'll remind you that I not only employ the subject, but I know him and have for a number of years. I'll know if he's lying."

Eve drummed her fingers on the table. She knew that look in his eye — cold, enigmatic, controlled. He would study and he would see, every bit as expertly as a veteran police interrogator.

"Observe only. You don't question him or comment unless I indicate otherwise."

"Agreed. Are you cleared for Maine?"

"We'll catch a shuttle as soon as we leave here."

"There's a jet at the airport. Take it."

"We'll take the shuttle," Eve repeated, even when Peabody's head came up and her eyes held all the hope of a puppy sniffing mother's milk.

"Don't be stubborn," Roarke said mildly. "The jet will get you there in half the time and with none of the frustration. You can pick us up a couple of lobsters for dinner."

The phrase *fat chance* trembled on her

tongue, but she bit it back when the knock sounded on the door.

"Showtime," Roarke murmured, and leaned back in his chair. "Come in."

Lamont had smooth, round cheeks, lively blue eyes, and a chin tattoo of a flaming arrow that was new since his ID photo. He'd let his hair grow some as well, Eve noted, so that it swirled in deep brown waves to his chin and gave him a slightly angelic look rather than the upright young conservative she'd viewed on-screen the night before.

He wore a white lab coat over a white shirt that was buttoned snugly to the Adam's apple, stovepipe black pants. She recognized his boots as being hand tooled and pricey, as Roarke had countless pairs in his endless closet.

He gave her a polite glance, gave Peabody's uniform a slightly longer study, then shifted his full attention to Roarke.

"You needed to see me?" His voice carried the faintest whisper of France, like a sprinkle of thyme over broth.

"This is Lieutenant Dallas of the NYPSD." Roarke didn't rise or gesture to a chair. It was his tacit shift of control to Eve. "She needed to see you."

"Oh?" The well-mannered smile was vaguely puzzled.

"Have a seat, Mr. Lamont. I have a few questions. You're entitled to have counsel present if you like."

He blinked twice, two slow movements. "Do I need a lawyer?"

"I don't know, Mr. Lamont. Do you?"

"I don't see why." He sat, shifted until he found comfort on the cushion. "What's this about?"

"Bombs." Eve gave him a small smile. "On record, Peabody," she added and read Lamont his rights. "What do you know about the bombing of the Plaza Hotel yesterday?"

"Just what I saw on-screen. They upped the body count this morning. It's over three hundred now."

"Have you ever worked with plaston, Mr. Lamont?"

"Yes."

"So you're aware of what it is?"

"Of course." He shifted again. "It's a light, elastic, highly unstable substance most commonly used as a detonation factor in explosives." He'd lost a little color since he'd taken his seat, but he kept his eyes on hers. They weren't quite so lively now.

"The explosives we manufacture here at Autotron for government contracts and some private concerns often employ minute amounts of plaston."

"How's your Greek mythology?"

His fingers linked together on the table, pulled apart, linked again. "Excuse me?"

"Know anyone named Cassandra?"

"I don't think so."

"Are you acquainted with Howard Bassi, more commonly known as Fixer?"

"No."

"What do you do with your free time, Mr. Lamont?"

"My — my free time?"

She smiled again. The change in rhythm had thrown him off, as she'd intended. "Hobbies, sports, entertainment. Roarke doesn't work you twenty-four/seven, does he?"

"I — No." His gaze flicked to Roarke, then back. "I . . . play a little handball."

"Team or solo?"

He lifted his hand, rubbed it over his mouth. "Mostly solo."

"Your father made bombs during the French War," she continued. "Did he work team, or solo?"

"I — he worked for the SRA — the Social Reform Army. I guess that's a team."

"I assumed he freelanced, worked for the highest bidder."

Color rushed back into Lamont's face.

"My father was a patriot."

"Sabotage for causes. Terrorists often call themselves patriots." She kept her voice mild, but saw the shimmer of anger in his eyes for the first time. "Do you believe in sabotage for causes, Lamont? In the slaughter and the sacrifice of the innocent for a just and righteous cause?"

He opened his mouth, closed it again, then took one long breath. "War is different. During my father's time, our country had been seized by exploitive bureaucrats. The second revolution in France was necessary to give its people back the power and justice that are their right."

"So . . ." Eve smiled a little. "I take that as a yes."

"I don't make bombs for causes. I make them for mining, for the demolition of old buildings. Empty buildings. For military testing. Contracts," he said, smoothly now. "Autotron is a respected and reputable company."

"You bet. You like making boomers?"

"We don't make boomers here." The tone was slightly scathing now and subtly more French. "Our devices are highly sophisticated, technologically advanced. We produce the best on the market."

"Sorry. You like making sophisticated,

technologically advanced devices?"

"Yes. I enjoy my work. Do you enjoy yours?"

A little cocky now, Eve noted. Interesting. "I enjoy the results of mine. How about you?"

"I believe in utilizing my skills."

"Me, too. Thank you, Mr. Lamont. That's all."

The little smile that had begun to form faded. "I can go?"

"Yes, thank you. End record, Peabody. Thanks for the use of the room, Roarke."

"We're always pleased to cooperate with the police at Autotron." He lifted a sleek eyebrow in Lamont's direction. "I believe Lieutenant Dallas is finished with you, Lamont. You're free to return to your work."

"Yes, sir." He rose, stiffly, and walked from the room.

Eve sat back. "He was lying."

"Oh yes," Roarke agreed. "He was."

"About what?" It came out before Peabody could stop it.

"He recognized the name Cassandra, and he knew about Fixer." Contemplatively, Eve scratched her chin. "He was a little shaky at first, but he started to warm up. He doesn't care for cops."

"A common emotion," Roarke pointed out. "Just as it's a common mistake to underestimate certain cops. He thought he was stringing you quite nicely toward the end."

She snorted, rose. "Amateur. Peabody, order a shadow for our friend Lamont. Roarke, I'll want you to —"

"Pull his work files, review his equipment and materials lists, any requisitions, and run a fresh inventory." He rose as well. "That's already being done."

"Show-off."

He took her hand, and because watching her work put him in the mood, nibbled on her knuckles before she could snatch it away. "I'll be keeping an eye on him."

"Keep your distance," she ordered. "I want him to think he pulled off the interview. Peabody . . ." She turned, then cleared her throat when she caught her aide dreaming into space. "Peabody, snap to."

"Sir!" She blinked, leaped to her feet, and nearly upended her chair. Seeing Roarke's clever mouth linger over Eve's fingers had made her wonder just what McNab would have in store for her later.

"Stay on planet, will you? I'll be in touch," she added to Roarke."

"Do that." He moved to the door with them, then caught Peabody's arm to hold her back a step. "He's a lucky man," he murmured.

"Huh? Who?"

"Whoever you were just dreaming about."

She grinned like an idiot. "Not yet, but he's going to be."

"Peabody!"

Peabody rolled her eyes and double-timed it to catch up with Eve.

"Take the jet, Lieutenant," Roarke called after her.

She glanced over her shoulder, saw him, tall, gorgeous, in the center of the wide doorway. She wished she'd had the time and the privacy to stride back and give those marvelous lips one quick little bite. "Maybe." She shrugged and made the turn for the elevator.

She took the jet — as much to keep Peabody from pouting as to save time. She'd been right. It was brutally cold in Maine. Naturally, she'd forgotten her gloves, so she stuffed her hands in her pockets as she stepped off the plane and into the bitter wind.

An airport official in cold-weather coveralls hustled over, handed her a vehicle coder.

"What's this?"

"Your transportation, Lieutenant Dallas. Your vehicle is in the green parking area, level two, slot five."

"Roarke," she muttered and jammed the code into her pocket along with her frozen fingers.

"I'll show you the way."

"Yeah, do that."

They moved across the tarmac and into the warmth of the terminal. The private transportation sector was quiet, almost reverently so, as opposed to the constant noise, bumping bodies and food and gift hawkers that crowded the public areas.

They rode the elevator down to green, where Eve was shown a sleek, black air-and-road number that made the all-terrains the illegals detectives drove look like kiddie cars.

"If you'd prefer another make or model, you're authorized for any available unit," she was told.

"No. Fine. Thanks." She waited until he'd walked away before she seethed. "He's got to stop doing this."

Peabody ran a loving hand over the glistening fender. "Why?"

"Because," was the best Eve could come up with, and she uncoded the door. "Map out directions to Monica Rowan's address."

Peabody settled in, rubbed her hands together as she scanned the cockpit. "Air or road?"

Eve spared her a steely look. "Road, Peabody."

"Air or road, I bet this baby moves." She leaned forward to study the on-board computer system. "Oh wow, she is *loaded*."

"When you finish being sixteen, Officer, map out the damn route."

"You never stop being sixteen," Peabody murmured, but followed orders.

The in-dash monitor responded immediately with a detailed map of the best route.

Would you like audio prompts during this trip? They were asked in the computer's warm, silky baritone.

"I think we can handle it, ace." Eve cruised toward the exit.

As you wish, Lieutenant Dallas. This trip comprises ten point three miles. Your estimated time to complete at this time of day on this day of the week, at the posted speed limits, is twelve minutes, eight seconds.

"Oh, we can beat that." Peabody shot Eve a quick grin. "Right, Lieutenant?"

"We're not here to beat anything." She drove decorously through the parking garage, into and around airport traffic, and through the gates.

Then there was a stretch of highway, long, wide, open.

Hell, she was human. She punched it.

"Oh man! I want one of these." Peabody grinned as the scenery blurred and flew by. "How much do you think this honey goes for?"

This model retails for one hundred and sixty-two thousand dollars, excluding tax, fees, and licenses.

"Holy shit."

"Still feeling sixteen, Peabody?" With a quick laugh, Eve swung onto their exit.

"Yeah, and I want a raise in my allowance."

They hit the commuter high-rises, strip malls, and hotel complexes that edged the suburbs. Traffic thickened on the road and overhead, but remained well-mannered and well-spaced.

That made Eve immediately miss New York with its nasty streets, rude vendors, and snarling pedestrians.

"How do people live in places like this?" she asked Peabody. "It's like somebody cut it all out of a travel disc, took a few thousand copies, and pasted it down outside of every goddamn city in the country. They're all the same."

"Some people like all the same. It's comforting. We took a trip to Maine when I was a kid. Mount Desert Island, the national park?"

Eve shuddered. "National parks are full of trees and hikers and weird little bugs."

"Yeah, no bugs in New York."

"I'll take a good honest cockroach any day."

"Come over to my place. Sometimes we have parties."

"Complain to your super."

"Oh yeah, that'll work."

Eve took a right, slowed as the street narrowed. The duplexes and triplexes here were old and shoved unhappily together. Lawns were quietly miserable, showing grass the bitter yellow of winter where snow had melted. She pulled up at a curb by a cracked sidewalk, shut off the engine.

Trip complete. Time elapsed nine minutes, forty-eight seconds. Please remember to code your door.

"You'd have cut another two minutes off easy if you'd gone air over that traffic," Peabody told her when they climbed out.

"Stop grinning and put on your cop face. Monica's peeking out the window." Eve headed up the bumpy, unshoveled walk and rapped on the middle door of the triplex.

It was a long wait, though she judged

Monica had about three steps to take to get from the window to the door. She didn't expect a warm welcome. And didn't get one.

The door opened a crack and one hard gray eye peered out. "What do you want?"

"Lieutenant Dallas, New York Police and Security, and aide. We have a few questions we'd like to ask you, Ms. Rowan. Can we come in?"

"This isn't New York. You've got no authority here, no business here."

"We have some questions," Eve repeated. "And we've been cleared to request an interview. It would be easier for you, Ms. Rowan, if we conducted it here rather than arranging for you to be transported to New York."

"You can't make me go to New York."

Eve didn't bother to sigh, and pocketed the badge she flipped out for Monica's study. "Yes, we can. But we'd rather not inconvenience you. We won't take up much of your time."

"I don't like the police in my house." But she opened the door. "I don't want you touching anything."

Eve stepped into what she supposed the architect had amused himself by calling a foyer. It was no more than four square feet of faded linoleum, ruthlessly scrubbed.

"You wipe your feet. You wipe your dirty cop feet before you come in my house."

Dutifully, Eve stepped back, wiped her boots on a mat. It gave her another moment to study Monica Rowan.

The image on file had been a true one. The woman was hard-faced, grim-eyed, and gray. Eyes, skin, hair were all nearly the same dull color. She was wearing flannel from top to toe, and the heat pumping through the house was already making Eve uncomfortably warm in her jacket and jeans.

"Close the door! You're costing me money letting the heat out. You know what it costs to heat this place? Utility company is run by government drones."

Peabody wiped her feet, stepped in, closed the door, and was rammed up tight against Eve. Monica stood glowering, her arms folded across her chest. "You ask what you got to ask, then get out."

So much, Eve mused, for Yankee hospitality. "It's a little crowded here, Ms. Rowan. Maybe we can go in the living room and sit down."

"You make it fast. I've got things to do." She turned and led the way into a doll-sized living area.

It was painfully clean, the single chair and

small sofa slicked with clear plastic. Two matching lamps still wore their plastic shields on the shades. Eve decided she didn't want to sit down after all.

The window drapes were drawn together, leaving a thin chink. The inch-wide slit brought in the only light.

There were dust catchers, but no dust. Eve imagined if a mote wandered in, it soon ran screaming in horror. A dozen little happy-faced figurines, gleaming clean, danced over tabletops. A cheap model cat droid rose creakily from the rug, gave one rusty meow, and settled again.

"Ask your questions and go. I've got housework to finish."

Eve recited the revised Miranda when Peabody went on record. "Do you understand your rights and obligations, Mrs. Rowan?"

"I understand you've come in my house unwanted, and you're interrupting my work. I don't need any bleeding-heart liberal lawyer. They're all government puppets preying on honest people. Get on with it."

"You were married to James Rowan."

"Until the government killed him and my children."

"You weren't living with him at the time of his death."

"Doesn't make me less of his wife, does it?"

"No, ma'am, it doesn't. Can you tell me why you were separated from him, and your children?"

"That's my private marital business." Monica's arms tightened on her chest. "Jamie had a lot on his mind. He was a great man. It's a wife's duty to give way to her husband's needs and wishes."

Eve only lifted a brow at that. "And your children? Did you take their needs and wishes into account?"

"He needed the children with him. Jamie adored them."

But he didn't think so much of you, did he? Eve mused. "And you, Ms. Rowan, did you adore your children?"

It wasn't a question she needed to ask, and Eve was annoyed with herself the moment it was out.

"I gave birth to them, didn't I?" Monica stretched her head forward aggressively on her scrawny neck. "I carried each one of them inside me for nine months, gave birth to them in pain and blood. I did my duty by them, kept them clean, kept them fed, and the government gave me a pittance for my trouble. A damn cop made more than a professional mother back then. Who do you think got up in the middle of the night with them when they were squalling? Who cleaned up after them? Nothing dirtier than children. You work your hands to the bone to keep a clean house when there's children in it."

So much for mother love, Eve thought, and reminded herself that wasn't the issue.

"You were aware of your husband's activities. His association with the terrorist group Apollo?"

"Propaganda and lies. Government lies." She all but spat it out. "Jamie was a great man. A hero. If he'd been president, this country wouldn't be in the mess it's in with whores and filth in the streets."

"Did you work with him?"

"A woman's place is to keep a clean house, to provide decent meals, and to bear children." She folded her lips into a sneer. "The two of you might want to be men, but I knew what God had put women on Earth to do."

"Did he talk to you about his work?"

"No."

"Did you meet any of his associates?"

"I was his wife. I provided a clean home for him and for the people who believed in him."

"William Henson believed in him."

"William Henson was a loyal and brilliant man."

"Do you know where I might find this loyal and brilliant man?"

Monica smiled, thin and sly. "The government dogs hunted him down and killed him, just the way they killed all the loyal."

"Really? I have no data that confirms his death."

"A plot. Conspiracy. Cover-ups." Thin beads of spittle flew out of her mouth. "They dragged honest people out of their homes, locked them in cages, starved and tortured them. Executions."

"Were you dragged out of your home, Mrs. Rowan? Locked up, tortured?"

Monica's eyes slitted. "I had nothing they wanted."

"Can you give me names of people who believed in him who are still alive?"

"It was thirty years ago and more. They came and they went."

"What about their wives? Their children? You must have met their families. Socialized."

"I had a house to run. I didn't have time to socialize."

Eve flicked a glance around the room. There was no view screen in evidence. "Do you keep up with the news, Ms. Rowan? Current events."

"I mind my own business. I don't need to know what other people are up to."

"Then you might not be aware that yesterday a terrorist group calling themselves Cassandra bombed the Plaza Hotel in New York. Hundreds of people were killed. Among them, women and children."

The gray eyes flickered, then leveled again. "They should have been in their own homes where they belonged."

"It doesn't concern you that a group of terrorists is killing innocent people? That it's believed this group is connected to your dead husband?"

"No one's innocent."

"Not even you, Mrs. Rowan?" Before she could answer, Eve moved on. "Has anyone from Cassandra contacted you?"

"I keep to myself. I don't know anything about your bombed hotel, but if you ask me, the country'd be better off if that whole city was blown to hell. I've given you all the time I'm going to give. I want you out of my house, or I'm calling my public representative."

Eve gave it one more shot. "Your husband and his group never asked for money, Mrs. Rowan. Whatever they did, they did for their beliefs. Cassandra is holding the city hostage for money. Would James Rowan have approved?"

"I don't know anything about it. I'm telling you to leave."

Eve took a memo card out of her pocket, set it on the table in front of a figure of a laughing woman. "If and when you remember or think of anything that might help, I'd appreciate it if you contacted me. Thanks for your time."

They headed out, with Monica dogging their heels. Outside, Eve sucked in air. "Let's get back to the whores and filth in the streets, Peabody."

"Oh, you bet." She shuddered for effect. "I'd rather have been raised by rabid wolves than a woman like that."

Eve glanced back to see that dingy gray eye peering through the chink in the drapes. "What's the difference?"

Monica watched them go, waited until the car had pulled away. She went back, picked up the memo card. Could be a bug, she thought. Jamie had taught her well. She hurried into the kitchen with it, dumped it in the recycler, and turned the whining machine on.

Satisfied, she went to the wall 'link. Could be bugged, could be bugged, too. Everything could be. Dirty cops. Lips peeled back, she slipped a small jammer out of a drawer, slid it onto the 'link.

She'd done her duty, hadn't she? Done it without complaint. It was long past time for compensation. She programmed the number.

"I want my share," she said in a hiss when she heard the voice answer. "The police were just here, asking questions. I didn't tell them anything. But I might next time. I might just have a few things to say to Lieutenant Dallas of the NYPSD that would perk her ears up. I want my share, Cassandra," she repeated, attacking a faint smudge on the counter with a tattered disinfectant rag. "I earned it."

Chapter Fifteen

Dear Comrade,

We are Cassandra.

We are loyal.

I trust you have received and are pleased with the latest progress reports transmitted to your location. The next steps of our plan are under way. Much like the chess games we used to play on those long, quiet nights, pawns are sacrificed for the queen.

At this time there is a small matter I would ask you to take care of for us, as our time is limited and our concentration must remain focused on the events unfolding. Timing over the next few days is vital.

Attached is the data you will require to arrange an execution long overdue. This is a matter we had hoped to handle ourselves at a future date, but circumstances require its implementation immediately.

There is no cause for concern.

We must keep this transmission brief. Remember us at tonight's rally. Speak our name.

We are Cassandra.

Zeke stayed in the apartment all day, afraid if he so much as stepped out to the corner deli for tofu, Clarissa would call, and berating himself for forgetting to give her the number of his pocket 'link.

He kept himself busy. There were a dozen minor chores and repairs around the apartment his sister had neglected. He cleared the kitchen drain, repaired the drip, sanded the bedroom door and window sashes so that they no longer stuck, dealt with the temperamental light switch in the bathroom.

If he'd thought of it, he would have bought a few kits and upgraded her lighting system. He made a note to do so before he returned to Arizona.

If there was time. If he and Clarissa weren't on a transport west that night.

Why didn't she call?

When he caught himself staring at the 'link, he moved into the kitchen and concentrated on the recycler. He took it apart, cleaned it, put it back together again.

Then he stared into space, imagining what it would be like when he took Clarissa home.

There was no question his family would welcome her. Even if it hadn't been part of the Free-Age dogma to offer shelter and comfort to any in need, without questions or strings, he knew the hearts of those who had raised him. They were open and generous.

Still, he knew his mother's eyes were sharp, and would see his feelings no matter what he did to hide them. And he knew she wouldn't approve of his romantic involvement with Clarissa.

He could hear his mother's counsel as if she were in the room with him now.

She has to heal, Zeke. She needs the time and space to find what's inside her. No one can know their heart when it's so badly injured. Step aside and be her friend. You've no right to more than that. Neither does she.

He knew his mother would be right to say those things. Just as he knew no matter how hard he might try to follow her advice, he was already too deeply in love to turn around.

But he'd be careful with Clarissa, gentle, treat her the way she should be treated. He'd coax her into therapy so she could find her self-worth again, introduce her to his family so that she could see what family was meant to be.

He would be patient.

And when she was steady again, he would make love with her, sweetly, softly, so she would understand the beauty between a man and a woman and forget the pain and fear.

She was so full of fear. The bruises on the flesh would heal, but he knew those on the heart, on the soul, could spread and fester and ache. For that alone he wanted Branson to pay. It shamed him to crave retribution; it was against everything he'd come to believe. But even as he struggled to concentrate only on Clarissa, on how she would bloom away from the city — like a desert flower — his blood called out for justice.

He wanted to see Branson in a cage, alone, afraid. Wanted to hear him cry out for mercy as Clarissa had cried.

He told himself it was useless to wish it, that Branson's life would mean nothing to Clarissa's happiness and recovery once she was away from him. His Free-Ager's belief that each should move toward their own destiny without interference, that man's insistence on judging and punishing his fellows only hampered their rise to the next plane, was sorely tested.

He knew he'd already judged B. Donald Branson, and that he wanted him punished. A part of himself Zeke hadn't known existed craved to mete out that punishment.

He fought to bury it, to erase it, but his

hands were clenched into fists as he looked toward the 'link once again and willed Clarissa to call.

When it beeped, he jolted, stared, then leaped on it. "Yes, hello."

"Zeke." Clarissa's face filled the screen. There were tears drying on her cheeks, but she curved her lips into a trembling smile. "Please come."

His heart sprang to his throat, swelled. "I'm on my way."

Peabody itched for the final team meeting of the day to be over. The fact was, she admitted, she just itched. Period. McNab sat across the conference table, sending her an occasional wink and bumping his foot against hers as if to remind her of what was going to happen if they could ever get the hell out of Central.

As if she could forget.

She had a couple of bad moments, wondering if she'd lost her mind, if she should call it off. It was torture trying to concentrate on the work.

"If we're lucky," Eve was saying as she paced the room, "Lamont will make a move tonight, try for some contact. We have two tails on him. My impression of Monica Rowan is that she's a basic whack, but I instructed Peabody to put in the request to tap her home and porta-links. Ordinarily, I don't think we'd get it, but the governor's jumpy, and he'll put pressure on the judge."

She paused a moment, dipped her hands into her pockets. It always unnerved her to bring up Roarke's name in official business. "Added to that, I have some hope that Roarke will gather some evidence from inside Autotron, without putting Lamont any more on alert."

"If it's there," Feeney said with a nod, "he'll find it."

"Yeah, well, I'll be checking in with him shortly. McNab?"

"What?" He was caught in the middle of another wink at Peabody, coughed wildly. "Ah, sorry. Yes, sir?"

"You developing a tic or something?"

"Tic?" He looked anywhere but at Peabody, who was struggling to turn a laughing snort into a sneeze. "No, Lieutenant."

"Then maybe you'd entertain us with your report."

"My report?" How the hell was a guy supposed to think straight when the blood kept insisting on draining out of his head and into his lap? "After contacting Roarke with your request for a long-range scanner, I took Driscol from E and B to the lab at Trojan

Securities. At that time we met with Roarke and his lab manager. They demonstrated a scanner currently in development. Man, oh man, it's a beauty, Lieutenant."

Warming up, he leaned forward. "It can scan, triangulate, and scope through six inches of steel with a range of five hundred yards. Driscol nearly wet his pants."

"We can leave out Driscol's bladder problems," Eve said dryly. "Is the equipment developed enough for use?"

"They haven't done the fine tuning, but yeah. It's more sensitive and powerful than anything we have available through NYPSD. Roarke put a round-the-clock in manufacturing. We can have four of them, maybe five, by tomorrow."

"Anne, will that be enough?"

"If the units are as sensitive as Driscol reported — and I'm pretty sure he did wet his pants — it'll go a long way. I've had teams doing scans on arenas and sports complexes all day. We haven't found anything, but it's slow work. I'm short of men with so many assigned to the Plaza site."

"Our problem is time," Eve put in. "If Cassandra sticks to the timetable used by the Apollo group, we've got a couple of days. But we can't count on that. At this point, we've got everything in place we can have in place. I suggest everyone go home, try to get a decent night's sleep, and be ready to kick back into gear in the morning."

Peabody and McNab sprang up immediately, making Eve eye them balefully. "Bladder problems?"

"I . . . I need to call my brother," Peabody said.

"Me, too. I mean . . ." McNab laughed nervously. "I've got a call to make."

"Just remember, you're *on* call until this is over." She shook her head as they hurried out. "What's with those two lately?"

"I didn't see anything, I don't know anything." Feeney got to his feet. "That warrant comes through, I'll arrange the tap."

"See what anything?" she demanded, but he was already heading out. "Something's weird around here."

"We're all wired." Anne got to her feet. "And, oh joy, it's my turn to put dinner on the table. See you in the morning, Dallas."

"Yeah." Absently, Eve picked up her jacket, and alone, turned to study the boards one last time.

McNab's apartment was three blocks away. They took it at a fast clip with the wind directly in their faces and the beginnings of an icy rain pricking their skin.

"Here's how it's going to be," Peabody began. She had to take control from the get-go, she'd decided, to avoid any chance of disaster.

"I've got a pretty good idea how it's going to be." Once they were far enough away from Central, he patted a hand on her butt.

"This is a one-time deal." Though she liked his hand where it was, she knocked it aside. "We go to your place, we do it, and it's done. Then that's it, that's all. We get back to the way things were."

"Fine." At that point, he'd have agreed to strip naked and walk on his hands through Times Square just to get her out of that uniform.

"I'm calling my brother." She pulled her palm-link out of her pocket. "To tell him I'll be a little late."

"Tell him you'll be a lot late." With that suggestion, he bit her ear and pulled her into the skinny lobby of his building.

Heat washed through her, nearly as annoying as it was arousing. "He's not home yet. Keep out of range, will you? I don't want my brother knowing I'm stopping off for a bounce on a bony EDD guy."

Grinning, McNab stepped back. "You've got a real strong romantic streak, She-Body."

"Shut up, Zeke," she continued when her 'link clicked to message. "I'm running a little late. Guess you are, too. I should be home in an hour . . ."

She trailed off as, still grinning, McNab held up two fingers.

"Or so. We'll go out to this club I think you'll like, if you're up for it. I'll call back when I'm on my way home."

She tucked the 'link away as they stepped into the creaky elevator. "Let's make this quick, McNab. I don't want him wondering where I am."

"Okay. Then let's get started right now." He grabbed her, had her up against the wall and his mouth fused on hers before she could squeak.

"Hey, wait." Her eyes crossed when his teeth closed over the cord in her neck. "Is this a secured elevator?"

"I'm EDD." He had fast hands and they were busy dragging open the buttons of her overcoat. "Would I live in an unsecured building?"

"Then cut it out. Wait. This isn't even legal."

He could feel her heart thudding, feel the frantic beat of it under his hand. "Screw it." He turned, jabbed the controls to stop the car between floors.

"What the hell are you doing?"

"We're about to live out one of my top ten fantasies." From his pocket he took a minitool kit, and went to work on the security panel.

"In here? In *here?*" Just the thought of it had the blood swimming wildly in her head. "Do you know how many city ordinances you're breaking?"

"We'll arrest each other after." God, his hands weren't steady. Who'd have thought it? But he grunted in satisfaction when the light on the security camera overhead went blank. He deactivated the alarm system, tossed the tools in the corner, and swung around to her.

"McNab, this is insane."

"I know." He jerked his coat off, flung it aside.

"I like it."

He grabbed her again, grinned. "I thought you would."

Ice slicked the streets and sidewalks by the time Zeke finished fighting traffic and arrived at the Branson townhouse. It fell in thin, bitter needles and shimmered in the streetlights.

He thought of the baking heat of home, the strong, clean sunlight. And of how

Clarissa would heal there.

She answered the door herself. Her face was pale and showed the ravages of tears. Her hand shook, just a little, as she reached for his. "You took so long."

"I'm sorry." She'd left her hair down, in a soft wave he wanted to press his face against. "This weather's slowed everything down. I don't know how anyone lives here."

"I don't want to. Not anymore." She closed the door, leaned back against it. "I'm scared, Zeke, and I'm so tired of being scared."

"You don't have to be anymore." Gently, swamped with love, he framed her face in his hands. "No one's going to hurt you again. I'll take care of you."

"I know." She closed her eyes. "I think I knew, the minute I met you, that my life was going to change." She lifted her hands to his wrists. "You're cold. Come in by the fire."

"I want to take you out of here, Clarissa."

"Yes, and I . . . I'm ready to go." Still, she walked into the parlor, close to the fire, shivering a little. "I packed a bag. It's upstairs. I don't even remember what I put in it." She drew a breath, leaned back into him when Zeke laid his hands on her shoulders. "I left a note for B.D. When he gets home tomorrow and reads it . . . I don't know what he'll do, Zeke. I don't know what he's capable of, and I'm afraid of what I've done by putting you between us."

"I want to be between you." He turned her to face him, his eyes quietly intense on hers. "I want to help you."

She pressed her lips together. "Because you feel sorry for me."

"Because I love you."

Tears glistened in her eyes again, shimmering like dew on wild violets. "I love you, Zeke. It seems impossible, incredible that I could feel like this. But I do. It's as if I'd been waiting for you." Her arms slipped around his waist, her mouth tilted toward his. "As if I could get through anything, survive anything, because I had to wait for you."

His mouth moved softly over hers, to soothe and to promise. When she laid her head against his heart, he drew her closer and simply held her.

"I'll get your bag." He brushed his lips over her hair. "And we'll go away from here."

"Yes." She looked up at him, smiled. "Yes, we'll go away from here. Hurry, Zeke."

"Get your coat. It's cold."

He walked out, up the steps. Now his heart began to pound. She was going with him. She loved him. And it was a miracle. He found the suitcase on the bed, saw the envelope addressed to her husband propped on the pillow.

That had taken courage, he thought. One day she'd understand how much courage she had inside her.

He was halfway down the steps again when he heard her scream.

Propped in a corner of the elevator, mostly naked, Peabody struggled for air. McNab had his face buried against her throat with his breath whistling like her mother's old teakettle.

They'd pulled, tugged, and torn at each other's clothes, bit, groped, and bruised each other's flesh. Then had finished the job exactly where they stood.

It had been, Peabody admitted as her brain began to engage again, the most incredible experience of her life.

"Jesus." His lips formed the word against her throat and had her pulse picking up speed again. "Jesus, Peabody."

He didn't think he could move if she'd stuck a stunner in his ear. Her body — oh my God — her body was amazing: ripe and lush, the kind a man could just sink into. If he could manage to get them both horizontal, he wanted to do just that. Maybe drown there.

She had her arms locked around him. Couldn't quite make herself let go. Just as she couldn't quite remember what they'd done or how they'd managed it. The last ten minutes were a whirling blur, a sexual haze. A quick walk through insanity.

"We've got to get out of here."

"Yeah." But he nuzzled at her neck another moment in a gesture she found scary and sweet. Then he stepped back, blinked, and stared at her. His gaze skimmed down, up, then made the trip again. "God, you look great."

She knew it was ridiculous. Her bra was hanging off one shoulder by one strap. She still had one uniform sock and shoe on, with her trousers caught on the ankle. She wasn't sure where her panties were, but thought they'd probably been torn to pieces.

And the two dozen ab crunches she suffered through every day still hadn't flattened her belly.

Despite it, she felt the sly feminine thrill slide up her spine at the approval in his voice and the heat in his eyes. "You look okay, too."

He was thin, she could nearly count his ribs, and his stomach was flat as a board.

Normally, that would have annoyed her. But just now, looking at him, seeing his long blond hair tousled, and the goosebumps starting to pop out on his skin from the chill in the elevator, she found herself grinning.

He grinned back. "I'm not done yet."

"Good. Neither am I."

Zeke raced down the stairs with Clarissa's suitcase tumbling after him. He burst into the parlor to see her sprawled on the floor, one hand holding her cheek. Through her splayed fingers an ugly red mark stood out against her skin.

B. Donald Branson stood over her, swaying, eyes glazed and furious.

"Where the hell do you think you're going?" He snatched her coat from the floor, swung at her with it. "I didn't tell you to leave the house. You think you can sneak out while I'm away, you bitch?"

"Stay away from her." Though fury was bubbling in his gut, Zeke's voice was calm.

"Well, well." Branson turned, stumbled a little, and Zeke caught the stink of whiskey. "Isn't this cozy. The whore and the handyman." He shoved Zeke in the chest. "Get the hell out of my house."

"I intend to. With Clarissa."

"Zeke, don't. He doesn't mean anything,

B.D." She pushed herself to her knees like a woman praying. "I was . . . just going out for a walk. That's all."

"Lying bitch. So you were going to help yourself to what's mine, were you?" He shoved Zeke again. "Did she tell you how many others she's whored with?"

"That's not true." Clarissa's voice broke on a sob. "I never —" She broke off, cringing when Branson swung back to her.

"Shut the fuck up, I'm not talking to you. Thought you'd put in a little overtime while I was out of town?" He sneered at Zeke. "Too bad I canceled the trip, but maybe you shoved your dick into her already. No." He laughed, knocking Zeke back a step. "If you'd had her, you'd know she's lousy in bed. Beautiful and a waste. But she's mine."

"Not anymore."

"Zeke, don't. I want you to go now." Her teeth were chattering. "I'll be fine. Just go now."

"We'll go." Zeke said it calmly as he bent down to pick up her coat. He didn't see Branson's fist fly out. He never expected violence. But it connected with his jaw, radiating pain, shooting sparks. Through the buzzing in his ears, he heard Clarissa cry out again.

"Don't hurt him. Please, don't hurt him.

B.D., I won't go. I swear I —" Then she screamed again when he grabbed her up by the hair.

It happened fast, in a kind of red mist. Zeke jumped forward, striking out with one hand, grabbing for Clarissa with the other. Branson fell back, feet sliding on the polished floor. He went down hard, and there was a sharp crack as his skull rapped onto the marble hearth.

Frozen, Zeke stood, one arm locked around Clarissa to support her, and stared horrified at the blood that began to seep and pool from Branson's head.

"Sweet God. Sit down, here, sit down." He all but carried her to a chair, leaving her huddled as he rushed over to Branson. His fingers trembled as he pressed them against Branson's throat.

"There's no pulse." He drew in air sharply, ripped open Branson's shirt, and began to pump the heart. "Call for an ambulance, Clarissa."

But he knew it was too late. Open eyes stared up at him, the blood was streaming. When he forced himself to look, he could see no aura.

"He's dead. He's dead, isn't he?" She began to shake, her eyes huge on Zeke's, the pupils contracted to needlepoints of shock.

"What will we do, what will we do?"

Nausea churned in Zeke's stomach as he rose. He'd killed a man. He'd left behind every belief and had taken a life. "We have to call an ambulance. The police."

"The police. No, no, no." She began to rock then, her face white and strained. "They'll lock me away. They'll send me to prison."

"Clarissa." He made himself crouch in front of her, take her hands, though his felt soiled and evil. "You didn't do anything. I killed him."

"You — you —" Suddenly, she threw her arms around him. "Because of me. It's all because of me."

"No, because of him. You need to be strong now."

"Strong. Yes." Still shaking, she leaned back and her eyes never left his face. "I will be strong. I will. I need to think. I know, I . . . But . . . I feel ill. I — Could you get me some water?"

"We need to call the police."

"Yes, yes, I will. We will. But I need a minute first, please. Could you get me some water?"

"All right. Stay right here."

His legs felt like rubber, but he made them move. His skin felt as slicked with ice as the streets outside.

He had killed.

The two servants in the kitchen barely glanced at him when he came in. He had to stand a moment, his hand braced against the door. He couldn't remember why he'd come in, but he could hear, as if it was happening again, the sickening crack of Branson's skull hitting the hearth.

"Water." He managed to get the word out. He could smell meat roasting, sauce simmering. Sickness reared up into his throat. "Mrs. Branson asked me to get her some water."

Without a word, one of the uniformed droids moved to the refrigerator. Zeke watched with a dull fascination as she poured bottled water into a heavy glass, sliced a fresh lemon, added it and ice.

Because his hands were shaking, he took the glass she brought him in both of them, managed a nod of thanks, and walked back to the parlor.

Water leaped over the rim of the glass and onto the back of his hand when he saw Clarissa on her hands and knees frantically wiping up blood.

There was no body beside her.

"What have you done? What are you doing?" Panicked, he set the glass down and ran to her.

"What has to be done. I'm being strong and doing what has to be done. Let me finish."

She was fighting him, shoving, weeping, and the smell of fresh blood was strong.

"Stop. Stop this. Where is he?"

"He's gone. He's gone, and no one has to know."

"What are you talking about?" Zeke pulled the bloody rag from her, tossed it back on the hearth. "For God's sake, Clarissa, what have you done?"

"I had the droid take him." Her eyes were wild, as with fever. "I had the droid take him out, put him in the car. He'll throw the body into the river. We'll clean up the blood. And we'll run away. We'll just go away and forget this ever happened."

"No, no, we won't."

"I won't let them put you in prison." She reached out, grabbed his shirt. "I won't let them lock you away for this. I couldn't bear it." She lowered her head to his chest, clung. "I couldn't stand it."

"It has to be faced." He gentled his hands on her arms. "If I don't face it, I couldn't live with myself." When she sagged against him, he took her back to the chair."

"You'll call the police," she said dully.

"Yes."

* * *

They'd finally made it to the bed. Peabody wasn't altogether sure how they'd managed to get from the elevator to his apartment to his bed without killing each other, but that's where they were. The sheets were hot and tangled, and even now when McNab rolled weakly off her, her body pumped heat like a furnace.

"I'm not done yet," he said in the dark with a voice that hitched.

Peabody snorted, then began to laugh like a loon. "Me, neither. What are we, crazy?"

"A couple of more times, we'll probably burn it all out of our systems."

"A couple of more times, we'll be dead."

He reached out to stroke her breast. He had long, bony fingers, and she was becoming very fond of them. "Game?"

"Looks like."

He rolled over, replaced his fingers with his tongue. "I love your tits."

"Gee, thanks."

"No, I mean . . . ummm." He began to suck, slowly now, bringing an odd liquid flutter to her belly. "I *really* love your tits."

"They're mine." She could have bitten her tongue, and was grateful for the dark that concealed the flush as he chuckled against her. "I mean, I didn't like buy them or anything."

"I know, Dee. Believe me, nothing improves on Mother Nature."

God, she wished he hadn't called her Dee. It made it all personal, and well, intimate, when it was — it had to be . . . otherwise. She started to tell him so, but his hand was sliding, not rushing this time, just lazily sliding down her rib cage.

"Man, you are so . . . female." He had an urge to kiss her, long and slow and deep. As he lifted his head, started to order lights so he could see her when he did, a 'link beeped.

"Shit. Lights. Yours or mine?"

All at once, they were both cops. She dived for her coat pocket. "Mine, I think. It shouldn't be from Dispatch, it's my palm-link. Block outgoing video," she ordered, shoving the hair back from her face. "Engage. Peabody."

"Dee." Zeke's face filled the miniscreen. By the time he'd drawn a breath, let it out, her heart had stopped. She'd seen that stunned and glazed look in too many other eyes.

"What's happened? Are you hurt?"

"No. No. Dee, I need you to come. I need you to call Dallas and come to Clarissa Branson's house. I just killed her husband."

* * *

Eve finished reading the printout Roarke had given her and sat back in the chair at her desk. "So, Lamont's been stealing material from Autotron, bits and pieces at a time, for the last six months."

"He covered his tracks well." It burned, oh, it burned to know he'd been paying the son of a bitch all along. "He had some autonomy, his requisitions would hardly be questioned. He just ordered a bit more than he required for the work, then obviously smuggled out the extras."

"Which were handed over to Fixer, I'd guess. This is enough to nail him on theft of hazardous material, anyway. And that's enough for me to haul his butt into interview and cook him."

Roarke studied the glowing tip of his cigarette. "I don't suppose you could hold off on that long enough for me to fire him. Personally?"

"I think I'll save myself the trouble of getting you out of assault charges and dump him in a cage out of your reach. I appreciate the help."

"Excuse me?" He turned back to her. "If you'd let me get my memo book, then repeat that for the record."

"Ha ha. Don't let it go to your head." Absently, she rubbed at a headache brewing in her temple. "We have to find the next target. I'll have Lamont brought in tonight, let him stew in a cage, but it's not likely he knows the where and when."

"He's bound to know a few of the whos." Roarke moved around the desk, stood behind her, and began to massage the tension from her shoulders. "You need to put this aside for a while, Lieutenant. Give your mind a chance to clear."

"Yeah, I do." She let her head fall forward as his hands worked magic. "How long can you keep that up?"

"A lot longer if we were naked."

She laughed and amused him by starting to unbutton her blouse. "We'll just see about that. Hell." She did up the buttons quickly when her communicator sounded.

"Dallas?"

"Jesus, Dallas. God."

"Peabody." She got to her feet quickly.

"It's my brother. It's Zeke. It's my brother."

Eve clamped a hand over Roarke's, squeezed hard, and forced her voice into a command. "Tell me. Say it fast and straight."

"He says he killed B. Donald Branson. He's at that address now. I'm on my way."

"I'll meet you there. Hold it together, Peabody. Don't do anything. Do you copy this? Do nothing until I arrive."

"Yes, sir. Dallas —"

"I'll be there in five minutes." She broke the connection and bolted for the door.

"I'm going with you."

She started to refuse, then remembered the terrified look in Peabody's eyes. "We'll take one of your cars. It'll be faster."

Chapter Sixteen

Eve wasn't surprised to arrive on scene ahead of Peabody, but she was grateful. One look at the parlor, the blood smeared on the hearth, and the possessive and protective way Zeke kept his hand on Clarissa's shoulder had her stomach sinking.

Oh shit, Peabody, she thought. *What a hell of a fix.*

"Where's the body?"

"I got rid of it." Clarissa started to her feet on legs that were visibly shaking.

"Sit down, Clarissa." Zeke said it softly while easing her back into the chair. "She's in shock. She should have medical attention."

Shoving sympathy aside, and for the moment doing no more than filing the bruises on Clarissa's face away, she stepped forward. "Got rid of it?"

"Yes." She drew a deep breath, locked her hands together. "After — after it . . . I sent Zeke out of the room, asked him to get me some water."

She glanced toward the glass still sitting

untouched on an inlaid table, the water that had sloshed out of it ruining the finish. "When he was gone, I got one of the droids to carry — to carry it out, drive it away. I programmed the droid. I — I know how. I instructed it to throw the body in the river. Off the bridge and into the East River."

"She was upset," Zeke began. "She wasn't thinking. It all happened so fast and I —"

"Zeke, I need you to sit down. Over there." Eve indicated the sofa.

"She didn't do anything. I did. I pushed him. I didn't mean . . . he was hurting her."

"Sit down, Zeke. Roarke, would you take Mrs. Branson in another room? She should lie down for a few minutes."

"Of course. Come on, Clarissa."

"It wasn't his fault." She began to weep again. "It was my fault. He was just trying to help me."

"It's all right," Roarke murmured. "Eve will take care of it. Come with me now." He sent his wife a long, silent look as he led Clarissa away.

"We're not on record yet, Zeke. No," she continued with a quick shake of her head. "Don't say anything until you listen to me. I have to know everything, every detail, every step. I don't want you to even think about leaving anything out."

"I killed him, Dallas."

"I said shut up." Damn it, why didn't people listen? "I'm going to read you your rights, then we're going to talk. You can call for a lawyer, but I'm telling you now — as your sister's friend — not to do that, not yet. You give it to me straight, then we go in and do a formal interview. That's when you lawyer up. I'm going on record here in a minute, and when I do, you keep looking me dead in the eye. You got that? You don't evade, you don't hesitate. I'm seeing self-defense here, I'm seeing an accident, but when Clarissa ditched the body, she put both of you in jeopardy."

"She only —"

"Quiet, goddamn it." Frustrated, she dragged her hands through her hair. "There are ways to get around that. That's what the lawyer's going to be for. And the psych tests I'm going to order. But right now, on record, you're going to tell me everything, leaving nothing out. Don't think by smoking any details you're protecting Clarissa. You won't. It'll only make it worse."

"I'll tell you what happened. All of it. But do you have to take her in? She's afraid of the police. She's so fragile. He hurt her. If you could just take me."

She moved forward, sat on the edge of the

coffee table to face him. Jesus, she thought. Sweet Jesus, he was little more than a boy. "Do you trust your sister, Zeke?"

"Yes."

"And she trusts me." Eve heard the commotion in the foyer and rose. "That'll be her now. Are you going to be able to hold it together?"

He nodded, got to his feet as Peabody burst in. "Zeke. God, Zeke, are you all right?" She nearly leaped into his arms, then yanked back to run her hands over him, face, shoulders, chest. "Are you hurt?"

"No. Dee." He pressed his brow to hers. "I'm sorry. I'm so sorry."

"It's all right, it's okay. We'll take care of everything. We'll take care of it all. We need to call a lawyer."

"No. Not yet."

Peabody whirled to Eve, eyes damp and terrified. "He needs representation. Jesus, Dallas, he's not going in a cage, he's not going into holding."

"Suck it in, Peabody," Eve snapped. "That's an order." The tears were already rolling, causing Eve to feel a slick sense of panic. *Oh God, oh God, don't fall apart on me. Don't do it.* "That's an order, Officer. Sit down."

She'd seen McNab out of the corner of

her eye and didn't stop to think why he was there. "McNab, take Peabody's recorder. You'll be acting as temporary aide in this matter."

"Dallas —"

"This one isn't for you," Eve interrupted. "It can't be. McNab?"

"Yes, sir." He came over, leaned down to Peabody. "Hold on, okay? Just hang. It'll be all right." He took the recorder still pinned to her uniform collar, fixed it on the lapel of his wrinkled pink shirt. "When you're ready, Lieutenant."

"Record on. Dallas, Lieutenant Eve, on scene at residence of B. Donald Branson, conducting interview with Zeke Peabody in regards to the suspected death of B. Donald Branson." She sat on the coffee table again, kept her eyes directly on his, and read him his rights. Both of them ignored Peabody's muffled moan.

"Zeke, tell me what happened."

He drew a breath. "I better start at the beginning. Is that all right?"

"That's fine."

He did as Eve had told him, kept his eyes on hers, never wavered. He spoke of the first day he'd worked in the house, what he'd heard, his conversation with Clarissa afterward.

His voice trembled now and then, but Eve simply nodded and let him continue on. She wanted the emotion in his voice, the obvious distress in his eyes. She wanted it all on record while it was fresh.

"When I started back downstairs with her suitcase, I heard her scream. She was on the floor, crying, holding her face. He was yelling at her, drunk and yelling at her. He'd knocked her down. I had to stop him."

Blindly, he reached out for his sister's hand, gripped it tight. "I just wanted to get her out, away from him. No, that's not true."

He closed his eyes briefly. Leave nothing out, Eve had told him. "I wanted him to be punished. I wanted him to pay for what he was doing to her, but I knew I had to get her away where she'd be safe. He yanked her up, yanked her up by her hair. Hurting her, just to hurt her. I grabbed for her, shoved him back. And that's when . . . that's when he fell."

"You stepped up to stop him." It was the first time Eve had spoken since he started. And she kept her voice quiet, even, expressionless. "To get Clarissa away when he hurt her again. You shoved him and he fell? Is that correct?"

"Yes, he fell, fell backwards. I watched. It was like I'd frozen, couldn't move, couldn't think. His feet went out from under him and he stumbled back, went down hard. I heard — oh God — I heard his head hit the stone. And then there was blood. I checked his pulse, and there was nothing. His eyes were open, fixed and open and his aura was gone."

"His what?"

"His aura. His life force. I couldn't see it."

"Okay." That was an area they could just leave alone. "What did you do then?"

"I told Clarissa we needed to call an ambulance. I knew it was too late, but it seemed right. And the police. She was shaking and terrified. She kept blaming herself. I said, I told her she had to be strong and she seemed to snap back a little. She asked me to get her some water, just to give her a minute and get her some water. If I'd known what was in her head . . ."

He broke off then, closed his mouth tightly.

"Zeke, you have to finish. Finish it out. You won't help Clarissa by covering up now."

"She did it for me. She was afraid for me. It was the shock, you see?" Those young, soft gray eyes pleaded with Eve for understanding. "She just panicked, that's all, and thought if there wasn't a body, if she cleaned up the blood, it would be all right. He'd hurt her," Zeke murmured, "and she was afraid."

"Explain what happened. You went to get water."

He sighed, nodded, and finished.

Eve sat back, considered. Calculated. "Okay, thank you. You're going to have to go downtown, make a full statement."

"I know."

"McNab, call Dispatch, report a homicide at this address." She shot Peabody a look as her aide sprang off the couch. "Believed self-defense. We need a team in here. And we need a team out, dragging the river. Zeke, I'm calling in a couple of uniforms to take you downtown. You're not under arrest, but you will be detained until this scene can be secured and swept and we get your statement."

"Can I see Clarissa before I go?"

"It's not a good idea. McNab." She indicated by a jerk of her head for him to stay in the room with Zeke. "Peabody, with me."

She strode out into the hall, saying nothing when Roarke slipped out of a door and shut it gently. "She's asleep."

"Not for long. Peabody, pull it together and listen to me. You ride with your brother. I'm going to order he be detained in an interview room, not a cage. And you're going to talk to him and explain that he's going to agree to truth testing and a psych and personality exam. Mira will do it. We'll put a rush on it and get it done tomorrow. We'll lawyer him up and get him out tonight. He may have to wear a bracelet until after testing results, but his end of the story is clean, and it's going to hold."

"Don't take me off the case."

"You were never on. Don't push this," she said in a fierce whisper when Peabody protested. "I'll take care of your brother. If I let you on, it's going to look shaky. It's going to be tricky enough for me to hang as primary."

She was struggling against the tears and losing fast. "You were good to him. You let him get it out on record clean, without the lawyer. You were right about that."

Eve jammed her hands in her pockets. "For Christ's sake, Peabody, a blind man could see the guy would trip over his own feet before he'd step on an ant. Nobody's going to argue with self-defense here." If they found the body. The goddamn body. "He'll be okay."

"I should've looked after him." Now she did begin to weep, in great gulping sobs. Helpless, Eve looked at Roarke, spread her hands.

Understanding, he turned Peabody into his arms. "It's all right, darling." He stroked her hair, rocked, watched his wife suffer more than a little. "You let Eve look after him now. Let her take care of him."

"I need to talk to the woman." Eve's stomach rolled every time a fresh sob shuddered out. "McNab will secure the scene and wait for the uniforms. Can you . . . handle this?"

He nodded and continued to murmur to Peabody as Eve slipped into the room where Clarissa slept.

"I'm sorry." Peabody's voice was muffled against Roarke's chest.

"Don't be. You're entitled to a good cry."

But she shook her head, eased back, and scrubbed at her wet face. "She wouldn't break down."

"Peabody." Gently, Roarke cupped her cheek. "She breaks."

Eve yanked all the chains she could reach, gathered strings and pulled each one. She argued, justified, debated, and came close to threatening. In the end, she was primary in the matter of the death of B. Donald Branson.

She booked two interview rooms, positioning Zeke and Clarissa in separate areas, put the fear of God into the crime scene team and sweepers, harangued the body retrieval unit that was already dragging the East River, put McNab to work on the Branson droid, and arrived at Central with a viciously brilliant headache.

But she had everything she'd wanted.

Her last step before taking statements was to contact Mira at home and arrange for both Zeke and Clarissa to be tested the following day.

She took Clarissa first. She imagined when the woman's initial shock passed, she'd want a lawyer, and the lawyer would shut her up. Self-preservation was bound to overshadow any concern Clarissa might have for Zeke.

But when she walked into the interview room, Clarissa was sitting pale and quiet, her hands clutched around a cup of water. Eve gestured the uniform outside, closed the door.

"Is Zeke all right?"

"Yeah, he's okay. Feeling any better?"

Clarissa turned the cup in her hands, but didn't lift it. "It's all like a dream. So unreal. B.D.'s dead. He is dead, isn't he?"

Eve walked to the table, pulled back a chair. "Tough to say at this point. We don't have a body."

Clarissa shuddered, squeezed her eyes tight. "It's my fault. I don't know what I was thinking. I guess I wasn't thinking."

"Now's the time to start." She left any sympathy out of her voice. Sympathy would only push the woman into tears again. She engaged the recorder, recited the necessary information, and leaned forward. "What happened tonight, Clarissa?"

"I called Zeke. He came. We were going to leave together. Go away."

"You and Zeke were having an affair?"

"No." She raised her eyes then, dark and bright and beautiful. "No, we'd never . . . we kissed once. We fell in love. I know it sounds ridiculous, we barely knew each other. It just happened. He was kind to me, gentle. I wanted to feel safe. I only wanted to feel safe. I called, and he came."

"Where were you going?"

"Arizona. I think. I don't know." She lifted a hand to her forehead, skimmed her fingers over her skin. "Anywhere, as long as I got away. I'd packed. I'd packed a bag, and Zeke went up to get it for me. I got my coat. I was getting away, I was going away with him. Then B.D. came in. He wasn't supposed to."

Her voice started to hitch, her shoulders to tremble. "He wasn't supposed to come home tonight. He was drunk, and he saw I had my coat. He knocked me down." Her hand drifted to her cheek where the bruise was raw. "Zeke was there, and he told him to stay away from me. B.D. said awful things, and he kept pushing Zeke, shoving him, shouting. I can't remember, exactly. Just shouting and pushing, and he grabbed my hair. B.D. grabbed my hair and yanked me up. I think I was screaming. Zeke pushed him away. He pushed him because he was hurting me. And he fell. There was a terrible sound and the blood on the hearth. Blood," she said again and huddled over her cup of water.

"Clarissa, what did Zeke do then, after your husband fell? After the blood?"

"He . . . I'm not sure."

"Think. Pull it back into your head and think."

"He . . ." The tears began to plop, in single drops, onto the table. "He made me sit down, then he went to B.D. He told me to call an ambulance. He told me to hurry, but I couldn't move. I just couldn't. I knew he was dead. I could see — the blood, his eyes. He was dead. Call the police. Zeke said we had to call the police. I was so afraid. I told him we should run. We should just run away, but he wouldn't. We had to call the police."

She stopped, shivering, then looked into Eve's eyes. "B.D. knows the police," she said in a whisper. "He said if I ever told anyone, if I ever went to them because he hurt me, they'd lock me up. They'd rape me and lock me up. He knows the police."

"You're with the police now," Eve said coolly. "Have you been raped and locked up?"

Clarissa's eyes flickered. "No, but —"

"What happened after Zeke told you he was calling the police?"

"I sent him away, into the other room. I thought if I could just . . . make it go away. I asked him to get me some water, and when he was gone, I got the droid. I programmed it to take the — the body, to drive it to the river and throw it in. Then I tried to clean up the blood. There was so much blood."

"That was fast work. Fast and smart."

"I had to be fast. And smart. Zeke would come back — he'd try to stop me. He did stop me." She lowered her head. "And now we're here."

"Why are you here?"

"He called the police. He called them and they'll put him in prison. It was my fault, but he'll go to prison."

No, Eve thought, he wouldn't.

"How long were you married to B. Donald Branson, Clarissa?"

"Almost ten years."

"And you claim he abused you during this period?" Eve remembered the way Clarissa had stiffened when Branson had put his arm around her at the will reading. "He hurt you physically?"

"Not the whole time." She wiped a hand over her face. "At first. It was all right at first. But I couldn't do anything right. I'm so stupid, and I never got anything right. He'd get so angry. He hit me — he said he hit me to knock some sense into my head. To show me who was in charge."

"Just remember who's in charge around here, little girl. Just you remember."

Eve's gut clenched as the words played back in her head, and the sticky fear from childhood that went with it. "You're a grown woman. Why didn't you leave?"

"And go where?" Clarissa's eyes were ripe with despair. "Where would I go that he wouldn't find me?"

"Friends, family." She'd had none, Eve thought. She had no one.

Clarissa shook her head. "I didn't have any friends, and my family's gone. What people I knew — the ones he let me know — think B.D. is a great man. He beat me whenever he wanted, raped me whenever he chose. You don't know what it's like. You can't know what it's like to live with that, with the not knowing what he'll do, what he'll be like when he walks through the door."

Eve rose, walked away to the two-way mirror and stared at her own face. She knew exactly what it was like, too much what it was like. And the remembering, the feeling, would only cloud her objectivity. "And now, now that he won't walk through the door again?"

"He can't hurt me anymore." She said it simply, causing Eve to turn. "And I'll have to live with knowing I caused a good man, a gentle man to be responsible for his death. Any chance Zeke and I had to be together, to be happy, died tonight, too."

She laid her head on the rough table. Her weeping, Eve thought, was the sound of a heart breaking.

Eve ended the recording and stepping out, instructed the uniform to arrange to have Clarissa taken to her health center until morning.

She found McNab by the vending machine, scowling at his choices. "The droid?"

"She did a good job with him. He followed orders. I ran his program back and forward and sideways. She inputted orders — retrieve the body by the hearth, transport it to the car, drive to the river, and dispose. There's nothing else in there. She wiped previous memory."

"Accident or design?"

"Can't tell. She'd have been rushed, nervous. It's easy to wipe out old with new programming if you're in a hurry."

"Yeah. How many other servants in that place?"

McNab took out his notes. "Four."

"And nobody hears anything, sees anything?"

"Two in the kitchen at the time in question. Personal maid upstairs, groundskeeper tucked in his shed."

"Tucked in his shed, in this weather?"

"They're all droids. The Bransons had full droid staff. Top quality."

"Figures." She rubbed her tired eyes. She'd think about that later, go through those steps and stages later. First priority was to clear Zeke of any chance of formal charges.

"Okay, I'm going to hit Zeke again. Peabody in there with him?"

"Yeah, and the lawyer. No way around running him through again?"

She dropped her hands and her eyes were cool. "We do this by the book. We fucking write the book with this one. Every step documented. This'll hit the media by morning.

'Tool and Toy Tycoon Killed by Wife's Lover. Suspect is the brother of a police officer assigned to Homicide. Investigation snagged. Body missing.' "

"Okay, okay." He held up a hand. "I can see the picture."

"The only way to avoid that is to beat them to it. We prove self-defense, quick and clean. And we find the goddamn body. Tag the sweepers," she said as she swung toward the interview room. "If they haven't finished yet, light a fire under them."

Peabody's head came up the moment Eve walked in. Her hand continued to grip Zeke's. On the other side of him was a lawyer she recognized as one of Roarke's.

The woman in her was grateful, the cop furious. *One more shadow on the case,* she thought grimly. *"Husband of investigating officer arranged for representation." Fabulous.*

"Counselor."

"Lieutenant."

Without a glance at Peabody, she sat, engaged the recorder, and got to work.

Thirty minutes later, when Eve walked out, Peabody was right on her heels. "Lieutenant. Sir. Dallas."

"I don't have time to talk to you."

Peabody managed to skirt around Eve, face her. "Yes, you do."

"Fine." Braced for a battle, Eve pushed into the women's room, marched to the sink, and ordered the water on cold. "Say it and let me get back to work."

"Thank you."

Off balance with the quiet words, Eve lifted her dripping face. "For what?"

"For taking care of Zeke."

Slowly, Eve turned off the tap, shook the excess water from her hands, and moved to the dryer. It ran with a nasty buzz and a chilly blow of air. "I've got a job to do here, Peabody. And if you're thanking me for the lawyer, you're off. That's Roarke, and I'm not happy about it."

"Let me thank you."

She hadn't expected it. She'd been prepared for anger, for accusations. *"Why did you push him that way? Why did you keep trying to trip him up? How can you be so hard?"*

And what she got was Peabody's shaky gratitude and unhappy eyes. Eve rubbed her hands over her face, closed her eyes. "God."

"I know why you were rough on him this round. I know how much stronger his story is because you were. I was afraid . . ." She had to suck in breaths, one at a time. "Once I got my head clear, I was afraid you'd give him room, go soft — the way I would. But you hammered him. So, thanks."

"My pleasure." Eve let her hands drop. "He's not going down for this. You can hold onto that."

"I know. Because I'm holding onto you."

"Don't do that." Eve bit off the words and turned away. "Don't."

"I've got to get this out. My family's the most important thing I've got. Just because I don't live close doesn't mean we aren't close. After them comes the job." She sniffled, rubbed a hand impatiently under her nose. "You're the job."

"No, I'm not."

"Yeah, you are, Dallas. You're everything that's right about the job. And you're the best thing that's happened to me since I picked up my badge. I'm holding onto you because I know I can."

Eve's heart quivered. The backs of her eyes burned. "I don't have time to stand here and get sloppy with you." She strode to the door, stopping briefly to tap a finger on Peabody's chest. "Officer Peabody, you're out of uniform."

As the door swung closed behind Eve, Peabody glanced down and saw the third button on her uniform jacket was hanging by a thread. McNab, she realized, hadn't quite torn it off.

"Oh hell." She swore again, viciously, and ripped the button free.

There was a manic dance troupe doing a foot-stomping jig inside Eve's head. She gave a passing thought to rooting out a pain blocker. Then she walked into her office and saw Roarke.

He sat in her ratty chair in his elegant suit. His equally elegant overcoat hung on her ugly coat rack. His eyes were clear, his voice smooth and alert, as he conducted whatever kind of business a man like him conducted at eleven o'clock at night.

On principle, she rapped a fist against the supple Italian shoes currently making themselves at home on the top of her desk. She didn't budge them, but she made her point.

"I'll have to get back to you on the details." His gaze skimmed over Eve. His sharp eyes saw everything. The fatigue, the headache, the simmering emotions held ruthlessly in check. "I have a meeting."

He disconnected, lazily swung his feet to the floor. "Sit down, Lieutenant."

"This is my office. I give the orders here."

"Um-hmm." He rose to go to her AutoChef, and knowing she'd complain, programmed it for broth rather than coffee.

"There was no point in your waiting."

"Of course not."

"You might as well go home. I'm not sure when I'll get there. I'll just bunk here."

In a pig's eye, Roarke thought, but simply turned and handed her the broth.

"I want coffee."

"You're such a big girl now. You must know you can't have everything you want." He moved past her to the door, shut it just as she bristled at him.

"What I don't need, in here, is a smart mouth."

He winged up a brow. "Are you having yours removed? I'm so fond of it."

"I can have two gorillas in uniform in here in thirty seconds. It would make their night to toss you out on your excellent ass."

He sat in her spare chair, stretched out his legs as far as the cramped room would allow, and studied her face. "Sit down, Eve, and drink your broth."

Because she caught herself, barely caught herself, before flinging the cup across the room, she did sit. "I just pounded on Zeke. For thirty minutes I beat him up the wall and down again. 'You wanted to fuck another man's wife. So you killed him to get him out of the way. He was a rich man, wasn't he? She'll be rich now. That oughta set you up just fine, Zeke. You get the woman, you get the money, and Branson gets a tasteful memorial service.' And that was before I got nasty."

Roarke said nothing, simply waited her out. Eve picked up the broth. Her throat was raw, and it was better than nothing. "And when I finished hammering him, Peabody follows me into the john and thanks me for it. For Christ's sake."

He rose because she'd dropped her throbbing head into her hands. But when his hands came down to rest on her shoulders, she tried to shrug them off. "Don't. I can't take any more understanding tonight."

"That's a pity." He lowered his lips to the top of her head. "You've been training Peabody for months now. Do you think she doesn't know how your mind works?"

"Right now *I* don't know how the hell it works. She — Clarissa — she said he'd beaten her, raped her. Whenever he wanted. For years. Over and over for years."

Roarke's fingers tightened on her shoulders before he controlled them, gentled them. "I'm sorry, Eve."

"I've heard it before, from witnesses, suspects, victims. I can handle it. I can deal with it. But every time, every goddamn time, it's like a fist in the gut. Right under the guard and into the gut. Every time."

For a moment, just a moment, she let herself lean back, into him, into the comfort. "I have to keep going here." She rose, moved away from him. "You shouldn't have called in your spiffy lawyer, Roarke. It's sticky. This whole deal is very, very sticky."

"She cried on my shoulder. Sturdy, stalwart Peabody. Would you ask me to turn away from that?"

Eve shook her head. "Okay." She pressed her fingers to her eyes, willing the headache away. "We'll deal with it. I'm going to call Nadine."

"Now?"

After blowing out a breath, Eve turned back. Her eyes were clear again. "I'm going to offer her a one-on-one, right here, right now. She'll jump at it, and we'll have our spin on this right out of the box."

She walked back to the 'link to make the call. "Go home, Roarke."

"I will. When you do."

Chapter Seventeen

He bullied her into going home. Or she let him think he did. Zeke had been released on his own recognizance and was to report to Dr. Mira's office at nine A.M. Clarissa was tucked in a private room at her swanky health center and sedated for the night.

Eve had stationed a guard at her door.

Nadine's story hit the air at midnight and carried exactly the brisk tone of a routine if tragic accident that Eve had wanted.

The crime scene evidence was in and would be fully analyzed the next morning. The body was still somewhere in the depths of the East River, and there was simply no more to be done.

So at two A.M. she stripped off her clothes and prepared to fall into her own bed.

"Eve?" Roarke noted her weapon and harness were now out of reach. When she turned her head toward him, he caught her chin and shoved a pain blocker into her mouth. Before she could spit it at him, he caught her close, clever hands roaming down to squeeze her naked ass, and crushed his mouth to hers.

She choked, swallowed in self-defense, and felt his tongue dance lightly over hers. "That was low." She shoved away, coughed a little. "That was despicable."

"That worked." He caressed her cheek and gave her an affectionate shove into bed. "You'll feel better for it in the morning."

"In the morning, after coffee, I'm going to smack you around."

He slid into bed beside her, cuddled her against him. "Mmm. I can't wait. Go to sleep."

"You won't think it's so funny when your head's bouncing off the floor." But she rolled hers onto his shoulder and dropped away.

Four hours later, she awoke in exactly the same position. Exhaustion had gobbled her up, and she'd slept like a stone. She blinked, saw Roarke's eyes were already open and on hers. "Time?" she croaked it out.

"Just past six. Take a few minutes more."

"No, I can get started from here." She climbed over him, then stumbled groggily into the bathroom. In the shower, she rubbed sleep out of her eyes, and realized — with some resentment — her headache was gone.

"Jets on full, a hundred and one degrees."

Water streamed out from half a dozen jets, billowing steam. She let out one low, appreciative moan, then hair dripping, narrowed her eyes as Roarke stepped in behind her.

"Lower the temp and suffer."

"I thought I'd boil with you this morning." He handed her a cup of coffee, amused by the suspicious look in her eyes, pleased that they showed no shadow of pain. "I'll be working at home myself for a few hours today."

He sipped his own coffee, then set the mug on a high shelf above the pumping jets. "I'd like you to keep me apprised of progress, in both the helpings you currently have on your plate."

"I'll tell you what I can, when I can."

"Good enough." He filled his hands with soap and began to slide them over her.

"I can manage this myself." She stepped back because the blood was already sizzling under her skin. "I don't have time for water games this morning."

He only moved in, gliding his hands up over her belly, torso, breasts, which made her shiver. "I said —" His mouth lowered to her shoulder, teeth nipping. "Cut it out."

"I love it when you're wet . . ." He took the mug out of her hand before she could drop it, set it next to his own. "And slippery." Nudged her against the wall running with water, dripping with steam. "And reluctant. Go up." He murmured against her ear as his fingers dipped into her, slipping in, slipping out in a smooth, lazy rhythm.

Her head fell back, her body took over. "Damn it." It came out in a moan as pleasure, dark and drugged, spread from her center to the tips of her fingers.

"Go over." He slicked his tongue down the side of her throat and gave her no choice.

Her hands were splayed against the wet tile, her body pulsing. Water rained over them, hot and needle sharp, as he felt the orgasm tear through her.

A kind of purging, he thought.

She was still gasping when he spun her around and closed his mouth greedily over her breast.

She was helpless against what he brought to her. Each time, every time, helpless, staggered. And grateful. She dived her fingers into his hair, twisting, tangling them in that thick wet silk while those good, strong tugs of desire in her belly followed the restless hunger of his mouth on her.

His hands, slick, skilled, strong, raced over her, took her to the edge and over.

Where he wanted her, where he needed her — shuddering, moaning his name, swamped in her own pleasure.

The nails biting viciously into his back thrilled him, the frenzied race of her heart against his incited him. More. All. *Now,* was all he could think as they savaged each other's mouths.

"I want you." His breath was heaving as he gripped her hips. "Always. Ever. Mine."

His eyes were a wild and burning blue. She could see nothing else. It should have been too much, this desperate, endless need for him. Yet somehow it was never, never enough. "Mine." She dragged his mouth back to hers, and when he drove into her, met him beat for urgent beat.

She had to admit, four solid hours of sleep, wet, wild sex, and a hot meal went a long way to put the mind and body back into fighting trim. At seven-fifteen, she was at her desk in her home office, ready to start her day with her head clear and alert, her muscles warmed, and her energy up.

Marriage was having a number of interesting side benefits she hadn't considered.

"You look . . . limber, Lieutenant."

She glanced over. "I'd better. I want to put in a half hour here before I head in.

We've still got Cassandra to deal with, and I need to keep Peabody's energies focused in that direction."

"While you juggle Zeke's case with your other hand."

"Cops are always juggling." She had some very definite ideas where she was heading in that particular area. "I'm going to split McNab's duties. We can spare him to put time into the Branson case until we smooth it out. It helped having him around last night."

She stopped, frowned. "What the hell was he doing around last night, anyway? I didn't take time to find out."

"I'd say that was obvious." When Eve only stared at him blankly, Roarke laughed. "And you call yourself a detective. He'd been with Peabody."

"With her? What for? They were off duty."

Roarke stared at her a moment, saw she was seriously at sea. With a chuckle, he walked over, cupped her chin, skimmed his thumb over the dent in it. "Eve, they were off duty and *on* each other."

"On each other?" It took her a beat, then two. "Sex? You think they had sex? That's ridiculous."

"Why?"

"Because — because it is. She thinks he's

a pest. He goes out of his way to irritate her. I know you thought they had some . . . thing developing, but you were off. She's busy fooling around with Charles Monroe and he's . . ." She trailed off, thinking of the odd looks, the silences, the blushes. The signals.

"Oh, Jesus Christ," was all she could say. "Jesus Christ, they're having sex. I don't need this."

"Why should you care?"

"Because. They're cops. They're both cops, and damn it, she's *my* cop. This kind of shit gets in the way, it messes things up. They'll moon over each other for a while, then something's going to go wrong, and they'll start spitting and slapping."

"Why do you assume it won't work?"

"Because it won't. It doesn't. Your energies and your focus get all split up when they need to be channeled on the job. You start mixing sex and romance and Christ knows what into it, everything gets tilted. They've got no business having sex. Cops aren't supposed to —"

"Have a personal life?" he finished, just a bit coolly. "Personal feelings and choices?"

"I didn't mean that. Exactly. But they're better off without them," she added in a mutter.

"Thank you so much."

"This isn't about us. I'm not talking about us."

"Meaning you're not a cop, and we haven't mixed sex, romance, and Christ knows what into it?"

She'd pushed a button all right, Eve noted and wished she'd broken her finger first. "This is about two cops working on my team and on two messy investigations."

"An hour ago I was inside you, and you were wrapped around me." His voice was more than cool now, it was cold. As were his eyes. "That was about us, and the investigations were still there, messy or otherwise. How long are you going to keep believing you'd be better off without that?"

"That's not what I meant." She got to her feet, surprised to find herself just a little shaken.

"Isn't it?"

"Don't put words in my mouth or thoughts in my head. I don't have time for some marital crisis right now."

"Fine, I don't have the tolerance for one."

When he turned and left her, snapping the door closed between their offices, she lifted a fist. Then, as the temper refused to build and spare her from guilt, she lifted the other and knocked them against her temples.

Heaving out a breath, she strode to the door, opened it, and faced him down. He was already behind his desk and barely acknowledged her.

"That's not what I meant," she said again. "But maybe it's part of it. I know you love me, but I don't know why. I look at you, and I just can't get why it's me. Every time I get my balance, I lose it again. Because it shouldn't be me, and I think it'd kill me if you ever figured that out."

He started to get to his feet, but she shook her head. "No, I don't have time. I mean it. I just wanted to say that, and to tell you it wasn't what I meant. Peabody — she got hurt before, she got bruised because she tipped for a cop — another cop, another case. I'm not going to see that happen to her again. That's it. That's all. I'm going in. I'll be in touch if there's anything you need to know."

She moved fast. He could have stopped her, but he stayed where he was and let her go.

Later, he told himself, he'd deal with her. And she would have to deal with him.

Eve strode into Central. The glowing mood with which she'd started the day was now tarnished. She thought it just as well.

She'd work better, sharper, if she was edgy. Spotting Peabody, she jerked her chin, then pointed a finger toward her office.

She could see the signs of an unhappy, sleepless night on her aide's face. She'd expected that. She held the door herself until Peabody moved through, then closed it. "As of now, you put Zeke out of your mind. It's being handled, and you have a job to do."

"Yes, sir. But —"

"I'm not finished, Officer. If you can't guarantee that I'll have all your energy and all your concentration on the Cassandra matter, I want you to withdraw from the team and request leave. Now."

Peabody opened her mouth, closed it again before something nasty could escape. When her control was back, she nodded briefly. "You'll have the best I can give you, Lieutenant. I'll do my job."

"So noted. Lamont should have been picked up last night. Arrange for him to be brought up to interview. When the scanners received from Securities arrive, I want to know about it." Keep her busy, Eve thought. Keep her swimming in grunt work. "Contact Feeney and see if the tap warrant came through on Monica Rowan. Did you sleep with McNab?"

"Yes, sir. What?"

"Shit." Eve shoved her hands in her pockets, paced to the window, back. "Shit." She stopped, and they stared at each other. "Peabody, have you lost your mind?"

"It was a momentary lapse. It won't be repeated." She intended to tell McNab so at the first opportunity.

"You're not . . . stuck on him or anything?"

"It was a lapse," Peabody insisted. "A momentary lapse brought on by unexpected physical stimuli. I don't want to talk about it. Sir."

"Good. I don't even want to think about it. Get me Lamont."

"Right away."

Delighted to escape, Peabody fled.

Eve turned to her 'link and began to run the incoming messages. When Lamont's name popped, she swore, punched the machine. "Why the hell wasn't this transmission forwarded when it came in?"

Due to a temporary lapse in the system, all transmissions received between one hundred and six hundred and fifty hours were placed on hold.

"Lapses." She smacked the machine again, for the hell of it. "We're just full of lapses these days. Transmit full report on Lamont, hard copy."

Working. . . .

While her unit hiccupped through the printout, Eve signaled Peabody on her communicator. "Don't bother to dig up Lamont. He's in the morgue."

"Yes, sir. The mail just came in. There's another pouch."

Eve's nerves hummed. "I'll meet you in the conference room. Tag the rest of the team. Let's move."

The pouch was tested, cleared. The disc was copied, secured. Eve took a seat at the computer, slid the disc into the slot. "Run and print," she ordered.

We are Cassandra.

We are loyal.

We are the gods of justice.

We are aware of your efforts. They amuse us. Because we are amused, we will warn you a last time. Our compatriots must be freed. Until these heros have liberty, there will be terror — for the corrupt government, the puppet military, the fascist police, and the innocent they suppress and condemn. We demand payment, as retribution for the murders and imprisonment of the righteous. The price is now one hundred million dollars, in bearer bonds.

Confirmation of the release of the unjustly imprisoned political prophets must be received by sixteen hundred hours today. We will accept a public statement from each individual listed, made live through the national media. All must be accounted for. If even one is not released, we will destroy the next target.

We are loyal. And our memory is long.

Payment must be made at seventeen hundred hours. Lieutenant Dallas is to deliver this payment, alone. The bonds are to be placed in a plain black suitcase. Lieutenant Dallas is to go to Grand Central Station, track nineteen, westbound landing, and await further instruction.

If she is accompanied, followed, tracked, or attempts to make or receive any transmissions from this position, she will be executed, and the target will be destroyed.

We are Cassandra, prophets of the new realm.

"Extortion," Eve murmured. "It's the money. It's the money, not those psycho jokers on the list. A public statement over national screen. A ten-year-old could figure we'd be able to rig that."

She rose to pace and think. "That's smoke. It's the money. And they'll blow the target whether they get it or not. Because they want to."

"Either way," Feeney pointed out, "it puts you in the crosshairs and some unknown target on countdown."

"Can you fix me up with a tracker they can't make?"

"I don't know what the hell they can make."

"Do your best." She turned to Anne. "You've got a team who can work these high-end scanners?"

"One of Roarke's geniuses is giving us a briefing on it in twenty minutes. Then we're in the field."

"Find the target. I'll deal with the drop."

"You're not going in alone." This time Feeney rose. "Whitney won't clear it."

"I didn't say I was going in alone, but we'd better work out how it'll look that way," she said again. "We're going to need a hundred million in fake bearer bonds." Her smile was thin, humorless. "I think I know someone who can deliver those in time for the deadline."

"Give Roarke my best," Feeney said with a smirk.

She sent him a bland look. "I need you to report to Whitney and rig me a tracker."

"McNab and I will get on that."

"I need McNab — for a bit."

Feeney looked at her, at his detective, nodded. "I'll get another man on it until I've finished with the commander." He took the hard copy. "We'll want a good hour to test it out on you beforehand."

"I'll be available. Peabody, you're with me. I'll meet you at my vehicle in five minutes. McNab." She signaled him out with the flick of a finger.

"I want you to check in with Mira," she began as they walked toward her office. "Get a line on Zeke's testing. Then I want you to put the squeeze on Dickhead in the lab. I'd do it myself, but I don't want to involve Peabody at this point."

"I've got it."

"Threaten him, and if that doesn't work, bribe him. Arena ball tickets should work. I can scope two VIP box seats for next weekend."

"Yeah?" His eyes went bright. "Gee, Dallas, how come you never share with pals? The Huds are squaring off against the Rockets next weekend. If I threaten him into shagging his ass, can I have the tickets?"

"Are you asking for a bribe, Detective?"

Because she'd stopped, because her eyes were flat and her mouth set, he sobered quickly. "Why are you pissed off at me?"

"Why did you have sex with my aide during a sensitive investigation?"

His eyes glistened. "Does she need your permission to date, Lieutenant?"

"This wasn't pizza and a video, McNab." She strode into her office, yanked her jacket off the hook.

"Oh, so she only has to clear who she goes to bed with."

Eve spun back. "You're insubordinate, Detective."

"You're out of line, Lieutenant."

It surprised her, she had to admit. It threw her off rhythm to see him standing there, eyes cold and fierce, body braced, teeth showing. She thought of him — when she thought of him — as a good cop with a sharp mind for details, a good hand with electronics. And as a man, a little foolish, vain, and glib, who talked too much and took nothing beyond his work seriously.

"Don't you tell me I'm out of line." Working on control, she put her jacket on slowly. "Peabody got kicked by a cop with a pretty face before. I'm not watching it happen again. She matters."

"She matters to me, too." The words were out before he could yank out his tongue and bite it off. "Not that she gives a damn about that. She brushed me off this morning, so you've got nothing to worry about." He kicked her chair, sent it skidding across the room. "Goddamn it."

"Oh hell, McNab." The anger she'd worked up so nicely dipped toward nerves. "What are you doing here? You're not getting sticky on her?" His only answer was one long, miserable stare. "I knew it. I knew it. I just knew it."

"It's probably just a blip," he muttered. "I'll get over it."

"Do that. Just do that, will you? This isn't the time — it's never the time, but this is *really* not the time. So forget it, okay?" Eve didn't wait for his reply — she wanted him to understand. "Her brother's on the hot seat, we've got bombs all over the damn city. I've got one body in the morgue and another in the river. I can't afford to have two members of my team tripping over heartstrings."

He surprised himself by laughing, and meaning it. "Christ, that's cold."

"Yeah, I know." She remembered the way Roarke had looked at her that morning. "I suck at this, McNab. But I need you on your toes."

"I'm on them."

"Stay on them," she told him and walked out.

* * *

Since she calculated she couldn't do worse on her record of offending, insulting, and injuring people who mattered to her that morning, Eve put a call through to Roarke as she headed to the garage.

Summerset answered, and her instinctive reaction of clenching her teeth felt a lot better than guilt. "Roarke," was all she said.

"He's engaged on another call at the moment."

"This is police business, you cross-eyed putz. Put me through."

His nostrils flared in annoyance, and her mood lightened just a little more. "I will see if he's available to take your call."

The screen went blank. Though she didn't doubt he'd have the nerve to cut her off, she counted to ten. And ten again. She was heading toward thirty when Roarke came on.

"Lieutenant." His voice was clipped, the Irish in it frigid temper rather than music.

"The department needs one hundred million in fake bearer bonds — good fakes, but not good enough to pass a bank check. Sheets of ten thousand."

"When's your deadline?"

"I could use them by fourteen hundred."

"You'll have them." He waited a beat. "Anything else?"

Yes, I'm sorry. I'm an idiot. What do you want from me? "That's it. The department —"

"Appreciates it. Yes, I know. I'm on an interplanetary conference call, so if that's all . . ."

"Yeah, that's all. If you'd let me know when they're ready, I'll arrange transport."

"You'll hear from me."

He cut her off without another word and made her wince. "Okay," she mumbled. "That hurt. Bull's-eye." She jammed the link back in her bag.

She remembered her advice to McNab. Just forget it. She did her best to follow it, but some of her feelings must have shown on her face. Peabody kept her mouth shut as Eve stepped up to the car. And they drove to the morgue in silence.

The dead house was packed like a lobby bar at a Shriners' convention. The corridors were full of techs, assistant MEs, and the medical staff drafted from local health centers to wade in during the current crisis. The stench of humanity, alive and deceased, smeared the air.

Eve managed to snag one of the morgue staff she knew. "Chambers, where's Morris?" She'd hoped for a five-minute consult with the chief medical examiner.

"Up to his eyebrows. The hotel bombing brought in a lot of customers. A lot of them in pieces. It's like putting a jigsaw puzzle together."

"Well, I need to see one of your guests who checked in early this morning. Lamont. Paul Lamont."

"Jeez, Dallas, we're working on priority here. We gotta get these stiffs ID'd."

"It's connected."

"All right, all right." Obviously miffed, Chambers scurried to a computer, ran the log. "We got him on ice in area D, drawer twelve. We're racking, packing, and stacking them for now."

"I need a look at him, his personal effects and the incoming report."

"Let's make it quick." His shoes slapped down the hall. He swung into area D, slid his key card in the slot, and led them inside. "Drawer twelve," he reminded her. "Just use your master, and I'll pull up the rest."

Eve uncoded the drawer and out came a puff of icy smoke and Lamont. Or what was left of him. "They did a job on him," she muttered, scanning his mangled, broken body.

"Sure did. Says here the vehicle, a black Airstream van, jumped the curve and ran right over him where he stood on the sidewalk. We haven't done anything on him yet, just stored him. He's not priority."

"No, he'll keep." Eve slid the drawer back in place. "What did he have on him?"

"Fifty couple in credits, wrist unit, IDs and key cards, pack of breath mints, palm-link, date book. Oooh, and a sticker." He examined the long, slim blade. "Over the legal limit, I'd say."

"Only by a mile or two. I need the 'link and date book."

"Fine by me. Sign for them and they're yours. Look, I have to get back. Hate to keep the customers waiting."

She signed the checkout log. "Have these effects been dusted?"

"Hell if I know. Enjoy."

Eve turned to Peabody as the area doors swung shut. "We'll dust and clean first. Let's go on record."

Peabody shifted her field kit on her shoulder. "Here? Don't you want to do this somewhere else?"

"Why?"

"Well, the place is full of dead people."

"And you want to be a murder cop?"

"I'd rather deal with one at a time." But she opened her kit and went to work. "Good clean prints on here."

"We'll run them after we check out his

'link and log. Probably Lamont's prints."

Eve took the 'link, turned it over in her hand. It was a top-of-the-line model, sleek and complex. She remembered his expensive shoes. "Wonder what Roarke pays these guys? She turned the control to replay all incoming and outgoing transmissions for the last twenty-four hours. "Note any numbers we hit. We'll need to run them, too."

She watched the numbers zip by on the display, then pursed her lips. Video was blocked. But the voices came through loud and clear.

Yes.

They're looking at me. Lamont, Eve decided, with the faintly French accent and the squeak of nerves in his voice. *The cops were here. They're looking at me. They know something.*

Calm down. You're shielded. This isn't something to discuss over 'links. Where are you?

It's all right. I'm secured. I slipped out to the grill down from work. They called me up, Roarke was there, too.

And what did you tell them?

Nothing. They got nothing out of me. But I'm telling you, I'm not taking the fall for this. I want out. I need more money.

Your father would be disappointed.

I'm not my father, and I know when it's time

to cut loose. I got you everything you needed. I'm finished here. I want my share now, tonight, and I'm gone. I did my part. You don't need me anymore.

No, you're right. It would be best if you finished out the day as normal. You'll be contacted later as to where to pick up your share. We still have to be careful. Your work is done, but ours isn't.

Just get me what I've got coming, and I'm gone by morning.

It'll be arranged.

"Idiot," Eve muttered. "Signed his own execution papers." She shook her head. "Greed or stupidity."

There was another call, Lamont booking a private compartment on the off-planet transport to Vegas II. He used a false name and identification number.

"Have a unit go by his place, Peabody. I bet our boy was all packed and ready to go."

The next was an incoming, a recorded voice giving brief instructions.

The corner of Sixth and Forty-third, one hundred hours.

Lamont made two more outgoings, received no answer from either.

"Run the numbers, Peabody," Eve instructed as she picked up the day book.

"Already running the first. It's a private code."

"Use my authorization number and get it. Whoever he was talking to didn't realize Lamont was on his own 'link. Had to figure he was on a public job, or he'd never have left this on the body. Even if he'd wanted it, the tails on Lamont were right on scene."

"The code's shielded," Peabody told her. "They won't release it."

"Oh yeah, they will." Eve whipped out her communicator. Within thirty seconds she had Chief Tibble on the line, and barely two minutes later, the governor's personal authorization.

"Man, you are good." Peabody looked on with admiration. "You snarled at the governor."

"Gives me that shit about privacy acts. Politicians." She set her teeth, flexed and unflexed her fingers as she waited for the last line of bureaucracy to tumble. "Well, son of a bitch."

"What is it? Who is it?" Peabody craned her neck to see the data on Eve's display.

"B. Donald Branson's private line."

"Branson." The blood drained out of Peabody's face. "But, Zeke. Last night . . ."

"Transmit that call to Feeney, get him to run a voice check. We need to know if that was Branson on the call." She was moving fast as she snapped out the order. "Contact the guard on Clarissa Branson's room," she continued as they strode down the corridor. "Tell him no one goes in or out of it until we get there."

She pulled out her own communicator as they swung outside into the cold. "McNab, get down to Mira's. I want Zeke brought back up. Tuck him away until you hear from me."

"Zeke wouldn't know anything about Cassandra, Dallas. He'd never —"

Eve spared Peabody a look as she jumped into the car. "Toys and tools, Peabody. I'd say your brother was being used as both."

Chapter Eighteen

Clarissa was gone. There was nothing to be gained by berating and browbeating the guard on duty, but Eve did it anyway.

"She looks at him, smiles tearfully, and asks if she can go sit in the gardens." Eve rolled her eyes and tapped the note Clarissa had left behind in her palm. "Then she uses the can I have a glass of water routine she did with Zeke and our boneheaded hero runs off to fetch."

She circled the conference room, waiting for Zeke to be brought in. "Oops, where'd she go? It takes him thirty fucking minutes to call it in because he's so sure a sweet little thing like her is still around somewhere. But does he check her room? See the tearful good-bye note?"

Eve unfolded it again while Peabody wisely remained silent.

I'm sorry, so sorry, for everything that happened. It was my fault. All of it. Please forgive me. I'm doing what's best for Zeke. He can't be held responsible. I can never face him again.

"So she leaves him holding the bag. Let's

hear it for true love." Though Peabody said nothing, Eve held up her hand and began to go through the steps and stages. "Zeke hears them fighting through the vent in the workroom. It's Branson's house, his workroom. He knows Zeke's down there. According to Clarissa, he was wild to keep anyone from knowing he knocked her around. So why doesn't he fix the damn vent? The staff's all droids, so he doesn't worry about them. But he's got a live one now."

"You think he wanted Zeke to hear?"

"Follow along, Peabody. I've been working this out since last night."

"Last night?" Peabody's mouth dropped open. "But, Dallas, there was nothing in the prelim report about —"

She broke off, winced, as Eve shot her a cool stare. "You read my prelim, Officer Peabody?"

"Strap me in irons," Peabody muttered, "and flog me. He's my brother."

"I'll reserve the flogging for a later date. No, I didn't put anything into the prelim because the main concern was getting Zeke's story down and putting him in the clear. But the whole deal screamed setup. Slick, organized, damn well-oiled, but a setup."

"I don't see it."

"You can't see past Zeke. Take the steps here. They pull Zeke in from out west. I don't care how good he is, they could've found somebody to do this work without transporting him in. But they pull him, a single guy, a Free-Ager. Branson kicks his wife to hell and back, but he lets her import a young, attractive man into the house. And he's diddling with having carpentry work done when, we suspect, he's laying plans for the biggest terrorist siege on the city since the Urban Wars."

"None of it makes sense."

"Not separately, but it does when you connect the dots. He needed a fall guy."

"But, for God's sake, Dallas, Zeke killed him."

"I don't think so. Why haven't they found the body? Why did this cowed, terrified woman manage to get rid of it in less than five minutes?"

"But — who died?"

"This time around, I don't think anybody did. Toys and tools, Peabody. I've seen several of the prototype droids Roarke's R and D department's got under production. You wouldn't make them at a glance, even a close look." She glanced around as Zeke came in, followed by Dr. Mira.

"Doctor?"

"Zeke's my patient, and he's under considerable distress." Gently, Mira walked him to a chair. "If you feel it's necessary to interview him, I want to be here."

"Zeke, do you want your lawyer?" Eve asked him, and he only shook his head. Sympathy threatened to surface. She knew firsthand how miserable Testing could be. She set the recorder, sat across from him. "I just have a few questions. How many times did you meet Branson?"

"I only saw him twice. Once over the 'link and then last night."

"Just once, over a 'link?" But he'd recognized Zeke instantly. Branson had reportedly been stumbling drunk, but he'd tagged Zeke at a glance. "The whore and the handyman," Zeke had quoted him as saying. "So most of your contact was through Clarissa. How much time did you spend together?"

"Not a lot. When she was in Arizona, we talked. We had lunch a couple of times." He looked up quickly. "It was harmless."

"What did you talk about?"

"Just . . . things. All sorts of things."

"Did she ask you about yourself?"

"I guess, yeah. She was so relaxed and happy. Not like she is here. She liked hearing about my work, and she was interested in Free-Agism. She said it sounded like such a gentle and kind religion."

"Zeke, did she come onto you?"

"No!" His shoulders straightened. "It was nothing like that. She was married. I knew she was married. She was just lonely. There was something there." He said it with a wonder that made Eve's heart sink for him. "Right away, and we both knew it, but we wouldn't have done anything. I didn't know how he treated her, I just knew she was unhappy."

"Last night was the first time you'd actually seen Branson in person. He never came down to the workroom, never called you up to discuss the projects?"

"No, he never came down."

Eve sat back. She was willing to bet Zeke had yet to meet B. Donald Branson in the flesh. "That's all I need for now. Zeke, you're going to have to stay here, in Central."

"In a cell?"

"No. But you have to stay here."

"Can I see Clarissa?"

"We'll talk about that later." Eve rose. "The uniform will take you up to the recreation area. There's a sleeping bin off the side. I think you should tranq up and use it."

"I don't use tranqs."

"Me, either." She softened enough to smile at him. "Use the bin anyway. Get some rest."

"Zeke." There was so much Peabody wanted to say, wanted to do, but she held it in and looked at him soberly. "You can trust Dallas."

"I'll be up in a minute." Mira patted his arm. "We'll use meditation." She waited until the uniform came to take him out. "My testing is complete enough for me to give you an evaluation."

"I don't need it." Eve cut her off. "It's for the record, not for me. He's not going to be charged."

Mira relaxed fractionally. In the last two hours, Zeke had slipped past her professional veneer. "He's suffering. The idea that he took a life, however accidentally —"

"It wasn't an accident," Eve corrected. "It was a setup. If I'm on target, B. Donald Branson's very much alive, and most likely with his wife. I can't get into the details, I don't have time," she continued. "You looked at Clarissa's statement, you viewed the recording."

"Yes. It's a classic case of abuse and shattered self-esteem."

"Classic," Eve agreed with a nod. "Like textbook. Like line for line out of a case study. She didn't miss a trick, did she?"

"I don't know what you mean."

"No friends, no family support. Delicate, helpless woman dominated by an older, stronger man. He drinks, he beats her. He rapes her. She sticks. 'Where will I go, what will I do?' "

Mira folded her hands. "I realize you would find her inability to change her situation a sign of weakness, but it isn't at all atypical."

"No, it's dead typical. And I'm saying that's just how she played it. Played Zeke, played me, and would have played you. I think you'd have caught on, and she probably figured the same. That's why she's gone. And when we check Branson's financials, I guarantee the money's gone, too."

"What possible reason would the Bransons have to fake his death?"

"The same reason they arranged his brother's. Money. The same reason they timed it to pull part of the team away from the central theme. More money, with a little payback thrown in. We'll tie them to Apollo. Sooner or later, something'll click. Take care of Zeke. If I'm right, we'll be able to tell him he didn't kill anyone. Let's move, Peabody."

"I can't keep up," Peabody told her. "I

can't get it straight in my head."

"You will, when we get the rest of the pieces. Check those financials."

Peabody scrambled to keep pace as they worked their way down to the garage. "Jesus, Branson transferred fifty million — that's most of the fluid cash in the business — to an off-planet, coded account. He did it last night, two hours before Zeke . . ."

"Check their personal accounts."

Working one-handed, Peabody slid into the car. "Six personals, between twenty and forty apiece. He cleaned them out yesterday."

"A nice little nest egg for Cassandra." As she drove, Eve contacted Feeney on her communicator.

"Voiceprints match," he told her. "Now how are we going to arrest a dead guy?"

"I'm working on it. Take a run by Branson T and T; take a look at the droids in development. Did we get the order for tapping Monica Rowan's lines?"

"They're tapped. Not a peep so far."

"Keep me up." She ended transmission. "Peabody, contact the locals up in Maine, get a black and white to do a runby. I want Monica under wraps."

Lisbeth wasn't pleased to see cops at her

door. She stared through Eve and ignored Peabody. "I have nothing to say to you. My counsel has advised —"

"Save it." Eve pushed her way in.

"This is harassment. One call to my lawyer, and I'll have your badge."

"How tight were the Branson boys, Lisbeth?"

"Excuse me?"

"J.C. must have talked to you about his brother. What did they think of each other?"

"They were brothers." Lisbeth shrugged. "They ran a business together. They had their ups and downs."

"Did they fight?"

"J.C. didn't fight with anyone, really." Something like grief flickered in her eyes and was quickly shut down. "They disagreed occasionally."

"Who ran the show?"

"B.D. ran the show." Lisbeth waved a hand. "J. Clarence was better with people, and creatively he enjoyed having input in new projects. It didn't bother him that B.D. held the reins."

"What was his relationship with Clarissa?"

"He liked her, of course. She's a charming woman. I think she intimidated him somewhat. She's very formal and aloof for all that air of fragility."

"Really, but you were friends?"

"Friendly. After all, we were both involved with a Branson. We socialized, with and without them."

"Did she ever tell you B.D. mistreated her?"

"Mistreated?" Lisbeth let out a short laugh. "The man fawned on her. All she had to do was bat her eyes and purr and he jumped."

Eve glanced toward the wall screen, noted it was turned off. "Not watching the news these days?"

"No." She turned her head and for a moment looked tired and strained. "I'm making arrangements to clean up some personal matters before I transfer to the rehabilitation center."

"Then you wouldn't have heard that B. Donald Branson was killed last night."

"What?"

"He fell during a struggle when he was beating his wife."

"That's ridiculous. That's absurd. He wouldn't lay a hand on Clarissa. He worships her."

"Clarissa claims he's been abusing her physically for years."

"Then she's a liar," Lisbeth snapped out. "He treated her like a princess, and if she says otherwise, she's lying through her teeth."

She stopped abruptly, went very pale.

"You didn't find the photographs in your mail slot, did you, Lisbeth? You had them handed to you by someone you trusted — someone you thought cared about J.C."

"I — I found them."

"No point in lying to protect the Bransons. He's dead, and she's gone. Who gave you the photographs of J.C., Lisbeth? Who gave them to you and told you that he was cheating on you?"

"I saw the pictures. I saw them with my own eyes. He was with that blond bitch."

"Who gave them to you?"

"Clarissa." She blinked once, twice, and tears started to stream. "She brought them to me, and she was crying. She said how sorry she was, how sorry. She begged me not to tell anyone she'd given them to me."

"How did she get them?"

"I never asked. I just looked at them, and I went crazy. She told me it had been going on for months, and she couldn't pretend not to know any longer. She couldn't stand to see me hurt and J.C. ruin his life over some cheap lay. She knew how jealous I was, she knew. When I got to his house, he denied it. He told me I was crazy, there wasn't any blonde. But I'd *seen!* And the next thing I knew, I was picking up that drill. Oh my God, oh my God. J.C."

She collapsed into the chair, wailing.

"Get her a tranq, Peabody." Eve's voice held no sympathy. "We'll have a car come by and pick her up. When she's pulled it together, McNab can take a statement."

"I know we're pressed for time." Peabody jumped in the car again. "But I feel like I'm three steps behind."

"Branson's connected to Cassandra. Clarissa's connected to Branson, Zeke's connected to Clarissa. We're led to believe that both the Branson brothers meet with untimely and violent ends within a week of each other. Meanwhile, the accounts are stripped. Zeke's brought in from clear across the country to work at the Branson house, and within a couple of days, he's tangled with Branson over Clarissa and supposedly killed him. But Clarissa, out of her fear and concern for Zeke, loses the body.

"That's the part that hung me up all along, but a guy tells you he kills another guy, you generally go with it. Still we've got no body, and there's nothing on the droid playback to indicate he was instructed to weigh it down. The search team's sensors don't pick another up, it doesn't bob up and float, but we know it got tossed in the river."

"Droids don't float, and the sensors are looking for flesh, blood, and bone."

"See, you're catching up. Now, we connect those dots. Zeke killed himself a droid. We have Lisbeth's statement that there were never any beatings, no rapes, and odds are she'd have known if there were. Through J.C., if not on her own. We have the coincidence that Zeke just happened to be in the right place at the right time to hear beatings and rapes, then Clarissa turns to him for help. She's already scoped him; she knows the kind of man he is, and very likely made the subtle kind of play for him he wouldn't see as a come-on."

"He doesn't understand women," Peabody murmured. "He's practically still a kid."

"He wouldn't understand this one if he'd hit the century mark. She trolled for him and reeled him in. She and Branson got rid of the brother, which leads me to believe he wasn't involved in Cassandra. He was weight, so they ditched him. I'm primary on the case, and they don't want me looking too hard, having just the kind of talk with Lisbeth I just finished having, so they tag me on the bombings. Blowing up the city's going to pull my attention away from a plea bargain I know I can't change."

"Whoever had pulled J. C. Branson's homicide would have been tagged? They moved to you because of that?" Peabody considered. "That was their big mistake."

"That was excellent sucking up, Peabody. Smooth, subtle."

"I've been practicing."

"The politics are more smoke — pull the attention away, waste our time. It's the money they're after and the sheer delight in destroying."

"But they have money."

"More's better, especially if you grew up on the run, hiding out, maybe scraping for the good life. What do you want to bet Clarissa Branson spent her formative years in Apollo?"

"That's a big leap, Lieutenant."

" 'We are loyal,' " Eve quoted as she zipped through the security gate to the parking area under Roarke's midtown offices.

Peabody gawked a little when they moved into the private elevator, but before she could comment, Eve's 'link beeped.

"Lieutenant Dallas? Captain Sully, Boston PD. The patrols just reported in from the Rowan address. Monica Rowan has been the victim of what appears to be a bungled B and E. She's dead."

"Damn it. I'll need a full report on that, priority level, Captain."

"I'll get you as much as I can as quick as I can. Sorry we can't be of more help."

"So am I," Eve murmured as she ended the call. "Goddamn it, I should've put a wall around her."

"How could you know?"

"I do know. Just a little too late." She strode out of the elevator, moved past Roarke's efficient assistant without stopping.

Efficiency prevailed, however. Roarke was opening the door for her himself when Eve got there.

"Lieutenant, I didn't expect you personally."

"I'm heading in. I'm pressed to the wall here." She looked in his eyes, wished she could say . . . wanted to. "Things are coming together, and the clock's running."

"Then you'll want your bait." He looked into her eyes. "I assume several million in counterfeit bonds is bait — with you as hook."

"We're closing in. With any luck, this should finish it. I — Peabody, take a walk," she said without looking back.

"Sir?"

"Step out, Peabody."

"Stepping out, Lieutenant."

"Look . . ." Eve began. "I'm really hitting the wire on this, so I can't get into stuff. I'm sorry about before."

"You're sorry I'm irritated."

"Okay, fine. I'm sorry you're irritated, but I have to ask for a favor."

"Personal or official?"

Oh, he was going to make it tough. She leveled her gaze, and a muscle in her cheek twitched. "Both. I need everything you can dig up on Clarissa Branson — everything — And I need it really fast. I can't spare Feeney, and even if I could, you'll be quicker and you won't leave fingerprints."

"Where do you want me to send the data?"

"I need you to call me with it, privacy mode, on my personal palm-link. I don't want her to know I'm looking."

"She won't." He turned and lifted a wide steel case. "Your bonds, Lieutenant."

She tried a smile. "I won't ask you how you managed this so fast."

He didn't smile back. "Best not."

She nodded, hefted the case, and felt miserable. She couldn't remember another time when they'd been together for five minutes and he hadn't touched her in some way. She'd gotten so used to it, so dependent on it, that she felt the loss like a backhanded slap.

"Thanks. I'll — The hell with it." She took a fistful of his hair, and swallowing what for her was a great gulp of pride, pressed her mouth hard to his. "See you later," she muttered and turned on her heel, stormed out.

Now he smiled, just a little, and walked to his desk to do the favor she'd asked of him.

"You okay, Dallas?"

"Yeah, shit. I'm dancing." She was stripped down to her undershirt and jeans, a fact which mildly embarrassed both her and Feeney.

"I can call in a female to, ah, finish this."

"Hell, I don't want any ham-handed EDD chick pawing at me. Just do it."

"All right, okay." He cleared his throat, rolled his shoulders. "The tracker's wireless. It's going to go right over your heart. We figure they'll scan you, but we're going to coat it with this stuff — it's like skin. They're using it on droids. If they pick it up at all, it'll look like a blemish or something."

"So they'll think I have a pimple on my tit. Fine."

"You know, Peabody could do this."

"Jesus, Feeney." Somebody had to get going, so keeping her gaze trained over his shoulder, she yanked up her shirt. "Put the damn thing where it goes."

The next five minutes were mortifying for both of them.

"You, ah, want to hold your shirt out for a couple of minutes, till the skin strip dries."

"I've got it."

"I'll be on the tracker myself. We'll be able to monitor your location through your heartbeat. We rigged this wrist unit." Relieved the worst was over, he picked it up from the table. "The mike's low frequency, so it shouldn't pop on a scan, but its range is a joke, and you're going to have to talk straight into it for us to pick you up. This is just backup."

"I'll take it." Eve removed her own unit, replaced it. "Anything else I should know?"

"We're positioning men all over Grand Central. You won't be on your own. Nobody moves in until you give the go-ahead, but they're there."

"Good to know."

"Dallas, any protective gear over your chest will jam the tracker."

She stared at him. "No vest?"

"Your choice. Gear or tracker."

"Hell, they're more likely to blast me in the head, anyway."

"Goddamn it."

"Joking." But she rubbed a hand over her

mouth. "Any line on the target?"

"Nothing so far."

"You looked over the droids at Branson T and T?"

"Yeah, they've got a new Brainiac line." He smiled a little now. "New shell covering, too. Next best to skin. But they're toys," he added. "I didn't see anything full size."

"Doesn't mean they aren't there. Those toys capable of acting out a scene like what happened at Branson's?"

"If they were six foot instead of six inches, yeah. I'd say. Creepy little bastards, you ask me."

"That's my personal 'link," she said when she heard the signal. "I have to take this. It's private."

"Okay, I'll be outside. We're ready to roll when you are."

Alone, she took out her 'link, engaged the privacy mode by unfolding and slipping on her headphones. "Dallas."

"I have your data, Lieutenant." Roarke's eyes narrowed. "Where's your shirt?"

"Somewhere. Here." She grabbed it up. "What have you got?"

"She checks out easily if you skim the first few levels. Born in Kansas thirty-six years ago, parents are teachers, pure middle class, one sister, married with son. She went through the local school system, worked for a short time as a department store clerk. She married Branson about ten years ago, moved to New York. I assume you have all that."

"I want what's under it."

"So I thought. The names her records show as parents did indeed have a daughter named Clarissa born thirty-six years ago. However, she died at the age of eight. Scraping off the levels, we find this dead child with school and employment records and a marriage license."

"Bogus."

"Yes, indeed. A little dip into Clarissa Stanley's medical files indicates she hasn't seen the age of thirty-six for some time. She's forty-six. Tracing the data input, it appears Clarissa was reborn twelve years ago. Whoever, whatever she was before, has been wiped. I might be able to jiggle some out, but it won't be quick."

"That's enough for now. She wanted a new ID, and not to carve ten years off her age."

"If you do a bit more math, you see that she would have been exactly the same age as Charlotte Rowan when Apollo headquarters was destroyed."

"I've already done the math, thanks."

"Since I followed your avenue here, I took it a bit farther."

"Farther where?"

"Some may disagree," he said with a long look at her, "but people in intimate relationships generally have some common ground and a general knowledge of each other's ambitions and activities."

Guilt fizzed back into her chest. "Look, Roarke —"

"Shut up, Eve." He said it so pleasantly, she did. "Since it appears Clarissa may have close ties with Rowan and Apollo, I did some back-checking on B. Donald. Nothing in particular there, except for a number of large and perhaps questionable contributions to the Artemis Society."

"Another Greek god?"

"Yes, and Apollo's twin. I doubt we'll find any data on it in the banks. However, looking a generation back, I found that E. Francis Branson, B.D.'s father, contributed large amounts to this same organization. He was also — according to CIA files — briefly an operative. He not only knew James Rowan but worked with him."

"Which closed the link between the Bransons and the Rowans. Branson grew up with Apollo; so did Clarissa. They hooked up and kept heading down the same path.

We are loyal." She let out a breath. "Thanks."

"You're welcome. Eve, how much of a risk are you about to take?"

"I'll have backup."

"That wasn't my question."

"Nothing I can't handle. I appreciate the help."

"Any time."

Words, many of them foolish, bubbled into her throat. And Feeney stuck his head in the door. "We have to move, Dallas."

"Yeah, right. I'm there. Time to saddle up," she said with a half smile at Roarke. "See you tonight."

"Take care of what's mine, Lieutenant."

She smiled again as she slipped the 'link away. She knew he hadn't meant the bonds.

Having backup and a tracker didn't stop her from feeling alone and exposed as she moved through the crushing crowd in Grand Central. She spotted some cops whose faces she knew. Her eyes passed over them, and theirs over hers, without interest.

The speakers droned overhead, announcing incoming and outgoing transports. Flocks of commuters lined the public 'links, calling home, calling lovers, calling their bookies.

Eve strode past them. In the surveillance

van two blocks away, Feeney noted her heartbeat was smooth and steady.

She saw the vagrants who'd come in from the cold and would soon be rousted out again by security. Vendors sold the news, on paper, on disc, as well as cheap souvenirs, hot drinks, and cold beer.

She took the stairs rather than the glide and moved down to check point. Lifting her arm as if to push at her hair, she muttered into her wrist unit.

"Leaving main level for check point. No contact yet."

She felt the floor tremble, heard the whining scream as a bullet train tore out of the station.

She stood on the platform, one hand firm on the suitcase, the other in plain view. If they were going to take her out, they would do it here, fast, taking advantage of the crowd waiting for their transport. One takes her out, another snags the case, and they're lost in the confusion.

That's what she would do, Eve thought. That's how she'd play the game.

Out of the corner of her eye, she saw McNab in a bright yellow coat, blue shoes, and ski hat, idling at a computer game while he sat on a bench in the waiting area.

They were scanning her now, she imagined. They'd find she was armed, but they'd have expected that. If she was lucky, and Feeney was good, they wouldn't make the tracker.

The public 'link behind her began to ring, loud and shrill. Without hesitating, she turned and answered. "Dallas."

"Take the incoming train to Queens. Buy a ticket onboard."

"Queens," she repeated with her mouth all but against her wrist unit. The caller had already disconnected. "Next train," she added. "Incoming."

Turning away, she moved toward the tracks as the rumble started. McNab pocketed his computer game and strolled up behind her. He'd been a good call, Eve mused. No one looked less like a cop. He was wearing headphones, doing a little head and shoulder dance as if he were listening to music that set him into motion. His body stood at Eve's flank like a shield.

The displaced air from the train blew over them. The whine shivered away, and people began to bump and shove their way on and off the train.

Eve didn't bother to try for a seat but gripped a security hook, planted her feet, and braced for the takeoff.

McNab squeezed in just down the line

and began singing lightly under his breath. Eve nearly smiled when she recognized one of Mavis's songs.

The trip to Queens was crowded, hot, and blessedly short. Yet even that short jaunt made Eve thankful she wasn't an office drone condemned to ride public transpo throughout her days.

She stepped off onto the platform. McNab moved by her without a blink and headed into the station.

They sent her to the Bronx next, then Brooklyn. Then shot her to Long Island, back to Queens. She decided she'd just throw out her arms and beg for a laser blast if she had to take one more ride.

Then she saw them coming. One on the left, one on the right. She ran Fixer's description through her head and decided these were the two who'd made his deliveries and cut out his tongue.

She backed up out of the crowd of weary commuters, noting the two-man team had slipped into a pincher pattern:

They were taking no chances, she mused, and as one flipped open his coat to show the police-issue blaster, she assumed they meant to take no prisoners, either.

She bumped deliberately into a man wai-ing behind her, lifted a hand as if to catch her balance. "Contact. Two. Armed."

"Lieutenant." One of them slipped a hand over her arm. "I'll take the payment."

She let him steer her back. Not a man, she realized when she took a good, hard look. Fixer had been right there, too. They were droids. You couldn't even smell them.

"You'll get the payment when I get the target, and it's confirmed. That's the deal."

He smiled. "New terms. We'll take the payment, my partner will cut you in half where you stand, and the target will be destroyed as a celebration to the cause."

She saw McNab barreling down the glide. He jerked his thumb up, signaling that the target had been made. Eve showed the droid her teeth. "I don't like those terms."

She swung back, slamming the case into the knees of the droid behind her. With the move she swung down and to the side, catching him by the ankles as he discharged the weapon. The blast put a fist-sized hole in his partner's chest.

Screaming for civilians to take cover, she reared up, clamped her fingers over his weapon hand, and twisted. The next blast hit the concrete, its path close enough to singe her hair. She could hear shrieks, stumbling feet, the roaring whine of an oncoming train.

Eve threw back her weight, brought the droid down with her. They rolled through running feet, toppling people like bowling pins.

She couldn't get her hand to her weapon, and his was lost in the stampede. Her ears were ringing with the noise, and beneath her, the ground shook like thunder. The droid reared up; something sharp and silver flashed in his hand.

Eve bucked back, swung up her legs, and slammed her feet into his groin. He didn't buckle as a man would, but teetered back, arms pinwheeling for balance. She rocked to her feet, made one frantic grab, missed.

He tumbled to the tracks, then disappeared under the silver blur of the train.

"Jesus, Dallas, I couldn't get through." Panting, red welts swelling on his face, McNab gripped her arm. "Did you take a hit?"

"No. Damn it, I needed one of them working. They're useless to us now. Call for a cleanup and crowd control here. Where's the target?"

"Madison Square, they're evacuating and defusing right now."

"Let's get the hell out of Queens."

Chapter Nineteen

The first charge went off in the upper deck of section B in Madison Square at precisely eight forty-three. The game, a hockey match between the Rangers and the Penguins, was in the bitterly contested first period. There'd been no score and only one minor injury when the offensive guard from the Penguins had cross-checked his man — a little on the high side.

The Ranger defensive lineman had been carried off, bleeding profusely from the nose and mouth.

He was already in the ER when the bomb blew.

The NYPSD had moved fast once the explosives had been detected. The game was halted, and the announcement was made that the arena was to be evacuated.

This was met with catcalls, profanities, and from the Ranger side of the stadium, a rain of recycled toilet paper and beer cans.

New York fans took their hockey seriously.

Despite it, the swarm of uniforms and officials had managed to move close to twenty percent of the attendees out of the Garden in more or less an orderly fashion. Only five cops and twelve civilians had reported minor injuries. There were only four arrests for assault and lewd conduct.

Below the Garden, Pennsylvania Station was being cleared as rapidly as possible, with all incoming trains and transpos diverted.

Even the most optimistic of officials didn't expect to scoop up every beggar and sidewalk sleeper who hid in the station for warmth, but an effort was made to sweep through the usual flop spots and hiding places.

When the bomb blew, spewing steel and wood and pieces of the drunk who'd been dozing on the floor of the bleachers along seats 528 through 530, people got the picture fast.

They flooded like a raging tide for the exits.

When Eve arrived on scene, it looked as though the grand old building was vomiting people.

"Do what you can," she shouted at McNab. "Get these people away from here."

"What are you doing?" He shouted over

the screams and sirens, made a grab for her, but his fingers skidded off her jacket. "You can't go in there. Holy God, Dallas."

But she was already pushing, punching, and peeling her way through the press of fleeing bodies.

Twice she was slammed hard enough to make her ears ring as she fought to get clear of the doors and the frantic rush for escape.

She swung up toward the closest set of stairs, climbing over seats as people leaped for safety. Above, she could see one of the emergency team efficiently putting out several small fires. The nosebleed seats were in smoking splinters.

"Malloy!" she shouted into her communicator. "Anne Malloy. Give me your location."

Static hissed in her ear, words hiccupping through it. "Three — cleared . . . scanned ten . . ."

"Your location," Eve repeated. "Give me your location."

"Teams spread . . ."

"Goddamn it, Anne, give me a location. I'm helpless here." Helpless, she thought, watching people claw their way over each other to get out. She saw a child shoot out of the crowd like soap from wet fingers, feet tripping over him as he slid out and bounced facefirst on the ice.

She swore again, viciously, and leaped over the rail. She hit the ice on her hands and knees, skidding wildly until she slammed in with the toes of her boots. She grabbed the boy by the collar of his shirt and dragged them both away from the stampeding crowd.

"Up to five." Anne's voice came through, clearer now. "We're clicking here. Update on evacuation."

"I can't tell. Shit, it's a zoo." Eve pushed a hand over her face, saw blood smeared on her palm. "Fifty percent clear, up here. Maybe more. I've got no contact with the team in Penn. Where the hell are you?"

"Moving toward sector two. I'm under the floor in Penn. Get those civilians out."

"I've got a kid here. Injured." She spared the boy under her arm a glance. He was sheet white with a lump the size of a baby's fist on his forehead, but he was breathing. "I'll get him clear and be back."

"Get him out, Dallas. Clock's ticking."

She managed to get to her feet, skidded, grabbed clumsily for the rail. "Move your men out, Malloy. Abort and move out now."

"Cleared six, four to go. Have to stick. Dallas, we lose it down here, we take out Penn and the Garden."

Eve dumped the boy over her shoulder in a fireman's carry and pulled herself onto the steps. "Get them out, Anne. Save lives, fuck property."

She stumbled through the seats, kicking aside the bags and coats and food people had left behind.

"Seven, down to three. We're going to make it."

"For God's sake, Anne. Move your ass."

"Good advice."

Eve blinked the sweat out of her eyes and saw Roarke just as he plucked the boy off her shoulder. "Get him out. I'm going for Malloy."

"The hell you are."

It was all he managed before the floor began to tremble. He saw the crack in the wall behind them split. Eve's hand was caught in his.

They leaped off the platform and ran for the door where cops in full gear were pushing, shoving, all but tossing the last of the civilians through. She felt her eardrums contract an instant before she heard the blast. The wall of sizzling heat slammed them from behind. She felt her feet leave the ground, her head reel from the noise and heat. And the tidal wave force of air shot them through the door. Something hot and heavy crashed behind them.

Survival was paramount now. Hands gripped, they scrambled up, kept moving blindly forward while rock and glass and steel rained down. The air was full of sounds, the shrieks of metal, the crash of steel, the thunder of spewing rock.

She tripped over something, saw it was a body trapped under a concrete spear as wide as her waist. Her lungs were on fire, her throat full of smoke. Diamond-sharp fists of glass showered down, propelled by vicious secondary explosions.

When her vision cleared, she could see what seemed to be hundreds of shocked faces, mountains of smoking rubble, and too many bodies to count.

Then the wind slapped her face, cold. Hard. And she knew they were alive.

"Are you hurt, are you hit?" she shouted to Roarke, unaware that their hands were still fused together.

"No." Somehow, he still had the unconscious boy over his shoulder. "You?"

"No, I don't think . . . No. Get him to the MTs," she told Roarke. Panting, she stopped, turned, blinked. From the outside, the building showed little damage. Smoke billowed from the jagged opening where doors had been, and the streets were littered with charred and twisted rubble, but the Garden still stood.

"They got all but two. Just two." She thought of the station below — the trains, the commuters, the vendors. She wiped grime and blood off her face. "I have to go back, get the status."

He kept her hand firmly in his. He'd looked behind as they'd flown through the door. And he'd seen. "Eve, there's nothing to go back for."

"There has to be." She shook him off. "I have men in there. I have people in there. Take the kid to an MT, Roarke. He took a bad spill."

"Eve . . ." He saw the expression on her face, and let it go. "I'll wait for you."

She crossed the street again, avoiding little pots of flame and smoking stone. She could already see looters joyfully racing down the block, crashing in windows. She grabbed a uniform, and when he shook her off and told her to move along, dug out her badge.

"Sorry, Lieutenant." His face was dead white, his eyes glazed. "Crowd control's a bitch."

"Get a couple of units together, get the looting stopped. Start moving the perimeter back and get some security sensors up. You!" she called to another uniform. "Get the medical teams a clear area for the wounded and start taking names."

She kept moving, making herself give orders, start routines. By the time she was ten feet from the building, she knew Roarke was right. There was nothing to go back for.

She saw a man sitting on the ground, his head in his hands, and recognized him as part of E and B by the fluorescent yellow stripe across his jacket.

"Officer, where's your lieutenant?"

He looked up, and she saw he was weeping. "There were too many. There were just too many, all over hell and back."

"Officer." Her breath wanted to hitch, her heart to pound. She wouldn't let them. "Where's Lieutenant Malloy?"

"She sent us out, down to the last two. She sent us out. Just her and two men. Only two more. They got one. I heard Snyder call it over the headphones, and the lieutenant told them to clear the area. It was the last one that took them. The last fucking one."

He lowered his head and sobbed like a child.

"Dallas." Feeney came on the run and out of breath. "Damn, goddamn, I couldn't get closer than half a block by the time I got here. Couldn't hear a damn thing over the communicator."

But he'd heard her heart on the tracker, loud and strong, and it had kept him sane.

"Sweet holy Jesus." His hand gripped her shoulder while he looked at the entrance. "Mother of God."

"Anne. Anne was in there."

His hand tightened on her shoulder, then his arm was around her. "Oh hell."

"I was one of the last out. We were nearly clear. I told her to get out. I told her to abort and go. She didn't listen."

"She had a job to do."

"We need search and rescue. Maybe . . ." She knew better. Anne would have been all but on top of the bomb when it went off. "We need to look. We need to be sure."

"I'll get it started. You ought to see a med-tech, Dallas."

"It's nothing." She drew in a breath, blew it out. "I need her address."

"We'll get done what needs to be done here, then I'll go with you."

She turned away, scanned over the huddles of people, the wrecks of cars that had been too close to the building, the mangled hunks of steel.

And below the streets, she thought, in the transpo station, it would be worse. Unimaginably worse.

For money, she thought as the heat rose in

her like a geyser. For money, she was sure of it, and for the memory of a fanatic without a clear cause.

Someone, she swore it, would pay.

It was an hour before she got back to Roarke. He stood, his coat rippling in the wind, as he helped MTs load wounded into transports.

"The kid okay?" Eve asked him.

"He will be. We found his father. The man was terrified." Roarke reached out, wiped a smear off her cheek. "The talk is casualties are light. Most were killed in the panic to get out. Most got out, Eve. What could have been a death toll in the thousands is, at this point, less than four hundred."

"I can't count lives that way."

"Sometimes it's all you can do."

"I lost a friend tonight."

"I know that." His hands lifted to frame her face. "I'm sorry for that."

"She had a husband and two children." She looked away, into the night. "She was pregnant."

"Ah, God." When he would have drawn her to him, she shook her head and stepped back.

"I can't. I'll fall apart, and I can't. I have to go tell her family."

"I'll go with you."

"No, it's a cop thing." She lifted her hands, pressed them to her eyes, and just held them there a moment. "Feeney and I will do it. I don't know when I'll be home."

"I'll be here awhile yet. They can use extra hands."

She nodded, started to turn.

"Eve?"

"Yeah."

"Come home. You'll need it."

"Yeah. Yeah, I will." She walked off to find Feeney and prepared to deliver news that crushed lives.

Roarke worked another two hours with the wounded and the weeping. He sent for oceans of coffee and soup — one of the comforts money could buy. As bodies were transferred to the already overburdened morgue, he thought of Eve and how she faced the demands of the dead every day.

The blood. The waste. The stink of both seemed to crawl over his skin and under it. This is what she lived with.

He looked at the building, the scars and the ruin. This could be mended. It was stone, steel, glass, and such things could be rebuilt with time, with money, with sweat.

He was driven to own buildings like this. Symbols and structures. For profit, certainly, he thought, reaching down to pick up a chunk of concrete. For business, for pleasure. But it didn't take a session with Mira to understand why a man who'd spent his childhood in dirty little rooms with leaking roofs and broken windows was compelled to own, to possess. To preserve and to build.

A human weakness to compensate, he supposed, that had become power.

He had the power to see that this was rebuilt, that it was put back as it had been. He could put his money and his energies into that and see it as a kind of justice.

And Eve would look to the dead.

He walked away, and went home to wait for his wife.

She drove home in the damp, frigid chill of predawn. Billboards flashed and jittered around her as she headed uptown. Buy this and be happy. See that and be thrilled. Come here and be amazed. New York wasn't about to stop its dance.

Steam spilled out of glida grills, belched out of street vents, pumped out of the maxibus that creaked to a halt to pick up a scatter of drones who'd worked the graveyard shift.

A few obviously desperate street LCs strutted their stuff and called out to the drones.

"I'll give you a ride, buddy. Twenty, cash or credit'll buy you a hell of a ride."

The drones shuffled on the bus, too tired for cheap sex.

Eve watched a drunk stumble along the sidewalk, swinging his bottle of brew like a baton. And a huddle of teenagers pooling money for soy dogs. The lower the temperatures fell, the higher the price.

Free enterprise.

Abruptly, she pulled over to the curb, leaned over the wheel. She was well beyond exhausted and into the tightly strung stage of brittle energy and racing thoughts.

She'd gone to a tidy little home in Westchester and had spoken the words that ripped a family to pieces. She'd told a man his wife was dead, listened to children cry for a mother who was never coming back.

Then she'd gone to her office and written the reports, filed them. Because it needed to be done, she'd cleaned out Anne's locker herself.

And after all that, she thought, she could drive through the city, see the lights, the people, the deals, and the dregs, and feel . . . alive, she realized.

This was her place, with its dirt and its drama, its brilliance and its streak of nasty. Whores and hustlers, the weary and the wealthy. Every jittery heartbeat pumped in her blood.

This was hers.

"Lady." A grimy fist rapped on her window. "Hey, lady, wanna buy a flower?"

She looked at the face peering through the glass. It was ancient and stupid and if the dirt in its folds were any indication, it hadn't seen a bar of soap in this decade.

She put the window down. "Do I look like I want to buy a flower?"

"It's the last one." He grinned toothlessly and held up a pitiful, ragged bloom she supposed was trying to be a rose. "Give ya a good deal. Five bucks for it."

"Five? Get a handful of reality." She started to brush him off, put the glass between them. Then found herself digging in her pocket. "I got four."

"Okay, good." He snatched the credit chips and pushed the flower at her before heading off in a shambling run.

"To the nearest liquor store," Eve muttered and pulled away from the curb with the window open. His breath had been amazingly foul.

She drove home with the flower across her lap. And saw, as she headed through the gates, the lights he'd left on for her.

After all she'd seen and done that day, the

simple welcome of lights in the window had her fighting tears.

She went in quietly, tossing her jacket over the newel post, climbing the stairs. The scents here were quiet, elegant. The wood polished, the floors gleaming.

This, too, she thought, was hers.

And so, she knew, when she saw him waiting for her, was Roarke.

He'd put on a robe and had the screen on low. Nadine Furst was reporting, and looked pale and fierce on the scene of the explosion. She could see he'd been working — checking stock reports, juggling deals, whatever he did — on the bedroom unit.

Feeling foolish, she kept the flower behind her back. "Did you sleep?"

"A bit." He didn't go to her. She looked stretched thin, he decided, as if she might snap at the slightest touch. Her eyes were bruised and fragile. "You need to rest."

"Can't." She managed a half smile. "Wired up. I'm going to go back soon."

"Eve." He stepped toward her, but still didn't touch. "You'll make yourself ill."

"I'm okay. Really. I was punchy for a while, but it passed. When it's over, I'll crash, but I'm okay now. I need to talk to you."

"All right."

She moved around him, shifting the flower out of sight, going to the window, staring at the dark. "I'm trying to figure out where to start. It's been a rotten couple of days."

"It was difficult, telling the Malloys."

"Jesus." She let her brow rest against the glass. "They know. Families of cops know as soon as they see us at the door. That's what they live with, day in and out. They know when they see you, but they block it. You can see it in their faces — the knowledge and the denial. Some of them just stand there, others stop you — start talking, making conversation, picking up around the house. It's like if you don't say it, if you just don't say it, it isn't real.

"Then you say it, and it is."

She turned back to him. "You live with that."

"Yes." He kept his eyes on hers. "I suppose I do."

"I'm sorry, I'm so sorry about this morning. I —"

"So you've said already." This time when he crossed to her, he touched, just a hand to her cheek. "It doesn't matter."

"It does. It does matter. I've got to get through this, okay?"

"All right. Sit down."

"I can't, I just can't." She lifted her hands in frustration. "I've got all this stuff churning inside me."

"Then get rid of it." He stopped her by putting a hand to hers, lifting the flower. "What's this?"

"I think it's a very sick, mutant rose. I bought it for you."

It was so rare to see Roarke taken by surprise, she nearly laughed. His gaze met hers and she thought — hoped — it might have been baffled pleasure she saw there before he looked down at the rose again. "You brought me a flower."

"I think it's sort of traditional. Fight, flowers, make up."

"Darling Eve." He took the stem. The edges of the bud were blackened and curled from the cold. The color was somewhere between the yellow of a healing bruise and urine. "You fascinate me."

"Pretty pitiful, huh?"

"No." This time his hand cupped her cheek, skimmed into her hair. "It's delightful."

"If it smells anything like the guy who sold it to me, you might want to have it fumigated."

"Don't spoil it," he said mildly, and touched his lips to hers.

"I do that — spoil things." She backed away again before she gave in and grabbed on. "I don't do it on purpose. And I meant what I said this morning, even if it pisses you off. Mostly, I think cops are better off going solo. I don't know, like priests or something, so they don't keep dragging the sin and sorrow home with them."

"I have sin and sorrow of my own," he said evenly. "It's washed over you a time or two."

"I knew it would piss you off."

"It does. And by God, Eve, it hurts me."

Her mouth dropped open, trembled closed again. "I don't mean to do that." Hadn't known she could do that. Part of the problem, she realized. Her problem. "I don't have the words like you do. I don't have them, Roarke, the kind you say to me — or even think, and I see you thinking them and it — my heart just stops."

"Do you think loving you to excess is easy for me?"

"No. I don't. I think it should be impossible. Don't get mad." She hurried on when she saw that dangerous flash in his eyes. "Don't get mad yet. Let me finish."

"Then make it good." He set the flower aside. "Because I'm damn sick and I'm tired of having to justify my feelings to the woman who owns them."

"I can't keep my balance." Oh, she hated to admit it, to say it out loud to the man who wobbled it so often and so easily. "I get it, and I cruise along for a while, realizing this is who I am now, who we are now. And then, sometimes, I just look at you and stumble. And I can't get my breath because all these feelings just rear up and grab me by the throat. I don't know what to do about it, how to handle it. I think, *I'm married to him. I've been married to him for almost six months, and there are times he walks into the room and stops my heart.*"

She let out a shuddering breath. "You're the best thing that ever happened to me. In my life, you're what matters most. I love you so much it scares me, and I guess if I had a choice about it, I wouldn't change it. So . . . now you can get pissed off, because I'm done."

"A fat lot of room you've given me for that." He watched her lips twitch into a smile as he went to her. His hands slipped over her shoulders, down her back. "I've no choice either, Eve. I wouldn't want one."

"We're not going to fight."

"I don't think so."

She kept her eyes on his as she tugged at the belt of his robe. "I stored up this energy in case I needed it to fight with you."

He lowered his head, bit her bottom lip. "It's a shame to waste it."

"I'm not going to." Slowly, she backed him toward the bed, up the short steps to the platform. "I drove through the city tonight. I felt alive." She tugged the robe away, closed her teeth over his shoulder. "I'm going to show you."

She tumbled to the bed on top of him, and her mouth was like a fever. The frantic burst of energy reminded her of the first time they'd come together on this bed, the night she'd thrown all caution and restraint aside and let him take her where they'd needed to go.

Now she would drive him, with fast, rough hands, hot greedy lips. She took exactly what she wanted, and what she took was everything.

The light was gray and weak, trickling through the sky window overhead, filtering down on her. His vision blurred, but he watched her as she destroyed him. Slim, agile, fierce, the bruises from the hideous night blooming on her skin like the medals of a warrior.

Her eyes gleamed as she worked them both toward frenzy.

Then, and then again, skin glowing, breath ragged, she lowered over him, sheathed him, surrounded him.

She arched back, arrowed with pleasure. He gripped her hips, said her name, and let her ride.

Her skin was slick with sweat when she collapsed onto him, melted into him. His arms came around her, holding her there. Her cheek to his heart.

"Sleep awhile," he murmured.

"I can't. I have to go in."

"You haven't slept in twenty-four hours."

"I'm okay," she answered as she sat up. "Almost better than okay. I needed this more than sleep — really, Roarke. And if you think you're going to force a tranq down my throat, think again."

She rolled off him and up. "I need to keep moving. If there's any down time, I'll catch a nap at the crib at Central."

She glanced around for a robe, took his. "I need a favor."

"Now would be an excellent time to ask for one."

She glanced over, grinned. He looked sleek and satisfied. "I bet. Anyway, I don't want Zeke stuck at the station the way he has been, but I need to keep him under wraps awhile longer."

"Send him here."

"Ah . . . if I took one of your vehicles in, I

could leave mine here. Working on it would give him something to do."

Roarke turned his head. Eyed her. "Do you plan to be involved in any wrecks or explosions today?"

"You never know."

"Take anything but the 3X-2000. I've only driven it once."

She made some comment about men and their toys, but he was feeling mellow and let it pass.

Chapter Twenty

Dear Comrade,

We are Cassandra.

We are loyal.

We are sure you've been watching the bleeding liberal media puppets report on the incidents in New York City. It sickens us to listen to their sobbing, their wailing. While we are nothing but amused by their condemnation of the destruction of their pathetic symbols of the blindly opportunistic society that now holds this country under its rigid thumb, we are angry at their one-dimensional and predictable stand on the issues.

Where is their faith? Where is their comprehension?

They still don't see, still don't understand what we are and what we will mean to them.

Tonight we struck with the fury of the gods. Tonight we watched the scrambling rats. But this is nothing, nothing to what we will do.

Our adversary, the woman that fate and circumstance deemed we face down for our mission, has proven difficult. She is skilled and strong, but we would be satisfied with no less. It is true that through her, we have lost a certain monetary payment, which we understand you had hoped to secure quickly. Do not concern yourself with this matter. Our finances are very solvent, and we will bleed this heedless city to its bones before we are finished.

You must trust that we will finish what he began. You must not falter in your faith and your commitment to the cause. Soon, very soon, the most precious symbol of their corrupt and weeping nation will fall. It is all but done.

When this is accomplished, they will pay.

We will see you, face to face, within forty-eight hours. The necessary papers are in order. This next battle to be waged and won in this place, we will complete personally. He would have expected this. He would have demanded it.

Prepare for the next stage, dear comrade. For we will be with you soon to drink to the one who set us on this path. To celebrate our victory and to set the stage for our new republic.

We are Cassandra.

Peabody strode toward the conference

room. She'd just left Zeke and was feeling a little shaky over the conversation they'd had with their parents over the 'link. Both of them had put the pressure on for their parents to stay out west, though each had separate reasons.

Zeke couldn't stand the thought of them seeing him under the current circumstances. He wasn't in a cell, but it was close.

Peabody was determined to clear her brother and put him back on the path of his life in her own way.

But her mother had struggled not to cry, and her father had looked dazed and helpless. She wasn't going to get the image of their faces out of her head any time soon.

Work was the remedy, she decided. Unearthing that lying, murdering bitch Clarissa. Then snapping her skinny neck like a twig.

It was with violence brewing under her starched uniform that she walked into the room and saw McNab.

Oh hell, was all she could think, and she marched straight over for coffee. "You're early."

"I figured you'd be." He'd also figured out what he intended to do, and he took the first step by going over and closing the door. "You're not kicking me out of your way without an explanation."

"I don't need to explain anything to you. We wanted to have sex, we had it. Done and over. The lab reports come up?"

"I say it's not done and over." It should be, he knew it should be. But he'd been thinking about that square, serious face and amazingly lush body for days. Weeks. Jesus, maybe months. *He'd* damn well say when it was done and over.

"I've got more important things on my mind than your ego, McNab." She took a deliberate sip of coffee. "Like my semiannual dentist appointment."

"Why don't you save up your lame insults until you have a better selection? They don't work. I've had you under me."

And over him, she thought. Around and through. "*Had*'s the operative word. Past tense."

"Why?"

"Because that's how it is."

He stepped closer, pulled the cup out of her hand, slammed it down. "Why?"

Her heart began to pound. Damn it, she wasn't supposed to feel anything. "Because that's the way I want it."

"Why?"

"Because if I hadn't been rolling around with you, I'd have been with Zeke. If I'd been with him, I wouldn't have just told my parents my lieutenant is trying to clear him on murder charges."

"That's not your fault. It's not mine." Her breath had begun to hitch, unnerving him. He was mortally afraid she might cry. "It's on the Bransons. And Dallas isn't going to let him take the heat from it. Get a hold here, Dee."

"I should've been with him! I should've been with him, not you."

"You were with me." He took her arms, gave her a quick, surprising shake. "You can't change that. And I want you with me again. Damn it, Dee, I'm not done."

He was kissing her, with all the helpless rage and lust and confusion that roared through him. She made some little sound, a sound caught between despair and relief. And was kissing him with all the vivid fury and need and bafflement that pumped inside her.

Eve walked in, stopped dead in her tracks. "Oh, jeez."

They were too busy trying to swallow each other to hear her.

"Man." She pressed her fingers to her eyes, half hoping they'd disappear before she lowered them. No such luck. "Break it up." She jammed her hands in her pockets and tried to ignore the inarguable fact that McNab's hands were clamped on her aide's ass.

"I said break it *up!*"

The shout got through. They leaped apart as if someone had snapped a spring between them. McNab hit a chair, knocked it over, then stared at Eve as if he'd never seen her before.

"Oh. Whoa."

"Clamp it shut," Eve warned him. "Not a word out of you. Sit down, shut up. Peabody, damn it to hell and back again. Why don't I have my coffee?"

"Coffee." Eyes dazed, blood screaming, Peabody blinked. "Coffee?"

"Now." Eve pointed to the AutoChef, then made a show of looking at her wrist unit. "You are now on duty. Anything that happened here before this mark was on your own time. Is that clear?"

"Uh-huh, you bet. Listen, Lieutenant —"

"Zip it, McNab," she ordered him. "I don't want any discussion, any explanations, any verbal pictures drawn of activities pursued on your own time."

"Your coffee, sir." Peabody set it down, shot McNab a look of dire warning.

"Lab reports?"

"I'll check on them now." Relieved, Peabody hurried to a chair.

Feeney came in. The bags under his eyes were in danger of drooping past his nose. Seeing him, Peabody got up again, ordered more coffee.

He sat, nodded absently in thanks. "The emergency teams managed to clear down to the site of the last explosion, Malloy's last known location." He cleared his throat, lifted his cup, drank. "The shield appeared to be in place, but the blast took it out. They said it would have been over quick."

No one spoke for a moment; then Eve got to her feet. "Lieutenant Malloy was a good cop. That's the best I can say about anybody. She died doing her job and trying to give her men time to reach safety. It's our job to find the people responsible for her death and take them down."

She opened the file she'd brought in, took out two photos, and moved to the boards to fix them in place.

"Clarissa Branson, aka Charlotte Rowan. B. Donald Branson. We don't stop," Eve said, turning, with eyes bright and cold. "We don't rest until these two people are in a cage or dead. Labs, Peabody. McNab, I want the report on Monica Rowan's 'link. Feeney, I need Zeke in interview one more time. Maybe if you take him, you'll push a button I missed. He might have heard something, seen something, that can give us a line on where to look."

"I'll take care of it."

"And I want another round with Lisbeth Cooke, too. Same deal. If you can spare the time, you'd probably get more out of her by going to her place and playing the sympathetic ear."

"She a weeper?" Feeney wanted to know.

"Could be."

He sighed. "I'll take extra hankies."

"There'll be a trail," Eve continued, scanning the faces of her team. "Where they went under, where they're going next, where and when they've targeted the next one. They'll know we're following the Apollo line now and probably know we've made — or will make — Clarissa as James Rowan's daughter."

She moved back to the board, pinning up another photo. "This was Charlotte Rowan's mother. I believe her daughter gave the order for her execution. If this is true, understand we're dealing with an individual with a cool and focused mind. A skilled actor who doesn't mind getting blood on her hands. She has, with her husband, arranged or carried out the murder of four people we are aware of, one tied to her by blood, one by marriage, and is responsible for the deaths of hundreds through terrorist acts that are no more than disguised blackmail for gain.

"She won't hesitate to kill again. She has no conscience, no morals, and no loyalty to anyone but herself and a man who's been dead for over three decades. This is not a creature of impulse but of calculation. She's had thirty years to plan what she's now setting out to accomplish. And so far, she's kicking the shit out of us."

"You took out two of her droids," McNab pointed out. "And she didn't get the bonds."

"That's why she's going to hit again and hit hard. Money's part of the motive, but it's not all. Mira's analysis indicated a large ego, a mission, and a sense of pride. Pulling from that, she *is* Cassandra." Eve tapped a finger on the photo. "Not just the woman, but the whole. And her ego and pride took a hit last night — and she hasn't yet accomplished her mission. She can't be dealt or bargained with because she's a liar, and she's enjoying playing the goddess, high on power and blood. She believes what she's saying. Even when what she's saying is a lie."

"We've still got the scanners," McNab pointed out.

"And we'll use them. E and B's going to be shaken up, and they're also going to want payback for Anne. They'll work their asses off on this one."

"Labs, Lieutenant." Peabody held out the copy. "Blood, skin, and hair samples from the Branson hearth match B. Donald Branson's DNA."

Eve took them, noted the fresh worry in Peabody's eyes. "They'd have been clever enough to think of that. They stored the blood, and she had plenty of time to plant the other samples while she was pretending to clean up the mess."

"They haven't come up with a body yet." When McNab spoke, Peabody turned her head to watch him. "They've got divers down now." He moved his shoulders. "I'll keep in touch."

Her mouth wanted to tremble, but she firmed it, nodded briskly. "Appreciate it."

"Maine's shooting me down the 'link unit from Monica Rowan's place," he continued. "They found a slew of jammers and code-spanners in the kitchen. Her 'link log's been blocked. I'll unblock it."

"Get it down. I'll take the Branson house and the offices. Anything develops, I want a tag, pronto." She yanked out her communicator when it signaled. "Dallas."

"Sergeant Howard, Search and Rescue. My divers found something. I think you'll want to see this."

"Send through your location. I'm on my way." She glanced toward McNab. As he rose, Peabody stepped forward.

"Sir, I know you have reason to keep me off this part of the investigation. I don't believe those reasons are valid at this time. I request, respectfully, to accompany you as your aide."

Eve considered, tapped her fingers on her thigh. "Are you going to keep talking to me that way? All tight-assed and formal, using long, polite sentences?"

"If I don't get what I want, yes, sir."

"I admire a good threat," Eve decided. "You're with me, Peabody."

The wind whipped like a nest of angry snakes and had the ugly water of the river churning. Eve stood on the scarred and littered dock, cold to the bone, as one of the search team uncovered the body.

"We probably wouldn't have come on it for days if you hadn't told us to start looking for a mechanical. Even with that, we got lucky. You wouldn't fucking believe what people dump in this river."

He crouched down with her. "Looks a

hell of a lot better than a floater would by this time. No bloat, no decay. Fish gave him a try, but they don't get off on synthetics."

"Yeah." She could see the nicks and dents where fish had taken nibbling samples. One had apparently given the left eye a hell of a go before giving up. But the diver was right; he looked a hell of a lot better than a floater.

He looked like B. Donald Branson — handsome and fit, if considerably bedragged. She used a fingertip on the chin to turn the head, then studied the massive damage to the back of the skull.

"When I saw it down there, I thought the sensors were whacked. Never seen a droid this good before. Wouldn't have known for sure it wasn't a fresh dead guy if it wasn't for the hand."

Somewhere along the line, the wrist had been injured enough to split the skin casing. The structure, riddled with sensors and chips, showed clearly.

"Of course, when we got him out and gave him a good look-see in the light —"

"Yeah, doesn't quite fit the bill. You get pictures?"

"Oh, you bet."

"We'll just get some to back up the record. Then I'll need it bagged and sealed and shipped to the lab. Get all angles, Peabody."

Eve rose, moved to the side, and called Feeney. "I'm sending this droid into the lab. I need someone from EDD to go in and work with Dickhead's team. I want to run his programming back. Can we interface with our system? Get a playback of the night Zeke was there?"

"Might."

"And can we dig in enough to get a time frame for the programming and the programmer?"

"It's not impossible. Much damage?"

She glanced back as Peabody got the crater in the skull on record. "Considerable."

"We'll do what we can. Does this put Zeke out of it?"

"No law against killing a droid. He could get it on destruction of property, but I don't think the Bransons will pursue that angle."

Feeney smiled. "Good work. Want me to tell him?"

"No." She looked back at Peabody. "Let him hear it from his sister." She pocketed her communicator and signaled to Peabody. "We're done here. Let's move."

"Dallas." She walked over, laid a hand on Eve's arm. "I was afraid when we came down here. Afraid you'd been wrong. I knew, in my head, that even if it was

Branson, it would go down as an accident, just the way Zeke said. He wouldn't have gone to jail, but he'd have paid for it. All his life."

"Now you can tell him he doesn't have to."

"He should hear it from you. You weren't wrong," she said before Eve could speak. "And it'll matter more."

Zeke's hands dangled between his knees. Slumped over, he stared at them as if they belonged to a stranger. "I don't understand this." He spoke slowly, again as if the voice were someone else's and just happened to come out of his mouth. "You say it was a droid that just looked like Mr. Branson."

"You didn't kill anyone, Zeke." Eve leaned toward him. "Get that in your head first."

"But he fell. He hit his head. There was blood."

"It fell, as it was directed to fall. There was blood because blood had been injected under its skin shield. Branson's blood. It was put there to make you think you'd killed him."

"But why? I'm sorry, Dallas, but that's just crazy."

"Part of a game. He's dead — his body

conveniently disposed of by his terrified and abused wife who's now run away. They can be anyone they want to be, anywhere they want to be, and with a big pile of money to hide in. They thought they'd have a lot more by the time we figured this out. If we ever did."

"He *hit* her." Zeke's head snapped up. "I heard it — I saw it."

"A show, an act. A few bruises were a small price to pay for winning the whole match. They'd already arranged for his brother's death. They had to be able to access all the fluid cash from the company. Once B.D.'s gone — branded, they'd hoped, as a wife beater, marital rapist, they pick up their new lives. He's cleaned out the cash flow from all accounts. We'd probably have looked at that as just one more vicious act on his part. But they left holes."

He shook his head, and fighting impatience, she tried to explain quickly. "Why does a man like that let his wife go off to a spa out west, spend time on her own? He doesn't even trust her out of the front door from what she told me in interview. But he lets her bring you into the house. He's insanely jealous, but it's fine and dandy to have a young, good-looking guy in the same house with his wife all day. And she can barely decide to get out of bed in the morning, but she gets in gear, orders a droid to ditch her dead husband's body, and gets it done in the time it takes you to get her a glass of water. All while she's in shock."

"She can't have been involved," Zeke whispered.

"It's the only way it can play. She's lived with a man she claims beats her for nearly ten years, but she's ready to leave him to go with you, someone she barely knows — and this after two conversations about her situation."

"We fell in love."

"She loves no one. She used you. I'm sorry."

"You don't know." His voice lowered and went fierce. "You can't know what we felt for each other. What she felt for me."

"Zeke —"

Eve simply lifted her fingers from her knee to stop Peabody's protest. "You're right, I can't know what you felt. But I can know that you killed no one. I can know that the woman who said she loved you set you up to take the fall. I can know that that same woman was responsible for the deaths of hundreds of people this last week. One of them was a friend of mine. That I can know."

She rose, started to walk out of the room, when Mavis burst in.

"Hey, Dallas!" Smile brilliant, hair a purple explosion of curls, eyes the disconcerting shade of copper, Mavis threw open her arms and sent the twelve-inch emerald fringe running from armpit to wrist flying. "I'm back."

"Mavis." Eve struggled to switch gears from the miserable to the absurd. "I thought you were back next week."

"That was last week, now it *is* next week. Dallas, man, I was seismic! Hey, Peabody." Her laughing eyes landed on Zeke and sobered even as she winced. Even someone dancing on Mavis's level of happy could sense the anger and grief. "Oops, bad timing, huh?"

"No. It's great. Come outside a minute." Eve jerked her head at Peabody, signaling her to deal with Zeke, and moved outside the office with Mavis. "It's good to see you." And suddenly it was more than good. Mavis, with her stupendously ridiculous wardrobe, her ever-changing hair, her sheer delight with herself, was the perfect antidote for misery.

"It's great to see you." Eve caught her in a fierce embrace that had Mavis giggling even as she gave Eve's back soothing pats.

"Wow. You missed me."

"I did. I really did." Eve stepped back and grinned at her. "You kicked ass, didn't you?"

"I did. I really did." The narrow corridor didn't stop Mavis from turning three fast circles on her platform airpumps. "It was orbital, it was mag, it was beyond the ult. I came to see you, but my next stop is Roarke, and I figure I should warn you I'm going to kiss him hard right on the mouth."

"No tongues."

"Spoilsport." Mavis shook back her curls, angled her head. "You look beat, wasted, absolutely dead."

"Thanks, just what I needed to perk up my day."

"No, I mean it. I caught some of what's been going on — didn't have much time for screen, but what I didn't catch, people were talking about. I don't buy this Urban Wars revival crap. I mean who wants to run around blasting people in the streets all the damn time? It's so, you know, last century. So what's up?"

Eve smiled and felt wonderful doing it. "Oh, nothing much. Just a whacked terrorist group blowing up landmark property and blackmailing the city for millions of dollars. Some droids tried to kill me, but I took them out. Peabody's brother's here from Arizona and got pulled into the mix because he fell for some lying slut bomber and thought he killed her husband by accident. But he only took out another droid."

"Gee, is that all? I've been gone for a while. I figured you'd be busy."

"Roarke and I had kind of a fight, then terrific make-up sex."

Mavis's face brightened. "That's more like it. Why don't you take a break and tell me all about it?"

"Can't. I'm busy saving the city from destruction, but you can do me a favor."

"Since you put it that way. What?"

"Zeke, Peabody's brother. I need to keep him under wraps. No media, no outside contacts. I'm sending him to my place, but I know Roarke's busy, and I don't want to stick the poor guy with Summerset. Can you take him over, hang awhile?"

"Sure, Leonardo's busy on some designs. I've got plenty of swing time. I can keep him happy at your place."

"Thanks. Just call Summerset. He'll send a car for you."

"I bet he'll send the limo if I ask nice." Delighted with the prospect, she turned for the door. "Well, intro me so Zeke knows who he's going to be playing with today."

"No. Peabody'll do it. He doesn't want to see me right now. He needs to be mad at someone — I'm it. Just tell her to meet me in the garage. We've got places to go."

"You've had a rough time, Zeke." Mavis licked pink frosting from her fingers and contemplated eating another of the pretty little cakes Summerset had served them. *Control, greed,* she mused. *Control. Greed. Let's hear it for greed,* she decided and plucked up another.

"I'm so worried about Clarissa." He sat, steeped in his unhappiness.

"Mmm-hmm."

He'd started out shy with her so that she'd had to pry every second word out of him. So she'd chattered away for the first hour, about her tour, about Leonardo, adding little anecdotes about Peabody that had wormed through his defenses.

When she'd seen him smile for the first time, Mavis had sensed victory. She'd drawn him into talking about his work. She didn't understand a damn thing, but she'd made interested noises and kept her glowing, copper-colored eyes on his face.

They'd settled into the main parlor in front of the fire Summerset had built in anticipation of her arrival. And when Summerset had brought in the tea and cakes, Zeke had taken a cup out of politeness.

By the time Mavis had charmed, nagged, and bullied the full story out of him, Zeke had gone through two cups of tea and three cakes.

He felt better. Then felt guilty because of it. When he'd been detained at Cop Central, it had seemed he was paying for his crimes, for not completing his ride to Clarissa's rescue. But here in the beautiful house, with the fire crackling and his body warm from fragrant tea, it was like being rewarded for his sins.

Mavis curled her legs under her and felt as comfortable as the cat who stretched out on the top of the sofa above her. "Dallas said you killed a droid."

Zeke jolted, set down his tea. "I know, but I don't see how that's possible."

"What did Peabody say?"

"She said — she said it was a mechanical they pulled out of the river, but —"

"Maybe she's saying that to make you feel better." Mavis turned her body toward him, nodded with her eyes wide and guileless. "Maybe she's covering up for you. Oh, and I know! She's blackmailing Dallas to go along with it so you get away with the whole thing."

The idea was so absurd, he would have

laughed. But he was too shocked to do more than goggle. "Dee would never do that. She couldn't."

"Oh." Mavis pursed her lips into a pout, then moved her shoulders. "Well, I guess she must have told you straight then, huh? I guess it must be like they said, and you knocked over a droid that looked like this Branson guy. Otherwise, Peabody'd be lying and breaking the law."

He hadn't put one and one together in quite that way before. Now that Mavis had, he stared down at his hands. Thoughts whirled inside his head. "But if it was a droid . . . Clarissa. Dallas thinks Clarissa did all this. She has to be wrong."

"Maybe. She's hardly ever wrong about this sort of thing though." Mavis stretched luxuriously, but her eyes stayed sharp on Zeke's. It was getting through, she thought. Poor guy. "Let's say Clarissa didn't know it was a droid. She really thought you'd offed her husband, and then . . . oh that won't work." She furrowed her brow. "I mean, gee, unless they ditched the body, the cops would've tagged it as a droid right off. She's the one who got rid of the body, right?"

"Yes." It was indeed getting through, and his heart cracked like an egg. "She was . . . scared."

"Yeah, well, who wouldn't be, but if she hadn't lost the body, it would've been all over that same night. Nobody would've thought Branson was dead. The cops wouldn't have wasted all that time and given Branson the lead to get clear and stuff. I guess, hmmm." She tilted her head. "I guess if Dallas hadn't figured a droid, they'd never have found the body anyway. Then everybody would think the guy was fish food, and Clarissa had run off because she was so weirded by the whole scene. Wow!"

She sat up as if the idea had just occurred to her. "That means if Dallas hadn't clicked to it and pushed until she had the proof, they'd have gotten away with it, and you'd still believe you'd killed a guy."

"Oh God." It didn't just get through now. It burst through, ripping out his guts. "What have I done?"

"You didn't do anything, honey." Mavis swung her legs off the sofa, leaned forward to lay a hand over his. "They did it all. Danced a number over you. All you did was be who you are. A nice guy who believes the best of people."

"I have to think." He got shakily to his feet.

"Sure you do. You want to lie down? They've got amazing guest rooms in this place."

"No, I . . . I said I'd work on Dallas's car. That's what I'll do. I think better when I'm using my hands."

"Okay."

She made him put on his coat, bundled him up, and added a motherly peck on the cheek. Closing the door behind him, she turned, and let out a squeak of surprise when she saw Roarke on the steps.

"You're a good friend, Mavis."

"Roarke!" This time she squealed and bounded up the steps. "I got something for you. Dallas said I could." With this, she threw her arms around him and gave him a hard, noisy kiss.

For a little thing, Roarke mused, she packed a punch. "Thank you."

"I'm going to tell you about the tour, every second of it. But not now, because Dallas said you'd be busy."

"Unfortunately, I am."

"So I thought Leonardo and I could take you guys out to dinner — maybe next week? Sort of celebrate and fill you in and thank you. Thank you, Roarke. You gave me the chance for everything I wanted."

"You did the job." He tugged on one of her curls, watched it, with some fascination, spring out and back. "I'd hoped to take Eve to your final show in Memphis.

But things got complicated."

"So I hear. She looked ragged out big time. I figure when she wraps this up, you can help me kidnap her. We'll get Trina to give her the full treatment — relaxation and beauty session. The works."

"It'll be a pleasure."

"You look a little tired yourself." And she couldn't remember ever seeing real fatigue in his eyes before.

"It was a filthy night."

"Maybe Trina should have a go at you, too." His only answer was a vague "Hmmm," and she grinned. "I'll let you get back to what you're doing. Okay if I take a swim?"

"Enjoy yourself."

"Always do." She danced down the stairs, grabbed her oversized bag, and headed for the elevator to the pool house. She was going to give Trina a call and make those appointments — including erotic therapy.

Since she'd tried it out with Leonardo, she knew it was mag.

Chapter Twenty-one

Eve scanned every file and disk in Branson's office. He'd covered his tracks well. Even his private 'link had been wiped clean. She'd send it to Feeney, but she doubted he'd find any overlooked data on the logs.

She pigeonholed his assistant, then his brother's assistant, but got nothing out of them other than shock and confusion.

He'd kept his area clean, she decided.

She did a run through the labs, examined the droids in development. She nailed another piece into place when the lab foreman, in the spirit of cooperation, told her they had produced replica droids of both Branson brothers. As a surprise, he explained, ordered by Clarissa Branson. A personal request, kept off the books and logs.

They'd been completed and delivered to the Branson townhouse only three weeks before.

Very slick timing, Eve thought as she wandered through production with its orderly shelves loaded with minidroids, tyke-bykes, and space toys.

She picked up an excellent reproduction of a police issue stunner, shook her head. "This sort of thing should be outlawed. You know how many 24/7s are knocked over with these every month?"

"I had one when I was a kid." Peabody grinned with nostalgia. "Bought it on the sly and hid it from my parents. No toys of violence allowed in our house."

"Free-Agers got that one right." Eve set it down, walked farther down the line and into the maze of souveniers. Her energy was flagging. It felt as though she were walking through a wall of water. "Shit, who buys this stuff?"

"Tourists love them. Zeke's already loaded with key chains and globes and friggie magnets."

The New York section was filled with replicas — the key chains, the pens, the dash figures, the magnets and trinket boxes that crowded the stores and stands for eager tourists.

The Empire State Building, the Pleasure Dome, the UN building, the Statue of Liberty. Madison Square, the Plaza Hotel, she noted, frowning at the detailed reproduction of the hotel inside a water globe. Lift it, shake it, and glitter rained like confetti on New Year's Eve.

Good business, she wondered, *or irony?*

"I bet that kind of thing is going to sell like crazy now." Peabody scowled at the globe when Eve replaced it. "Hot ticket item."

"People are sick," Eve decided. "Let's do the house." Her eyes were feeling gritty now from lack of sleep. "Got any Alert-All in your bag?"

"Yeah, I've got the official limit."

"Give me one, will you? I hate that stuff, makes me edgy. But I'm losing focus."

She swallowed the pill Peabody handed her, knowing the false energy would annoy her.

"When's the last time you caught some shut-eye?"

"I forget. You drive," Eve ordered. God, she hated to give up the control, but it was Peabody or auto. "Until this crap kicks in."

She slid into the passenger seat, let her head fall back, her body relax. Within five minutes, her system was on the gallop. "Man." Her eyes popped open. "I'm awake now."

"It'll give you a good four hours — maybe six — then, if you don't get horizontal, you'll crash hard. Go down like a tree after 'timber.' "

"If we don't close up some of these holes in four to six, I might as well crash." Revved now, she contacted McNab at EDD. "Did you get the 'link from Maine?"

"Working on it now. She had a class-A jammer on it, but we're getting there."

"Bring everything you get to my home office. Bring the whole 'link if you don't have clear data by five. Save me a call and tell Feeney I've sent him Branson's personal. It's been wiped, but he might jiggle something."

"If there's anything, we'll jiggle it."

She put the next call through to Whitney. "Commander, I've finished at Branson T and T and am en route to his residence."

"Progress?"

"Nothing solid at this point. However, I suggest steps be taken to scan and secure the UN building." She thought of the pretty, pricey souveniers. "Apollo's next hit was the Pentagon. If Cassandra continues to follow the theme, that location is the logical choice. Time-wise there would be a lag of several weeks, but we can't risk them sticking to the schedule set by Apollo."

"Agreed. We'll take all necessary steps."

"Do you think they'll make contact again?" Peabody asked when Eve broke transmission.

"I'm not counting on it." She made one last call, to Mira.

"Question," she began as soon as Mira's face came on-screen. "Given the tone of the demands, the fact that those demands have not been met. Adding on that the targets were not destroyed and loss of life was kept minimal, will Cassandra contact me again to play guess what's next?"

"Doubtful. You haven't won the battles, but neither have you lost. Their goals have not been accomplished, while yours have come closer to the mark in each instance. According to your report, which I've just finished reading, you believe they are now aware of your line of investigation. Aware that you know their identities and their pattern."

"And their response to that would be . . . ?"

"Anger, a need to win. A desire to thumb a total victory under your nose. I don't believe they'll feel compelled to issue any sort of warning or jeer the next time. The rules of war, Eve, are, there are no rules."

"Agreed. I have a favor to ask."

Mira tried to hide her surprise. Eve rarely asked for anything. "Of course."

"Zeke's been informed of the setup, Clarissa's part in it."

"I see. This will be difficult for him."

"Yeah, he's not taking it well. I've got him at my place. Mavis is with him, but I think he could use some counseling. If you've got time for a house call."

"I'll make time."

"Thanks."

"Are unnecessary," Mira said. "Goodbye, Eve."

Satisfied, Eve ended the call, and glanced over to see that they'd arrived at the Branson townhouse. Peabody had already parked. "Let's get started." Then she saw that Peabody was clutching the wheel, and tears were swimming in her eyes. "Don't even think about doing that," Eve snapped. "Dry it up."

"I don't know how to thank you. For thinking of him. After he acted that way, with all that's going on, for thinking of him."

"I'm thinking of me." Eve shoved her door open. "I can't afford to have my aide's concentration split because she's worried about a family member."

"Right." Knowing better, Peabody sniffled as she got out of the car. But she'd blinked her eyes clear. "You have my full attention, sir."

"Let's keep it that way." Eve disarmed the police seal and entered the house. "The droids have been deactivated and taken into holding." But she hitched back her jacket so her weapon was in easy reach. "The place should be empty, but we're dealing with people with solid tech and electronic skills. They could have gotten through the seal. I want you on alert while we're in here, Peabody."

"Full alert, sir."

"We'll start with the offices."

Branson's was masculine, distinguished, in burgundy and green with dark wood, leather chairs, heavy crystal. Eve stopped in the doorway, shook her head.

"No, she's the force, she's the one who's driving this train." Her mind was clear again, achingly so. "I shouldn't have wasted time at his plant. She's the button here."

She strode across the hall and into the feminine grace of Clarissa's office. Sitting room, Eve decided it would have been called, with its rose and ivory tones, its dainty chairs with pastel cushions. There were pretty little vases lining the marble mantel, each with tiny flowers tucked in. The flowers were faded and dying and added a sick scent over the fragile fragrance of the air.

There was a day bed with a white swan painted on the cushions, lamps with tinted shades, curtains of lace.

Eve walked to the small desk with long curved legs and studied the small-scale communication and data unit.

The disc collection proved to be filled with fashion and shopping programs, a smatter of novels — heavy on romance — and a daily journal that spoke of household matters, more shopping, lunch dates, and social events.

"Got to be more." Eve stepped back. "Roll up your sleeves, Peabody. Let's take this creepy little room apart."

"I think it's kind of pretty."

"Anybody who lives with this much pink has to be insane."

They went through drawers, searched under and behind them. The small closet held more office supplies and a filmy robe. Again pink.

They found nothing behind the watercolor paintings of formal gardens, not even dust.

Then Peabody struck gold. "A disc." Triumphant, she held it up. "It was in this swan cushion."

"Let's run it." Eve slipped it into the slot, then looked less than pleased when it immediately engaged. "She hides it, but doesn't bother to passcode it. Oh, I don't think so."

It was a diary, written in the first person, and detailing beatings, rapes, abuse.

"I heard him come in. I thought — he'll

think I'm asleep, he'll leave me alone. I've been so careful to do everything right today. But when I heard him coming up the stairs, I knew he was drunk. Then I could smell it as he came to the bed.

"It's worse when he's drunk, when he's just drunk enough.

"I kept my eyes closed. I think I stopped breathing. I prayed he was too drunk to hurt me. But no one listens when you pray."

"Playing possum, little girl." The words, the voice, the memory snapped out at Eve like fangs. The smell of liquor and candy, the hands pulling, bruising.

"I begged him to stop, but it was already too late. His hands were on my throat, squeezing so I wouldn't scream, and he was pushing himself into me, hurting me, his breath hot on my face."

"Don't. Please, don't." It hadn't done Eve any good to beg. Hands on her throat, yes. Squeezing until red dots danced in front of her eyes, and the burning, tearing pain of another rape. With that sick-sweet breath on her face.

"Lieutenant. Dallas." Peabody took her arm and shook. "You okay? You're really pale."

"I'm all right." Damn it, goddamn it. She needed air. "It's a plant," she managed.

"She knew someone would find it during the investigation. Scan through to the end, Peabody. She wants us to finish it."

Eve walked to the window, unlocked it, threw it open. She leaned out, had to lean out and breathe. The frigid air stung her cheeks, scraped her throat like little bits of ice.

She wouldn't go back there, she promised herself. Couldn't afford to go back there. She would stay in the now. In control.

"She talks about Zeke," Peabody called out. "It goes on — pretty flowery love language here — about meeting him, how she felt when she knew he was coming."

She looked over, relieved to see color in Eve's face again, though she suspected it was mostly from the slap of cold wind. "She talks about going down to the workshop; it runs with what they'd told us before. Then she's saying that she found her strength because of him, and was leaving her husband at last. It stops with her writing that she was packed and about to call Zeke and begin her real life."

"She covered her ass. If she decided not to run straight off, she'd have the disc, dated and logged, as verification of the story. I guess she figured Testing was too big a risk."

"Doesn't help us any. Everything here's

just as you'd expect it to be if her story was on the up."

"But it's not, so there's more. This is a front." Eve closed the window, turned to wander the room. "This is image — what do you call it — veneer. Under this we've got a tough, determined, bloodthirsty woman who wants to be treated like a goddess. With awe and fear. She's not pink." Eve lifted a satin pillow, tossed it. "She's red; rich, powerful red. She's no delicate flower. She's poison — exotic, sensual, but poison. She wouldn't have spent any more time in this room than it would have taken to set it up."

Eve stopped, waiting for her racing mind to slow. *Damn chemicals,* she thought. She deliberately closed her eyes. "She'd come in here, probably sneer at all the little trinkets. False front. Society's trappings. She hates it. Uses it. She goes for the bold, but this is part of the stage. She's been acting for years. This room is to show people how soft and female she is, but it isn't where she works."

"The rest of the house is guest rooms, baths, living and kitchen area." Peabody sat where she was, watching Eve, watching her work. Watching her mind. "If she didn't work here, then where?"

"Close." Eve opened her eyes, studied the little closet. "Master bedroom's on the other side of that wall, right?"

"Yeah. Big he and she walk-in closet takes up the facing wall."

"All the closets are big. Except this one. Why would she settle for this little corner here?" She squeezed herself in, started running fingers over the wall. "Go around the other side, into the closet. Knock on the wall. Give it three good raps, and come back."

While she waited, Eve crouched, dug her minigoggles out of her field kit.

"Why did I do that?" Peabody asked when she came back.

"You knock hard?"

"Yes, sir. Rap, rap, rap. Stung my knuckles."

"I didn't hear a thing. There's got to be a mechanism, a control."

"Hidden room?" Peabody tried to angle it. "That's so iced."

"Back up, you're in my light. It's got to be here. Wait. Hell. Give me something to pry with."

"I've got something." Peabody dug in her bag for her Swiss Army knife, selected the slim opener, and offered it.

"Were you a Girl Scout?"

"All the way to Eagle level, sir."

Eve grunted, slid the opener into the

minute crack in the glossy ivory wall. It slipped out twice before she got some leverage, and hissing out an oath, she shoved it hard. The little door swung open to reveal a control panel.

"Okay, let's bypass this sucker." She worked for five cramped minutes, shifted her weight on her knees, wiped sweat off her face, and started again.

"Why don't you let me have a go at it, Dallas?"

"You don't know any more about electronics than I do. Hell with it. Step back." She rose, her shoulder bumping solidly into Peabody's nose. Peabody had a minute to yelp, check for blood, then Eve had her weapon out.

"Oh, sir, you don't need to —"

Eve blasted the control lock. Circuits sizzled, chips flew, and the panel of ivory slid smoothly apart.

"What's that fairy tale code? Open sesame." Eve stepped inside a small, pie-slice room, eyed the sleek control panel, the snazzy equipment that reminded her, a bit uncomfortably, of what Roarke had behind a locked door. "This," Eve said, "is where Cassandra worked."

She ran her fingers over controls, tried manual and verbal commands. The machines stayed silent.

"They'll be passcoded," she murmured, "and unregistered, and likely have a couple of traps laid in."

"Should I send for Captain Feeney?"

"No." Eve rubbed her cheek. "I've got an expert only minutes from this location." She dug out her 'link and called Roarke.

He took one look at the fried control panel and shook his head. "You'd only to call."

"I got in, didn't I?"

"Yes, but there's something to be said for finesse, Lieutenant."

"There's something to be said for speed. I don't mean to rush you —"

"Then don't." He moved into the room, let his eyes adjust to the dim light. "Set up your night flash until I can get the room controls working."

He took a slim penlight out of his pocket and, sitting at the controls, clamped it between his teeth in a technique favored by burglars.

Eve saw Peabody's eyes register appreciation and speculation, and moved between them. "Take the vehicle and get to my home office. Get ready to receive data. We'll send through what we find here. Put the rest of the team on alert."

"Yes, sir." But she craned her neck to see over Eve's shoulder. Roarke had removed his jacket, rolled up the sleeves of his white silk shirt. The man had fabulous definition in his arms. "Are you sure you don't want me to assist here?"

"Beat it." Eve bent to dig a light out of her field kit. "I still see your shoes," she said mildly. "Which means the rest of you has yet to follow orders."

Her shoes pivoted smartly and marched away.

"Do you have to look so sexy when you do that?" Eve demanded. "You distract my aide."

"Just one of life's little hurdles. Ah, I won't need that flash after all. Lights," he ordered and the room brightened.

"Good. See if you can find the controls that open this paper file over here." She turned to a cabinet. "I'd blast it, but I might damage the data inside."

"Try a little patience. I'll get to it. She had excellent taste in equipment. These are my units. Locks, yes, here we are." He keystroked and Eve heard the click.

"That was easy."

"The rest won't be. Give me some quiet here."

She pulled out a drawer, hefted it, and carried it into the sitting room. She could hear the beeps and hums of the machines as Roarke worked on them. His occasional terse voice commands. Why she should have found it soothing, she couldn't say, but it was oddly satisfying to know he was in the next room working with her.

Then she started going through the paper files and forgot him, forgot everything else.

There were letters, handwritten in bold, sprawling script from James Rowan to his daughter — the daughter he didn't call Charlotte. The daughter he called Cassandra.

They weren't the sentimental or fatherly correspondence between parent and child but the rousing, dictatorial directives from commander to soldier.

"The war must be fought, the present government destroyed. For freedom, for liberty, for the good of the masses who are now under the boot of those who call themselves our leaders. We will be victorious. And when my time has passed, you will take my place. You, Cassandra, my young goddess, are my light into the future. You will be my prophet. Your brother is too weak to carry the burden of decision. He is too much his mother's son. You are mine.

"Remember always, victory carries a price. You must not hesitate to pay it. Move like a fury, like a goddess. Take your place in history."

There were others, following the same theme. She was his soldier and his replacement. He'd molded her, one god to another, in his image.

In another file she found copies of birth certificates. Clarissa's and her brother's, and their death certificates as well. There were newspaper and magazine clippings, stories on Apollo, and on her father.

There were photographs of him: public ones in his politician suit with his hair gleaming and his smile bright and friendly; private ones of him in full battle gear, his face smudged with black and his eyes cold. Killer eyes, Eve thought.

She'd looked into them hundreds of times in her life.

Family pictures, again private, of James Rowan and his daughter. The fairylike little girl had a ribbon in her hair and an assault weapon in her hands. Her smile was fierce, and her eyes were her father's.

She found all the data on one Clarissa Stanley, ID numbers, birth date, date of death.

Another picture showed Clarissa as a

young woman. Dressed in military fatigues, she stood beside a grim-faced man with a captain's hat shading his eyes. Behind them was a dramatic ring of snow-covered mountains.

She'd seen that face before, she thought and dug out her magnifying goggles again to get a better look.

"Henson," she murmured. "William Jenkins." She pulled out her palm unit and requested data to refresh her memory.

William Jenkins Henson, date of birth August 12, 1998, Billings, Montana. Married Jessica Deals, one child. Daughter Madia, born August 9, 2018. James Rowan's campaign manager . . .

"Right. Stop." She rose, took a turn around the room. She remembered, she'd scanned the data before. He'd had a daughter Clarissa's age. A daughter who hadn't been accounted for, hadn't been mentioned since the bombing in Boston.

A female child's body had been identified in the ruin of that Boston home. Henson's daughter, Eve thought. Not Rowan's. And Willian Jenkins Henson had taken Rowan's child as his own.

He'd finished her training.

She sat again, began to push through the papers looking for another letter, another photo, another piece. She found another stack from Rowan to his daughter and began to read.

"Eve, I'm in. You'll want to see this."

Taking the letters with her, she went to Roarke. "He'd been training her since she was a kid," Eve told him. "Brought her up through the ranks. He called her Cassandra. And when he died, Henson took over. I've got a photo of her and Henson taken a good ten years after the bombing in Boston."

"They trained her well." Damned if he hadn't admired her skill with the units and the codes and mazes she'd planted within them. "I have transmissions from here to a location in Montana. It may be to Henson. No names are used, but she's kept him up to date on her progress."

Eve glanced down at the monitor. "Dear Comrade," she read.

"I don't understand politics," she said after she'd read the first transmission. "What are they trying to prove? What are they trying to be?"

"Communism, Marxism, Socialism, Fascism." Roarke jerked his shoulders. "Democracy, republic, monarchy. One is the same as the other to them. It's power, it's glory. It's revolution for the sake of it. Politics, religion, for some it remains their own narrow and personal view."

"Conquer and rule?" Eve wondered.

"To feed. Have a look. On-screen," Roarke ordered, and the wall unit flashed on. "We have schematics and blueprints, security codes and data. These are the Apollo targets, starting with the Kennedy Center."

"They kept records," she murmured. "Property damage and cost, number of dead. Jesus, they list the names."

"War records," Roarke said. "So many for them, so many for us. Tally the count. Without blood, war's losing its sexuality. And here . . . secondary data, split screen. This is the data and images of Radio City. Note the red dots indicate the positioning of the explosives."

"Following in daddy's footsteps."

"I have names and locations for members of the group."

"Feed them to my home unit, to Peabody. We'll start rounding up. Are all the targets listed?"

"I haven't gone past the first two. I thought you'd want to see what we've got so far."

"Right. Get the data to Peabody first, then we'll go on." She glanced down at the letter in her hand as he started the transmission. And her blood froze.

"Jesus, the Pentagon wasn't the next target. They had an abort between the arena and the Pentagon. It doesn't say what it is here, just equipment problems, financial difficulties. 'Money is a necessary evil. Line your coffers well.' " She tossed the letter aside. "What's after the arena? What was next on Apollo's list?"

Roarke called it up and they both stared at the white spear on-screen. "The Washington Monument, targeted for two days after the complex."

She laid a hand on his shoulder, squeezed. "They'll move tonight, tomorrow the latest. They won't wait, they won't contact. They can't risk it. What's the target?"

He called it up. Three images popped. "Take your choice."

Eve yanked out her communicator. "Peabody, get an E and B team to the Empire State Building, another to the Twin Towers, one more to the Statue of Liberty. You and McNab cover the Empire State, get Feeney down to the Towers. Have one of the long-range scanners ready for me. I'm on my way home. I want everybody to move, move fast. Riot gear and armed. Evacuation immediately, cordon off entire sectors. No civilians within three city blocks of locations."

She jammed the communicator into her

pocket. "How fast can that jet-copter of yours get us to Liberty Island?"

"A lot faster than those toys your department uses."

"Then shoot this data off, add your copter's computer to the spread. Let's go fire it up."

She raced through the door, out and down the steps. Roarke was behind the wheel of his car and had the engine engaged before she could slam her door.

"The Statue's your target."

"I know it. They'll go for the symbol. The biggest one we've got. She's female, she's political." He took the blocks home at a speed that had Eve pressed against the seat. "And I'm damned if they're going to take her down."

Chapter Twenty-two

"Lieutenant! Dallas! Sir!" Peabody scrambled out the front door as Eve leaped out of the car.

"Go," Eve told Roarke. "I'm right behind you."

"Your data's still coming in." Peabody slid over the frost on the lawn, grabbed her footing. "I relayed to Central. Units are being mobilized."

Eve took the scanner. "Full protective gear. You scan before you go in. I'm not losing anyone else."

"Yes, sir. The commander wants your destination and ETA."

Eve whirled around as the silky drone of the jet-copter blurred the air. She watched it sweep out of the minihangar, purr. "God help me, I'm going up in that. Liberty Island. You'll know my ETA when I do."

She crouched to avoid the blast of air, tossed the scanner to Roarke, then hooked a hand on the door opening, propped a boot on the runner. She gave Roarke a brief glance. "I hate this part."

He grinned at her. "Strap in, Lieutenant," he advised as she boosted herself through the door. "Secure the door. This won't take long."

"I know." She hooked the strap across her body, braced. "That's the part I hate."

He went into a steep vertical lift that had her stomach flopping as she contacted Whitney. "Sir. En route to Liberty Island. Data should be coming through to you now."

"It is. Mobilizing backup and E and B teams to each location. ETA to Liberty Island, twelve minutes. Give me yours."

"What's our ETA, Roarke?"

They rose over trees, buildings, engine purring. He sent her one quick look out of wickedly blue eyes. "Three minutes."

"But that's —" She managed not to scream when he punched in the jets. The purr turned to a panther roar and the copter ripped through the sky like a pebble shot from a sling. Eve gripped the seat with white-knuckled hands and thought, *Shit, shit, shit*. But her voice was relatively controlled. "We'll be there inside of three minutes, Commander."

"Report in on arrival."

She clicked off and struggled to breathe steadily through her teeth. "I want to get there alive."

"Trust me, darling."

He banked over the city, adjusted course, and the copter tilted dramatically. Eve felt her eyes roll back in her head. "We'll need to scan the site." She picked up the instrument, studied it. "I've never used one of these."

Roarke reached over, flipped a switch on the base of the scanner. It let out a mild hum.

"Jesus Christ! Keep your hands on the controls!" she shouted at him.

"If I ever want to blackmail you, I can threaten to tell your associates of your phobia of heights and high rates of speed."

"Remind me to hurt you if we live." She wiped a clammy hand on her thighs, then took out her weapon. "You'll need my clinch piece. You can't go in unarmed."

"I've got what I need." He sent her a grim smile as they flew out over the water.

She let that go and called up the data on the in-dash. "Five locations, from base to crown," she said, studying the image. "If they follow these plans, how long would it take you to deactivate them?"

"Depends. I can't say until I see the devices."

"Backup's nine minutes behind us. If this is the target, it's going to be mostly up to you to take the explosives down."

"Activate long-range sensor and screen," he ordered. The in-dash monitor blipped on. Eve saw lights, shadows, symbols. "That's your target. Two people, two droids, one vehicle."

"Have they activated?"

"I can't read explosives with this equipment." He made a mental note to add that capability. "But they're there."

"Droids here, and here?" She tapped a finger on the screen, indicated the black dots on the screen.

"Guarding the base. Ever been in the lady?"

"No."

"Shame on you," he said mildly. "Museums in the base. She's on a pedestal, several stories high. Added together, she's got to be twenty, twenty-two stories, easy. There are elevators, but I wouldn't recommend them under the circumstances. There'll be stairs. Narrow, winding metal. Up to the crown. Then a jag and they follow up to the torch."

Eve wiped a hand over her mouth. "You don't, like, own her or anything?"

"No one owns her."

"Okay. Go in low." Gritting her teeth, she unstrapped. "I'll need you to get close to give me a shot at taking the droids out."

He pressed a button under the dash. A compartment opened. In it was a long-range laser rifle with night scope. "Try that instead."

"Christ, you could get five years in maximum lockup for transporting one of these."

He only smiled when she pulled it out, checked it for weight. "Or you could get two droids before we land. My money's on you, Lieutenant."

"Just keep this thing steady." She opened the door, gritted her teeth against the blast of wind, then bellied down on the floor of the cockpit.

"We've got one at three o'clock and one at nine. We'll take three o'clock first, then I'm going to swing around. So brace yourself for it."

"Just get me in range," she muttered and sighted in.

Out of the dark, out of the delicate mist, the lady rose up. Torch held high, face serene and somehow kind.

Lights glowed in her, around her, charging her with brilliance, with purpose. And how many, Eve thought, had seen that welcome, that promise, when they'd crossed an ocean to a new world? A new life?

How many times had she seen it herself

and thought nothing more of it than that it was there? Had always been there. And by God, she vowed, there it would stay.

She saw the other copter first, the cargo unit cloaked in the shadows of the statue. Through the scope it burned red through a green background.

"Coming into range," Roarke warned her. "Do you see it?"

"No, not — Yeah. Yeah, I got the bastard. Little more, little more," she murmured, then engaged the target lock. She fired, took him clean, midbody. She had a moment to see the mechanical implode, a moment to register the shock of the rifle's power sing up her arm to her shoulder, then Roarke was going into a hard turn.

"They'll have made us now," he told her. "So let's make it two for two. Droid's moving, coming around to six o'clock. One of the marks inside is heading down, fast."

"Then we'll be faster. Come on, come on, come on."

"He's got a long-range himself," Roarke said mildly as a blast of light skimmed inches from the windscreen. "Evasive maneuvers. Take him out, Eve."

She hooked a boot around the base of her chair as the copter swung and danced. "I've got him." She fired, watched the light stream explode onto the ground as her target swerved. "Fuck it. This time."

She drew in breath, held it, ignored the flash and flare of fire outside. She caught him in the crosshairs, locked, and sheared him off neatly at the waist.

"Get this thing on the ground!" she shouted, crawling up to grip the door. "If you get the chance, take out their transpo." She dropped the rifle onto her seat. "They'll think twice about blowing up this site if they're stuck on it."

She watched the ground speed up toward her, began to breathe in fast pants to pump adrenaline. "I'll keep them off you as long as I can."

"Wait until I land." A spear of panic arrowed into his gut as he understood what she meant to do. "Goddamn it, Eve, wait until I put down."

She watched the ground come, felt the speed slow. "Clock's ticking," she told him and jumped.

She kept her knees loose, absorbing the shock. Still, she felt the bright pain careen from her boots up her legs as she hit and rolled. She came up, weapon drawn, and ran in a zigzag pattern for the statue's entrance.

A stream of heat singed past her. Eve hit the ground, rolled again, and returned fire.

Even as she came up, she released the harness on her calf, pulled her clinch piece. She hit the door with sweeping blasts from both weapons and dived through.

The return fire came from above. Eve saw Clarissa in full combat gear, an assault laser in her hands, two hand blasters strapped to her side.

"It's done!" Eve called out. "It's over, Clarissa. We found your room, your data. Your transmissions to Montana are going to lead us right to Henson and the rest. There's a hundred cops on their way to this location."

A huge blast rocked the ground. Light exploded outside the door. Roarke, Eve thought with a cold smile. He'd come through. "There goes your transpo. You can't get off the island. Give it up."

"We'll take it out. We'll take it all out. There'll be nothing left but the ashes." Clarissa fired another round. "Just as my father planned."

"But you won't be there to take his place." Eve plastered herself to the wall. Across the room was the first device, set in a slim metal box. She could see the red lights blinking. Time? she thought. How much time?

"It falls apart, everything he wanted falls apart if you don't take his place."

"I will take his place. We are Cassandra." She laid down a stream of heat and light as she raced up the stairs.

Sucking in a breath, Eve pounded after her. The heat burned her lungs, had tears streaming from her eyes and blurring her vision.

She heard Clarissa screaming for her husband, calling for death, for destruction. For glory. The old metal stairs circled, circled up the body of the statue. She saw the second device, hesitated for a heartbeat with some thought of deactivating it herself.

And hesitating saved herself a laser blast full in the face. The blast shrieked past her and blew out three of the metal treads.

"He was a great man! A god. And he was assassinated by the Fascist forces of a corrupt government. He stood for the people. For the masses."

"He killed the people, killed the masses. Children, babies, old men."

"Sacrifices of a just war."

"Just, my ass." Eve swung from cover, fired high and blind toward the shouts. She heard a howl of rage or pain; she couldn't be sure which. She hoped it was both.

Then they were racing up again.

She saw the third device. Roarke had already dealt with the first, she told herself.

Had to. She could hear no sounds of fire or struggle from below. He was in the clear, doing what needed to be done.

She took a quick look at her wrist unit. Six minutes to backup.

Her calves burned, her breath came short. For a moment, her vision wavered and the weapons clutched in her hands grew weighty and awkward.

The crash was coming on. She leaned back against the wall to catch her breath and her bearings. *Not now, not now.* She could hold out against it, would hold out against it.

Finally, she heard movement behind her. "Roarke?"

"The first is down." He called up the stairs, his voice brisk and cool. "Moving on to two. We're on timers with these. Set for eighteen hundred. Locked and loaded."

"Okay. Okay." She scrubbed the back of her hand over her mouth. It was seventeen-fifty.

She pushed away from the wall, climbed. She didn't give the fourth device so much as a glance. Her job was the Bransons.

She was running on pure nerve when she reached the top. Her legs were jellied. As she slid along the wall, she saw the dazzling view out of the observation windows. The last device was set dead center of the lady's crown.

"Clarissa."

"Cassandra."

"Cassandra," Eve corrected, shifting slightly, trying to scan as much of the area as she could manage. "Dying here isn't going to finish your father's work."

"It will be a great moment in history. The destruction of the city's most beloved symbols. She'll crumble in his name, and the world will know."

"How will they know? If you're buried under tons of stone and steel, how will they know?"

"We are not alone."

"The rest of your group is being searched out and picked up right now." She looked at her wrist unit again, felt sweat slipping down her spine. "Henson." She tossed the name out, hoping it would shake her quarry. "We know where he is."

"You'll never take him." In fury, Clarissa fired. "He was my father's most trusted friend. He raised me. He completed my training."

"After your father was killed. Your father and your brother." Roarke was moving up, she told herself. They'd take out the last device together. There was time. "You weren't in the house."

"I was with Henson. Madia died for me. It was right that she did. We heard the explosion from blocks away. I saw what those pigs had done."

"So Henson took you under. What about your mother?"

"Worthless bitch. I wish I could have killed her myself, watched her die. I would've enjoyed that, loved it, remembering all the times she berated me. My father used her as a vessel, nothing more."

"And when her usefulness was over, he left her, and took you and your brother."

"To teach us, to train us. But I was his light. He knew I would be the one. Others saw me as just a pretty little girl with a soft voice. But he knew. He knew I was a soldier, his goddess of war. He knew, as Henson knew. As the man I chose to marry knew."

Branson. Eve shook her head to clear it. Dear God, she'd forgotten about him. "He's been in on it all along."

"Of course. I would never give myself to a man who wasn't worthy. I could make them think I would — like Zeke. What a pathetic boy, starry-eyed, gullible. He made those last steps work. The Bransons dead, most of the money in closed accounts, me running out of guilt and fear. B.D. and I would continue our mission from another place, with other names. And all the wealth of this corrupt society to back our cause."

"But that's over now." She heard feet slapping the stairs beneath her. It was time to move.

"I'm not afraid to die here."

"Good." Eve dived across the opening, firing a sweeping blast. She saw the impact knock Clarissa down, and the blood bloom on her thigh. She came in low, kicking the weapon from Clarissa's still shuddering hand. "But I'd rather you live in a cage for a long, long time."

"You'll die here, too." Clarissa gasped for breath as Eve disarmed her.

"The hell I will. I've got an ace in the hole."

Roarke came through the door. She started to grin at him, then saw the movement behind. "Your back!" she shouted.

He pivoted, swung out. The flash from Branson's weapon smoked his sleeve. Eve saw the line of blood, sprang to her feet. They were already struggling, locked in close hand-to-hand. With no way to get a clear shot, she prepared to leap.

Clarissa swung her legs out, caught her behind the knees, and sent her sprawling. Eve was cursing when the next blast shattered the glass. Wind poured in, and the roar of copters, the scream of sirens.

"It's too late!" Clarissa shrieked, and her lovely eyes were wide and wild. "Kill him, B.D. Kill him for me while she watches."

Roarke's hand slipped off the weapon. Pain fired up his arm. The scent of his own blood had his teeth bared. From somewhere behind him, he heard Eve shouting, the sound of racing feet. But all he could see was the vicious thirst for death in Branson's eyes.

The weapon swung again, shot blasts into the ceiling. Debris rained down, whirled by the wind into his face like tiny bullets. When a hand closed hard over his throat, he saw small stars and spun his body into Branson's. The impact sent them both over the rail and through the jagged glass.

Eve heard screams, couldn't separate them. Hers, Clarissa's. She was halfway across the room when she saw Roarke fall. Her heart froze, her mind went helplessly, hopelessly blank. The lights from the incoming copters blinded her as she dashed to the window.

Roarke. His name shrieked through her mind, but only a choked sob pushed its way out of her throat. The dizzying height had her head reeling, but her wavering vision could still make out the small, crumpled body on the ground below.

She was halfway out the window, with no idea what she would do when she saw him. Not dead and broken on the ground, but clinging to a narrow fold of weathered bronze with bloody hands.

"Hang on. For God's sake, hang on."

She started to swing out when Clarissa rammed into her back. Her balance teetered, her breath heaved. Almost as an afterthought, Eve spun into a back kick and planted her boot in Clarissa's chest, a second in her face. "Stay away from me, you bitch."

There was wailing and sobbing behind her as Eve leaned into the teeth of the wind, braced her midriff on the window ledge, and held out a hand to Roarke.

"Reach up. Grab hold of me. Roarke!"

He knew he was slipping. Blood was dripping down his arm, through his fingers. He'd faced death before, was no stranger to the sensation of knowing this breath, this one breath, could be the last you drew.

But he'd be damned if it would. Not when his woman was watching him with terrified eyes, calling to him, risking her life to save his. He set his teeth, gave his injured arm his weight. Pain swam sickly into his head, into his gut as he reached up to her.

And her hand gripped his, firm and strong.

Eve rammed the toes of her boots into the wall for purchase, and muscles screaming, held out her other hand. "I'll pull you in. Give me your other hand. I'll pull you in. Hurry."

When her fingers closed over his, slipped once as the blood slickened them, his vision grayed. Then she was locking her hand over his wrist, hauling up. He bore down, pulled his body up, an inch, then two. He saw the sweat run down her face, into her eyes. Concentrated on her eyes.

Then his arm was on the window ledge, braced there. With one last heave he was tumbling in on top of her.

"God. Roarke. God."

"Time!" He rolled free, all but fell on the last explosive. The readout showed forty-five seconds. "Get out, Eve." He said it coolly as he began to work.

"Get it down." She fought to get breath back in her body. "Get it down."

"There won't be time." Battered, bloody, Clarissa dragged herself to her feet. "We die here. All of us. Both men I loved, martyrs to the cause."

"Fuck your cause." Eve yanked her communicator. "Keep this area clear. Keep it clear. There's a hot one left. Working now." She shut it down as shouts and orders buzzed through. "Live or die," she said, looking into Clarissa's eyes. "You still lose."

"Die," she said. "My way."

Screaming her father's name, she leaped through the window.

"Jesus Christ." Eve wanted to sag to her knees, but braced against the device. "Kill this thing, will you?"

"I'm working on it." But his fingers were slippery, his system screaming to shut down from loss of blood. The readout clicked down twenty-six seconds, twenty-five, twenty-four.

"It's going to be close." He shut off the pain, as he'd learned to do as a child. Get through, get by. Survive. "Start out. I'll be behind you."

"Don't waste your breath." She moved to his side. Seventeen, sixteen, fifteen. Laid a hand on his shoulder. Unified them. Lights from a circling copter speared through the windows, lighted his face. Doomed angel, with a mouth of a poet, the eyes of a warrior. She'd had a year with him, and it had changed everything.

"I love you, Roarke."

His answer was a grunt, and it nearly made her smile. She took her gaze from his face, looked down at the readout. Nine, eight, seven . . .

The hand on his shoulder tightened. She held her breath.

"Would you mind repeating that, Lieutenant?"

She whooshed out her breath, stared down at the readout. "You killed it."

"With four seconds to spare. Not bad." He pulled her against him with his good arm. Those wild warrior's eyes were brilliant on hers. "Kiss me, Eve."

She let out a whoop of laughter and ignoring the circling lights, the shouts from bull horns, the incessant beep of her communicator, crushed his mouth with hers. "We're alive."

"And staying that way." He buried his face in her hair. "By the way, thanks for the lift."

"Any time." In joy, she threw her arms around him, squeezed, then leaped back when he yelped. "What? Oh God, your arm. Looks bad."

"Bad enough." He wiped blood from his face, then hers. "But it'll hold."

"Uh-uh." She tore his sleeve, frowned at the wound, and quickly bound it up. "This time I get to drag your ass to a health center, pal." She staggered, shaking her head as he grabbed her.

"We'll get a big bed. Are you hit?"

"No, crash city." Her mind went on float and she giggled. "I got my four to six out of the goddamn chemicals though. I'm okay. I've just got to lie down really, really soon."

But she hooked her arm around his waist, turned. Together they looked out over the water, toward the city lights that flashed and blinked against the dark. "Some view, huh?"

His arm came around her. It was debatable who was holding whom upright. "Yeah, it's a killer. Let's go home, Eve."

"Okay." She pulled out her communicator as they hobbled toward the doorway. "This is Dallas, Lieutenant Eve. We're secure here."

"Lieutenant." Whitney's voice came through as a mild buzzing as fatigue washed over her. Even the echo of adrenaline had faded. "Report?"

"Ah . . ." She shook her head, but didn't quite clear it. "The explosives are down, E and B teams can dispose. The Bransons took a leap. We'll need body removal to scrape up what's left of them. Sir . . . Roarke's injured. I'm transporting him to a health center."

"Is his condition serious?"

They teetered on the stairs, shifted grips, and continued down. Eve had to swallow down a chuckle. "Oh, we're pretty much a mess here, Commander, thanks, but we'll hold. Do me a favor, will you?"

On the miniscreen, Whitney's brows drew together in surprise. "Yes?"

"Will you tag Peabody and McNab and Feeney? Tell them we're okay here. Mostly okay, anyhow. They worry, and I'm feeling a little too flaked to triangulate our status. Oh, and tell Peabody to go get Zeke and maybe get him drunk or something. He'll handle what went down here better that way."

"Excuse me?"

She swayed as they came to the entrance level, shot Roarke a puzzled look as he shook with laughter. "Um, sorry, Commander, I think we're running into some interference on this channel."

Obligingly, Roarke took the communicator and shut it down. "There, before you ask your superior to join the drunken revelry."

"Jesus, I can't believe I said that." She stepped out into the teeth of the wind, winced against the brilliant spin of lights from landing copters. She rubbed a hand over her face as the teams began to leap out and race toward the statue. "Let's get out of here before I say something else stupid."

By the time they dragged each other into the jet-copter, she wanted nothing more than to curl up in a corner, any corner, and sleep for a week. Yawning, she turned her head and looked at Roarke as he took the controls. He was bloody, torn, and gorgeous. Through the fatigue, the worry, she grinned.

"Roarke? Nice working with you."

His eyes glinted wild and blue and his grin flashed in return as the jets roared to life. "My pleasure, Lieutenant. As always."

The employees of Thorndike Press hope you have enjoyed this Large Print book. All our Large Print titles are designed for easy reading, and all our books are made to last. Other Thorndike Press Large Print books are available at your library, through selected bookstores, or directly from us.

For information about titles, please call:

(800) 257-5157

To share your comments, please write:

Publisher
Thorndike Press
P.O. Box 159
Thorndike, Maine 04986